The Man
in the
Red Jacket

MICHAEL REEVES

Lulu Publishing Services rev. date: 01/03/2014

TO CAROLINE, KATIE AND SARAH

About the Author

Michael Reeves was born in Feltham, Middlesex in 1961. He read English at Swansea University, and has been teaching since 1986, latterly as an assistant headteacher at a special school in South London. He and his wife, Caroline, have two grown daughters. This is his first published novel.

Prologue

October 2009

T he captain looked across the city through his binoculars, crouching alongside his men behind a low wall. There had been gunfire for almost half an hour, followed by three loud explosions and palls of smoke. At the centre of it all was one small building.

He was not sure about the building. It might be a police station, or it might not. He had called in, and nobody else seemed to know either. Earlier, a rocket had been fired at the Serena Hotel, but he was sure it had landed harmlessly in a garden. The Palace had also been fired at, but he knew that the President was not in the city this week. All in all, it seemed like the usual activity.

From his rooftop position, he could make out a flashing of blue and red, and he could just hear the wailing of sirens. Now the firing had stopped, ambulances had started to arrive in clouds of dust, and then headed back roughly in his direction. They would be going to the hospital at Bagram, he thought. So they obviously weren't locals.

He heard a shuffling behind him and turned. The sergeant's face was expressionless as he came to the edge of the roof and looked across at the smoke. He leaned his SA80 upright against the wall and lit a cigarette. The captain passed him the Otterburns and he scanned the city in his turn, taking a heavy drag on the cigarette every now and then.

'Seems as though it's dying down,' said the captain.

'Let's hope so, sir. What do we do now?'

'I'm afraid we wait. Again, I can't raise anybody.'

The sergeant handed him a peach wrapped in paper. He bit into it, and wiped the juice from his chin.

The sergeant finished his cigarette, picked up his weapon and pointed it at the floor. He crouched tensely, looking away to the west. The new viewpoint did him good.

The captain finished his peach and flicked the stone over a garden wall below. It was becoming a habit. As usual, he hoped the stone would grow.

Chapter One

December 1855

Mr Dickens often walked at this time, sometimes right through the night for thirty miles. His body was like a coiled spring, and he walked with long, energetic strides. He always had a purpose. First he would clear his mind, and then he would seek out new nooks and crannies and rooms, and then imagine new little souls to put into them.

But he also had to revisit the dark but magical places where so many of his folk had already come into being. Today he had walked north of the river, through Hosier Lane and Finsbury Square and Long Lane and through Smithfield Market. Twice he had seen Fagin, and once he had thought ... But no, it wasn't him. It couldn't be, not really. And so Mr Dickens had come back to the world around him.

This afternoon, he had kept close to the river. Nowhere in the world was there a river more important to a city, and nowhere in London was there a feature more important to Mr Dickens. All his life, water had lapped at his feet. His third name was Huffam, who had been a sail maker in Portsmouth docks. Just upstream from here, right on the river at Hungerford Stairs, he had pasted labels on boot-blacking bottles for six shillings a week, and twenty-five years later he had made David Copperfield do just the same.

Many of his souls, such as Quilp and Captain Cuttle, had sprung from the river. Many would be carried away by it: to Australia or to

3

their deaths. Mr Dickens had laid dear little Paul Dombey into his death bed near here, and made Paul's mind wander off to *the waters, black and deep, reflecting the stars and rolling inevitably to the sea.* Ten years from now, although he did not know it yet, he would have Gaffer Hexham keep his family warm by bringing home lumps of wet coal dropped from coasters. One night, Hexham and his daughter Lizzie would pull a bashed and bloated body from the water.

The walking was also a search for something else, though. Yes, he sometimes earned £5000 in a year. A fortune. And yes, he could be the life and soul of a place, and fill a room with light. Once, before he had married Catherine, he had leapt into the Hogarths' front parlour through the window, disguised as a sailor, and danced a jig and jumped out of the window again, only to ring the door bell minutes later, dressed as himself and looking terrifically serious. How they had laughed, Catherine and Mr and Mrs Hogarth!

But always there was that sense of something missing in his life, a yearning. A yearning for what? He really didn't know. That was why he was in the East India Dock today, looking across the water into the setting sun. The place was full of ships and full of seekers. A small boy – perhaps we could call him Oliver or Artful or David or Tommy Traddles – looked up at the majestic hull of an East Indiaman, just berthed after a ninety-three-day journey from Canton with an early cargo of tea. Men lowered large chests to the dockside with chains and pulleys which clanked loudly as the weight was taken by the ground. Dockers from the sooted, wart-like houses of Blackwall stacked it ready for the short journey to the great warehouses. Men stood with papers, pencils poised or wedged behind their ears, watching carefully, counting and ticking and marking. Everywhere there was running and shouting and heaving, and the air was thick with the smell of tar and spices and tea and sweat.

Mr Dickens turned away from the setting sun and the forests of masts and rigging, and looked down river. A clipper was approaching the dock, a light breeze in its piled-up sails and a delicate double bow-wave peeling towards the dock walls. The river was like a rippled sheet of silk under a cooling iron. He guessed that the ship was carrying tea, but he was wrong. It was from Bombay, and carried a mixed cargo of silks, Persian carpets, spices, even a little opium for those who would find escape in the dark dens of Field Lane and Cripplegate. There were passengers too: a few soldiers returning from service in India, and merchants looking after their goods. As the clipper manoeuvred gently into the dock channel and waited in the lock, Dickens saw its name: *Aurora*. The dawn.

From the deck, two people seemed to look straight at him, even at this distance and through this crowd. One was much taller than the other, but not especially tall himself. The shorter looked no more than a boy. Both were wearing the costume of distant lands: dark grey turbans, sheepskin jackets and loose-fitting, lighter trousers and shirts.

The two travellers and Mr Dickens watched one another as the clipper came out of the lock. Hassan had picked Mr Dickens out because of his silk top hat glistening in the late sun, a hat such as Hassan had never seen before. There was a sort of exactness in the cut of his beard and in the way he stood and stared. Hassan's uncle had noticed him too, and they held their gaze until the ship turned and the masts cut Mr Dickens from view.

Hassan and his uncle turned to each other. Anybody could see the blood-connection between them. They had familial chestnut eyes, the same pointed chins. They even had the same stillness, the same ability to look intently and to say nothing. But of course there were differences between them, too. Hassan was not yet fifteen, and his Uncle Ahmet was more than forty. Ahmet's white hair had only traces of the original deep red, but Hassan's was silky as a child's. Ahmet's brown face was deeply lined, especially around the eyes and in the cheeks, by squinting into the sun and being chilled by icy winter winds and snows; Hassan's was still fresh, except for a furious scar running from under his left eye almost to the corner of his mouth.

And what of their lives? There was too much to tell at once. Ahmet Qaderi had known the golden quality of some men's hearts and the darkness in others. In Kabul he had known both the love and the treachery of friends, and the occasional kindness of those who were supposed to be his enemies. He knew what it was like to flee and to start again.

Ahmet knew more of Hassan than Hassan knew of himself. He had travelled the Jugdulluk pass, that freezing crack through the mountains, just two months ahead of Hassan and the slaughter that went with him, walking through three feet of snow, his feet wrapped in cloth, his body in his *poshteen*. Hassan was too young – probably – to remember that horror of broken people and the whiteness reddened with blood, but Ahmet had known how many had died there, and thought of it often.

They looked down at the dockside. Already there were swarms of men waiting to unload *Aurora*. The crew, English and Indian, were lowering the trapezoid sails. The Company flag flapped limply, as though exhausted. Hassan looked across the dockside. Like a traveller coming on foot from Kent or Essex, he had been able to see the white-grey dome with its cross on top from a long way off. Now it was almost hidden from view by the red brick walls and grey slate roofs of the three-storey warehouses, with their little arched windows and great gaping doors twenty feet from the ground. Cranes with oaken jibs lifted barrels and chests to platforms up the walls, where they were hauled in under cover. In between these and St Paul's were hidden the poor homes of Whitechapel and Spitalfields and Holborn, grimy with soot and glistening with recent rain. Ahmet put his hand on Hassan's shoulder.

'So. Are you well now?'

'Yes, uncle. But still ...' He was lost for a moment, looking across the docks. Then he turned and looked at Ahmet. 'Yes, my uncle, I am well. And I thank you again for your care of me, and for all your many kindnesses. Perhaps ...'

'Enough, my dear child. The holy Qur'an tells us it is a man's duty to care for the orphan, and to pay the poor due. And now perhaps, together, we will find the fortune that we seek!' He raised his eyebrows and smiled. It was a frequent joke between them.

'Let us hope. Have you seen the mosque?'

The uncle smiled, just a little. 'That is not a mosque, my nephew. It is the temple of the ... of the English. I almost said of the *feringhees*, but here it is we who are the *feringhees*. The English call their temple a church.'

'If we are lost, uncle, if we are separated, we shall meet at the English church!' Hassan looked a little worried. 'I hope that we will not be lost, Uncle. But such a big city! So many buildings along the river! Is it a dangerous city? More dangerous than Calcutta or Bombay? More dangerous than Kabul?'

'I cannot say, Hassan. It is best to be careful: and remember that you have only a little language. And the language you know is the language of the soldier and the language of the man who has been to school. It is not the language of the working man or the language of the poor.'

'So they have different languages here? As they do in Bombay?'

'I believe so. Your...' He seemed to catch himself. 'I was once told, many years ago, that the English themselves speak in many different ways.'

'And who told you that, Uncle?'

'I do not remember. It was long ago.'

'And where will we pray tonight? It is almost sunset.'

'For tonight, where we have prayed for the last three months. We must pray now, for Allah has brought us to safety again.'

And they turned together, the uncle's hand still on his nephew's shoulder, and strode the twenty feet across the deck to the opposite rail, with their backs to the sun. Both raised their hands beside their heads, their palms forwards. Hassan yearned to feel the dying sun on the backs of his hands, but felt only the icy breeze. They then held their hands together on their stomachs, and as usual Uncle Ahmet spoke.

'*In the name of Allah, the kind, the merciful. Praise be to Allah, Lord of the worlds, the kind, the merciful. Owner of the day of judgement. You alone we worship, you alone we ask for help.*

'*Show us the straight path, the path of those you have favoured, not the path of those who earn your anger nor of those who go astray.*'

Uncle Ahmet had spoken these words at dawn and at sunset every day, and at Friday prayers. He had also spoken them when they had dedicated themselves to this journey, when they had boarded the ship in Bombay, when they had come through the late monsoon winds, and also around the Cape of Good Hope and across the Bay of Biscay. Indeed, Ahmet's was a life full of prayer. Sometimes prayer could sound like a conversation. One day off the coast of Madagascar, on a calm sea and under a sky of cornflower blue, Hassan had been amazed at the sight of a flock of gulls soaring and swooping for fish. Ahmet had shared his wonder.

'Have they not seen the birds obedient in mid air?' he asked. *'None holdeth them save Allah. Here, truly, are portents for a people who believe.'*

They bent, until their hands were on their knees, and then knelt and placed their foreheads on the deck for a few moments. And then they stood.

Once, when they stood on the deck looking up at the stars on a beautiful clear night off west Africa, Ahmet had said *'He it is that hath set for you the stars that ye may guide your course by them amid the darkness of the land and the sea. We have detailed our revelations for a people who have knowledge.'*

Hassan had been puzzled by this at first. He knew he was not supposed to question the words, but he had questions about himself.

'I am afraid, Uncle. How shall I set a course in this strange country? You have always set the course for me, and the captain sets the course for you, and the stars are given by Allah to the captain. What must *I* do?'

Uncle Ahmet was silent for a moment, for he never spoke before thinking, especially when the question was awkward. He knew that Hassan was thinking of the great gap in his life, of the mystery at the centre of his being. They both looked up at the pale moon.

'Have I not always taught you to follow the right path? If you do so, you will never be lost. And so it will always be. Follow what is in your heart, and all will be well. And if you need to follow the stars, and do not know how, you must ask the sea captain. And then you will have followed Allah, for the sea captain's knowledge comes from Him. And in any case, I am by you.'

Hassan had been dreaming of this moment, this arrival after a two-month voyage. In fact, this moment had been buried in his heart all his life. For he too was a seeker, and he had prayed that here he would find the truth at last. Or something more than just the truth, perhaps even the drop of blood that he was looking for. After all, we are all made by Allah from a drop of blood, and where was his?

Now it was his turn to pray.

'*The Lord says that you must worship only him, and that you must show kindness to your parents. If one of them or both of them reaches old age with you, do not defy them and do not push them away, but speak gracious words to them. When they are old, lower to them the wing of mercy and obedience, for they cared for you when you were little. The Lord knows what is in your minds. He will forgive those who are righteous and who turn to him. Do not squander your wealth, but give what is due to your kinsman, and to the traveller and the poor.*'

They bowed, straight legged and with their hands on their knees, then knelt and placed their foreheads on the deck again. Then they stood. Hassan turned again to look westwards into the setting sun. The sky was now darkening, and he thought that the reddish globe shimmered a little.

At times like this, Hassan often reached inside his jacket for his dearest possessions. One was a knife, which Akbar Khan had given to him when he was three or four years old. Hassan hardly remembered those times. He remembered some of the *feringhees* – men and women, and he remembered the distant mountains, capped with snow. He remembered the panicked voices during the earthquakes, and the heat and the dusty goats. But Akbar he had forgotten: it was his uncle who had told him about the knife. He felt it now, its smooth and comfortable handle, cold steel inlaid with brass, and with an emerald on either side; the edge, as sharp as it had ever been; the solid, tapering point which might once have broken a rib as it headed for the heart.

Hassan looked at the knife and realised that Uncle Ahmet was watching him. He replaced the knife, reached into another pocket and pulled out a book. It was bound in brown calfskin, with gold across the spine. For the thousandth time, Hassan opened it carefully and looked in wonder at its yellowing, marble-edged pages. There too many tiny words, but also many pictures of *feringhees* – a bald man with a paunchy belly making what looked like an angry speech at a dining table. The same man chasing his hat in a gale; struggling out of a crashed carriage; sitting in a wheelbarrow in a pigsty; doing the splits on ice. 'So these,' he had often thought, 'are the great *feringhees* in their own country!' Often, he was caught half-way between disappointment and contempt. He prayed that the *feringhees* would not all be like this. And then he remembered that he did not know very much about the book. He had started to read it many times, but had found that the pictures were easier than the words. How could he guess what was meant by a *varnished hat*, or a *roast potato*, or a *village green*? And perhaps the man in the barrow was a good man. It was difficult to tell just from the pictures. He breathed deeply and smelled the paper.

Then he turned to the back of the book to make sure that the letters were still there, with the grim remains of their waxen seals. They always were, of course, because there was no way they could fall out. Nevertheless, he liked to be sure.

One was written in Pashtu, neatly, but with a few crossings out, as though it had been rushed. The other was in English, in a clear and rounded hand, almost like that of a determined child.

As he always did at these times, he cast his mind back to his very earliest memory. The mental image that still meant so much to him was always cast in sunlight. Why was that? It must have been cloudy sometimes. The edges of it were blurred; he could hardly see the surroundings, but knew he was in a room, and that there was snow on the ground outside. By the fire, sitting on a small divan, was a man in a red jacket. Every now and then he looked over the book at Hassan and winked. Sometimes he whistled or grinned, or made a sound like an owl.

There was a shelf of books behind the man. Ahmet had said that all of them were burned later. Hassan had always assumed that the man was reading from the same brown book that Hassan now kept in his pocket; he had never wondered whether this were true. Later, as he found out more of his own history, and about his half-remembered parents, he became sure that the imagined picture, and some of his dreams, were an echo of the real past. It happens sometimes. So even nowadays, Hassan sometimes felt laughter rising in his throat, and an aching sorrow in his heart.

Sometimes, he imagined the man and the woman - he could tell she was beautiful, even though he never saw her face - turned away from him, both writing. They sat very close, and sometimes their hands would touch. Every now and then, they would try to look at each other's writing. Once, he remembered, the woman had snatched up her sheet and run shrieking with laughter across the room, chased by the man in the red jacket.

Now, Ahmet again placed his hand on Hassan's shoulder and guided him back across the deck towards wooden steps which were roped to the dockside.

'I must see to my merchandise,' he said. 'And then, *inshallah*, we shall find a *serai* to spend the night in. You must come along with me: do not leave my side.'

As they reached the top of the gangway, a deep voice spoke quietly in Hasan's ear.

'We shall meet soon, *inshallah,*' said a crewman. It was Khodar, a man from his own country, the country he had left a dozen years earlier. They had met Khodar and his cousin Aziz in Bombay, and Ahmet had seemed to like them at first. He had even helped to arrange for them to work their passage on *Aurora*, for he knew the captain. But something had happened – Hassan did not know what – and Ahmet now seemed very wary of them. And for reasons he didn't understand, Hassan had changed his mind as well. Now he turned and felt his spirit quail under the man's height and breadth. His eyes looked deep and powerfully into Hassan's, twinkling and unwelcome. 'We shall meet soon.' He grinned a ghastly grin, showing six teeth and a wad of betel-nut.

Hassan had often seen Khodar and Aziz, who nearly always worked together and sometimes, when it was calm, looked out over the seascape together, deep in conversation. Every now and then their voices had been raised a little, but the words were always carried away by the wind.

They were big men, Khodar slightly the taller, but both surprisingly agile on the ropes. They had often exchanged a few words with Hassan, and had sometimes given him small presents: perhaps some nuts or some dried peach. But they had said little to Uncle Ahmet, and had usually been separated from him by yards of deck and wary glances. Hassan found this strange. After all, there were very few Pashtun about, and they were far from home. Surely some conversation would be welcome?

Hassan looked straight up at Khodar and gave a nervous smile, more with the mouth than with the eyes. Ahmet very gently nudged Hassan forward. Aziz was usually quieter and much more appealing. For one thing, he knew how to keep his distance, and for another he had teeth. He had rarely spoken to Hassan, but now he smiled.

'Allah is good to us,' he said, and gave a little nod to Uncle Ahmet. He seemed to be struggling to say more, but his mind wilted and he grinned again.

For once, Ahmet replied. *'And when prayer is ended, disperse in the land and seek of Allah's bounty, and remember Allah much, that you may be successful.'*

Somehow, the cousins were silenced by this.

Uncle Ahmet nudged again, firmly this time, and they were soon on the dockside. A slightly-built Indian joined them, with a small carpet rolled up under his arm and a canvas bag over his shoulder, bulging at the seams. This was Kajan. As usual he said nothing, but smiled broadly at the other four in turn. Uncle Ahmet made a point of returning the silent friendship. The Indian walked down the gangway, and Hassan noticed that Khodar watched him carefully.

Khodar and Aziz came down the gangway and disappeared together into the crowd. Hassan stood and watched as ropes and pulleys lowered more wooden chests and enormous crates to the ground. Ropes hissed into the water. Uncle Ahmet quickly identified his merchandise, and found which warehouse it was heading for. Then it was time to look for somewhere to sleep.

They walked. It was now getting quite dark, and the gas lamps were being lit one by one. As each came on, a boy, younger than Hassan, was illuminated from above. The light revealed a long taper beyond its glowing tip, and a cap and a jacket just too large for their owner. Each time, he stepped out of one light and on to the next, where he would suddenly be revealed again. The dockside was now heaving with labour, and it was all Uncle Ahmet and Hassan could do to keep out of the dangerous rush. Still there was the smell of tea and spices and tar and old rope. The wind played in the forests of masts and rigging like a harp. There was a fierce hammering and the rolling sound of barrels and the occasional squawk of a gull. There was the thrumming of iron-hooped wheels on cobblestones, and the odd yell of a carter or a docker, lucky enough to find work today. 'Watcherself, young 'un,' shouted one man at Hassan, and Hassan leapt aside as a barrow lumbered past. Constantly there were cries of 'Watcher backs! Mind yerself! Move over!'

That was why Hassan and Uncle Ahmet almost missed what happened next. Just as they reached the dock gates, and walked towards the red-brick arch and the clock-tower, Hassan noticed a knot of people just outside, looking intently at the ground. They were held in a bubble of silence for some time before screams and cries and shouts broke out. Something was wrong deep within the crowd. Uncle Ahmet took Hassan firmly by the upper arm, determined to avoid trouble. He tried to skirt the edge of the crowd to pass through the gate and beyond the fourteen-foot red brick walls that surrounded the dock. But as he did so, a large woman in a black blouse, a grubby bonnet and an apron that opened like a bell beneath her enormous bosom, caught Uncle Ahmet's eye and beckoned to him. She shouted something Hassan could not understand and pulled Ahmet into the crowd. There was a great jabbering of voices as people noticed Ahmet's turban, his lined skin, his white beard and his *poshteen*, but there was no anger. They drew him into their midst. A man with terror on his face and blood on his hands pointed to the floor, and it was then that Uncle Ahmet saw the body. Or not just a body, because the soul had not quite left it. It was a man, dressed in the pea jacket of a sailor, slashed open. Underneath the jacket was a white shirt, with a great gout of blood centred just beneath the breastbone and spreading slowly under the arms.

Hassan recognised him at once. He was Kajan, the little man from *Aurora*, the Indian who had sparkled wordlessly above the gangway. Uncle Ahmet looked around: surely Khodar and Aziz could help. But there was no sign of them in the crowd. The wounded man lifted a weak hand as if to beckon at Hassan, but it was Uncle Ahmet who knelt by his side. He had lived in Bombay for nearly fourteen years, and hoped that he knew enough Hindi to understand the man's sighing words. For he knew that these would be his last. After all, he had seen this sort of thing before, in Kabul and in Bombay. And he knew that the *wazifeh,* the duty, was his. So he and the man were alone with each other, an invisible shell around them. Uncle Ahmet strained to hear, and the words hovered. And then, the man's breath faded away and the shell suddenly dissolved, and once more Uncle Ahmet was one of the silent crowd. It was all over with the Sparkling Indian. Uncle Ahmet stood up and looked around him at the pale faces and the parted lips.

Later, Hassan would remember the way his uncle looked out of the crowd, scanning the dockside, the berths and the stream of workers heading towards the gate.

'Come. This is no place for you. We must leave.'

Again he stood and observed, and again Hassan watched him. Then he started to look outwards for himself.

Chapter Two

December 1855

A hoarse whistle blew just beyond the crowd, and three men pushed through to the centre from different directions. Hassan thought at first that they were soldiers, because they wore black boots, dark blue trousers, jackets almost down to their knees and dark helmets on their heads, pointed like the white ones the *feringhees* had worn. They ran up carrying large batons, their silver helmet badges, rows of buttons and whistle chains flashing under the gas lamps. A large, red-faced man with three stripes on his sleeve, a bushy brown moustache on his face and a great deal on his mind spoke first.

'Now. Who saw what happened? Does anybody know this … this genelman?' There was a brief silence from the crowd, until the bosomed lady spoke.

'I seen him first. 'e was … poor creatur. Such wickedness there is, down 'ere.' She wrung her hands, and like many others, looked at the man on the floor. There is such a thing as grief for a stranger.

'I have asked, madam, if you know this man. Do you?'

'Well no, but I saw 'im fall. Right here, as God's my witness. I saw 'im fall, and I thought I seed someone running away. Couldn't make 'im out, mind. Dark, see. But there was shouts over there.' She pointed. 'Over there. Up towards the Dock Road. Then I see this man fall, poor love, and tried to help. But 'e were long past help then.'

15

'And now I ask all you 'spectable folk again. He looked up and around at the crowd, and made himself as tall as he could. 'Did ... anybody ... see ... what ... hoccurred?'

Silence again. The Sergeant stretched up again.

'Well. Quite a mystery, ain't it, in one of the most crowdedest parts of Lunnon?'

'Well,' said a man with a barrow. Reckon he must've bin 'tacked somewhere else, quiet like, like by a 'sassin. And then just staggered over 'ere an' fell.'

'Obliged to you, sir, I'm sure,' said the sergeant. 'Any more? Did the genelman say anythink before 'e passed on?'

And now the crowd looked with a compound eye at Uncle Ahmet. The sergeant's head turned slowly towards him and stared into Uncle Ahmet's eyes, expecting something. Uncle Ahmet hunted for words.

'The man dying, good sir. Very quiet. Not hear him.'

'Most helpful, sir, I'm sure. Well, all we can do now is remove the genelman to the dispensary. There is a room for the purpose. Now you, young feller ...' He looked Hassan up and down, from turban to boots, and changed his mind. His eye cast around the crowd. 'No, you.' He pointed at the lamplighter, who had by now reached the edge of the crowd. 'Your name, young sir?'

'You know my name, Pa. What's with the gammon?'

'I'll gammon you proper, young man. What's yer name?'

'Tommy.'

The Sergeant's eyes widened. He had to win this one.

'Tommy what?'

'Tommy Jackson'.

The sergeant's moustache twitched.

'Tommy ... Jackson ... what?'

'Tommy Jackson, sergeant.'

The sergeant looked ready to explode. Just in time the lamplighter understood.

'Tommy Jackson, Sergeant Jackson.'

'Better. Now off you go to Mr Lovelace for a coffin. Quick, now. You, Constable 'Arris.' Harris was young and rather thin. He paid complete attention. 'Stand guard. Remember that last corpse we found down West India? The one that got up and run away?' Harris looked at his boots. 'Well this one ain't goin' nowhere. Clear?'

'Yes, Sarnt Jackson.'

'Now then.' Again, Jackson looked at the crowd. 'Last question. Where does this man come from? Who saw him?'

Uncle Ahmet stepped forward. 'I know him. Kajan. Not his family name, but I know him. *Aurora.*' And he pointed across the dock.

'As I thought. A sailor. And you, sir. You a sailor?'

'No, sir. I am Ahmet Qaderi. Merchant. Carpets, silk, spices. This my nephew, Hassan'.

'And where are you staying?' Jackson put his hands together on the side of his face, miming sleep. Uncle Ahmet smiled at the play-acting. He had understood perfectly well.

'I have nowhere.'

'In that case, you will come with me to the station.'

A woman spoke up. It was Mrs Bosom again. 'You can't do that, Thomas. He's not a felon. You can see that clear as day.'

'And who is this Thomas, might I ask?' Yet again, he drew himself up. The constable allowed the corners of his mouth to twitch a little.

'You can't do that, Sergeant Jackson. It ain't right.'

'And what do you suggest, Madam?'

'If you need the genelman, he can stay with me.' Uncle Ahmet looked at Hassan. 'And the boy, too.'

'Most irreg'lar, Madam. But let me see. I s'pose you'll do. I shall need your address, though.'

'28 Evans Street, off the Dock Road.'

'Ah, yes. Four rooms, terrace, on Limehouse Reach, ain't it?'

'Yes, Sergeant Jackson.'

'And your name, madam?'

'Molly Jackson, Sergeant Jackson.'

There was a confused ripple of laughter from the crowd, but it did not last, and sombreness descended like a cloak. A space had cleared around the Indian, who still stared up at the night sky.

Sergeant Jackson looked down at him, with just a little tenderness. He crouched, and closed Kajan's eyes with his fat thumbs.

Molly Jackson took Hassan by the hand and led him and Uncle Ahmet away from the gates, away from the towered entrance to the docks and towards the traffic of London. A poor coffin went the other way, tottering on a handcart.

'Not long dears, said Mrs Jackson. You'll be in the warm in two shakes of a lamb's tail. An' now I remember - there's a lamb stoo ready when we get there, and you'll want some rest.'

'You are very kind,' said Uncle Ahmet, smiling at her.

'Ooh, no sir, when you've been married to a police sergeant for seventeen year, you gets used to all sorts of things. You should hear what Sergeant Jackson – Thomas – tells me of an evening. There's all sorts. Bodies in the river, fights in the taverns, the opium dens. Not that I've seen much of it meself, you know. It's hidden, mostly. But you go good and steady and careful, like. Stay clear.'

Hassan understood little of what Mrs Jackson had said, and none of the nouns, but something in her face made him trust her. Perhaps it was the pity. They soon reached the East India Dock Road and turned left. Wagon after wagon headed into London, to the grocers and spice merchants and tea houses. Soon, on their left, another forest of masts and vine-like rigging appeared on their left, and through a gap between two buildings Hassan could just see green land stretching to the river. He did not know it, but this was the Isle of Dogs, where Kings had kept their hunting packs in kennels at the water's edge. They passed buildings that grew on the outer edges of the West India Dock, the coffee merchants and the sail makers and the ironmongers and rope makers and ship-chandlers. And then they crossed the road, and were met by a boy selling pies and another roasting chestnuts, and a third selling song sheets. A man played a game with another, hiding a coin under one of three cups. The other man guessed wrong, and stomped away. Three foul-smelling men stumbled out of Grimson's Stout House, and sat in the street, arguing.

Finally, they turned right into Stansby Street, then on and into Gatesby Street, and then right again into Evans Street. It was a tidy street of terraced brick houses with shiny slate roofs and brightly painted doors opening straight onto the pavement. From each house, two windows looked out at the street from the ground floor, and two from the first. At number 28, Mrs Jackson unlocked the door with a large key and ushered Ahmet and Hassan in.

'So here we are, then. As you see, we're not rich, but we're comfy. Come and sit in the parlour.' Hassan followed Mrs Jackson into the gloom, down a passageway and through a door on the left. There were tallow candles on the mantelpiece and on side tables, casting monstrous flickering shadows on the walls. Hassan's eyes picked out a Bible, a few other books and a rack of clay pipes. They reminded Hassan of the pictures in his mind. The man in the red jacket might have been there, reading his book and reaching up for a pipe. A low fire flickered in the hearth, lighting the fire-dogs, a tremendous clutter of little tables with round spindle legs, oak elbow-chairs, toby jugs and endless ornamental items. On a sofa there were stockings, half-darned, a gigantic needle and thread and a pin cushion. A cheap, dark Dutch clock ticked loudly above the crackling of the fire.

On a small table covered with green baize there were plates and tin mugs, a cheese board and a knife, but no cheese. Just visible through the clutter was a small patterned carpet which also reminded Hassan of Bombay. On the walls there were colourful but poorly-drawn pictures, probably bought from a street-pedlar: men handing out fish to a large crowd, a man about to kill another man in front of a burning bush; and woman with a baby holding a cross. Hassan understood none of them.

Mrs Jackson returned with a lamp and mugs, which she filled from a black iron pot standing on a trivet in front of the fire.

'There now. Something to warm you up. Don't mind me father. Johnson, 'is name is. If he snores just nudge 'im a little. 'Bout every ten minutes should do at this time o' day. Try not to surprise 'im, though. 'E don't like it.'

Uncle Ahmet looked confused, and Mrs Jackson pointed into a dark corner. There, barely visible and perfectly still, was an elderly man with a bushy grey and yellowed beard and half-moon glasses hanging on a string. He wore grey breeches and a waistcoat with brass buttons, both of which had seen better days. Every now and then his chin dropped onto his chest, and his top lip quivered and rasped noisily.

Then there was an explosion of noise from the hall – shouting, laughing, running and the scraping of a table. As the door banged, the old man leapt forward, reaching for his stick. He staggered to his feet, shouting, and launched himself at Uncle Ahmet.

'They're in the orchards! In the trees, coming straight for us. Down there, look, below the walls! Quick – fetch ammunition! His hands reached for Ahmet's throat, then he reached to his waist for an imaginary sword, and then he looked confused for a moment, looking at his hands, then at the floor, and then out of the high window which looked out onto the street.

'I am sorry, sir. You have been disturbed,' said Uncle Ahmet.

'Not at all, sir,' said Granddad. 'Right you are. Are you selling grain? Can you make a spade?'

He stood still as Tommy Jackson, still holding the taper he had used to light the lamps, came into the room with two girls. One was perhaps a couple of years younger than Tommy, and wore a dark grey dress with a white collar. Her brown hair was gathered at the back. She looked at Hassan and uncle Ahmet with amazed blue eyes. The older girl, whose hair was strawberry blonde and who had a scattering of small freckles across her nose, seemed about the same age as Hassan. She looked straight at Hassan and frowned a little, before smiling and making a little curtsy.

'Lucy, sir, pleased to make your acquaintance'.

She nudged her sister, who did the same.

'Lizabet, sir, pleased to make your acquaintance likewise, I'm sure.'

Tommy spoke for the three of them.

'You well, Granddad? See our new wisitors: 'assan and Mr Qaderi. They've had such adventures to tell you about. 'Ope you like 'em, guv'nor.' And off he went again.

A few minutes later there was a knock on the door, and Lizabet went out to answer it.

'Good afternoon, miss,' said a familiar voice. 'Fetch Mrs Jackson, if you please.'

'Yes, Pa. You coming in, then?'

'I'll remind you, young lady, that I'm not over the doorstep just yet.'

'Sorry, Sergeant Jackson'.

Then there were two firm steps on the tiles in the hall, and a shriek of helpless childish laughter. Sergeant Jackson came into the room carrying the child, her arms round his neck. He kissed the elder daughter and ruffled the son's hair.

'Did you get Mr Lovelace, Tommy?'

Yes, Pa. He went there straight'.

'Good lad.' He looked around at the clutter, seeming to have forgotten about Ahmet and Hassan. Finally, he saw them. 'Now! Visitors! Ah yes! I 'ope you finds yourselves come-for-table. These are my two girls, Lucy – she's fourteen, and Lizabet. She's ten.'

'Oh, yes, sir, thank you,' said Uncle Ahmet.

'Good. Good. Let's find some stoo.'

Soon the eight of them were sitting at the baize-covered table. As the stew disappeared, Sergeant Jackson turned to his wife.

'Thank you for that, my dear Molly. Most satisfactory. 'Ave you 'ad sufficient. Mr Qaderi?'

'I never eat sufficient,' said Uncle Ahmet. 'What is it, please?' And he wondered why Tommy roared laughing.

'No,' said Mr Jackson. 'I mean, 'ave you 'ad enough?' He patted his stomach.

Now it was Uncle Ahmet's turn to smile. 'Oh yes, yes. Thank you. Very good and delicious, Mrs Jackson.'

'Very well, sir,' said the Sergeant. 'Now we need to speak about what 'appened earlier.' He looked meaningfully around the table, and Mrs Jackson and the girls went into the scullery, and the old man shuffled back into his corner seat, lit a pipe and watched the street outside silently. Tommy sat deadly still and silent, hoping not to be noticed.

'Now. Who was this man?'

21

Michael Reeves

'He was crew on *Aurora*.'

'From?'

'From Bombay. Merchant ship and some soldiers'.

'D'you know his name?'

'Kajan. Indian. I know no Hindi.'

'Me neither. But the captain knows him?'

'Oh yes. Captain Butterworth. On *Aurora* now.'

'Good. I shall visit Captain Butterworth early in the morning. Did you see the dead man after he left the ship?'

'I look for my merchandise.'

'I see. What have you brought from Bombay?'

'Spice, some dye, some silk, some carpets.'

'And did the dead man bring anything valuable?'

'Oh no. He a poor man. Crew on boat.'

'Yes, but plenty of poor folk are killed for next to nothing on those docks: and outside, away from them gas lamps. Anyhow, who might have done this 'orrible thing?'

'I not know'.

'Really? No arguments on the boat?'

'Oh no. No arguments. And the dead man leave alone. Went into crowd'.

'Very well, Mr Qaderi. I'm obliged to you. Now, will you stay with us for a few days? I am sure Grandpa will appreciate the company.'

'You very kind, sir. We pay you. We pay in London'.

'No, no'. He thought a moment. 'Well, perhaps you can ask my wife. We do sometimes have paying guests. Now let me show you to your room. It's only one pair of stairs'.

Hassan and Uncle Ahmet were shown to a room with an iron bedstead, two chamber pots, a fireplace and a pine wash stand with a big tin jug and a basin.

'It's the children's room, usually, but they'll sleep in the parlour with granddad'. And Sergeant Jackson trod softly back down the stairs.

Hassan lay with great relief on one side of the bed, and Uncle Ahmet sat on the other looking out of the window. He looked troubled by something.

'What is it, uncle?'

'Do not worry yourself, Hassan. We are both tired.' He looked into Hassan's eyes, as though he wanted to ask him something. And then he looked out of the window again, stroking his beard.

Hassan was still curious.

'Uncle?'

'Yes, my child?'

'What did the man say?'

'Which man? When?'

'Why, the man who died, of course.'

'I am not sure, Hassan. It was hard to hear.'

Hassan wondered at this, and again was left watching his uncle's back. He would ask again tomorrow.

As always at this time, Hassan placed his knife under his pillow. There was no need, but it had become habit now. And then he reached for the book. This time he opened the cover and looked at the title page. *The Pickwick Papers* by Charles Dickens. London, Chapman and Hall, 180 The Strand, MDCCCXXXVII. And a picture of a different fat man, trying to duck the head of a little thin man in a water trough outside a public house.

Hassan gazed into the picture. So this was what the *feringhees* did in the evenings. But no – he somehow knew that the man in the red jacket had never done anything like this. The man in the red jacket was a good man. And he had written in the corner of the page, in black ink, perhaps with the pen that Hassan vaguely remembered.

'To my dear Hassan, whom, God willing, I shall one day see again. Your loving father. January 1842.'

He took out the envelope. *A Story for Hassan on his Fifth Birthday.* He read it only occasionally, because he did not want it to lose its power, but now seemed a good time.

It was not so much a letter as a story.

*

My dear nephew Hassan,

I do not know where you will be when you are old enough to read this story. I cannot foresee the man you will become, or the woman you will marry, or the sons you will have. Nor can I know what will become of your loving father and mother. For there is much danger in the world.

What will become of you, I wonder? Perhaps you will have grown into a prince, or a rich merchant, or a Mullah. It is all in the hand of Allah. But whoever you are, and wherever you are, I hope that you will often read what I have written for you. Perhaps one day you will read it to your own children, and perhaps they will read it to theirs. Perhaps you will read this to yourself, or perhaps your mother or father will read it to you.

Always remember, Hassan, that some stories are true, and some are not. And stories are true in different ways. Was there really anybody called Ali Baba? Did forty thieves ever hide in pots and get boiled alive? Perhaps not. But is it true that there is honesty and treachery? Is it true that there can be love in a servant-girl's eyes? Of course it is true.

The story I have to tell you is true, but it is for you to discover how it is true, and also how true it is. But there is one thing you must remember always: if the treasure that is yours can be found, it is for you to find it, and nobody else.

*

There was once a boy in a great city who was rich beyond the wildest dreams of men. Like many men (and women and children), he did not know that he was rich, and nor did he know what had made him rich. He was the son of a good man and a good and beautiful mother, and he was born in a fine city one beautiful night in the winter, when the stars shone brightly and the air was icy cold. The moment he was born he acquired a treasure, by a power that is known only to Allah. It was a treasure born in a drop of blood, and which grows and grows.

Some of the treasure had come from across the seas, in a ship that sat as proudly on the waves as a fortress on its hilltop, and some had come from his own country. His mother and father knew of the treasure, but nobody else in the great city knew about it. Not the King, not the Vizier, not the Imam. Even the wisest knew nothing of the boy's riches.

Except, that is, for one other man. He was the uncle of the boy, a poor trader. Once, he had been loved by the people of his city, for he paid the poor due and cared for the widow and the orphan. They loved to see him wrestle, and to look into his kind and happy face.

Yet soon, the uncle became much abused by the people of the city. He had done what he thought was good and right, and thought he may, inshallah, be rewarded by God for it. But the people did not understand what he had done. He had to leave his nephew and his sister and his sister's husband, and the city that was his home. He had to flee for his life across plains and mountains, under the boiling sun and through the freezing wind, looking for a place where he would be safe.

And there he is today, inshallah, as you listen to this story, or as you read it yourself. The uncle hopes to live a good life and to be rewarded with the thanks of his new countrymen and the blessings of heaven and the love of a woman and his children. But always he will think of what he left behind, and wonder what happened to the treasure and the boy. He lives in fear of travellers, knowing that any one of them might bring him the news he dreads.

When the uncle left the nephew in the city with his mother and father, he knew that there were terrible times ahead. For the people had begun to hear of the treasure, and some started to envy the boy. The treasure was an evil thing, they said. It must leave the city, and be returned across the seas before it could do them harm. Some even thought that the treasure should be destroyed before it could be taken away. The boy would be happier without it.

The uncle who fled did not hear of the treasure again. Some told him that it was destroyed. Others said that it lost its beauty and is now worthless. And others said that it had been returned to the place from which it came, closely guarded by good and loyal men. Some believe that it is buried in the sands somewhere nearby, guarded by a poor shepherd who has been bewitched into silence. Nor does anybody know where the little boy is.

Perhaps, my dear nephew, you are with your own treasure now. And if not, I pray to Allah that you will find it one day. I hope that one day we shall meet again. If ever you are in trouble, send a letter to Ahmet Qaderi the Afghan merchant in Bombay. Then, inshallah, *I shall come to you. And, if Allah wills it, you will be reconciled with what you have lost.*

Your loving uncle, Ahmet Qaderi

*

Hassan closed the book, wondering when his search would begin. Then he slept, and his uncle still sat looking out of the window.

Chapter Three

December 1855

In the shadows outside, as far from the nearest gaslight as they could be, two figures looked up at a window and watched carefully. Seated just inside was the man Ahmet Qaderi, his eyes searching up and down the street like those of a hunted man. Somewhere in the house was the boy, Hassan.

Sometimes Khodar and Aziz spoke, with their faces bent towards one another, as they had on *Aurora*. Here they were much quieter, because there was no rushing and heaving of the sea and no wind to carry their words away. Even now, well after dark, there were a few people going about their business: the odd delivery of coal; a boy heading for the Dock Road to sell newspapers; a sailmaker and a lamplighter on their way home. It was worth being cautious.

*

They had first seen Ahmet long ago, of course, but had never got to know him. They had been sent to Kabul by Aziz's father, and had come through the mountains from the east in November 1841 with a cargo of rich red cloth to sell to the British, and the most wonderful hand-fashioned carpets which they hoped the soldiers would want to send home to their wives or mothers. Khodar had come partly to earn a living, but also partly as a family favour. After all, somebody had to look after Aziz.

But by the time they had arrived it was too late. Nobody wanted red cloth or beautiful carpets. The beautiful things were already being burned: Lady Sale's mahogany table had gone in small pieces into her fire, and the books had mostly been sacrificed for a feeble, short-lived warmth. Khodar had dreaded the prospect of returning home to explain this to his uncle. So they, or rather Khodar, had decided to stay and hope for good fortune.

They remembered Ahmet as the man of strength, the wise man, the man people admired, and loved even. The wheat merchant, the man's man, the friend of the *feringhees,* the wrestler. He had run from Kabul, fled for his life, two weeks after they had arrived. They didn't quite know why, but when they spoke about him in Kabul, they were met with sorrow in some people and loathing in others.

Aziz thought that Ahmet may have done some terrible thing which had roused the blood of some powerful Kabuli, but Khodar always believed that everything was connected to the treasure.

They had found out about the treasure after the *feringhee* army had departed. What chaos it had been as they had left and headed into their Hell, the coldest and most miserable hell the world had ever known!

After the slaughter of the fifteen thousand in the passes, many in Kabul had gone to rake through the English and Indian ashes for anything of value: men and women who had half-starved because of high grain prices, magpie children looking for bright and shiny things, opportunists searching for what they could sell, rifled through the cantonments, through Sir Sikundur's house; and later, after he was dead, through the Shah's palace. A few had even gone into the passes, into the blood and the snow. Latecomers waited for the spring before looking through the bird-picked corpses and scattered debris.

Dozens of scavengers had returned from the Khoord Kabul and Jugdulluk passes, with odd little scraps for sale. Rings and watches, some crusted with blood. Weapons – a sword, a rifle. An empty wagon, a half-dead camel. Clothing from the dead – men's, women's and children's - which had escaped the bullets and swords.

Some had even brought back documents: after all, who knew what they might be worth to the British, should they ever return? It was Aziz who had first come across it, that letter which had somehow escaped the destruction. Khodar had told Aziz that papers can be valuable, and more than anything Aziz wanted to please his cousin. This arose in part from his fear of Khodar.

He was given it: not by a genie fresh out of a bottle, not by an archangel or a ghost or a spirit, but by a real old man with real whiskers on his face and real hunger in his belly. He had been a farrier, and had done well for a while under the *feringhees*, but then his own people had deserted him, and the *feringhees* had left. Now he had joined the scavengers. The letter had cost Aziz a bowl of rice. The farrier, suspecting that his property was worthless, would not allow him to see the letter before the rice was handed over.

Aziz could make no sense of the letter, of course, beyond its simple-minded story. He had laughingly balled it up and thrown it at Khodar, pretending that he understood it. After all, it did him no harm to show that he could learn. But Khodar was more cautious, and quickly unrolled it. He was pleased that the writing was in his own language, and he started to read.

There was no date on the letter, but Khodar knew exactly when it had been written: in November, two months ago, just as they were settling in Kabul. Ahmet had fled in November, as the snows had started, and had not been seen since. This was his last message to a Kabuli. Here was a letter worth keeping! He put it under his *poshteen* and said nothing to Aziz until later. They had eaten rice and gee and fried mutton and were sitting alone, strangely enough, in the dismal remains of some *feringhee* house. They had lit a fire out of some pointless bric-a-brac.

'Aziz, what have you heard of *feringhee* treasure?'

Aziz thought for a moment. 'The *feringhee* army brought much treasure. Wagon loads of treasure. You know where it was: in Captain

Johnson's treasury house. You have seen much of it. And now it is gone: into the hands of women and children.'

'Yes. But is there not a greater treasure somewhere, do you think? A treasure ...' He struggled to remember the words. '... beyond the wildest dreams of men?'

Aziz frowned, and closed his eyes as he thought again. 'But my dear cousin Khodar,' he laughed, 'you must understand that if they could bring the treasure here with them, they could have taken it away again. Or... or perhaps it was given to the King, or to Akbar Khan, or to the Dost.'

'That may be. Of course it may. And if it were the great Mogul diamond, the Koh-i-Noor, which the Shah stupidly gave to Ranjeet Singh, it could easily be put into a small bag and carried over the Hindu Kush. But perhaps there is a still greater treasure. What do you think? Is it possible?'

Aziz looked at Khodar quizzically. He had seen this enthusiasm in his cousin before, and when they were boys it had often led to trouble. Aziz had always followed on the current, unresisting. Still, he thought, now that they were men Khodar was usually quite wise: and certainly cleverer than he was. What was he thinking?

'I am thinking,' said Khodar, 'that there may be a great treasure here in Kabul, and that only we know about it. Listen to this.'

And he had read the story to Aziz, who listened intently with one eye shut.

'Do you not see? It is a secret message, a message to the boy, Hassan. *A great city.* Why, cousin, it is Kabul!'

'Perhaps,' said Aziz. 'And perhaps it is just a story. Like *The Thousand Nights and One Night'.* You don't believe all this! Do you believe in Ali Baba, also?'

'But do you not see? We know who Hassan is, and we know who his uncle is. Surely it is Ahmet the wrestler, whose sister married the *feringhee.* The uncle who fled for his life into the mountains. All we need now is to find Ahmet and Hassan. One or the other.'

'And then?'

'And then they tell us where the treasure is, and then we find it.'

'But how do we find them? Why would they tell us? What will do if we find the treasure – the Koh-i-Noor, or whatever it is?'

'Let us see. Perhaps it has been destroyed. Perhaps it has been returned across the seas. Or perhaps it has always been here. Do you see? Here in Kabul! *Others believe that it is buried in the sands close to the city.* Perhaps we do not need to look. Let us see firstly if it is here in the city. Here in Kabul. If not, why, we can look in the feringhees' favourite places outside the walls.'

Aziz still looked doubtful.

'The treasure was *born in a drop of blood,*' he said. 'What treasure could be born in a drop of blood?'

'Why, *feringhee* treasure, of course. All of their treasure is born of blood and war, can you not see? And no treasure that is born of bloodshed can belong to the *feringhee*. It is ours!'

Khodar laughed and lay on his back, making a pillow of his *poshteen*. But Aziz felt troubled.

'This treasure does not belong to us,' he said simply. It belongs to the child. Or to his father and mother if they are alive. You remember the words of the Holy Qur'an: *Give unto orphans their wealth. Exchange not the good for the bad in your management thereof, nor absorb their wealth into your own wealth. That would be a great sin!*'

'Your conscience!' sneered Khodar. 'The boy is not here. His father and mother are not here. Nobody knows where they are – perhaps in the land of the *feringhee*, perhaps in Jalalabad, perhaps in the garden where rivers flow, perhaps in hell. Any how, when have you ever heard of the poor due being paid in Kabul? And you think a *feringhee's* child will pay the poor due?'

He thought for a moment. Then he was calm again. He put a hand on his cousin's shoulder.

'Very well. You are right, my cousin. We must make sure that the treasure, or some of the treasure, is used for the poor. But we can be sure of that only if we are the ones who find it!'

He got up and walked away, and Aziz watched him anxiously.

*

They had searched all of the obvious places: Captain Johnson's house, Lieutenant Smith's house, Sir Sikundur's house, the treasury and every part of the cantonments, even the buildings that had been gutted by fire. They tried to make friends with the thirty-odd sick and wounded *feringhees* who had been left behind, but they were too tired, too ignorant or too suspicious. In desperation, Khodar had even skirted the lake where, he had heard, people had been walking on the ice. He looked for disturbed rocks and behind boulders. He found nothing.

The last place to look would be Bombay, but even Khodar accepted that Bombay was a long way to go to ask such a question. One day, he thought, he would more prosperous, he would have regained his losses from this terrible expedition, and he would go there. And when he was there he would find Ahmet, the treasure-boy's uncle.

What was it, Aziz wondered, that made Khodar so unhappy that he could think of nothing else?

Chapter Four

December 1855

Still, Khodar and Aziz looked up at the windows of number 28, until after the candle had been snuffed out between Uncle Ahmet's wet fingers. Khodar thought of the treasure, and Aziz thought of Bombay. He had been happy there.

They had left for India a long year before, Khodar in search of his obsession and Aziz looking for a little innocent adventure. They had approached Bombay from the south, and the seven islands, all joined together by causeways to make one united city, had appeared in the afternoon like slivers of green. Then they had seen the silver beaches curving gracefully inland, and then were round Colaba and heading for the harbour. The monsoon was over, the lawns and palm trees were freshly radiant and the air was newly scented by fresh growth.

After a few days, trade had gone well, and they had little left to sell. It was time to think of returning, or of moving on elsewhere. Either way, they had to buy things to take back with them. Aziz was keen to head for home, but Khodar seemed slightly excited and restless. Every evening he was at the dockside, looking at the clippers and the Eastindiamen and the new steam ships spouting smoke as they set off southwards towards the point. Perhaps, he thought, we should see England. Perhaps we will find something there. Perhaps the treasure, whatever it is.

He watched groups of blue and scarlet soldiers disembarking, most of them new to Bombay. He wondered what they knew of the slaughter in the Khoord-Kabul and Jugdulluk passes, or the burning houses in the cantonments of Kabul. Had they heard that Sir Sikundur's body had been cut into pieces and hung up in the bazaar?

'These *feringhees*!' he said, and spat into the dust.

'My father was a *feringhee*.'

Khodar turned sharply to see a boy standing close by.

'You are an Afghan? A Pashtun?'

'I was. A long time ago. Now I live here in Bombay. With my uncle. Sometimes he tells me about Afghanistan. Often I come here to look out for Afghans so that I can ask them about Kabul.'

Khodar was on the alert instantly.

'And you are from Kabul?'

'I was born in Kabul.'

'And your father was a *feringhee*. A soldier?'

'Yes. My uncle has told me so.'

'And your mother?'

'She was a Kabuli. My uncle's younger sister.'

Khodar had to work hard to hide his excitement.

'She was? So she is now with Allah?'

'Yes. I believe so. I never knew her. '

'And your father?'

The boy looked absently out to sea.

'I do not know where he is. Perhaps he too is in the garden where rivers flow. My uncle has told he me was wounded in Kabul. My uncle was beside him when it happened. And the Good Man Leary was killed. So when the Bombay army returned here, they had to leave my father behind in Kabul. Then he fell in love with my mother, and she cared for him. He was sick, and then he got well again, and they married. And then I was born!'

He opened his eyes wide, grinned and spread his arms, as though to tell Khodar that his life was a miracle.

Then he became more serious. 'And then, when I was just a year old, the rest of the army left. My mother died I think, and my father went away. I don't know how, and nor I think does my uncle. And we do not know what happened to him. I believe he is very far away, in another land.'

Khodar smiled and looked into the boy's eyes.

'It is an interesting story. And what do you do here? How do you live?'

'My Uncle Ahmet is a merchant. He has a fine house on Malabar Hill. Near the General's house. He buys and sells all sorts of things. At the moment he is very excited. The railway is being built from here to Thane, and he says there will be new cotton mills and lots of money.'

Now it was Khodar's turn to look out to sea. He could not believe what he was hearing. Uncle Ahmet! It was fate!

'And what is your name, my friend?'

'Hassan. Sometimes I am called Hassan Qaderi, and sometimes Hassan Smith. For in Bombay they like to hear your family name also.'

'And which do you call yourself?'

'I prefer Hassan Qaderi. For it is my uncle's name.'

'Hassan Qaderi. So, Hassan, your uncle will trade in cotton? He will make lots of money? He will build a treasure house?' he laughed, but Hassan was still serious.

'My Uncle Ahmet wants to trade across the sea.'

'Oh? Where to?'

'To the country my father came from. England. Uncle Ahmet says that the port of London is the greatest port in the world, and there are fortunes to be made. Soon we will go there. Uncle Ahmet says that there is something...'

He stopped abruptly. He had said too much.

'Tell me. Your uncle. Might I meet him? I have been away from Afghanistan for a year, almost, and I would like to hear Pashtu. It is as though the breeze has stopped, not hearing your own language.'

'My Uncle Ahmet will be here shortly. But you must understand that he does not often speak to Afghans, especially Kabulis. I do not know why. He has never told me."

Hassan's eye caught something behind Khodar, and Khodar turned to see a man approaching, well but not expensively dressed, a neatly trimmed beard, mostly white now, even though he was probably only forty. Hassan called out.

'Uncle Ahmet! I have found a friend!"

Khodar recognised Ahmet at once: the calm poise, the stillness even as he walked. It was Ahmet the wrestler, Ahmet the grain merchant. Khodar watched for a moment as man and boy talked, Ahmet's hand on the boy's shoulder. Ahmet Qaderi glanced at Khodar. There was no recognition, but this was no surprise: after all, Ahmet was the famous one.

He was not the man he was, thought Khodar. A little older. A little sadder, a little slower. What had happened to him? There was still energy in the eyes, and strength in the shoulders and arms. It would be a brave or foolish man who leapt out at him in the dark. But there was also an exhaustion of the spirit, it seemed.

'Greetings, my friend!'

Khodar had been just a little too enthusiastic, and a flicker of suspicion crossed Uncle Ahmet's face. But it was soon gone, and he recognised the need of a man in a strange land. For once, he smiled at a Kabuli.

'And also to you, my friend. Hassan has often told me of his meetings and his adventures on the dock, but this time I have seen it for myself. Will you take some tea with us?'

'You are kind to the traveller! First I must find my cousin. He is often a wanderer: not a wanderer from the straight path, praise be to Allah, but difficult to keep an eye on!' He put a finger to his temple and looked at the sky.

Hassan pointed urgently at a man sitting on a sack under the bows of a steamship, looking up at the funnel.

'There! Is that him?'

Sure enough, it was Aziz, and Hassan rushed off to introduce himself and invite Aziz to tea.

An hour later, they were seated in a garden filled with birdsong and the fragrance of hibiscus and bougainvillea.

That was where, after a series of hints and plenty of flattery from Khodar, all of it pointedly ignored by Ahmet, they came to their arrangement. They would travel together to England, the centre of the known world, where there were fortunes to be made. They would leave in five months. Ahmet had already made his own plans. Aziz and Khodar would stay in a small house near the port, buying and selling, earning enough to buy wares to make their journey worthwhile.

As they left the house the sun was setting. Uncle Ahmet fixed them with one of his looks.

'As I have said to you, my friends, you will not be employed by me. You will be employed by Captain Butterworth. That means that he can throw you into the sea whenever he likes, without asking my permission.'

Aziz was sure that Ahmet was serious. Even Khodar was not quite sure that he was joking.

*

Now that the lights were out at 28, Evans Street, Aziz wondered what would happen next.

'We must find somewhere to rest our heads,' he said. Khodar still stared at the house, as though the Koh-i-Noor diamond was sitting on a first floor windowsill. Aziz nudged him.

'What is it, Aziz?' He was irritated.

'Are we to stay here all night, Khodar?'

'We have to watch.'

'But why? We can return early tomorrow.'

'Yes, perhaps that would be best.'

'Let us return to the road and look for a *serai*.'

Soon they were back in the clattering traffic of the Dock Road, with its horses and wagons, shops and lodging houses, nooks and corners. Aziz noticed that always Khodar was looking around him, as though he were watching for somebody. At every corner, at every crossing, he would do the same. He had been doing this since they left the dock, since just after he had sent Aziz off on an errand to the warehouse.

Aziz thought it likely that something had happened while he had been gone.

Chapter Five

Lieutenant William Smith and his platoon had not seen Ghazni properly until dawn. Last night they had seen only a vague outline of the citadel, since they had pitched camp almost in the dark. This morning, they had struck camp at five soon after the fortress was in view, dull, brown and dusty against a steel-grey sky. At first it had shimmered darkly, hardly visible in the chill dawn. But as the sun had strengthened, it positively shone, in a light as clear and clean and hard as any light in the world. It had been many miles off, but Sergeant Leary said that it seemed a few steps away.

'Like a picture on the wall, sir. Couldn't you just reach out and touch it!'

'Perhaps, Leary. But just wait until we are in the picture proper. We shall certainly touch it then. And perhaps Ghazni will touch us. Just look at her. I believe the walls are eight feet thick.'

By eight o'clock they were within two miles, and Ghazni seemed to be rearing up in front of them. The city was built on raised ground, and its walls were built some way up a slope. Inside the walls, a great sand-coloured rock rose up, and atop this was the citadel – another circular wall containing more mud-brick buildings and a great tower.

Soon they heard a British gun battery firing at the walls, and Ghazni's brass cannon firing back. The entire army, except for two regiments of Native Infantry, was ordered to skirt around the city, out of range of the Afghan guns, on narrow, rocky mountain paths. After many hours, they reached the Kabul side.

The Native Infantry were ordered to clear the enemy out of surrounding villages, orchards and gardens, and the threat soon melted away into the city, a threat that could appear and disappear like shadows on a wall.

As the army swung slowly around the city, the height of Ghazni's central citadel and surrounding walls, and the steepness of its rocky seat, became more and more sharply engraved on the mind. Half a mile from the walls was a mighty pillar, perhaps some symbol of the city's power aimed at its enemies. Smith and his men arrived late in the afternoon, under a blazing sun and a luminous blue sky. Long before they could see any sign of human life – smoke, a flag – or hear anything from within, Ghazni seemed to have a power and life of its own, unmoving and everlasting, and quite beyond the wit of man. Surely it could not be defeated. Leary was the first to say so.

'It's impregnable, sir. How do we get in there? I never seen anything like it, sir, not in all my days in the Army, sir.'

'There are ways, Leary. Three ways to break a fort. What are they?'

'Siege it, sir. But they've p'raps got food for months, we've got food for three days, sir.'

'Quite. And?'

'Escalade it, sir. Ladders, sir. But they'll kill us. With their big hitter sir, and their *jezails*. Much better 'n our rifles, begging pardon, sir. Better range, an' more accurate. An' we'll be in the open. They'll pick us off.'

'Hmmm. And?'

'Artillery, sir. But we left the big guns in Kandahar, sir. And after we'd dragged 'em through the passes! All we got now is the little guns. Wouldn't get in there with 'em. Sir'

Smith smiled and looked at Leary with his eyebrows raised just a little ironically.

'Well, I'm sure the General has thought of a way. We shall soon find out, I am sure.'

Smith liked Leary, perhaps more than an officer should like his sergeant. Leary didn't have Smith's education, or his military training, or a country estate waiting for him in Surrey. And he certainly didn't have a scholar for a brother. In fact, his life story was still a blank page to Smith, except that he was a Londoner. Leary never mentioned his past and Smith, of course, had never asked. So he could only imagine one of those dark places in Whitechapel, and the younger Leary who had run from it years ago.

Leary's strength was his extra ten years of experience in the Queen's 13th Light Infantry. In Smith's early days in India, Leary had given him all sorts of quiet advice, without letting anything slip to the men. It had been a helpful and subtle sort of loyalty.

But even if Smith was green, he was far from weak. So eventually, the tables had been turned. The Regiment had been in a mess for months: disease had killed hundreds of men in Burma, and replacing them was urgent work. So the Regiment cleared the young and fit out of London's prisons and shipped them across the oceans for a new life. They were hardened, difficult men. There was too much drinking and too much gambling, and there were too many fights in the barracks. At least one sergeant was stabbed to death, for there were too few officers who could keep a grip. Those who could yearned for a commander who would knock things into shape.

And then Colonel Robert 'Fighting Bob' Sale took charge. The dregs from the goals soon realised that things were going to change, but many fought on. Daily floggings – four men each morning, four each evening, regardless of the crime – took place in front of the parading troops. Sale soon received death threats, but had handled these with typical bravado – lunacy, almost. He ordered the whole parade to load blanks and fire at him. Any of the six hundred men could have put a live round into his rifle, but nobody did. And Sale would leave on his horse, laughing. The floggings continued, but then slowed as the Regiment became one of the finest of the Indian units.

During this time, Leary had fallen foul of Fighting Bob. Half a bottle of rum was not a good way to prepare for a parade, and one afternoon Leary found himself staggering about in a sea of blurred crimson and dust before waking up under a mango tree. Four of his brother sergeants carried him to his bed. His excuse was that the heat had caught him out. Smith, although only a lieutenant, politely requested that the Colonel show mercy to Leary.

'I believe, sir, that the sergeant was ill.'

Sale stood still as marble, epaulettes perfectly balanced, sword hanging from his belt. His right eyebrow lifted just a little, and he looked steadily at the bridge of Smith's nose.

'Ill, Smith? What can you mean? The man was drunk. Drunk on parade.'

'I believe, sir, that the effect of his liquor was made the greater by the heat, sir, and also by his illness, of course. Moreover, sir, Leary is a fine sergeant, loyal and brave. I would request, sir, that you limit his punishment somewhat, and make me responsible for his future conduct'.

'Responsible for him as you were this afternoon, what? What d'you propose to do with the man? Discipline, Smith!'

'I have been in error, sir. But Leary will know not to play this game in my platoon again, sir. He shall make amends, I guarantee it.'

The Colonel did not ask Smith how he knew about Leary's bravery. After all, the two had never seen action together. But he was impressed by Smith's loyalty to his junior, told him not to make a habit of it and reduced Leary's punishment to twenty lashes, in private. By the time his wounds had healed Leary was putty in Smith's hand.

Now, in Afghanistan, they were both on strange ground, but it was Smith who knew a little more about sieges and scaling ladders, and who had read something of the country and the people. He had even learned a little Pashtu. They had left Bombay by ship last November, landed at Karachi and joined with the Bengal Army at Kandahar in June.

It made for a fine army: fifty thousand men and thirty thousand transport camels. Plodding along with them were thousands of head of cattle, enough to feed the army for three months, and dwindling by the day. If you could have stood and watched as the army passed, you would have stood and watched for half the day. There were English soldiers with their white breeches and red tunics, their rifles and their feathered hats. There were Indian soldiers and nearly forty thousand followers: servants, cooks, stewards, cleaners and porters. The camels were over-laden with all things imaginable, and squealed in pain as they crossed the harsh ground through the mountain passes, for their hooves were more suited to dust and sand than rock and flint, and many went lame. They starved, and ate poisonous plants by the wayside. They died in their thousands. Many carried tents, of course, but others were used more frivolously. Two carried nothing but fat cigars; dozens carried crisp white bed linen for the crisp white officers; they carried jars of pickles and jams; several carried mahogany dining tables, white table cloths, silver candelabras, knives and forks, champagne, beer and whisky. Some officers, even the lieutenants, had forty servants and a dozen camels each. As Lieutenant James had said, 'No point in taking civilisation to the wilderness and leaving the essentials behind'. So even in the Bolan Pass, hemmed in by rocks and gloom, and often dying in their dozens at the hands of scampering *jezailchees*, they had laid out their picnic blankets, and eaten beef, fish and pickles from fine crockery, and passed round wine in pewter goblets.

Now Smith watched a rather grand train of horses, ambling slowly in the heat. At its head was an Afghan with a fine black beard and deep and mellow chestnut eyes. He wore a full length, tobacco coloured robe which even as he sat in the saddle almost covered his boots. He had thrown a fine cloak of Persian blue across his shoulder, and must have held it there for hours after the damp chill of the dawn had been burned away. As his horse stood still he squared his shoulders, lifted his chin a little and stared across at the city. A servant helped him dismount, looking downwards all the while.

Shortly behind was an Englishman dressed in white trousers, a white tunic with splendid epaulettes, and a pith helmet to shade his head and neck. He too dismounted and walked to the Afghan, bowing ever so slightly, as though the Afghan were half way between a king and a friend in Oxford Street. Here was the man in charge, bow as he might. They were shortly joined by a large, white-haired man in a red tunic and feathered helmet, and a younger, efficient looking officer. Perhaps a little fearfully, and certainly with surprise, they all gazed across at the walls of Ghazni for some time before the younger officer spoke.

'It is unfortunate, Sir John, that we left the heavy guns in Kandahar. They appear now to be just what is needed!'

'Big guns be damned, Major Havelock,' retorted the General, a little red-faced. 'There are other ways!'

'If we do not need them now, Sir John, it seems strange that we should have hauled them through the passes to Kandahar. Where could we have needed them more than we need them here?'

'Poppycock, sir! Wait and see!' Sir John glared dismissively at Havelock, who then made his retreat, giving orders for the pitching of camp. The General turned to the Afghan with a smile and a little, barely respectful bow.

'Your Majesty has seen Ghazni before?'

'Indeed, Sir John, but some time ago.'

'And what are they like, the people? How will they resist us?'

'They are a brave people. There is none braver in Afghanistan. They fight for their city, of course, and for themselves, but you see the flags?'

The two Englishmen peered searchingly at the distant walls. The white-suited gentleman cleaned his little round glasses on a crisp linen handkerchief and looked again.

'Ah, yes. I can just see them.'

'Mr Macnaghten, they are green. You know this quarter of the world well. You have translated many of *A Thousand Nights and One Night* into your own tongue. You know the meaning of a green flag.'

'Indeed,' said Macnaghten. These are the fearsome Ghazees, fighting under the flag of Islam. He smiled slightly, as though unconcerned.

'Just so. And that, praise Allah, gives great additional strength.'

'And you think it a good thing to praise Allah for the strength of your enemies?' asked the General, with just a little scorn.

'That is a fine question,' said the Shah. 'But yes - look at what Allah has given me: two British armies, two fine generals and Mr William Hay Macnaghten. Shortly the people will be my loving subjects, and the Persians will not dare to come down upon Afghanistan again. There will be a wondrous powerful people between the Russians and your glorious possessions in India!'

The Shah roared, briefly, with laughter. General Sir John Keane and Mr William Hay Macnaghten smiled a little and avoided Shah Soojah's chestnut eyes. He had made it all sound so simple. Smith sensed a great gulf between the Shah and the English.

Later, as the sun set, Smith set his guard at the edge of the camp. Leary handed him a battered tin mug of tea; it was so much more military than porcelain, Smith had always thought. The mountains to the east were painted with a dark umbra and turned from tallow to orange to grey as the sunlight chased up their sides. They had all seen such sunsets a hundred times since Karachi, but still this time of day moved them. And as their eyes and their hearts chased the last of the sun, and as the dark closed in on them, they all dealt in their own ways with their fears.

Smith left Leary and three men and went to his tent. At this time of day he thought briefly of a myriad of things, most of them to do with Surrey. He thought of his father and his brothers. He remembered the small domestic details that come into the mind when we are far from home: the cherry blossom in April, a new litter of spaniels, incense in the village church on Sundays. The Lord's Prayer and communion as sunlight streamed like arrows through the stained glass. His mother's hair mottled with green and red and amber. Conkers, roast goose, a roaring fire.

And then it felt chill again. Even in July, night time temperatures were sometimes not so far above freezing at this altitude. Smith trimmed his oil lamp and picked up his book. Perhaps he would read for five minutes.

'Well, Sam,' said Mr Pickwick as that favoured servitor entered his bed-chamber with his warm water, on the morning of Christmas Day, 'still frosty?'

'Water in the wash-hand basin's a mask o'ice, sir, responded Sam.

'Severe weather, Sam,' observed Mr Pickwick.

'Fine time for them as is well wropped up, as the Polar Bear said to himself, ven he was practising his skating,' replied Mr Weller.

'I shall be down in a quarter of an hour, Sam ...'

Suddenly, Smith was startled by yelling outside. It sounded like Leary, then the voice of one of the men. There were panicked cries in a foreign tongue, and then a slapping sound and a 'shaddup'.

'Mr Smith, sir, Mr Smith!'

Smith leapt for the opening in the tent, tunic all undone, the oil lamp in his left hand and his sword in his right. He soon came across a scrawny man, held by the scruff of his neck between Jones and Sergeant Leary.

'Caught him, sir, near the edge of the camp. Thieving, I'll warrant. Or spying. What shall I do with him, sir?'

'Let him go, Leary.'

There was a delay as Leary absorbed Smith's words.

'Go, sir?'

'Yes, Leary. Unhand him, I mean.'

The man almost collapsed to the floor as he was freed. Jones and Leary held him under the arms, now more kindly. It was hard to tell his age: he could have been anything between thirty-five and sixty. He had small walnut eyes which might have looked kinder had he not lived such a harsh life. And Smith saw the harshness at once. He may have been dressed well, if plainly, in a clean *poshteen* and lunghee, with neat sandals on his feet, but his face told another story. It was a face that had spent months in the sun, and then months in the ice and snow, and then again and again, year after year. Cracked leather. He had been terrified when Smith first saw him, but as Smith looked into his eyes he subsided and was quiet.

Smith spoke, and the man was amazed to hear his own language from the lips of the European.

'What is your name?'

'Malik, good sir. Poor shepherd, sir'.

'What are you doing here?'

'Want to help, sir'.

'Help? How? You can see that we have enough to eat.'

'Not food sir. To defeat Ghazni sir!'

Smith found this hard to believe. This was not what he'd heard about the valour of the men of Ghazni. He looked down at the wizened little man, into his frightened eyes, and wondered what use he could be in a war. Still, there was more to war than fighting.

'Shall we take him outside, sir? And shoot him, sir?'

'Good God! Certainly not, Leary. Do you really think we shall get the Afghans to support the new king if we start shooting little old men? Remember when we were going hungry the other side of Kandahar, out on the plains?'

'Yes sir, very well, sir.'

'Well, the Shah wanted us to take all the green crops for the army, and let the locals starve. Mr Macnaghten informed his majesty he had to treat his people better if he wanted to remain Shah for any length of time. Do you know what they do to kings here? To make sure they don't come back? To destroy their power?'

'Kill them, sir?'

'No. At least, not always, and not straight away. They put their eyes out. As they did to the last Shah. Then everybody knows what an ex-king looks like. Do you know any Shakespeare, Leary?'

Leary bit his lip. 'No, sir. Not in particklar.'

'*When lenity and cruelty play for a kingdom, the gentler gamester is the soonest winner.* King Henry V.'

'Yes, sir. Thank you, sir.'

Leary looked at the floor, and Jones whistled softly and mysteriously. Smith reverted to Pashtu.

'Now then, Mr Malik, how will you help us?'

Malik's face brightened just a little, as if with moonlight. Smith wondered about his life. His family, his friends, what he talked about round the fire on winters' evenings. He soon had his answer.

'To defeat the city. The walls, sir. The Kabul gate. Your army great, sir. And you can save my sons and my father and my brothers and sisters. I serve you. And perhaps ...'

His brown eyes flickered in the light from the oil lamp. His mouth quivered a little.

'Perhaps what?'

'Perhaps you give me rupees, great sir. For my help.'

'Hmmm. What about the Kabul gate?'

'Not finished, sir. Can be broken.'

'Very well. Come with me.'

Perhaps now they could avid the horrors of a siege or scaling ladders. Smith dragged Malik to the General's tent, where he was sitting drinking sherry with Colonel Sale and some younger officers. The air was filled with the smell of cigar smoke.

'Good Lord! What is it, Lieutenant? What have you got there?'

'It's a who, sir. A prisoner, sir. He came to report that the Kabul Gate is weak and might be brought down. He wishes to help, but wants sanctuary for his family. And money.'

'A reasonable request, I should say. I should be less than honest if I did not admit that breaking Ghazni is somewhat urgent. We are already short of provisions, after all, and these raids are not improving our situation. We saw the Dost's forces at Belanti Ghilzyee, and again yesterday morning. Remember, gentlemen – time is on his side, not on ours. The raiders will take our provisions, our horses, our camels five at a time if we sit still for too long. Especially if we do nothing to punish them.' He sipped his brandy and examined the glowing end of his cigar. 'Do you know, Sale, that the Shah is keen to take two camels from the local villages for every one we lose, and to shoot every thief and murderer we catch? What do you think of that?'

'It may deter them, Sir John. Like all sensible men, the Ghilzyees will take their own safety into account.'

'Indeed. And do you know why we cannot do so? Why we are not allowed to do so? Do you know why, Smith?'

Smith was rather thrown by this. He thought he was the last person to ask for advice.

'Well, General, perhaps it is to ensure that we remain the better men.

'Hmmph!'

'Or to put the case another way, Sir John, he continued, 'perhaps the Envoy thinks it unwise to stir up hatred against us.' He thought of Shakespeare again, but this hardly seemed the time or the place.

'It hardly bothers the Shah. And he has his eyes to lose.'

'His majesty does not see things, even with his eyes, as we do, Sir John.'

Sir John Keane laughed at this, and looked around him. Smith was very much the centre of attention now. There was a lengthy silence. Some men looked at their boots, some at the ends of their cigars, and one closed an eye, lifted his glass and looked at the flickering candlelight through swirling brandy.

Sale spoke again.

'Sir John, there remains the question of how we bring the gate down. With respect, that seems to be our first task at present.'

The brandy-swirler, a young captain, broke in just a little excitedly.

'If I may speak, sir?'

'Go on, Thomson.'

'We have heard of this weakness already, sir. From some prisoners taken in one of the gardens. Frankly, Sir John, I gave the reports no credit. And yet ... Well, sir, the gate is timber, set in a wooden frame, I suppose. If that frame is not keyed fully into the brickwork, perhaps it might be removed by nailing bags of powder to the door, setting them off with fuses and running for it.'

'Running for it?'

'Yes, sir. To avoid the blast, of course. I've seen it done. The fortifications here are somewhat more impressive than others, but if the gate is weak ...'

'By Jove! Yes. Are you volunteering, Thomson?'

Thomson's attention was diverted away from his glass, and he looked keenly at the General. He thought for a moment.

'Certainly, sir.'

'And how much powder do you need?'

'Eight or nine hundred pounds, I should say.'

'Excellent! Excellent! Tomorrow night then. Under cover of darkness. Let's hope for a cloudy night. Sale, you are in charge.'

'Thank you, sir.'

Sir John Keane took a long draw on his cigar, smiled contentedly, refilled the brandy glasses of his brother officers and leaned back in his chair.

Chapter Six

22nd July 1839

The following afternoon the sky was a clear blue, and behind the citadel the mountains were sharp as ever. After four weeks' travel, the men had a chance to rest, and preparations for the storming of Ghazni were well under way. Captain Thomson had set aside twelve seventy-five pound bags of gunpowder, and ordered up some camels to carry them to the Kabul gate on the far side of the city. Lieutenant Durand was busy making the fuses, sausages of cloth filled with gunpowder. Smith, like most of the officers, was watching the plain through his brass spy-glass. Lieutenant James had spotted movement across the plain – at first a cloud of dust with the naked eye, and then, through his spy-glass, horses and green flags. There was no order as yet, and no sound, but the green flags were ominous.

Many of the men were lazing pensively, but the Reaper's sharp shadow was strolling through the camp. Those who were touched by his hand suddenly felt the need to instruct their more literate comrades about letters to wives and parents. A few wrote their wills, although Smith could never understand why this was suddenly necessary now, when they had left Bombay eight months ago. Moreover, he often wondered what they had to leave behind them.

The enemy cavalry was now forming into a line. The distance and the spy glass had created an optical illusion. As the line of horses became thinner and longer, Smith realised the size of the threat.

'My God, James. Look at them. How many d'you think there are?'

James looked out and said nothing. All he could manage was to suck his teeth. Then they saw a gigantic cloud of dust rising from the ground, and it all but obscured the Kabul gate behind. James found his voice.

'Enemy approaching!'

As the horses stormed forward ahead of their own dust, Smith could just make out the green banners and the curved scimitars, and the men's heads clothed in their *lunghees*. Then, by the time Smith had ordered his men to fix bayonets, load rifles and stand ready, he could hear clearly the rumble of hooves, gradually growing in volume. There must have been two thousand of them, and they were heading straight for the Shah's camp, just a few hundred yards to the left of the 13th. Soon he could just hear the battle cries of the enemy.

Never before had Smith, or most of his men, experienced what happened next. They had fought off the odd band of raiders, and had come across the occasional bloodied remains of a scout or a waylaid messenger, but never this. Even at this distance, his mouth was dry, his eyes widened and an icy hand seemed to grip his intestines. But it was what happened to his mind that he would remember later. It wasn't true that your life flashed before you at moments like this. Surrey was four thousand miles away, and his past was a different world. His mind was emptied of everything, except for the dust, the pounding of his blood and the steel in his right hand.

In no time at all, the enemy force had almost reached the Shah's camp, a few hundred yards to Smith's right.

Smith gave the order.

'Fire!'

Rifles rang out, and a few of the enemy cavalry, carrying only swords and daggers, fell from their horses. Smith was relieved to hear the Shah's Light Infantry raining fire on the enemy, and then to see the Shah's cavalry ride out to meet them. He briefly saw Afghan foot soldiers, but the fighting was soon hidden by clouds of dust.

There was a flash of fire from the walls of Ghazni, more than a mile away. Smith felt something grip his ankle, and looked down to see Malik looking up at him, wide-eyed.

'The *Zubur-Zun*, Mr Smith. The *Zubur-Zun*!'

Smith saw two puffs of dust on the plain, the second closer than the first, and caught sight of a cannon ball bouncing into the Shah's camp. Smaller flashes from other guns followed soon after. Malik stayed on the floor.

The cavalry skirmishes in front of Smith dizzied him as he tried to follow the action. Eventually, almost directly ahead of him and about a hundred yards away, three or four soldiers had been splintered from the main column and were engaged with half a dozen Afghans. Swords flashed in the sunlight, horses reared and the dust rose. Two of the officers aimed their pistols and fired, and two of the Afghans fell to the ground, along with a British lieutenant, who seemed to have been wounded by a swordsman.

Smith could watch no longer.

'Thirteenth! Prepare! Charge!'

Smith was first to head for the dust cloud ahead, as he had to be. Leary was hot on his heels. They soon came across a soldier wrestling on the floor with an Afghan. Smith swung his rifle butt against the Afghan's head. The British officer struggled clear, and Smith gave one swift, furious downward jab between two ribs. His victim looked at him with pitying eyes, whispered 'Ne Allah!' frowned at the sky and lay still. Smith had to stand on the man's chest to get the bayonet out, and saw a bubble and trickle of blood oozing from the side of the man's mouth. Again, a pinpoint of fear filled his whole world.

And then all his senses rushed back to him. There was the clashing of sword and sabre, cries and screams, yells of rage. He looked around and saw another man fall from his horse and roll in the dust, momentarily stunned. Leary bayoneted him, thinking of the corpses and the severed limbs he had seen in the Bolan Pass. More and more Ghazees fell to rifle fire, and some of their horses fell under them, crushing their riders' pelvises or breaking their backs. Later, when he was skating on a frozen mountain lake, the silence coming over him like a sheet, Smith wondered how he could have felt pleased at this. But here, in the thick of things, he wanted to live. Victory, and to live.

Soon he sensed a lull, and the Afghans started to retreat, not in panic but slowly, with a quiet defiance. One stood tall in his saddle and looked straight at Smith for a long, long time. He dismounted and took up the body of the man Smith had killed, so that it could be buried before sunset. He lay the body behind his saddle and then looked at Smith again, even as he remounted. He continued to glance behind him as he trotted back across the plan, as though wanting to fix an image of Smith in his mind.

As the dust settled, Smith could see dozens of dead Afghans lying around him, and a few British staggering under the usual wounds from close fighting against swordsmen – cuts to the arms, the odd missing finger. Later he heard that the *Zubur-Zun* had claimed a trooper and a camel. But in the end the rifle had defeated the sword.

Smith and Leary accompanied prisoners back to the Shah's camp. Altogether there were forty or fifty of them, dotted in small groups, each under a heavy guard. As they walked, they came across Captain Outram, commander of the Shah's infantry.

'Well done, old man. But what brought you into all this? We *were* managing, you know.'

'Indeed, sir. I could see that. But no man is averse to a little assistance, surely?'

'Quite so. And your name, sir?'

'Lieutenant Smith of the Thirteenth at your service.'

'Delighted to make your acquaintance. How many d'you have? Six? Good. Now His Majesty has requested that they be shown to his tent. Don't worry – there are plenty of infantry in there. I would warn you, however, that you will find the Shah somewhat discommoded.'

As Smith marched his prisoners through the camp, Leary became just a little too enthusiastic with his bayonet, and a prisoner with blue eyes and rather surprising reddish hair and beard turned to face him. This was the fiercest face either of them had seen in Afghanistan. There were no great scars, no bared teeth, no wrinkled brow or angry sneer. But there was a quiet, still ferocity in the eyes. Leary blanched a little, and Smith told him to be a little more restrained. The bayonet was lowered, and immediately the Afghan's mood lightened, although he resisted the temptation to smile at his captors.

As they approached, the sound of raised voices came from the Shah's pavilion, and Smith went in to see five prisoners in front of Soojah. He had expected the prisoners to be afraid of the Shah, at least respectful. He was their conqueror, even if he had been assisted by the British army. But the prisoners stood tall, glaring straight at the Shah, and the enraged Shah's *lungee* shook as he shouted.

'Take them away!'

And the Royal guard escorted them through the back of the tent. Smith could see their silent shadows on the canvas, and he imagined them sitting in the blazing sun, covering their faces to keep the dust out of their throats.

The Shah caught sight of the new party of prisoners, and recognised Smith, who had been decorated with all the other officers on the day Soojah was declared King at Kandahar. He spoke to Smith in Pashtu.

'You are welcome, Lieutenant. How do you happen to be here?'

'I am merely assisting with the prisoners, your majesty.'

'And a good day's work!'

Smith's prisoners scowled. Soojah glared back, and the air was thick with rage and hatred. Smith felt a tension in the air again.

'And how is it that these wretches do not bow to their new king?'

The red-haired prisoner spoke for the rest.

'Soojah al-Moulk is not our king. Our king is Dost Mahomed, who reigns still in Kabul. And his son reigns over us in Ghazni. What kind of a king are you, to come to power on the shoulders of the infidels?' he spat and looked straight at Smith. 'There will be a heavy price in blood – your own blood and the blood of the infidels – if you ask non-believers to assist you against your own countrymen. This is not Ferozopore, a place for parades and circuses. You can play none of your great games here. This is our Ghazni!'

And he waved his dagger at the king. There was no question of him striking at the king – there were too many to intervene. But Smith was furious with himself. How had the man not been disarmed?

'This is our Ghazni!' the man shouted again, and the other prisoners cheered briefly. Another prisoner sprang at a royal guard, whose shoulder was soon covered in blood. He paled and fell. The royal guards and the infantry started to grab the prisoners, and Soojah ordered them out of the tent. As they left, he summoned the chief of the royal guard and spoke in his ear, quietly but with obvious fury.

*

Later, Smith had arranged sentry duty with Leary, and was smoking a pipe behind his tent, out of view of the fortress. He listened to the usual sounds – the cry of an animal, the breeze through guy ropes, the beginnings of rain. Then something else: footsteps. Nothing unusual in that. He listened again. Stumbling footsteps, and a rasping breath. And sobbing, perhaps? A man running from something.

It was James. He looked into the tent, and Smith heard his name whispered.

'James? Here!'

Smith hardly recognised the face of the man who came around the tent. James was not wounded, but appeared to be ill. He was sweating and wild-eyed, un-helmeted, and with his short hair swept into spikes. He gripped Smith's shoulder and stared, unable to speak.

Smith briskly tapped his tobacco onto the ground and stood on it. He led James to the tent, pushed him into a chair and gave him a tumbler of brandy and water. James's hand shook as he took it.

'Now take your time, old man. There's no hurry.'

Gradually, James became calmer. His breathing returned to normal, and he took in his surroundings.

'I've just seen the most horrid thing,' he said. 'The prisoners. D'you know what's happened?'

Smith waited, silently.

'I had to take a message to Outram. Should have sent one of the men, I suppose. Wish I had. I couldn't find Outram anywhere. And then I came across that awful place.' He gulped. 'Behind the Shah's tent.'

And James described a scene beyond the imagination even of most soldiers. Even Smith, who had been there earlier, and had seen the prisoners, could not quite imagine what James was telling him.

For thirty men lay dead, and the ground was soaked with blood.

'There was a giant of a man with a red beard,' he said, and Smith knew that it was the man he had taken in. 'He just lay there, looking up at the sky. I thought he was alive at first, and then I realised his throat was cut, and the ground beneath his head was soaked with blood. Some were still bleeding slowly to death, Smith. Just lying there quietly in the sun. They weren't talking or crying. I couldn't even hear their breathing. They were just waiting for the executioners to come around and finish them off. One of them looked at me and just pointed, and ran a finger across his throat, and then he died. And the men who'd done the killing – almost – they were standing around laughing. There was no rush for them. One man had lost both hands and a leg: the Shah's men must have done it. He'd never have got off the battlefield like that. And he just sat and stared as they all laughed at him.'

'My God, James. What did you do?'

'I could do nothing, Smith. What would you have me do?'

'But the executioners. How many were there?'

'Half a dozen or so. What sort of executioner doesn't know how to kill a man quickly? They half killed them, and then went back half an hour later to finish the job.'

'So what did they do in the meantime?'

'In one corner,' said James, 'the executioners were hacking off the fingers and arms and heads of the dead. Dishonouring the dead. That is how things are done here. And as they did it, they laughed like maniacs.'

'And we allowed it to happen. Did you find Captain Outram?'

'No. I shall try again tomorrow.'

Perhaps, Smith thought, the prisoners' souls were now in a garden under which rivers flow. Perhaps they were being waited on by virgins, and fed with fruits. Perhaps there were wearing green robes of the finest silk and golden amulets, and reclining upon their thrones. That was how Smith made sense of it at the time.

But behind the Shah's tent, he thought, must have been like the fires of hell.

'May God be with us all,' he thought.

Gradually, the brandy warmed James's blood, and he slept. Smith wondered what he must be dreaming of, and decided, not for the first time, to tell his commanding officer that one of his fellow soldiers was ill.

Chapter Seven

22nd July 1839

A s Smith had hoped, the moon was obscured that night by thick cloud, and it was dark as pitch. In Surrey he had always loved the moon, especially on a frosty night in early spring. But that was the romantic in him; in Afghanistan he was a soldier and all he needed was to be made invisible by the darkness. After what he had been told by Lieutenant James, and what he had seen in his face the following morning, he decided to tell Sale that James was sick. He hoped that after the obvious lie he had told about Leary in Bombay, the Colonel would believe him. In any case, he made sure that James's servants would look after him.

Smith and his men had slept like the dead from sundown, apart from the few who had been posted on picket-duty. At one o'clock, Leary had touched his shoulder and handed him a mug of tea and some dry biscuits, and he had awoken immediately. They had marched from the camp and assembled behind the gigantic pillar which stood on a little mound above the city. Perhaps it had once been a minaret standing at the corner of a mosque; perhaps once there had been a muezzin standing at the top, calling the faithful to prayer. Now there was rubble around the base, and the mosques were all within the city walls.

Just as it started to rain, Fighting Bob spoke to the officers out of the darkness.

'I trust that the task ahead of us will be quite clear to you. Shortly, the 16th Bengal Native Infantry will make a feint attack on the Kandahar gate to create a diversion from our assault on the Kabul gate, which is deemed to be considerably weaker. Soon after that, the 13th Light Infantry will line the ditch which runs parallel to the walls. The walls are some forty feet in height at that point, and dotted all along with loopholes for the Afghan *jezails*. You may wish to know that the *jezail* is a most beautiful weapon, with a longer barrel than our rifles. It is thus considerably more accurate, and also has a somewhat greater range. The stock is often engraved or inlaid with mother-of-pearl, and it is my earnest desire to take one back to Simla as a souvenir!'

His eyes flashed as he said this, and there was a strange sort of muffled cheer.

'Thus, the ditch party's task is a highly important one: to keep up as rapid and as long a covering fire upon the loopholes as your supplies of ball and bullet will allow. This should greatly reduce the fire on the remainder of the 13th as they advance to the gate. The artillery will assist in this from behind by firing on the walls, and also into the citadel in order to flush the enemy out.

'The Royal Engineers, led by the redoubtable Captain Thomson, are presently at the gate. His sappers have carried some nine hundred pounds of powder which will by now be fixed to the gate, and which will detonated at three. That is the signal for the storming party, led by Colonel Dennie, to enter the city. They will take the streets on the left and clear them completely. They will then take the walls above and return to the gate, clearing away any inhabitants still firing upon us. As firing from the walls ceases, as I expect it soon shall, the remainder of the 13th will enter at the gate and strike for the ultimate prize, which is the citadel. We must hope that the enemy see the sense in not taking refuge in a tower which contains several tons of powder.

'Those of you in the storming party may have heard that you have been given a new moniker by one of the wits in camp. You are now known as the Forlorn Hope. This is, of course, a matter for some pride. I ask only that you do your duty, and wish you all the very best of fortune.'

A few men cheered, but many, including Smith, smiled grimly. This, surely, was the best built and the best defended city in Afghanistan. It was now, in that momentary emptiness, that he filled his mind with pictures from the past. His mother, now dead, smiling at him as she passed him a cake or embroidered a handkerchief. His father glancing across the drawing room from behind a leather-bound book. Fishing on the pond last summer, chatting in a clever way with his brother, desperately trying to keep up with the brilliance of his ideas. And Sophia Hunter, her eyes flashing as she played the piano. It was strange how powerfully such pictures can draw us back, he thought. He had never realised that such small things would become life-long memories. He had experienced them only very fleetingly at the time, before they had passed. And here they were again, out from behind the veil.

Soon his memories were interrupted by a gigantic explosion from the gate which flash-lit the steel in soldiers' faces. Swords and muskets glinted, and the men were left with a white imprint on their retinas as the darkness returned. Something scampered away under a bush.

'There!' called Brigadier Sale. 'It is time for us to leave.'

'I say. He makes it sound like a charabanc trip to the seaside,' whispered a young officer of the Queen's Royals.

And off they went.

Smith's platoon marched a brisk half mile to the ditch, and settled either side of a small wooden bridge which carried the road northwards to Kabul. Some of Smith's men had acquired *poshteens* in the criss-crossed streets of Kandahar, and used these to shield themselves from the dew. Many shivered, perhaps with the cold, as they peered upwards. A hundred yards or so ahead of them, the outer wall of Ghazni rose, just visible in silhouette against the navy sky. Three or four stars twinkled a fifty thousand-year-old message.

Colonel Dennie soon arrived at the head of the storming party, and crossed the bridge, a rapid patter of boots following him towards the wall. Then, like the opening of hell, the artillery battery opened up over Smith's right shoulder, and he would later swear that he could feel the breeze from a cannon ball as it went just overhead. The whole arena was lit by a flood of white light from the magnesium flares sent up by the defenders. There were flashes of yellow gunfire, and smaller flashes from matchlocks and rifles. Dennie's Forlorn Hope dashed towards the gate, slightly uphill as they got closer. There was a fierce cross-fire from the towers on either side, and in the light from a flare Smith saw two men fall, and only one scramble to his feet. Fire from the ditch increased in intensity as the men saw their comrades under attack, and got into the rhythm of loading and firing, loading and firing. A heavy gun fired back, but the ball sailed well over Smith's head.

Finally, the guns on the walls of Ghazni were silenced, and Smith ordered his men to fix bayonets and advance on the gate. Some, he later remembered, were keen as mustard; others took some goading. Leary had to prod one or two with his bayonet before they scampered clear of the ditch.

The gate was vast: twenty feet high and nearly a foot thick. And it had not been blown in completely. There was still a tangled mess of debris, and the bottom frame of the doors, twenty feet across, was still intact. The men had to clamber through a portico, working around burning beams which had fallen from above. Smith heard voices, and picked out three faces looking down. A bucketful of earth showered down on him, and he staggered blindly for a moment. Then he was violently shoved to the floor.

'Down, Mr Smith, and keep still!' There was a splash of tepid water on his face, and the first thing he saw on regaining his sight was the pallid face of Leary. 'They're throwing beams down on us, sir. Must be the wreckage from above.'

They stood and made cautious steps towards the barricade, stepping across a soldier on his back with an arrow through his neck. He gurgled desperately, his hands clutching the air, and then lay still. Three Afghans in sheepskins were pinned to the floor by the burning beams, screaming in terror as they were slowly roasted under the flames. As Smith tried to lead the way into the city, a burning hail of fire came from the walls above, and he ducked back under cover. He could now see stars through a great hole in the portico roof.

There was another lull in the firing, and Smith and his platoon made a mad dash for the tiny passageway ahead. Smith scanned the openings left and right, and was amazed to see forty or so lamp-lit Afghan men sitting on their *poshteens* in a tiny fruit garden. As twenty rifles pointed at them, they raised their hands.

'Please, sir, no shooting.'

Smith and his men rushed past. The citadel, rather than prisoners, was the priority. On the left, there was only sporadic firing as the Queens and the Engineers cleared the streets.

The street ahead had, just a few hours before, been busy. Now, the wooden shutters were closed, and faces peered down from above. The cross-battened, wooden doors of a shoemaker's workshop had been broken open to reveal a wiry, elderly man sitting in the back of it. A couple of hundred pairs of shoes hung from nails, clinging together in neat rows, and his awl and an assortment of knives, gimlets, hammers and nails stood on a bench at the front. Smith imagined him talking to his neighbours, tapping away.

Another shop seemed to be a tailor's, for there was a pile of animal skins outside, as though ready for cutting and trimming. A family looked down from above, a mother and her three round-faced children of different sizes, all with the same dark eyes and coal-black hair. The woman yelled at Smith through her tears:

'When we meet the unbelievers in battle, we shall hack off your heads! We shall have the victory and we shall bind you in ropes! That is the command of Allah! Allah could have destroyed you alone, but we are being tested! And those of us who perish will not perish in vain! *Allah is owner of the day of judgement!*'

Smith looked up at her. She was rather beautiful, and he caught himself wondering what she looked like when she smiled: perhaps as she passed her son a cake, or looked up from her sewing. And then he felt what his father had warned him against in one of his rare harsher moments: a wave of pity for the woman and children above. The words echoed in his mind: *It's an awful thing to say, my boy, but there's precious little room for pity when you live a soldier's life.* How would his father have known? He was the one who had inherited the land; his brothers were the soldiers.

So far, the woman had spoken automatically, as if from memory, as though from a poem or a prayer. She had been shouting at all of Britain. Now, she almost seemed to recognise Smith, looked steadily at him, and spoke to him alone.

'We shall have the victory, and the infidel and the unbeliever will leave this land, and take his puppet-king with him! We shall have his eyes! My husband will not have suffered in vain!'

As they passed the woman was overcome by her grief and rage, and stood wailing at the world. The tallest boy, perhaps aged eleven or twelve, joined in: he shouted something that Smith could not hear, something angry. Perhaps he was thinking of own future as a *jezailchee*, or a cavalryman fighting under the green banner. Perhaps he was thinking of his own one-day sons, or of a conflict stretching out ahead, perhaps to the edge of time.

The sky to the east lightened with the promise of dawn. They soon found the streets clear, and in the dawn light the citadel rose grimly above them. After an exhausting march up steep hills, through the now-silent streets, they arrived at the walls of the citadel. Soon it was theirs, and Fighting Bob was proved right: none of the inhabitants had wanted to sit in a tower full of gunpowder.

Smith entered the most magnificent hall he had ever seen. The floor was covered in a dark marble, and the walls were spangled with mosaic patterns of lapis lazuli blues and emerald greens. Whoever had built this place was clearly devout; there were no pictures, no imitations of Allah's world. Instead, there were scripts around the tops of the walls. Smith could not read them, but he knew that they must be verses from the Qur'an. He tried to conjure up images of St. John's Church at home, or St Paul's Cathedral, but his memory was blinded by the present.

He found a smaller room, skirted by divans and cushions, each with its own low table, and gorgeous silk screens. A sea of carpet lapped at the divans. Smith noticed that other officers had removed their boots, as much out of a desire for comfort as respect for the surroundings, and he did the same. The carpet caressed his feet and he felt joy surge through his veins. Such were the little comforts of the soldier.

A small group of officers was gathered in front of a divan on the far side of the room, and Smith joined them. Sale was lying there, a ghastly livid slash from the corner of his mouth. A surgeon was dressing it. Captain Robinson had a bloody face, and a young Lieutenant in the Queen's Royals was proudly displaying his bruised ribs.

'I tell you, if I'd been a foot to the left, it would have landed plum on my head, and it would all have been up with me. As it was, Sergeant McKay thought I was a goner. I heard him yell in the dark. 'Gawd,' he said, poor Mr 'oldsworth's gorn down!' Next I knew they were dragging me away.'

Sale spoke up. 'Anyone here from the 13th?'

'Quiet, now sir,' said the surgeon. This won't heal if you talk. If you must talk, at least try to do so with your mouth closed.' He turned to look at the officers behind him, a flicker of a grin on his face. 'There are plenty from the 13th, and I would advise that you communicate with them later.

'Nonsense! Send one to me directly.'

Smith stepped forward. 'Lieutenant Smith, sir.'

'Ah, yes. Smith. Smith of the treacherous prisoner, as I remember. Good work. And good work today, also. Casualties?'

'None in my platoon, sir.'

'Good. You should know that Ghazni is ours. I trust that the Shah will be delighted. The Young Dost is captured, and those who would insist on fighting to the last have been shot. There are three hundred prisoners, and I trust that the Shah and the Envoy will agree to spare them. Now get yourself back to camp. Someone has to look after things down there. And get yourselves a hearty breakfast. And some rest.'

'Thank you, sir.'

Smith marched his platoon back to the citadel gates, and then back down to the Kabul gate. Some of the soldiers were horrified to see the prize agents there. Smith had taken nothing from the city, but Leary had to hand back a beautiful dagger he had somehow acquired, not having any money to pay the refund due on it, and a couple of men were caught with little bronze sculptures that they thought may one day be valuable in the streets around Charing Cross. Somehow, Lieutenant Holdsworth managed to get through with a decorative spear he had taken from a chief. Smith wondered whether the Brigadier had been able to take charge of a *jezail*.

Later, after he had obeyed all of Fighting Bob's orders, including the hearty breakfast, he settled down in his tent with his book.

'What's that you've got there, Smith?' It was Lieutenant James. He looked cheerful, but there was something disturbed about him, Smith thought. The cheerfulness was rather forced, driven by some sort of mania.

'It's by a new writer. Dickens. Have you heard of him?'

'Never. But then I'm not a man for novels. Nonsense, mostly.'

'Yes. Quite.'

It was best not to argue, and soon Smith had dived back into the peaceful, calming waters of Dingley Dell. It seemed that Mr Pickwick was going ice-skating, and Smith could hardly wait to see what disasters would befall him.

Chapter Eight

November 1839

'Steel and leather straps, Leary. That's the way.'

'Won't it hurt, sir? And won't we feel the cold? It's been bitter, especially outside the city.'

'Yes, Leary, so I have gathered. Soon it will be icy inside the city as well. We shall need to get used to it. The whole point is that they have to be fixed outside the boots. With the straps, you see. So your boots will still keep you warm.'

Leary was unconvinced.

'Yes, sir. I see...'

'In any case, consider this an experiment. We cannot expect it to be perfect at the first attempt.'

They watched the smith at work, hammering over a small anvil in his darkened shop in the north of Kabul. Two strips of steel were welded together in a T shape. Each side of the top of the T had two slots in it, and the bottom of the T had a finely flattened edge. The edge glowed in front of the smith as he worked it, and flecks of glowing orange metal fell to the floor. Another identical piece, already finished, lay on the floor near a collection of spades and ploughshares. Malik, apparently in pride of place, sat next to the smith, and they talked intermittently.

Lieutenant Smith had brought the metal here two days earlier, and the smith had looked blankly at him as he explained what he wanted. Two blades with a flat edge – what use would they be?

and with slots to pass leather straps through – why no handle? The *feringhee* must be mad, he thought.

Malik, whenever silence descended, saw things the same way. The *feringhees* were mad. They had brought their packs of dogs with them. All the way from Hindustan. And for what? To hunt. What was the point of dogs? Arrows and *jezails* and horses were so much better. In the name of Allah, they were strange people.

Malik loved the horse racing, though. And the costumes. He remembered Mr William Macnaghten and Mr Alexander Burnes (Sikundur, they called him, like Sikundur the Great) as they came into the city four months ago. Fine horses, beautiful hats with feathers, beautiful coats and trousers with gold edging. They were so much finer than the Shah. Anyway, what sort of a Shah needed a *feringhee* army to bring him to power? And the Shah had given medal after medal to the *feringhees*. And Mr Burnes was Sir Sikundur now. Such a lot of honour for one so young. No wonder they had been met by the Kabulis with such a silence.

Malik had found that horse racing was a great sport in the *feringhees'* own land, just as it was in his. And there was much betting, and much money had been taken from the men in red jackets. All this just a few days after they had arrived. Only a week later, the Afghans had watched as the *feringhees* played a mysterious game with bats and a very hard ball. They were all dressed in brilliant white, with little blue caps to keep the sun out of their eyes. And they wore soft armour on their legs. A strange kind of game, where you had to show the world what a coward you were. Malik found the whole thing a mystery, and had always refused when he was asked to join in.

Then another Afghan had asked Malik to invite Leary to a wrestling match. Leary had not been enthusiastic. It was early days, and Leary still remembered the killings, infrequent though they were. Messengers disappearing, stragglers found covered in blood, and the hacking to death of Lieutenant Inverarity as he came back to Kandahar from a picnic in the hills.

So Leary had taken precautions. Or, to be more exact, he had taken five of his platoon, and made sure the wrestling match was in a public square. After two or three bouts, Malik had appeared and sat next to him. In no time, he was on his feet, yelling at the top of his lungs. Money again, thought Leary, and he was right: there was a small knot of people under a tall pine in the corner of the square. A gentleman of the turf, he thought. He reached into a pocket and found two coins, even before he had looked at the next two contestants. But there was only one contestant, a short, wiry Afghan with the most enormous shoulders and glistening biceps. The man roared at the crowd, and the crowd roared back. The only word Leary recognised made him shudder: it was the word *feringhee.*

Then Malik prodded Leary and whispered urgently in his ear.

'You, Mr Leary, sir. They want a bout with a *feringhee.*'

Now the man was looking at Leary and his platoon, looking from man to man, weighing them up. His gaze soon caught the imagination of the crowd, and they too turned to look. A boy leapt to his feet and pointed at the gold sergeant's stripes on Leary's arm, and the wrestler smiled gently. He spoke in the sort of new-found, necessary English that had been picked up by many in the city.

'You, sir? You want?'

Leary soon realised that he had little choice. The crowd wanted him to go into the arena, and so, it seemed, did the men. They turned to him wide-eyed, grinning and expectant.

He got slowly to his feet and approached the wrestler, who took him by the hand and drew him closer, laughing. Soon he was in a vice-like hug, and was then spun around to face the crowd, a strong Afghan hand on his shoulder. Then his hand was lifted into the air and he involuntarily saluted the crowd. The crowd cheered the sportsmanship of the Afghan.

There was then a pause as Leary removed his tunic. He intended to pass it to his Corporal, but Lomax had vanished. In a moment, Leary picked him out, way over to his left, making bets under the tree in the corner of the square. The other men had followed him.

The bout began, and the pair grasped each others' shoulders. Within seconds the Englishman found himself in the dust, the wind knocked out of him. As far as he could tell, there were no rules, although he had seen no weapons and no punching or slapping. He would have to rely on his *feringhee* strangeness. He had to be unpredictable. So he made a dive for the Afghan's knees, and made him tumble. He lay across the Afghan's chest, leaving him pinned to the ground. Honours even. The crowd complained vehemently, and the red tunics cheered.

This was just the provocation the Afghan needed, and Leary had no further opportunities. He was pitched to the floor again and again, until eventually he could put up with no more of it. He stood and bowed, and lifted the Afghan's hand. There was delirium in the crowd; Lomax had said later that there were tears in the eyes of some of the old men. Then Lomax said he would buy rum for everyone back in camp. He had plenty of money now, he said –for he had bet on the Afghan.

As the English left the square, they noticed the admiring glances of the Afghans, and a woman rushed up to Leary with a bowl of water and a cloth and started to wash his face.

She appeared at first to be concentrating on her task, but gradually Leary felt something else in her touch. The last time he opened his eyes, he caught her looking straight into his. Embarrassed, she looked back into the bowl, and squeezed a little lime juice into it. Leary smiled.

'You are a fine nurse, miss. I shall be healed quickly, I'm sure.'

She smiled, not understanding a word he said.

'Not too quickly, mind. I wouldn't want to heal too quickly. Wouldn't be right, of course. Mind you, Major Havelock says not drinking helps with the wounds. But if it healed too quickly there'd be no more nursing, would there?'

He had hardly known what had happened. She lowered her eyes, again concentrating on the lime juice, and he reached up and touched her cheek. She turned her eyes away quickly, and was gone.

Leary thought about nothing but her over the next few days.

*

Now, in the blacksmith's workshop, the task was nearly complete. Two perfectly identical blades had been beaten and beaten, and then dipped into a bucket of water. They still steamed.

'See what we've achieved, Leary?'

'I am looking forwards to being convinced, sir.'

'You shall be, rest assured. And remember – it is not merely a question of getting the blades themselves: it is the other consideration.'

'Other consideration, sir?'

'Yes. Don't you see? Have you never read the Book of Isaiah?'

'Not closely, sir. And a very long time ago, sir.'

'*Their swords will be beaten into ploughshares.* Remember that? *And nation shall speak peace unto nation. There will be no more preparing for war.*'

'Sir.'

'Well, we have beaten somebody else's swords... Into something else.'

'Yes, sir.'

Smith held up the blades in the light, and ran his finger over the flat edge. He spoke in Pashtu to the smith.

'Beautiful,' he said simply. 'I need twenty-five pairs more.' The smith grinned delightedly. And to Leary, 'Now back to the citadel.'

And they left the shop, followed at some distance by Malik. They passed through the bazaar, a great market along a narrow, roofed-in street. The buildings to either side were the same timber-framed, shuttered mud-brick as they had seen in Kandahar and Ghazni, and the shopkeepers were selling the same things in the same way: birds shot on the plains outside the city, dried peaches and apricots, spices, knives both for killing and for cooking with, woollen yarn and rugs, silks, and sheepskins ready for the coming winter. There was a phenomenal noise: arguing, bargaining and laughing. Often, there was a hush as Smith passed. They liked him, he sensed, but at the same time were unsure of him. The divide between the Afghans and the army was very difficult to cross.

Prices were rising all the time. With thousands of soldiers and their servants in the city, there wasn't enough to go round. The army had brought wagon loads of money with them, and could pay anything. So many of the traders, especially those who sold wheat, meat, ghee and animal feeds, started to hold some back, then protest there was a shortage and charge even more. And the Shah was raising taxes. Smith sighed as he thought of how they were collected – at the end of a British bayonet. He had heard that the Shah was disappointed with the state of his palace: Soojah, it was said, remembered it from his childhood as a building of great space and beauty, and had returned to find it dilapidated and tired out. He had to restore it to its former glory. And then he needed a buffer against troubles ahead: to prepare against the enemies who lay beyond the snow-capped mountains of the Hindu Kush. How much might that cost? They knew that Dost Mohammed had fled as the *feringhees* arrived, but he was out there somewhere.

And for how long would the British protect the Shah? Already the Bombay part of the force was preparing to head for Jalalabad, a hundred miles to the east. This would leave less than half of the original force to secure Kabul.

The passage of the Bombay force to Jalalabad would be a difficult one: Smith was not looking forward to it. He had heard that Macnaghten was having to pay the Ghilzyee chiefs to the east and the west just to let messengers and patrols through the mountain passes. Later, if ever the passes were cut off, they would never get back to save Kabul. Smith felt an ever-darkening cloud over his head. Perhaps it would be better when they had built some proper fortified barracks and got the stores, money and ammunition properly safe. Then they could leave men behind with a little less fear in their hearts.

But as they built the barracks, they were bringing their families here. To this place, to Kabul! Smith could not imagine bringing a wife here. Perhaps, he thought, it was a good thing he didn't have one after all. Just imagine if he had married Sophia, and brought her out!

And what did the Kabulis think of all this building? It made the Bombay force look more like a permanent army of occupation every day, and that wasn't why they were supposed to be here. They were supposed to get Shah Soojah settled, create a stable buffer between India and the Russians, and leave. Smith could not see how it was going to happen. They would never make peace with the men in the mountains, or with the people of Ghazni. Even in Kabul, Smith could see the iron entering Afghan souls.

Smith caught sight of the gates to the citadel ahead of them. The citadel's Pashtu name was soon engraved on the minds of every British soldier: they all came to call it the *Balla Hissar*, the fortress on the hill, just as the Kabulis did. It rose up above the city and beyond its walled eastern edge. Its gate, angled walls and rounded towers were strung across the hillside and around the hill and out of sight. Today the world was in shades of brown and grey, the earth, the dull walls of the fortress and the stormy sky piled up in varieties of monochrome.

Now Malik started to hang back, hoping that Smith would at least say something to him before he left. He stopped and watched, and Smith turned, the new blades swinging at his side.

'Malik. Thank you for your help. You have been very kind.'

Malik's eyes glittered and his face split into a crooked-toothed grin. Then he looked again at the blades and looked curious. He had already committed one act of treachery against his people, and much as he liked Smith, did he want to commit another? Seeking out and negotiating with the smith was one thing. But what had they created? What were these new blades?

'I would like to repay you,' Smith continued. 'I would like you to try these out with us. Tomorrow.' He pointed to the floor. 'Meet us here. An hour after dawn.' Malik looked sorely troubled, and Smith laughed. 'Do not worry. You will be perfectly safe!'

Malik smiled uncertainly. Smith walked away and rejoined Leary, and they re-entered the citadel. Malik watched until they were out of sight.

*

The following morning was crisp, to say the least. By ten o'clock, Smith, Leary and Malik had slipped out of the city and ridden west-north-west for an hour or so, the white teeth of the Hindu Kush over their right shoulders. They were now at a lake, utterly flat and crusted in ice. It was probably the flattest thing Leary had ever seen. A few stiff rushes stood around the edge, and a hungry-looking hawk swooped and dived behind them. Otherwise there was no sign of life.

Smith took a *poshteen* from a horse and walked cautiously onto the lake. It was completely solid. He folded the *poshteen* in half and laid it on the ice, and then called to Leary, who tottered over in a T-shape, clutching the air for balance.

'Come, come Leary! You can do better than that. Quickly! We've only an hour. You heard what the Brigadier said.'

'Moving as fast as I can, Mr Smith.' He always said *Mr Smith* when he was a little cross.

'Now. Sit on the blanket. Listen carefully to your orders, because this mission is of vital importance.'

Leary did as he was told, very slowly. As soon as he was seated, Smith brought out the pair of blades, now with added leather straps, from his haversack. A double strap was soon in front of and behind Leary's ankle, and a single one just behind his toes. Smith pulled them as tight as he could. Then the other blade went on, and Leary knew that his commanding officer would brook no further delay.

'Now, I still remember doing this when I was five years of age. The simplest way is just to ... well, stand up as you normally would.'

Leary could hardly believe what he was hearing. Was this a jape? Was the rest of the platoon waiting behind a rock to have a good laugh at him? But no – The Lieutenant would never do that to him. So, as quickly as he could, he staggered to his feet. Smith knelt and looked at the skates and Leary swayed jerkily.

'Splendid! Solid as anything.' He almost smiled at the sergeant. 'Now. The next thing is to start skating. Dip your left shoulder, put your weight over the left foot. Now then, are you right-handed? Or sinister?'

'Sinister, sir?'

'Sinister. Left handed.'

'Oh, right you are, sir. Right-handed.'

'Good. Dip your right shoulder, put your weight over the left foot, lift the right and slide it over the ice. Transfer your weight to the right foot, and slide the left.'

And off he went, very shakily at first and then, gradually, a little faster. Within half an hour, he was making great traverses of a hundred yards and more, his whoops of delight ringing from the mountainsides. As he came clattering into Smith for the final time, he was almost speechless.

'It really is awful strange, sir. When you stop ...'

'Yes, Leary?'

'Well, you're still, stiller than you've ever been. So still that the mountains seem to be sailing past you. Makes me quite giddy.'

'So you've read your Wordsworth, then?'

'Well, no sir, not really.' As before, Leary showed that slight embarrassment about himself.

Smith, feeling great delight himself now, quoted the relevant lines.

'Then at once Have I, reclining back upon my heels, Stopped short; yet still the solitary cliffs Wheeled by me – even as if the earth had rolled With visible motion her diurnal round!'

'Sir.'

And with a feeling that was half relief and half regret, Leary sat and removed the skates. Smith was excited now, spreading his arms as if to hug the Hindu Kush. He took the skates and called Malik.

'Your turn, Malik! Use Leary's boots.'

But as Smith had expected, Malik was unwilling. He had shown huge delight as he watched Leary, but watching was his limit.

'No, sir! Tomorrow!'

He waved a dismissive hand, tittering.

'Very well. Now it's my turn. Now that you've risked your neck to show they are safe, Sergeant Leary, your commanding officer will take a spin himself.'

'Yes, sir.'

Smith was on the ice for only twenty minutes, but this was long enough to tell that his plan would work. He spoke little on the way back to Kabul, except to give a warning to Leary.

'Not a word about this in the city, Leary. And especially not a word about my screeching and caterwauling. I would not wish the platoon, or my brother officers, to think that I were mad.'

'Course not, sir. You can rely on me sir.'

'Yes, Leary,' said Smith, smiling. 'I know I can.'

*

Over the next week or so, Smith sent Leary on several trips into the bazaar. Eventually, they had gathered the twenty-five pairs of skates.

'Now,' said Smith at dusk one evening, after Leary had brought him a plate of fried lamb and a glass of port, 'it is time to make arrangements. Get the platoon to fall in, will you?'

'What, now, sir?'

'Yes, Leary, now.'

'Well, sir, before I do, might I ask you something?'

'Certainly. Make it quick, though.'

'Well, sir, it's a little awkward. It's … well, sir… it's a woman, sir.'

'Oh, dear.'

Smith was still young, of course, and sometimes in matters like this he still jumped to conclusions.

'Are you in some sort of trouble, Leary?'

Leary stood tall and looked straight at a picture of Queen Victoria nailed to the wall behind Smith. Smith's imagination allowed all sorts of horrors into his mind: a maddened father, a proud brother with a knife, or a fight with a corporal in a cavalry regiment.

'No sir. It's not like that. Not at all, sir. It's just that I have formed an understanding, sir. An attachment, if you will. And I'm not the only one: you'll be aware sir, that Captain Warburton is to marry an Afghan lady, sir? One of the Dost's nieces, I believe.'

'Good heavens! No, I had no idea.'

'It's like this sir. I wish to marry her, sir. There's nobody at home, sir, except mother. And we've … well, we've never been close, like. In fact, tell the truth, sir, India's home now, in a manner of speaking. And my plan is to take the lady back afterward, sir. But my difficulty is with the men sir. You'll know what some of them are like. Begging pardon, sir. They'll not understand. They're happy queuing up.' He looked embarrassed for a moment. 'You know, sir. Outside that house near the bazaar when the fancy takes 'em. But they still think of the Afghan as the enemy, sir. I should appreciate your advice, sir.'

'I'm sure you would, Sergeant Leary. But ... well ... I've really no experience of all this at all. Not as an officer, not as a chap. It really is rather ticklish. I suppose you're thinking of a way to make it public. And you need my support? To spike their guns and all that?'

'Yes, sir. In a manner of speaking.'

This was not what he had planned for the evening at all. He wanted the ice skating arranged.

And then it clicked.

'I have it, Leary! We have twenty-five pairs of skates, yes?'

'Sir.'

'And if we skate turn and turn about, we could take ... how many? Forty, fifty people?'

'Yes sir. But...'

'But me no buts, Leary! The platoon are twenty five. It was my intention just to ask a few Afghans: your wrestling friend for one. But we can invite your young lady and twenty other Afghans. A mixed party. We cannot run the risk of the General, or the Shah, or the Dost for that matter, getting the wrong idea about this.'

So ten minutes later, Smith spoke to the platoon. They lined up in the yard in front of his office, perhaps a little more relaxed and a little more respectful than other troops Smith knew. It was a sign that they admired and liked him. They would look out for him in battle, he was sure of that.

'Now men, on Wednesday – the day after tomorrow – we shall have an extra day of leisure.'

The men cheered.

'However, this leisure will have a purpose beyond the usual cards, betting, wrestling and gambolling about the city.'

Some of the men groaned a little. They thought it might be another of Lieutenant Hallet's mind-improving lectures on English history.

'On Wednesday, we shall seek to improve relationships with the local population. We shall be taking a mixed group of Kabulis ... ' He stopped to prepare the moment. '... ice-skating.'

He paused, waiting for a reaction. But he was met with silence. There was no reaction whatever, not even a look or a frown. Nobody spoke, so Smith continued. Otherwise, he might have laughed, and that would have been fatal.

'The purpose of this is many-fold. First, it is always useful to know a little of the surrounding country. We never know when we might need such knowledge. Second, we shall demonstrate to the Ghilzyees and others that we are not to remain cramped in our little barracks for ever. Most important, we shall show to the Kabulis that we wish to befriend them and to look after their interests as well as our own.'

'May I speak, sir?' It was Pooter, always precise, often difficult and usually right. Sometimes, his education made him challenging. Why wasn't he an officer?

'Yes, Pooter.'

'Presently, so I hear, the local folk pay more in taxes than ever before so that the Shah can protect himself against the man they want as their ruler. Sir'

'Perhaps, Pooter.'

'And we are taking twenty Afghans ice-skating.'

'Correct.'

'Do we expect, sir, that will stop 'em shooting us at the first opportunity?'

There was a murmur of agreement.

'Probably not, Pooter. But it will hardly *encourage* them to shoot us, either. In any case, do you have an alternative for forming good relations with the local people? Other than queuing up outside the white house near the bazaar?'

Leary guffawed at this, because Pooter was always at the front of the queue. Pooter blushed and was silent. Smith did not like treating his men like this, but he had run out of choices.

'So,' he said. 'We leave on Wednesday at nine sharp. We shall be at the lake at ten, and leave at two to arrive back here before dark...'

The men trudged off, leaving Leary and Smith alone.

'How was that?' asked Smith.

'I think they all understand the position, sir.'

'Yes. Now you look after those skates. Sabotage remains a possibility.'

'Right you are, sir. And thank you, sir.'

As he turned to leave, Smith remembered one last detail.

'Leary?'

'Sir?'

'This lady of yours. Does she have a name?'

'Yes sir. Jamila, sir. Not sure how you spell it, though.'

Chapter Nine

November 1839

S hortly after dawn on the next day but one, Smith and his platoon mustered at the Kohistan Gate. They waited for just a few minutes until the first of the Kabulis started to arrive, and Malik strapped the skates behind saddles. Leary's eyes lit up as he recognised one of the women walking towards him. She seemed hardly more than a girl, and had a laughing mouth and large dark eyes beneath a silk scarf. She moved with the typical grace Smith had seen so often before, ahead of a small group of friends. Leary was a little distracted by the tall young man accompanying her; he bore down on the sergeant with a friendly smile and they shook hands, but Leary's friendship was rather strained, for it was the woman he wanted to speak to, and it was she whose eyes he looked into even as he spoke to her companion. One or two of the other soldiers looked askance at their sergeant. Some smiled, but Pooter's face was unreadable.

Soon another small group arrived, and at its centre were Ahmet Qaderi the wrestler and a much younger woman, perhaps his wife. As soon as he saw her, Smith felt compelled to shake Ahmet's hand.

'I am pleased to see you, sir.'

'I am also pleased to see you, Lieutenant Smith. And I am most interested to see what you have planned for us.' There was a pause, and Ahmet noted that like Leary, Smith was doing a rather bad job of looking at the man speaking to him.

'This is my sister,' said Ahmet. 'Nasrin Qaderi. Nasrin, this is Mr Smith. It was he who invited us to this... this adventure.'

Nasrin was well wrapped against the cold, her feet bound in many layers of cloth, and just a hem of thick blue and yellow cotton showing below a long, heavy sheepskin. She wore a thick headscarf which hid the shape of her face. In an instant, Smith found that the lines of eyes, nose and mouth were engraved on his mind, so that Ahmet Qaderi's words were lost. Nasrin bowed a little, and said nothing, after the local custom on a first meeting.

'Yes,' said Smith, absently. 'Shall we get underway?'

Soon the horses were readied, and the party mounted and set off. Once out of the gates they headed north for a while, between two tiny forts and past a vast walled plot known as the King's Garden. Soon the land was divided into little squares and planted out with plum, apricot, lime, olives and figs, and watered by the canal over to their right. This was the area already set aside for the Cantonments, the barracks and family living quarters which would soon be built for the occupiers.

They soon entered the village of Beymaroo, with its poor mud houses built on either side of the road. Smith assumed that the Qaderis must be from near here. Behind the houses to their left, the Beymaroo Heights rose into the early sunshine. One day, Smith thought, this would be a key objective in any rebellion. He could see Afghan soldiers on the hills, taking control of the grain stores in the village, harassing any family who had been supplying the British. Here the people made their livings from the land: from fruit, from mutton, from wool. Already there were men at work, and fires were lit in the fronts of workshops and stores. Smith caught a whiff of smoke from a forge, and imagined the village ablaze.

A weak sun rose behind them, and did little to warm them. The horses steamed a little, and everybody pulled their *poshteens* close. They bore left and headed across the plain, Smith and Leary at the head of the column. A gentle wind blew, and dusty snow swirled thinly across their lines of vision. Soon the *poshteens* met the *lunghees* which swathed their faces.

As Smith had feared, the English and the Afghans were distant and unconnected. He thought about asking Leary to break the ice, but quickly realised that such an order might be dangerously misunderstood. So for the next half hour the column moved in silence and slowly. Smith and Leary led, followed by the bulk of the platoon. The Afghans seemed to be led by Ahmet Qaderi, who sat as tall as he could in the saddle and seemed to attract his fellow Kabulis like a magnet. There were a dozen other Afghan men, looking as varied as Chaucer's Canterbury pilgrims. There were a few with hands marked by physical labour, and small eyes with crows' feet born of the sun and wind. Perhaps they were farmers or shepherds. There, at the back, was the smith from the bazaar.

Every now and then, Smith caught Leary turning to look for the woman he loved. He turned with great subtlety, feigning some military purpose. Whenever Smith lifted a spyglass to his eye, or took a look at the Hindu Kush, he saw Leary's movement on the edge of his vision. Smith himself had sneaked such glances at Sophia – in church as the stained light caught her hair, at village dances and at unexpected sightings near the river. And then, all of a sudden, she had married, and Smith had soon taken a commission and sailed for Bombay.

It was the wrestler who broke the silence. He called loudly from behind, and startled a nervous soldier.

'So, Mr Leary. How are you? Will you take another bout today?'

'No more bouts, Mr ...' He realised that he did not know the man's name. Why would he?

'My name is Ahmet.' He smiled. 'There are many Ahmets. Perhaps there are more Ahmets in Afghanistan than there are *feringhees*.' And he laughed. 'Tell me, Mr Smith, sir, what is the purpose of our journey? Why are we visiting the lake in such cold weather?'

'Because, Mr Ahmet, our plans will be impossible in hot weather.' The nervous soldiers laughed a little too loudly. Smith smiled, trying to look mysterious.

'Plans? But your army has no plans.' He drew alongside Smith and lowered his voice. 'Listen, my friend. There are no plans. How will you defend yourselves when the Dost comes down from the hills? Your Shah – yes, your Shah, for he was not wanted by us –will not allow you to live under the Balla Hissar for long. By the spring you outside the walls of the city. They build you mud houses with a little wall around you. Have you been through the passes? He turned and pointed to the mountains.

'Not as yet, I haven't. Yet I have seen the Bolan pass, before we arrived at Kandahar.'

'The Khoord Kabul is very safe … now. But you know how much you *feringhees* are paying the Ghilzyees to keep the passes clear? You cannot pay for ever. Your masters not allow it. And then? And what you eat?'

'Why, the same as you.'

'Yes. So why you pay three times? And what happen to you if the Kabuli stops selling to you? And stops making you weapons and tools? How you build your town with no tools and no food? How can you defend yourselves with no weapons?'

'It's not for me to say, Mr Ahmet.'

'You must take care. There are many who will seek your blood. I shall help if I can, my friend, for I have no family and I welcome the *feringhee.* But I am only one.'

Smith, as usual, did not know whether to believe him or not.

At last, they crested a rise and saw the lake below them. A few white-encrusted cedars stood solidly on its shores, and the powdered snow raced across its surface like little ghosts. They all stopped for a moment and looked down, their pale shadows stretching down the scree in front of them. Leary led them all in a scramble to the lake, and Smith watched the Afghans as they passed. Jamila looked at him from behind her scarf, and quickly looked away. Smith heard scraping close behind him, and a horse came alongside. Nasrin looked straight at him, and spoke experimentally.

'I am Nasrin.' She laughed and spurred her horse down the slope.

Smith, taken aback, followed at a distance. Perhaps, he thought, Nasrin thought of this as a second meeting, so that speech was now possible.

At the lake, they were soon dismounted, and Malik hurried to unhitch the blades. He called for the attention of the Afghans, and Smith ordered Leary to sit on a boulder and show everybody how to fit the skates. He did not need so much persuasion this time, partly because he had to play the conquering hero, and partly because he knew what he was doing. As soon as his skates were on, he launched himself onto the ice; the Afghans looked on in wonderment, still mystified. And then Leary was off, his voice ringing from the mountainsides. Malik looked at the audience, smiling to himself. He had to show that he had seen it all before.

For a few moments, a silence descended. Then some of the women shrieked, and there was a little laughter. But it was Ahmet who cheered first, and demanded a pair of skates. Smith handed him a pair, and realised that there was a difficulty: Ahmet was not wearing boots. Instead, he had criss-crossed cloth strips, like the puttees Smith had seen in India, up to just below the knee. Smith knew what to do: he took off his boots and handed them over. Ahmet smiled, unbound the puttees and squeezed the boots on, and then added the skates, wincing a little as he pulled the straps tight.

Soon the mountains tinkled with screams and laughter. Even Pooter was now convinced, and swept a little shakily back to the shore, whooping with glee and seeking out Leary to pat him on the back with a sort of insolent respect. Both ended up on the ice, dazed. Malik too made a tentative effort, not wanting to admit that he had never done this before.

It was some time before the women entered the fray. Leary kept looking back for Jamila, and once collided with Lomax. Both lay on their backs, bellowing with laughter. Jamila and Nasrin patted their knees and pointed, their laughter muffled beneath their headscarves.

This was the signal Leary needed. He hailed the women loudly through his hands, and beckoned them onto the ice before gliding back to the shore. He grabbed a pair of skates, and Jamila sat on a boulder. Leary gently put skates on over her puttees, and pulled the straps as tight as he could. She looked for her brother, and when she saw that he was not looking, she put a hand on Leary's shoulder. Soon, she got up and wobbled onto the Lake, and Nasrin took her place.

Smith did not know that he would remember this moment for the rest of his life. Just for a moment, he saw Sophia, but was surprised by how quickly the image vanished. He knelt before Nasrin, and then took up the skates, all the while sensing her looking at the top of his head, and watching his hands. She was utterly silent.

He offered his arm, and she took it and they stepped onto the ice. She tottered at first, hanging on to him. He taught her just as he had taught Leary, and yet in a completely different way. For one thing, she had no English, so all was done with gentle touch and gesture. And then finally she set off, doddery at first, but soon with a graceful confidence. She went a short distance, turned around and headed back towards him, faster and faster, sliding into his arms and shrieking with laughter. And then she was away again by herself.

Leary had become proprietorial, and took Jamila by the arm. Together they glided in long, long, silent sweeping arcs across the whiteness of the lake. Smith watched them for a moment before hearing Nasrin shriek and seeing her tumble. She stood quickly and brushed off the frost.

Instinctively, without a thought for his position, Smith skated out to where Nasrin stood alone. He hardly thought that he had skated only once in five years. He sailed past her and cut back sharply, with a spray of chipped ice and a blur of blue coat with his sword still hanging at his side. He put his hand on her elbow to support her, and showed her again, quite unnecessarily, how to place her weight on one foot, push away and transfer the weight to the other foot, and gradually, oh so gradually, she found her balance again and slid across the ice in a slow, graceful straight line. Only when she stopped could she turn to him and smile, and then she headed back towards him. He could not avoid catching her as she wobbled to a halt, and looked into her face to find that the headscarf had slipped to reveal an inexpressible loveliness. She glided off again, and Smith caught Leary and the other men looking across at him and nudging each other.

'Thank you Mr Smith. You kind.'

He was amazed to hear her speaking English – and not just the sort of English that the Afghans had quickly learned to make money: *God bless the Queen* and *best quality* and *two rupees please.* This was a personal English, a language that made contact just as her eyes did.

'You speak a little English! How did you learn?'

But now he had lost her, and she laughed nervously, looking back at the shore. Still the men were watching. Had Leary planned this as a way of preparing the ground for his news? If so, the man was a greater genius than Smith had imagined.

'You are well on ice, sir.'

'And so are you, Miss Qaderi. I am most pleased to make your acquaintance.'

She smiled as she heard her own name, but looked blankly at the rest.

When they got back to the shore, Smith felt that a spell had been broken as the noise of the men and the chatter of the Afghans intruded. Again there was that little bubble, that narrow focus of the senses. But this time it was beauty instead of fear.

'So how did I do, Pooter?'

'Most wondrously well, sir. We were just saying, sir, that you have the finest, most graceful technique of all, sir. A joy to behold, sir.'

'Why, thank you, Pooter. Thank you, men.'

But Pooter had not finished.

'And Jones was saying sir, begging pardon, sir, that your skating was most impressive, too, sir.'

And the men, and those few of the Afghans who understood, roared with laughter until the mountains tinkled.

They had a picnic lunch of salted mutton, rice and fruit, with coffee. It was not quite the same as the Bolan pass or the Kandahar plain, with their candelabra and pewter mugs and silver cutlery, but it was altogether happier. For the first time since he had arrived at Kabul, Smith felt at his ease. He could see the men felt it too as they sat on boulders, smoking and looking at the far-away mountains.

All too soon, it was time to leave. The journey back was very different from the journey out. The column had become more fluid as pairs formed and reformed, and jokes and comments were passed back and forth in a combination of broken English and broken Pashtu.

'You very good, Mr Pooter!'

'He'd be better sliding on his feet than on his back, though!'

English laughter.

'And Malik. Well done Malik!'

A little applause.

'And Sergeant Leary. What a gem you are, Sergeant. I could see you cutting a dash on the Thames next time it freezes over.

'Fat chance of that, I'd say.'

'Why's that, Sarge?'

'I'm never going back to Lunnon.'

'No? Why ever not?'

'Nothing to go back for. No family. At least, none to speak of. And I'm proud to be a soldier.'

'What, here, for the rest of your days?'

'And why not, pray? There's some of us as has a cause to stay in the east.'

He looked back at Jamila significantly, and then forwards to see that he was not too far from Smith. Nobody reacted, so Smith had to move things on.

'Really, Sergeant? Why's that?' There was a lengthier pause, and Smith smiled to himself as he imagined the honest face of the man behind him, and the gulp and the lump in his throat.

'Listen, you fellas. It is my intention... my firm intention ... I have decided ... to ... to marry. In short, and make no bones about it, I am to marry Jamila. It is all arranged. An' I shall stay in the east. *We* shall stay in the east, I should say, in India, p'raps. I've been 'ere a long time, nearly half my life, to tell the truth. I can make a home here now. So, whatever you think... there we are.'

To Smith's surprise, Pooter was the first to speak.

'Congratulations, Sergeant Leary, old chap.'

He seemed almost to lead the rest, and his reaction spread like fire. Soon congratulations and cheers were being poured upon him in a warm deluge, and as they crossed the plain the men drew close to him one by one and shook his hand. All the while, Jamila kept herself apart, exchanging nervous glances with Nasrin and the others.

By four the village of Beymaroo was in sight. The sun was now reddening just a little as it sank towards dusk; there were faint stars in the sky. And soon they would have dry feet, cocoa and a roaring fire, and they and the Kabulis may, Smith thought, have found small places for each other in their souls.

The village was quiet; the inhabitants were obviously indoors, perhaps eating and perhaps at evening prayers. As they rode through the main street, the Afghans and the British were again somehow separated, with Smith at the very head of the column and Malik some way behind it. They came out of the village in single file, the Afghans now leading the way, and the Kohistan gate ahead of them.

*

And then the shots rang out. Two of them, their whip crack echoing off the hills. Smith could not tell where they came from, until Pooter yelled from behind.

'From the Beymaroo hills!'

They were sitting ducks. If the men in the hills – however many they were – were *jezailchees*, they would have the accuracy and the range to pick them off one at a time. The gate was still nearly two miles away. Smith gave the order to dismount, and just as he did so there were a third and fourth shot.

He heard a groan from behind him, and a muffled thump. As he took the front of his saddle to dismount, he felt a searing, burning pain in his right shoulder, and slipped down the horse's left flank.

'Sir! Sir! The sergeant's fallen, sir.

'Leary! Were you hit?'

He looked along the ground and saw Leary, bare-headed, on his back. A blackish pool was spreading from his side.

'I'm all right, sir. I think I have a bullet in me, though. Top of my leg somewhere. It hurts.'

'All right, Leary. Get to him, somebody. Tell me what's up. Anybody else hurt?'

There was no answer. He saw two of the men look at the Sergeant, and then crawl towards him. It was Johnson, the youngest member of the platoon.

'I don't like the look of him at all, sir.'

'All right Johnson, you stay here. I'll go.'

He tried to crawl back down the column, and cried out in pain as his shoulder took his weight.

'Sir! You're hit, sir!'

'Yes. Nothing much. Just my arm, I think. Give me a hand.'

And together they shuffled and scraped their way ten yards to where Leary lay.

'Leary. Let me look at you.'

Smith almost gasped when he saw what had happened to Leary. It was the first time he had seen a bullet wound up close. The ball had gone in at the hip, a nice neat hole in the side of his trousers. But it was what had happened next that had done the damage. Smith could only imagine. Through the pelvis, through the abdomen and out the other side. He leant across Leary's legs to see. There was a gaping hole in the other leg, just a little lower down.

'I'm all right, sir, aren't I? Where's Jamila?'

'You'll be fine, old chap.'

He could have bitten his tongue. He had never called Leary a chap before, and Leary knew exactly what it meant. Smith had to gabble on to cover it up.

'Jamila's fine. You – we – are the only ones hurt, I think. Johnson! Go and get Jamila, will you? Use the horses for cover. She'll want to know the Sergeant's all right. She's at the back of the column.'

'No sir.' Leary touched Smith's hand. She's safer where she is. Keep her with her own people. We'd all be better to keep still, I'd say. We can get back under cover of darkness, sir. It's only two miles or so.'

'Just so, Leary'. His voice was caught on grief.

'Don't worry, sir. You will get back, you know. In the dark. '

'Of course we shall. All of us.'

'Sorry about the skating, sir.'

'Sorry? But why, Leary?'

'Didn't believe in it, sir. Should have, from the start, sir. It was great officering, sir.'

'Thank you, Leary.' He looked at Leary and smiled. The light was fading fast.

'Good luck with it all, sir. I...... look after Jamila, sir.'

And then he looked glassily at Smith, touched his hand, and breathed no more.

Chapter Ten

November 1839

They buried Leary in the new cemetery beneath the Beymaroo Heights. The cortege headed out of the Kohistan gate at noon, the coffin draped in a union flag on a cart, pulled by two docile black horses. The platoon took a dead march behind; Smith, his left arm in a sling and his right holding his sword upright, walked ahead.

They turned left beside a garden, its fruit trees winter-dead. Smith was still in pain, and the surgeon had told him that there was no question of riding for several months. The Bombay army was shortly to leave, but both Leary and Smith would be staying in Kabul.

There were few people on the route to the cemetery. An elderly shepherd bowed his head as they passed, and a group of young boys stared in silence. Way over to the right, nearly a mile away, a few unidentifiable faces gazed from the square tower of Mohammed Shereef's fort, and the Heights were dotted with curious onlookers.

A grave had been dug already, as a last favour to the Sergeant from Corporal Lomax and Pooter. They seemed to have taken a strange pride in the task, Smith thought.

They gathered around the grave and the chaplain began. The words were the same as they would have been in London or Brighton or Birmingham, and in the grip of an icy wind, the graveyard too reminded Smith of England. He had been to enough funerals, even there.

'I am the resurrection and the life, saith the Lord. He that believeth in me, though he were dead, yet shall he live. And whosoever believeth in me shall never die...'

Smith knew what it meant, but found it hard to open his heart to the words. A part of him followed the chaplain, and looked for something beyond the world, beyond this dismal place. But at the same time a part of him knew that Leary was gone, never to return. Wherever he had gone, he was gone.

Smith did not know the Sergeant's family, of course. Leary had hardly mentioned them. He did not know how well Leary had known them, how well he had loved them or whether he had loved them at all. Smith had written the usual letter to Mrs Leary. She did, as it turned out, live in Whitechapel. He imagined her as he imagined his own mother: much too young, of course. His mother had died at forty-one, and Mrs Leary must be older than that. Perhaps she had a white pinafore and grey hair. Perhaps she made buns and cakes for tea. Perhaps she still had a wizened old mother sitting by the fire wondering what had happened to her grandson.

One day, Smith would visit her: when he returned. He would find out about her, and he would tell her the things an officer could not write in such a letter. He would tell her that Leary had been the better man, that he had known so much more than Smith had known about almost everything that mattered. That once he had danced on the ice. That he had been in love, and within a deuce of being married and staying in India for the rest of his life.

'... we brought nothing into this world, and it is certain we can carry nothing out. The Lord gave, and the Lord hath taken away; blessed be the name of the Lord.'

Smith looked across the grave and was surprised to see Jamila and Nasrin there, quite calm and still. Jamila looked across at him, her black eyes alight with tears, but she gave no other clue to whatever was in her heart.

'...man that is born of a woman hath but a short time to live, and is full of misery. He cometh up, and is cut down, like a flower. He fleeth as it were a shadow, and never continueth in one stay. In the

midst of life we are in death. Of whom may we ask for help, but of thee, O Lord, who for our sins art justly displeased?'

For a long time after this, Smith's mind was elsewhere. Is life full of misery? Really? True, he had seen the roasting bodies in Ghazni's Kabul Gate; he had seen the shoemaker's family within. He had lost his mother, he had lost the man who had been his greatest friend in the army. He knew that in the capital city of his own country, the hub of the world, half of all funerals were for children. When in London, he had seen the soot and smelled the rottenness and putrefaction for himself. He had felt the grubby hand tugging at his sleeve, and heard the words: *penny for a loaf, guv'nor.*

Yet still there was beauty here. The mountains, the orchards in bloom as they had left Kandahar, the flowers on the plains. No, he thought. Neither the flowers nor the men he led were just waiting for the scythe. They were still here, now. The flowers on the plain and the men around the grave. There was hope in that. And there, opposite him, were Nasrin's kohl-black eyes.

He watched the platoon remove the flag, lower the coffin into the grave and take it in turns to cast a spadeful of earth on top of it. Pooter and he shared a spade, one hand each.

'For as much as it hath pleased Almighty God of his great mercy to take our dear brother here departed, we therefore commit his body to the ground, ashes to ashes, dust to dust, in sure and certain hope of the resurrection to eternal life, through our Lord Jesus Christ ...'

The service was soon over, and the group left the small mound that had once been Leary and moved for the gate. As he turned, Smith was surprised to see that Ahmet and Malik had been standing behind him. Ahmet looked at Smith, his eyes unwavering.

'Allah brings forth the living from the dead, and he brings forth the dead from the living, and he revives the earth after her death. And just the same, you will be brought forth. He created us of dust.' Smith was struck by the words. He felt that he somehow knew them already.

'Allah shaped you out of weakness, then gave you strength, and then, after the strength, he gives you weakness and grey hair.'

Malik looked far away to the south, not at Kabul but at the hills beyond: *over* the hills beyond, thought Smith, as though he were looking for Ghazni.

'Leary a good man,' said Ahmet. 'It is a shame that good men had to come to Afghanistan and give their lives.'

'Of course. But these things are necessary. Without us, perhaps the Dost would have made peace with the Russians. Perhaps they would have threatened India.'

'And your country? Would they make war with your country?'

'India is my country. A part of it.'

'Ah.' He smiled. 'You want protect your country – London and Manchester and Bombay and Calcutta!'

'Exactly.'

'And what did Leary know of this? About your country's great plans?'

'Like all of us, he could have known if he had asked. Indeed, he did ask. We discussed it often. My men know why they are here.'

'Well, I still say it senseless. You lost a good man, and a mother lost a good son. And Mr Leary has lost … whatever life he would have. I wrestled with him, you know. He could not wrestle well, but he was strong: strong in the arm and strong enough to stand up when he did not want to. You know what they are saying about you now?'

'Certainly. That we have placed an unwanted Shah on the throne, that we have brought our families here, and that we shall stay here until we are put to the sword. We understand that also.'

'And you will be happy to die? For that? For nothing? In a country that knows nothing of you and does not want you? We Afghans beat off one invader and then another for hundreds of years? Will you never learn?'

'I know only a little of your history. But I know that I must stay here. I have no choice. I cannot return to Bombay with my men, and I cannot return to my home.'

'Well, remember that I know more of Kabul than you. I have lived here all my life. Thirty years. Perhaps you will not believe me, but I want to be your friend.'

Smith was not sure whether to believe it or not, for he had seen soldiers lulled into friendship and then put to the sword as soon as they had dropped their guard. He had heard of messengers invited into a peasant's house for refreshment and never seen again. He had seen the naivety of Inverarity, killed on the way back from a picnic. He had, of course, gone ice-skating with the Afghans, but had taken a platoon of soldiers with him.

'I know you have seen the Afghans' friendship. Good and bad. We not untrustworthy, my friend. But we have to live. Life is hard. You came into this country thinking you could feed thirty thousand of your soldiers – that you would buy meat and rice and bread for thirty thousand men at the roadside!' He laughed. 'There is little enough here for us. Do you know people in this country starve? And you are surprised when an Afghan who is perhaps your friend decides to kill you as soon as you have given to him. And you are surprised when Dost Mahomed is friendly to you, and then to the Russians, and then to you again. If only you had given him what he wanted! Then he would have been your country's friend, and you, Captain Smith, would not have needed to come here and Leary would be still alive. And only Allah knows what will happen to you next. Only *the one God, the beneficent, the merciful*, knows how long you have to live. You – the man who loves his men – yes, I see that – the man who loves to dance on the ice, the man who looks into the mountains as though his soul is somewhere else. I know you, Smith. That is why I can be your friend. If you are in need, ask. And I do not want your money. I would not betray you for a *lakh* of rupees.'

'For two *lakhs*?'

They had laughed at this, and Ahmet had touched Smith's shoulder. But as they re-entered Kabul, Smith had a dreadful foreboding. He should shortly be heading back to the warmth of Bombay. Perhaps next summer he would see Delhi, or even visit Simla, where the air was fresh and where the British lived in splendour during the hottest part of the year.

Ahmet Qaderi had read Smith's thoughts.

'And when you leave here. You go to Bombay?'

'Perhaps'.

'Tell me. How is Bombay? You like it?'

'It is a beautiful place – in parts. And very prosperous. There are fortunes to be made there.'

It was the first time Ahmet had heard the word.

'Fortunes?'

'Money. Trade. Bombay is a good place for the merchant. There are many mouths to feed, and many people to clothe. And, of course, there are the British. There are uniforms to be made, ammunition to be provided and stored, and all those thousands of soldiers' stomachs. And, of course, the cotton. And some men I have spoken to are talking of railways.'

'So,' said Ahmet. Might there be room for one more grain merchant?'

And they laughed again, neither having any idea what the future might hold.

As he looked up at the citadel above him, Smith could not be optimistic. There were mountains to climb before the summer. The first of these was the building of the new British settlement outside the city, between the Kohistan Gate and Beymaroo. Almost as soon as the Shah had settled into the palace, he had decided that the British could not bunker down in the Balla Hissar. His people seemed to hate him enough already – the silence had been deadly as he and Macnaghten and Burnes had entered the city in August. They could not be allowed to see him in the palace with the British looking down on him from the citadel. Instead, they had built a crowd of little mud brick houses which now clung to the ground next to the citadel like barnacles.

*

Now that families were arriving, they needed more space and more security. Mrs Macnaghten would be the first to arrive: her husband had already sent for her. Soon Lady Sale would follow. The plan was to build living quarters outside the city, on the Kohistan road beneath the Beymaroo heights. Cantonments, they called them. One day Smith had come across Lieutenant Sturt of the Royal Engineers and Lieutenant Eyre, the Horse Artillery's Commissar of Ordnance, looking out across an orchard, surrounded by a troop of their own cavalry.

'What do you think, Smith?' asked Eyre.

'Think? About what, exactly?'

'Same old Smith, ever cautious!' joked Eyre. 'What do you think of building our little piece of England right here?'

'Right here,' said Sturt. 'We'll give you a clue. It's surrounded by orchards. What does that tell you?'

'Good cover for marauders.'

'Top marks. Walls will be ten feet high and a mile and a half around.'

'A lot of wall to defend.'

'Quite so. And outside the northern wall, in a separate enclosure, Mr Macnaghten's splendid Residence, with his Residence offices and his Residence gardens. So?'

'So that wall cannot be used to fire from.'

'Indeed. Now look about you. What else do you see?'

Smith turned slowly, anticlockwise, taking in the view. He saw a ruined, tumbledown fort and the Seeah Sung Heights rising beyond. Then, a mile away, the Balla Hissar beneath a feeble white sun. The city of Kabul, standing crisp in the icy air. The Kabul river and a canal built for watering the crops, both glinting and chill. Between Smith and the city there were four more forts, one either side of the Kohistan road, one a half-finished pile of mud brick in the orchards and one held in the vee of the river and the canal. Further round were the Beymaroo Hills, the village and the new cemetery which was Leary's last home. Smith took it all in.

'Who commands the forts?' he asked.

'We do. At present. Like the look of them?' Sturt's eyes were more serious than his voice.

'At that short distance? No, not at all. A gun mounted on any one of them might be directed straight into the barracks. What is their purpose?'

Eyre and Sturt looked at one another.

'You are most perspicacious,' said Eyre.

Sturt smiled.

'Do you see the fort to the left of the road?' he asked. 'It is at the junction of the road to Jalalabad. That will be the commissariat fort. That is where we will store all our food and other items. The treasury, of course, will remain in the city.'

Smith was stunned.

'Our food supplies will be outside the barracks?'

'Exactly.'

'And our ammunition?'

Eyre pointed to another fort.

'Over there.'

'But that is madness! In every way: the length of the walls, the position of essential supplies, the orchards, the surrounding forts, the ditches … In every way, we would be quite unable to defend ourselves! They can shoot us, starve us, rob us of everything. And that is before the Bombay force leaves us.'

'Yes. We thought so, too,' said Sturt. 'A child could see it. The three of us have seen it straight away. Perhaps that is why we are not generals.'

Over the next three months, the building of the cantonments proceeded rapidly. The outer walls went up first, with a road leading through a gate to the east, towards the river. They were a rich golden brown, made of bricks brought by a hundred or more Afghans. Then the homes were built, little bungalows with flat roofs, a fine house for the Sales and Sturt, who had married the Sales' daughter, and a bigger and almost palatial house for the Macnaghtens. Sir Alexander, for reasons Smith could not quite understand, elected to stay in his house in the city. He had always boasted of knowing the Afghan mind, and Smith wondered if he thought he could do his job better if he stayed closer to the people. He certainly knew them well, and spoke the language like a Kabuli: everybody had heard the tale of his one-man invasion of Afghanistan, disguised as a horse trader.

*

Smith's wound healed only slowly, and the cold seemed to get into the bone and made it ache agonisingly, especially at night. During the day, he could only wander about, his arm in its sling. He learned to observe many things, from the vast sprawl of the cantonments to the exact positions of the surrounding forts, and the moods in Sturt's face as he worked. Smith had seen the quiet joy created by the work, and the frustration when his sensible advice was ignored. Eventually, Sturt learned to follow his orders without question. This was not difficult, for he was a good engineer. Yet there was often a slight moroseness about him: that of intelligence defeated by a powerful stupidity.

Shortly before Christmas, everything changed. European women started to arrive: Lady Macnaghten, the Envoy's wife; Fighting Bob's wife Lady Florentia Sale and her daughter, Mrs Sturt; Eyre's wife, and a host of others. Sturt's mood swung almost imperceptibly back to contentment. Despite the difficulties, this was a golden time: Sturt was busy, efficient and skilled. He seemed to think that he was put on earth for this purpose, and basked in the loving admiration of his wife.

Smith found a purpose, also. New life had sprung up in him since Leary's death, in those same black eyes that Smith had glanced at from across the open grave. Despite what had happened on the homeward journey, Smith had not forgotten his moment with Nasrin as he had supported her on the ice, or the delicacy of her voice. He had seen her several times since, and she had seemed determined to act as an occasional nurse, helping Smith to regain the mobility in his shoulder, acting as a go between for Smith and the surgeon, fetching new bandages, helping him with things he couldn't reach. Of course, there were others who could have done this, but Smith was always happy to see her.

She seemed too to have been learning English, for she spoke to him more and more often, mostly in a fairly elementary way of weather or food or her uncle. Smith soon learned that her parents were dead, and that she had been taken under the wing of her older brother, Ahmet the wrestler-merchant. One day, she dressed Smith's wound as he sat in a chair in his office. Ahmet acted as chaperone, and passed her bandages, ever watchful.

'It hurt?' she had asked.

'No, not at all,' Smith had lied, gritting his teeth.

She laughed at him in his obvious lie, and he laughed because she had noticed. He felt that from the first time they had met, she had somehow seen his real self, or that he had unwittingly revealed his own true self to her.

'When you ride your horse? Soon?'

'I fear not.' She looked blank, and he shook his head.

'When you be a brave soldier again?' She smiled, perhaps a little mockingly.

'I am not a brave soldier.'

'But yes! I see you in your red tunic.'

'That is quite true, madam, but one does need to be brave to wear a red jacket.'

This time, her brother Ahmet had to translate, and she laughed again.

And so the questions went on, with their simple answers, and all the questions were hers. Smith had no idea how hard she had practised them with her uncle.

Once she had brought him some sweetmeats tasting powerfully of aniseed, and then disappeared for more than a week. He found this hard to understand, and during the time Nasrin was away, something gnawed at him. Was her closeness to him typically Afghan, helpful and hospitable? Occasionally his heart leapt in a kind of panic when he thought of her. Once, to his shame, he wondered if she might betray him in some way.

Ahmet continued to play the role of protective older brother, and usually came with her when she visited. He might stand at Smith's office door or outside in the bustle, talking to a sergeant, or he might take a cup of mint tea with them. Always there was the ramrod bearing as he stood, pouring great spouts of hot tea into cups on the floor, and the glint in the eye as he passed around great rocks of crude sugar.

The thaw started early that spring, and the flow of the Kabul river increased gently in the middle of March. One day Ahmet, Nasrin and Smith had ridden briefly along it, Smith stiff and cautious in his saddle. They went on other excursions as the sun's arc got gradually higher, and sunset was later by fifteen minutes or so each week.

The cantonments were now nearly finished, but Smith sometimes felt unaccountably anxious. It was not quite fear, but something like it. What if he had to leave Kabul suddenly, and never returned? What if this peace was shattered? Some days, even a passing cloud throwing Kabul into shade would chill his guts.

And then suddenly, one morning, he *could* account for it. If he were to move soon into the cantonments, how often would he see Nasrin? He had once felt like this about Sophia, with his timid glances in church and his vague hopes of seeing her in a lamp-lit window. He could hardly make sense of it.

Ahmet became ever more mysterious. '*Allah created you helpmeets from yourselves that you might find rest in them, and he ordained between you love and mercy,*' he might say, with a twinkling eye and a little cough.

Then, one evening, Nasrin spoke to him seriously for the first time, looking straight into his eyes.

'When you will leave.'

'Yes?'

'When?'

Smith reverted to Pashtu. 'I do not know. Perhaps a month. Perhaps two years!'

She looked downwards, sorrowfully.

'Why you are here, and why you are leaving?'

'I am here to keep your Shah on his throne.'

'Your Shah, not my Shah.'

'I am leaving when the new Shah is safe on his throne, and when Afghanistan is safe from the Persians and the Russians.'

'What are Russians, my William?'

'They are a very strong people from the north. They would like to take Afghanistan from you.'

'And they would like to take your India from you?'

'Yes. And when Afghanistan is safe from them, we shall leave.'

Nasrin looked sorrowful again, but managed a sort of a smile. Smith's heart leapt.

From that evening onwards, they saw a great deal more of each other. One evening in April, under a sky scattered with fast-moving clouds and occasional specks of stars and moonlight, they spoke of Captain Warburton and his Afghan wife. Smith had often been surprised by the forwardness of Afghan women: they spoke so much more freely than the English women he had known at home, more freely than the officers' wives in Kabul.

'Captain Warburton is a good man?'

'Of course. He is a captain.'

She had laughed at that, as though Smith had been joking. He was, but only partly.

'Is he a *good* man?'

'He is a good soldier, I think. And a gentleman.'

'A gentleman? What is it?'

'It is difficult to say, but being a gentleman is important in my country. And very important in the army. A gentleman is a man who keeps his word, and pays his debts, who tells the truth and who is good to others.'

'And good to his wife? Would he punish his wife?'

Smith smiled at her.

'No! Wives are not punished in England.' He knew this to be a lie: he knew that there was a Bill Sikes in every town and village. 'Well sometimes, but it is not allowed.'

'And will the captain take his wife away when he leaves?'

'Of course. He will take her to Calcutta, I should think.'

'You know that she is a niece of the Dost Mohamed? And that Akbar Khan, her cousin, will want to kill her for marrying a *feringhee*?'

'Perhaps.' And he looked at her face as it was turned upwards towards his. 'But for love they must take their chances.'

He looked at her and saw that her eyes were rimmed with tears. He cupped her chin in his hands and kissed her gently on the forehead.

*

They married just a month later, in the middle of April, as the orchards burst into bloom. The cantonments were complete, and they were given a tiny house near the south west corner. Immediately, they went on their wedding visits. They saw Lieutenant and Mrs Eyre, Captain and Mrs Warburton, Lieutenant and Mrs Sturt and Lady Sale, who was already dreaming of an English cottage garden with geraniums and sweet peas, and red English cabbages and hairy Afghan lettuces – not when she returned home, but here, in Kabul.

'We shall create a little life here,' she said, 'and the Afghans will come to regard my garden as something of a spectacle.'

Life went on like this for some time, with only occasional tremors from beyond the mountains. There might be a Ghilzyee chief unhappy with his tribute money, the occasional dead messenger, but they might have lost as many in camp at Bombay. Smith heard Mr Macnaghten speak many times of the peace they had created, and of the army's increasing control of the country. And how he hated the 'croakers', as he called them, the men who constantly pointed out the danger they were in, and complained about the design of the cantonments, who worried all the time about security and could not see things as they really were.

This was the world in which Nasrin conceived a child. He was born in January, and they called him Hassan.

Chapter Eleven

November 1855

Shortly before dawn, Hassan was awoken by his uncle's snoring. Sometimes in Bombay he had heard the ghastly sound from the other end of the house but had managed to ignore it. Here, in the same room, it was impossible. It seemed to make the windows rattle. He looked into the street below, wondering what his uncle had been so worried about last night.

Nobody.

He shivered as he saw the lightening greyness in the sky over the roof tops and decided he would like to light the fire. He had watched Tommy doing so the night before. But he soon realised that the coal scuttle was empty and there were no lucifers. He probably wouldn't have managed it anyway.

He heard steps on the stairs, and a squeaking sound, then a knock on the door. Uncle Ahmet woke immediately, fully alert. He sat up in bed as though galvanised, and then got up. It was Lucy with an empty bucket and Tommy with a huge and steaming ewer of hot water which he poured into a tin bowl on the washstand. Lucy seemed determined to give out instructions.

'We don't tip the pots in the yard here, like they do in some parts,' she announced. Just tip 'em in the bucket when you're done. Ma says breakfast will be in a 'alf hour. Eggs an' toast.'

With that, she turned and left. Tommy waited a moment and looked at Hassan.

'When you're washed, why don't I show you the street? I've an errand any'ow. Then we'll come back ter breakfast. P'raps later I'll show you the city.'

He had gabbled too quickly and too long for Hassan, who could not keep up. He just stared blankly. Tommy tried again, and this time used some actions.

'You wash.' He pointed to the bowl and Hassan nodded. 'We go out.' He pointed at himself, at Hassan and out of the window, and his fingers walked on air. 'Then we come back and eat.' He opened his mouth wide and pointed into it, and then patted his tummy. Hassan smiled. His scar made a crease in his skin, and Tommy stared at it for a second before turning away, a little embarrassed.

Ten minutes later they were out in the street. Tommy's errand was very simple. He walked to a house four doors along from the Jacksons' and found a piece of string hanging from an upper window. He told Hassan, again using sign language, to give it a pull. Hassan pulled gently, but nothing happened.

'No. Harder!' Tommy mimed a great wrench, like a bell ringer's. Hassan felt doubtful, having no idea what the effects of this might be. He wrapped the string around his hand and looked at Tommy. Tommy nodded enthusiastically, and Hassan pulled hard.

There was a scream of pain from the room upstairs, which they could hear clearly even with the casements shut. Then the window was flung open, and a red-faced Constable Harris looked furiously down on them. Hassan quickly dropped the string, but not quickly enough.

'You! Tommy Jackson! Brought your 'prentice along with yer, 'ave yer? P'raps you should train him proply first. What's he tryin' to do, nip me toe off? I said wake me up, not give me a ampy-tation. Off with yer! I shall 'ave words with yer father!'

'And tell 'im 'is best officer has to be woke up wiv a bit of string tied on his toe? By a twelve year old? For a farthin' a day?'

'All right, all right. Off wiv yer.' And he threw a farthing down.

'Hush money,' whispered Tommy, putting the farthing in his pocket.

Hassan looked at Tommy, astounded. Tommy looked back, and roared laughing. Eventually Hassan laughed a little too, although he still had little idea what had happened.

Breakfast was a busy affair. Mrs Jackson had already eaten, it seemed, and was now at the mangle, squeezing water out of sodden clothes between the two rollers. Hassan watched, fascinated. What a strange way they had to dry clothes, in this country with no sun! In Bombay, they would have been dry in an hour. Two little irons were sitting on a grate above the fire, and Lucy passed one of them to her mother. Mrs Jackson held it close to her cheek to make sure it was warm, spat on it, and then put a collarless white shirt on a table and ironed the creases out.

'Put that on the 'ook for your pa, Tommy, there's a good lad. And Lucy, pass me the other iron from the fire. Now sit down all of you, and get on.'

Just then Sergeant Jackson breezed in, and kissed each of his daughters in turn, and ruffled Tommy's hair, looking down at him carefully.

'Aw, leave off me, Pa.'

'Certain I shall. When you tell me where the farthing came from.'

'What farthing, Pa?' He made a very bad job of looking innocent.

'The farthing in your jacket pocket.'

'Yes, Pa. Change from the baker's, yesterday.'

'I see. In that case, it's housekeeping. Give it to your mother.'

'Yes, Pa.'

'And you'll give tomorrow's farthing to her as well.'

Tommy paused, not sure whether to question this. He thought better of it.

'Yes, Pa.'

'And Tommy?'

'Yes, Pa?'

'If Constable 'if Harris ever needs any more string, tell 'im there's plenty in the office.'

Tommy looked stunned. Sergeant Jackson winked at his wife, and Mrs Jackson roared laughing.

In the middle of this, uncle Ahmet appeared, still a little preoccupied. He ate slowly, and Mrs Jackson was disappointed that he didn't touch the ham. She smiled quietly and took his plate away.

As Sergeant Jackson lifted one last piece of glistening fried egg into his mouth, carefully avoiding his whiskers, he looked at Uncle Ahmet more seriously.

'Mr Qaderi, there's one or two things I still need to ask you. Shall we take a turn along the street? There's things I've to see to, if you take my meaning. Seems a nice crisp morning.'

'Yes, most certainly.'

The sky had now brightened, although the sun was still below the houses opposite. They could see their misty breaths on the air, and as they reached the end of the street, several steaming horses passed them by.

'Not as warm as you're used to, I'm sure.'

'No, Mr Sergeant Jackson. But not as cold as I am used to. I doubt that you have four months of deep snow every year in London?'

'You have snow in Bombay? I thought it was more a desert than that. Tell me a little about your country.'

'There is no snow in Bombay, sir, indeed not!' He laughed. 'But Bombay is not my country, sir. I left my country in your year 18 … 1841. Fourteen years. Almost fourteen years.'

'Why was that? Just on account of I find it interesting, mind. And my wife's father is especially interested.'

'I am an Afghan. From Kabul. You have heard of it.

'Why yes. Everyone in England knows Afghanistan – 'eard of it, I mean. We 'ad a show about the Afghan war at Astley's Circus. Ten years ago, it was. Saw it with Molly. Tommy was jest a little lad, like.' And suddenly there was just a little of the circus ringmaster underneath the policeman's uniform, threatening to get out but never quite able to. '*The Captives at Kabul*, they called it. Lady Sale, as I remember, beat off a dozen Afghans with a great 'eavy sword, and all the prisoners rescued. A great triumph, it was! Most inspiring!'

Ahmet said nothing. He knew what had really happened.

'Beggin' pardon, Mr Qaderi. We was yer enemy, arter all.'

'Not my enemy. I had many *feringhee* friends.'

'*Feringy?* What does that mean, then?'

'Foreigners. Your soldiers.'

'Ah.' He thought for a moment. 'And you left Afghanistan?' asked Jackson.

'Yes, sir.'

'And why would that be?'

'I left for my own reasons. I did something which made many people hate me. I had to flee for my life. They would have killed me, and put my head and my hands on spears in the bazaar or outside the gate. As a warning, you understand. I have returned only once. Perhaps it would be safe there now: for me and for Hassan. But I cannot be sure, and my life is now in Bombay.'

The sergeant had winced as Ahmet spoke of spears and heads and hands. 'Was what you did a crime?'

'Not a crime in England, I think, nor in the eyes of Allah. I sold what I should not have sold. To the wrong people. It was mine to sell. And they needed it. But there was suddenly much hatred in Kabul, and I had to leave and cross the mountains in the snow. And soon after, Hassan had to follow with his mother and father.'

'And you are here to trade?'

'Yes. And also ...'

'Also what?'

'We are also seeking ... what is it? I have always thought of it as a treasure. That is the story I told Hassan. I know that I can trust you, Mr Jackson. There are things I did not tell you. Now that Hassan is not here, I should tell you now.'

'If you would, Mr Qaderi.'

'Good sir, Hassan and his mother also left from Kabul in the winter of 1841 and 1842. His father was also with them, but he had his duty as a soldier, and could not care for them as a husband and father would like.'

'And you are here to find him?'

'I am here for trade. But yes, also to see what I can find. I know that Hassan wants the same, but he does not speak of it often. There are small things he does … things which tell me much. Always I have worried about this.'

'Tell me about the father.'

'Smith. Captain William Smith. The 13th Light Infantry.'

'P'raps I can help you. I know a man who may be of assistance to you.' He stopped, looked at Ahmet and smiled knowingly. 'But there is also the question of that murder. You say you knew this man.'

'Yes, a little. It was a long journey: more than ninety days.'

'The dead man was not a rich man.'

'No.'

'And he was the not the sort of man to fight?'

'No, no.'

So if he was not wealthy, and if he did not fight, and if he was a decent fellah, why would he be murdered? Not for theft, not for hatred, not in a fight. So why? And who was it?'

'I cannot be certain.'

'But you doubt somebody?'

'Yes, perhaps. There are two men. I met them in Bombay: or I should say Hassan met them. They are Afghans. I am not sure where from. I do not remember seeing them in Kabul. Perhaps they were there once: Kabul is a busy city. Sometimes you see a man who is always watching. You understand?'

Sergeant Jackson stood a little taller.

'Course I understand. Twenty years a constable, sir. What were their names?

'Aziz and Khodar. I do not know their family names. They are cousins, I think. They watched us on the ship. I think they watching us in the street last night.'

'What, here? You ought to have told me, Mr Qaderi.'

'I know that. I am sorry. But I cannot be sure. '

'You met these men in Bombay, you say? What were they like?'

'Good men, I thought. And Hassan liked them. He is a good judge, I think. But later I think he like them less: they always watching.'

'And how did they come to be on *Aurora*?'

'I arrange it. They say they wanted to come to London. To seek their fortunes. I ask the captain. I know him a little.'

'Well, p'raps you did not arrange it with them, Mr Qaderi. It is also possible, I should say, that Mr Aziz and Mr Khodar arranged it with you.'

Ahmet frowned.

'To me, Mr Qaderi, it's as clear as daylight. They meet Hassan in the docks in Bombay, they watches you all the way to Lunnon and they follow you here to Evans Street. Now why? If you see 'em again, you must tell me. Clear?'

'Yes, Mr Jackson.'

'What a story this could turn into! Like one of your Arabian Nights!'

'You like stories? The Arabian Nights?'

'Oh yes. Since I was knee high.' He stooped a little and put his hand out to demonstrate.

'You know Arabic?'

Sergeant Jackson laughed.

'No. In English.'

'I left a story, little like the *Tales of Thousand Nights and One Night*. I left a story for Hassan. May I show you?'

'That would be most interesting. Mr Qaderi, I'm sure. May I read that letter?'

'I regret not, sir.'

Sergeant Jackson stood just a little taller again.

'And why not, may I ask? Would you prefer me to command you to 'and it over?'

Ahmet smiled.

'This is something I have never shown to anybody before. Something very private. Private to me and Hassan.'

'Nothing's that private, I should say. Not when there's been a murder.'

'Yes, Mr Sergeant Jackson. So I can help you. But there is more why you cannot read it. Even if it help to find a killer, you cannot read it.'

'Then why?'

'Because I wrote it in Pashtu. Hassan has his copy also in Pashtu in the back of a book his father left him. I have told him the story many times, especially when he was small.'

Mr Jackson looked disappointed.

'So you must translate it for me, Mr Qaderi!'

'Not necessary. For Hassan and I also have a copies in English.'

'But why the copies, if it's so private?'

'Because this is written by my dear sister, Nasrin. The most beautiful and the best of women. As I have said, she was married to Captain Smith. I wrote two letters three days before I left Kabul. One for my sister, and one for Hassan. I gave them to a trusted friend from Ghazni, for he knew where I was hiding and helped me to complete my business. He help me to sold everything I owned. But my last night in Kabul, I must see my sister. I take a big risk. Nasrin gave me this.'

He pulled a buff piece of paper from his pocket, very worn at the corners and with slits where it had been folded. He gave it to Sergeant Jackson, who stood against a wall and took out a pair of steel-rimmed half-moon glasses. He opened the letter gently.

'She learning English. She wrote this English, and she gave it me. I kept it, only because it was the only thing I owned that was touched by her. I have never read it, for I speak better than I read. Please read here.' And he pointed to a point half way down the first page, careful not to touch the ink.

Sergeant Jackson glanced over his glasses at Ahmet, and then started to read silently.

*

Once upon time, boy in big city was so very rich, he had the riches other men dream about. He did not know he was rich, and he did not know why he was rich. His father was good, and his mother was good and beautiful, and he was born in the winter, when the stars shine bright and it was cold. He had the treasure when he was born, and Allah gave it to him. It was a treasure born with blood which grows.

Some of the treasure came from another land, in lots of ships that were as strong as castles on the hills. And the other treasure came from his own country. His mother and his father knew of it, but nobody else, not the Shah or the Wasir or the holy man or even the wisest of men.

But only one man. The uncle of the boy was a poor trader who was loved by his people, for he gave to the poor and cared for the widow and the orphan. His people saw him wrestle, and loved the kindness and happiness in his face.

But suddenly the people hated the boy's uncle. He did a good thing and he hoped, inshallah, *to get a big reward. But his people did not understand, and he had to leave his sister and his nephew and his country. He ran away to save his life over the deserts and mountains. And in the hot sun and the cold wind, hoping to be safe one-day.*

Inshallah, *he is safe today, still hoping for his reward, and working for the thanks of his new countrymen and the blessings of Allah and the love of a woman and his children. But he is sad to leave behind, and he questions what happened to the treasure and the boy. He is afraid of men who visit, for perhaps they give him terrible news.*

The uncle knew that bad things would happen in his country. The boy was with his mother and father, but the people started to envy the boy his treasure, and many started to hate him. The treasure was bad they said, and they wanted it to be taken away across the seas. It would make the boy and the city unhappy.

The treasure was never heard of again. Some men said it had no worth. Some men said it had been taken away across the seas, and was guarded by good brave men. Some men think it is in the sand, looked over by a Silent Shepherd. And the boy is lost.

But the uncle knows where the treasure is, and he knows that one day he will meet the boy and together they will find the treasure.

*

Sergeant Jackson smiled kindly at Ahmet, folded the letter as though it were a sacred relic and handed it back.

'A wonderful tale, and well told, Mr Qaderi. I can see that this was not written by an English lady. But still the English is quite good, and I understand all of it. Was the lady helped with it, do you think?'

'Yes, I am sure she was. It was one of her lessons, I am sure. Captain Smith would not have left her to write it all by herself. That would not be a good lesson. But perhaps he wanted the letter to be a little imperfect, so that it was her work, not his. To remind him later, you understand? Like a love letter. '

'And the treasure. What is the treasure?'

Ahmet hesitated, and decided the answer would sound ridiculous. He had never quite been convinced himself.

'I never decided. It is just a story.'

'Just a story, you say? This is more than just a story, Mr Qaderi. You need to be plainer with me about it.'

Sergeant Jackson put away his half moon glasses and looked straight into the chestnut eyes of Ahmet Qaderi. The chestnut eyes looked straight back, unblinking. But suddenly Ahmet seem to struggle with his English.

'I sorry again. You right. Hassan needed an idea. I never know what would happen to him, or his mother and his father. Perhaps his father leaves his wife in Kabul. Perhaps she dies for marrying the *feringhee*. It happened before. Perhaps his father die in a battle. Hassan need something over the mountains for him. Perhaps I may even come back for him. And if his parents still living, then all is well. That was the reason of my story. Perhaps it was a foolish idea. Perhaps I wrote the story really for myself.'

'Perhaps some people would see it different. And there was a copy of this left in Kabul, you say?'

'Yes. Hassan has it now.'

'I wonder if this might help us to explain things. Treasure, if there is any treasure, and mountains and bloodshed and murder and a story. Hmmm.' He stroked his beard.

Again, Ahmet frowned. Mr Jackson looked as though things were beyond him, and gave the game away by fiddling with his whiskers.

111

A door banged in the distance, and Hassan and Tommy came running down the street. It was the first time Ahmet had seen Hassan running since they had left Bombay. He put the letter back in his pocket quickly, but not before Hassan had seen him. Hassan said nothing. Like Ahmet, he rarely asked questions. It was Tommy who spoke next, casually.

'Pa, can I show 'assan the sights for a bit? Take 'im up to St Paul's maybe, look at the river? And look at 'oundsditch and Cheapside and Ludgate Hill? Quiz some people?'

'Quiz some people? Meaning?'

'Well, you know, pa, watch the world go by. Get 'assan used to London, like.'

'What do you think, Mr Qaderi? You're the lad's guardian. But Tommy's a good lad, knows his way around, keeps out of trouble. And we could talk...' He winked. '... about the east.'

'Very well. If it is safe. And if ... the watchers are not here.' He looked carefully up and down the street. Aziz and Khodar were nowhere to be seen.

'Of you go then. But take care, and stick close together. You 'ear, Tommy Jackson?'

'Yes, pa.' Tommy frowned a little, thinking he had let his chance slip by saying the wrong thing. 'Yes, Sergeant Jackson, as you're nearly on duty, sergeant.'

Mr Jackson the father watched the two of them go off down the street. Ahmet, the uncle, recognised the pride in his heart.

'Now,' said Sergeant Jackson. 'Let's go and talk to granddad about his Afghan days. It might be as interesting to you as it is for him. He may just be able to help you. He should be out of bed by now, poor old fellah.'

Sure enough, there was granddad at the scullery table. For the third time that morning he heard the door bang, and as he had done last night, was suddenly caught in his own private drama.

'Lieutenant Revel, sir! *Jezailchees* up above! They're firing on us! Can't see 'em anywhere. Up there! Up there! Chase 'em off the 'eights. Up there after 'em!'

He tore at his hair, like a man desperate to escape the nightmare. The enemy was as invisible now as it had been to him at the time. Mr Johnson's right hand shook wildly, and his face grew pale and clammy. He dashed madly to the window, as he had done last night, sank to his knees and peered over the sill into the street. Then the shuddering stopped, and he mopped his forehead, stood up and asked about breakfast.

Ahmet had never seen such madness, but the Jacksons saw it almost daily and showed no surprise. They had simply waited as though nothing was happening.

'Don't you worry now,' said Mrs Jackson kindly. She was speaking to Ahmet, not to granddad. He's always like this when the door slams. I always tell the children to be quiet, but you know what they are. They never listen for long.'

'Please do not worry,' said Ahmet. 'You have shown great kindness to the traveller, praise Allah. And this noble man and I have seen the same things. I understand him.'

'I was suggesting to Mr Qaderi, my dear, that he should speak to your father about the old days. Perhaps it would help him to speak to someone who might unnerstand him a bit, like.'

'So you're Afghans! Lord, I never thought to ask you. Sit with granddad, pray, and I'll fetch some tea.' Granddad fell completely silent, sitting in his elbow chair and looking out of the window, as though waiting for somebody. Or something.

Mrs Jackson was soon back, and her husband looked at her significantly.

'Now father, do you know where these visitors are from? They are from Afghanistan. Will you tell 'em about Jalalabad? Do you remember Jalalabad?'

'Of course I remember Jalalabad. I'm not daft. Just a bit distracted sometimes, that's all.' It was the first time, apart from the moments of madness, that he had spoken in front of Ahmet. He turned his head to look at him, as though seeing him for the first time. He looked surprised, and then beamed at them like an old friend.

'We're not concerned about Jalalabad at present,' said Sergeant Jackson. 'We want to know about before that – at Kabul.'

'Come now, Thomas. You know how he likes to tell the story: starting at the end and backwards to the start.' She looked at Ahmet. 'It's his way, you see. And you'll find it makes perfect sense in a peculiar sort o' way. P'raps you'll hear all of it if there's time.'

'Very well,' said Mr Jackson. He stood taller, and rocked back a little on his heels. 'But before we continue with the hevidence, I would point out that I ham at present going about police business, Madam.'

'Of course, sergeant. Quite right.'

'Very well. Now pray continue, Mr Johnson.'

Granddad Johnson took a deep breath and looked straight at Ahmet.

'This time I'll tell the right way around, since there's visitors. We came to Jalalabad from Kabul in the Autumn of '39. Kabul was settled, and we was ordered to Jalalabad. Bitter cold it was, and it was bad news all the time. We 'eard every now and then the next two years that the chiefs had blocked the passes. Their way of getting a bit more money to keep 'em open. In 1841, I think it was, I 'eard as Mr. Macnaghten – Sir William he was by then – had stopped paying the Ghilzyee altogether. And we was cut off from the army in Kabul. Or they was cut off from us, to tell the truth.

Anyway, the chiefs rose up against the Shah and the army in Kabul. We couldn't get there. Soon we heard they was on the way to Jalalabad. Fourteen thousand of 'em. Officers, men, the Indian soldiers. Sepoys they called 'em. Good men, faithful. They stood out in the cold night after night, looking after things. And women and children and servants: thousands of em. So they told me later, you never saw such a queue through the passes. We'd done it on the way to Kandahar in '39, through the Bolan pass, but it was warm then. This was winter. And they all headed for Jalalabad in the ice and snow.'

A tear sprung into his eye.

'And how many of 'em arrived in Jalalabad?' He looked at Mr and Mrs Jackson, and then at Ahmet. 'You must know that, don't yer?'

'Indeed,' said Ahmet. I have heard of it.'

'One. Surgeon Brydon.' He left a long and meaningful silence. 'And Mr Banness, a Greek merchant who rolled in three days later, and died as soon as he got to us. Cold and exhausted. We was up on the walls, everything ready, waiting for them all. Fourteen thousand. Fighting Bob was up there all the time, looking out. He had one of these.'

He took a brass telescope from his pocket, walked to the window and looked out through it.

'Picked this up in the bazaar in Kandahar. Don't know 'oo it belonged ter. Any ways, it was Dr Brydon what come in. Slumped on 'is 'orse, he was, like he was dead. But he lifted his 'at to us, an' 'e lived. Still alive now. Lives in Scotland, so the Lieutenant tells me. I remember the look on Fighting Bob's face. His wife should have been there, you know, and his daughter. Where were they? Dead, we all thought. So what did we do?'

'You lit a great fire above the Kabul Gate and you sounded the advance,' said Mr Jackson solemnly.

Granddad Johnson looked very distant, lost in another world and another time. Often they had wondered what he was thinking at this point in the story. Actually, he was remembering the silence: the dark of the night, a half-dead doctor in a bunk. The silence of total destruction, broken only by the Forlorn Hope of a bugle, sounding every half hour.

'We sounded the advance. Every 'alf hour for three days. Who turned up? Just a few sepoys who had managed to survive the bullets and the swords and the snow and the hunger. Later we heard there were prisoners, sick and wounded who had been left in Kabul and some of the ladies and children and married men, and some 'ostages in case we never gave up Jalalabad.

'And now we knew. We worked out one night, as we was on picket duty, me and Chalky and Plum, that now they'd done for Kabul they'd come for us. We could have run for it: back to Peshawar and India. But we'd never do that. Know what they called us? Do you? Thomas?'

'They called you,' said Mr Jackson, not wanting to insist on his rank this time, 'they called you ...' He built up to it. 'They called you

The Illustrious Garrison. They called you the Light Bobs. They called you the Bleeders. And they called you ... The Heroes of Jalalabad!'

'Yes! And we never run. We stopped and fought. Specially after Kabul. That was when the siege started: Akbar Khan came down on us like a ton of coals. But he never beat us, no sir.'

He laughed exultantly, like a man who had won a game of double or quits, and grew conspiratorial, and winked at Ahmet.

'He besieged us. But you know what we did? Well, Akbar brought shepherds and a great flock of sheep with him. Just like we'd done with the cattle: your grub marches with yer. One afternoon, we saw they'd let the sheep and goats graze near the city walls. I told Colonel Dennie, and he said we should go out and collar 'em. So we sneaked out after dark and brought 'em in. Five 'undred of 'em. Kept us in food for weeks!

'A week later, though, we got more serious. Out we went, and smashed Akbar's army and burnt all his tents and off he went. But then the Governor-General told the army to leave. And did we leave? Did we leave the prisoners to die? Or did we go back to defeat Kabul?'

'Defeat Kabul! Defeat Kabul!' cried Lizabet as she came into the room. Ahmet looked at her sadly.

'That's what we did. Back we went through the passes: and what a sight we saw. There were thousands and thousands, in their red tunics and their blue greatcoats. All dead. Sepoys, little two and three and four year old Indians, officers, men and women. All of them. In some places they were piled in their hundreds. I recognised some of them from when we'd been in Kabul together. They'd been preserved by the cold in some places. In other places they'd been picked clean by birds and dogs. Some had hands missing: p'raps to get rings off. Some places, more in the open, where the sun had got to them, the smell was terrible. They were strewn all over the way, everywhere you looked. Our cart wheels rode over them and you'd sometimes hear a cracking sound as a skull split open and the brains were let out, like. I saw little dead Indian kids with no clothes on, sitting in the snow, stripped and left to freeze to death.'

Ahmet cast his mind back fourteen years, when he had left Kabul and headed through these passes in the opposite direction, little knowing what was about to happen. He had missed it by just eight weeks.

'But we was triumphant in the end!' He exploded in glee again. 'We soon saw the insides of Kabul again. Oh yes, by God! We won in the end! It wasn't the same as when we'd left it: half the shops shut and the traders gone, but we were back. We 'ad our Army of Retribution. We 'ad our justice.'

Ahmet felt pity for this man: for his experiences, for what he had seen, and for the half-mad creature he had become. But even as a guest he had his limits.

'A strange kind of justice. Strange for you and for Afghanistan,' he said, simply and quietly. 'Twenty thousand dead!'

Granddad Johnson was lost in his thoughts again, and peace descended on the room. Mr Jackson was the one to break it.

'Mr J, we wanted to ask you something. Do you remember, when you were in Afghanistan, a man called ... Who was he?'

'Smith. Captain William Smith of the 13th Light Infantry,' said Ahmet.

'Smith? Why, there are lots of Smiths, of course.' He paused. 'But I 'eard of one special one. A young man. Lieutenant when I knew 'im. Friend of Lieutenant Eyre and poor Captain Sturt '

'He made ice-skates?' said Ahmet.

Mr Johnson was silent, staring at the floor. Then there was a flash of memory.

'I eard that. Yes, that was the special story! The very same genelman, maybe! A good man, I 'eard. And I 'eard of a Smith what married a Afghan.'

'Why, so did our Smith! And Hassan is his son.'

Granddad was silenced for a moment as though by a *jezail*.

'E's the son of Lieutenant Smith? Well, strike me down! And you?'

You will not remember me. I was born in Kabul. I was still there after you left, but I had to leave too, just before Mr Smith did. Did you ever see the wrestling in the town? The wrestler who took turns with the soldiers?'

'I can hardly credit it! You're not the man who had a bout with poor Sergeant Leary?'

'I am. I am Ahmet Qaderi.'

Mr Johnson was thrilled. He put out his hand, and Ahmet took it in both of his.

'Have you heard of Smith? Since you came back to England in '44?' asked Mr Jackson. It's very important, Mr J.'

'Well no.' He paused. 'But I have seen Lieutenant James, poor man. 'E spoke of him, said as he'd 'ad a letter off him. A long time ago.'

'James. Were you in Sukkur with Mr James? With General Sale?' Ahmet spoke quickly now, excited at this news.

'That I was.'

'And you still see Mr James now?'

''E's come down in the world since the wars. I haven't seen him for a long time.'

'Granddad, this is important. Please help us. When did you last see him?'

'Mr James? A long time ago.'

'Yes, but when?'

'A very long time ago. I think it was last Tuesday, or maybe Wednesday.'

Chapter Twelve

Hassan was worried. A day out in London with Tommy Jackson sounded exciting, but even after the freedom Uncle Ahmet had given him in Bombay, he still found the idea rather unnerving.

He also worried about his uncle: in Bombay Ahmet had always been open with him – about everything from his business affairs to the little stories about his sister. He had been both teacher and loving guardian. But since they had left, he had been quieter, and much less forthcoming. There seemed to be things that Hassan did not know and could not ask about. Whenever he thought of his uncle now, there were other pictures in his head: his uncle looking out of the window, his face etched in thought; the way he looked at Khodar and Aziz as they left the boat; the way he had thought of walking away from the dying Indian.

What was Uncle Ahmet worried about? Was there more to the little Indian's death than Ahmet had told him?

*

Tommy led Hassan quickly to the end of Evans Street. Just as they turned left into Gatesby Street, there was a shout from behind.

'Tommy! Wait for me!'

They both turned around, and there was Lucy running towards them, her hair streaming behind her and one boot still undone.

'What do you want?' asked Tommy, his voice and his face shot through with irritation. 'Pa did give us permission, you know. Or d'you want somefink?'

'I'm not checking up on you, Tommy,' she said, looking straight at Hassan. 'It's just Pa said I could come with you. He did, honest. Come on, let me come with you.'

Still she looked at Hassan. And then, as if to give her brother no choice, she took Hassan's hand and marched him to Stansby Street, and then the Commercial Road.

The day before, Hassan had thought the docks were the noisiest place he had ever been in, but the Commercial Road, Whitechapel High Street and Leadenhall Street were far noisier: noisier than a monsoon deluge on the roofs in Bombay; noisier than the roaring sea as they had rounded the Cape; noisier than the half-dozen church bells ringing out at once in the streets they had passed through. It was impossible to talk as the iron-rimmed wheels of carts and wagons and the lighter wheels of hansom cabs rattled on the cobblestones and echoed from the walls. Tommy and Lucy found all this completely natural, but the onrushing crowds and traffic turned Hassan into a bag of nerves. Bombay was busy too, but the Commercial Road was not like Malabar Hill.

The pavements were already busy, although it was still only just after nine o'clock. Men in varnished hats, boys in woollen caps of grey and brown, and women in cheap mob-caps of every colour bustled along, trying to keep out of the filthy gutters and away from the traffic. A drawn-looking woman in a lavender dress drawn tight above the waist shouted at Hassan and Tommy as she barged past them. Boys pushed noisy hand-barrows piled up with pies and peppermints and roast chestnuts. Everywhere there were the cries of trade, of the hollow-eyed, thrusting poor desperate for a few small coins. 'Walnuts sixteen a penny! Take a penny loaf! Pork pies! Best pork pies!'Everywhere there were people shouting above the din. Lucy disappeared for a moment, and then silently slipped a chestnut into Hassan's hand.

As they got to Aldgate High Street, closer to the hub of the city, the traffic became denser and denser. In Whitechapel High Street, it finally came to a clogged and noisy halt. A dozen or more large wagons carrying great bales of wool or timber or barrels of fish met at a junction. An omnibus advertising whisky and surmounted by eight or nine top-hatted, shouting men, brushed wheels with a carter's wagon, and the driver yelled furiously, waving his whip in the air as if about to lash out at somebody. A constable tried desperately to direct the traffic, and was almost crushed between two grey horses. A lady and gentleman in a tiny gig watched nervously, and a parson in a hansom cab read a book in complete peace, for this seemed a normal part of his everyday journey.

The noise had changed totally: the rattling of wheels had suddenly ceased, and had been replaced by scraping, screams and yells. Pedestrians struggled to find elbow room at the sides of the road, and small scruffy children were pressed against shop fronts and into doorways. Every so often, Hassan caught a view of St Paul's, looming hugely above buildings ahead and to the left, its stone dome and its little gold cross shining in the brightening sky. Looking back down at the street, he had lost sight of Tommy, but then felt the scruff of his neck being grabbed, and he was pulled into a quieter alley.

'Quick, 'assan. In 'ere. Issafer. We'll take another way. Where's Lucy?' Then he put two forefingers in his mouth and whistled shrilly. An elderly woman gasped and put her hands over her ears. 'Lucy! Lucy!'

'Awright, Tommy. I'm 'ere, aren't I? Open yer eyes! Come on, 'assan. Follow me.' And she grabbed his hand again.

In an instant they were in another world. Or not quite another world, but certainly a very different part of the same world. The street was very narrow, and no wheeled vehicles could get in. The fronts of the houses (or shops – it was hard to tell the difference) were draped with old clothes. There were stalls selling turnips, marrows and pies. Outside one house, lined up neatly along the street, were twenty pairs of old shoes. One of each had been turned over to show painstaking repairs, but the uppers were exhausted by the dance they had been led. Outside almost every house was a group of children: girls, mostly, it seemed to Hassan. Some families were like little Russian dolls all lined up: identical except in size. Identical eyes, identical curls, identical grime and rags and bare feet. A child a year for ten years to be added to the front step and the grind of life.

A girl younger than Hassan, covered in dust and filth, nursed a baby. Then he saw the same pattern repeated up the street. There were many things Hassan didn't know about this scene. Just as this little street had been hidden from Whitechapel High Street, so this street masked the thousand stories which lay in the rooms behind the high walls. Hassan did not know – how could he? – that the babies belonged to the girls who were often younger than he was.

Nor did Hassan know about the dead in the houses south of here as the land sloped down to the river. He had never seen a family gathered around a father who had died three days earlier, not having the energy or the wit or the money to remove him from the house and have him buried.

He wondered where the boys were. Working? Ill? Not all of them, surely? There was still the bustle of business and the street cries – 'slice of plum cake, only a penny'– but everything was a little slower. People were not on their way to somewhere else, as they had been on the main road. They were simply here, and they were staying here, cut off from any idea of a destination. A woman looked up at Hassan as he passed, and stared vacantly at him. She put a hand out, not caring whether or not anything would be put into her palm. Never had Hassan seen such hopelessness.

Tommy took a few dives into alleys, and Hassan and Lucy followed blindly. Soon they were back in a busier street: busier, but hardly safer or more pleasant.

'Oundsditch,' Tommy announced.

It was a street full of old clothes and the smell of a tavern. They passed a butcher's shop, and a fishmonger's with barrels of herring and crab and sole outside, and the fishmonger yelled 'poor hake a penny' as they strode by. They tore past an old clothes dealer, who jumped back in alarm as he saw Hassan. There was stall after stall of handed-down clothes, and Hassan now understood why he had seen so many people dressed in what had once been very fine clothes indeed, but were now threadbare and out-at-elbow. Clothes were passed from the rich, to the middle classes and then to the poor, and it was probably amongst the poor that they had spent more time than anywhere, stitched and patched over and over again until they were hardly cloth at all. How old were they, some of them? Twenty years old? Thirty? Perhaps, thought Hassan, some of these coats could last for fifty years. Nothing was wasted, even after the clothes had completely fallen apart. At the end of the street they came across a rag merchant, his scraps and tatters piled high, with a baby asleep on the top.

They then turned left again, and Tommy made another proud announcement.

'Bishopsgate Street.' He seemed to know everything.

Hassan was confused by the shops here. There was one with a gigantic cheese in the window and nothing more; one with a very lonely and very dead pheasant hanging up by its feet; one with a single loaf on a plate. He thought of Bombay, with its wild colours and its goods piled high and open to the street. Uncle Ahmet had told him many times that the shops in Afghanistan were the same, at least when the *feringhee* money was still there.

Why in this country was everything hidden away? He had seen nothing of the *feringhee* God, just heard Him clanging in the streets. He seemed to be hidden away and silent, and nobody spoke of Him – not when *Aurora* docked after ninety days, not when the Indian had died, not when the sun rose or when it set. Perhaps he had just not looked hard enough. Perhaps He would leap out at him soon: perhaps a muezzin would blast the call to prayer from a tower at the end of the street, or perhaps he would be invited in to the *feringhee* mosque – church, his uncle had called it – to wash himself and be refreshed and to pray. He heard distant music, and wondered whether that was it.

They crossed to the other side of the road, and several people gave farthings and half-pennies to the crossing sweeper who kept the street free of mud and dust: or as free of it as possible.

'God bless yer, Guv'nor! Thank you kindly, ma'am!'

Here there were shops selling odd decaying items of furniture and domestic odds and ends: washstands and sideboards and bedsteads. The pavements were blocked completely by them. There was a stout house, and a man fell out of it as they passed, still reeling from the night before. Everywhere there were people pushing barrows or carrying trays. In the middle of the street a small boy struggled with a large bucket, and Hassan watched him. Every now and then the boy stopped, scraped something from the road with a tiny shovel and hauled the bucket a few more yards, where he did the same thing again. Hassan looked at Tommy and frowned. Tommy and Lucy laughed at him.

'What he is doing?' asked Hassan.

'Dog muck,' announced Lucy indifferently.

The boy wrestled with the bucket again, and dragged it through a narrow arch next to *Piffkins Glove Manufactory, est 1847.*

'What is Piffkins Glove?' asked Hassan.

'Piffkins is a man. A glove is ...'and he mimed the action of putting on a glove.

'And why the boy picks up dirt for?'

'For making the gloves with. It gets the 'air out of the leather, and makes it nice and soft.' He pulled a hair on the back of his hand. 'Now you see why I don't wear gloves. The rich folks can wear 'em if they wants!'And he laughed.

Hassan was none the wiser. Why did they make gloves only for the Piffkins, and not for the women?

Further along, the music grew louder until the air was full of it, discordant and clashing. A group of young men played tunes on marrowbones of different sizes, and a small band played trumpets and a euphonium and an ophicleide, a brass instrument like a coiled serpent, with keys and pads and a mouthpiece. The blaring noise, which made Hassan want to laugh, echoed up the sooted fronts of shops and houses, and felt its way into every room to the tops of the buildings. Hassan looked up at the dusty windows, all firmly shut against the cold, except for one where an elderly woman dressed in black was beating a small carpet, the dirt falling in little clouds onto the people below.

'Ungry?' Tommy did the usual mime. Hassan nodded.

They stopped at a breakfast stall made from two trestles and a sheet of deal, covered with sheets of newspaper as a cloth. It was late now: nearly ten o'clock, and the trade was winding up. The woman who made her living here wore a faded grey shawl, a black dress as though she were in mourning, and tatty shoes. She had done her best with the stall: there was a tarpaulin to keep the worst of the wind off, and little muslin sheets to keep the dust off the bread. Hassan was grateful for the warmth of two big tins of hot coffee and tea, and he and Tommy quickly wolfed down some coarse brown rolls. Lucy ate nothing.

A man just up the street was selling chestnuts from another stall, where smoke and steam rose from the fire he had lit inside a gigantic brazier. It was Lucy who had to make the conversation.

'Bread all right, Hassan?' She pointed. Hassan nodded.

'Coffee all right?' Hassan smiled.

'You like London?' Hassan grinned and nodded again.

Lucy leaned forward and brushed a breadcrumb from Hassan's cheek.

As they stood to leave Hassan heard shouting. He looked back up the street, the way they had just come, and saw Khodar and Aziz. They seemed to be arguing with two small men dressed in aprons and caps. There was an up-ended board on the pavement, and half a dozen shining, steely fish under their feet. The small men were the ones doing the shouting.

Tommy caught the look on Hassan's face, and followed his stare. The view was blocked by a Hansom cab which took a while to squeeze between a barrow and a knot of pedestrians, and when it had gone the men had vanished.

'Wassup?' asked Tommy.

Hassan looked at him blankly, and Tommy tried again. 'Trouble?'

'No. It is nothing.'

'It don't look like nuffink to me,' said Tommy. 'Wassup? Pa did tell me to be careful with yer, yer know. Why did Pa ask me to be careful? You in trouble?'

And almost before he had finished, there was Khodar, standing right behind him and asking for coffee. He looked at Hassan, grinning broadly, but with a glint in his eye that was not just good-morning humour. Again, Tommy saw the look on Hassan's face and turned around. Khodar ignored Tommy and spoke to Hassan in Pashtu.

'Good day to you, my good friend. You are following the straight path today?' The smile vanished. 'Or are you making friends with the unbeliever?' He flashed a look at Tommy, who refused to blink. 'Why do you not seek the friendship of me and my cousin instead?'

Hassan thought about this.

'Because he has invited me to spend this day with him, and you have not.'

Khodar put his hand on Hassan's shoulder and lowered his face to look him straight in the eye from inches away. Hassan shrank away a little. He still did not know why he should fear this man, but he felt it anyway. How had Khodar found him? Had he followed him all the way from Evans Street? He couldn't have done, surely?

'Get yer 'ands off 'im,' shouted Lucy, and pulled Hassan away.

'Watch yerself!' shouted a man with a pie tray suspended from a leather neck strap. 'Yer'll 'ave me day's bi'ness all over the floor, young 'un!'

Hassan then noticed, on the other side of the street, a man in a brightly coloured waistcoat, fine boots, a tailed coat and a top hat. Where had he seen him before? He was watching Khodar and Aziz carefully, and then his head turned and looked straight at Hassan, just as Tommy yelled and the three of them ran hell-for-leather down Bishopsgate Street. Hassan found it harder to get through the crowds than Tommy did, so Lucy held back for him.

The man across the street thought for a moment, the vee of his thumb and forefinger running down his beard. What had just happened could be seen here almost everyday, of course: often, the running children had been thieving and were running from shopkeepers or the police.

But most of these children were victims too. Up-river were the Adelphi arches, where every day children were taken into slavery of one sort and another, and which every night became the haunt of whole dens of drunks and opium smokers and card sharps. And worse. Yet there was something different about this. These boys were running from something different from the usual. Clearly they knew those men, and were afraid of them. Otherwise, what had made them run? He walked with a very unusual briskness, along the route that the boys had just taken.

Strangely, Khodar and Aziz made no attempt to follow, and as Hassan looked back he saw them standing in the street. Aziz seemed to be complaining to Khodar, and Khodar was shouting back at him. The words were lost in the rattle of the traffic.

Hassan and Tommy turned right and ran down to the junction of Leadenhall Street and Cornhill. By the time they felt they were safe, they were well into Cheapside. Still the man in the top hat kept them in view.

'Tell you what,' said Tommy. 'I'll show you St Paul's. Should be safe there. 'But keep 'em peeled!' he wagged a forefinger at his own eyes.

'What is pilled?' asked Hassan.

'Never mind.' He pointed at his eyes and beckoned, telling Hassan to follow him. They were off again, keeping close to the grimy walls, watching out for their pursuers. No sign of them so far. Through Cornhill, under the splendiferous façade of the Bank of England – what a building to find, just a two minute run from Houndsditch! – and into Cheapside. Again the bells rang out, almost but not quite together, and again Hassan and Tommy were assailed on all sides by the noise of people making a living. Tommy bought a few peppermints for two farthings. Then, very suddenly, the buildings opened out on the left, and Hassan was stunned by the sight of the cathedral. He had seen it only from a distance: from the river, then the merest glimpse of its dome as they walked from the docks, and just now from Aldgate High Street. Now it became the biggest building he had ever seen: bigger than anything in Bombay and bigger, though he did not yet know it, than any of the buildings in Kabul. The white dome, made of Portland stone, stood out against a brightening sky, and the little gold cross – far less little than he had imagined – just began to gleam as the sun broke through. What, he wondered, was the point of the little cross? He had seen them everywhere.

They walked around St Paul's Churchyard to the West Front of the Cathedral, and stood together and looked up at the steps and the columns and the vast wooden doors.

'Grand, innit?' said Tommy. It was perhaps his proudest moment of the day.

'Splendid!' said Hassan.

Tommy laughed loudly.

'Splendid! Where did you learn that one, all on a sudden?'

'A word of a soldier. I know many soldier words: my father a soldier.'

'What, an English soldier? Nah!'

'Yes. Ask my Uncle Ahmet. He tell you.'

'All right, if you say so. Where is he now?'

'I not know. In England perhaps. Perhaps dead. Perhaps one day I find him.'

'And your ma?'

Again, Tommy's language failed to get through, and Hassan looked blankly, than frowned.

'Mother. Your mother.'

'Allah took her to the garden where rivers flow.'

'Who's that? What garden?'

'Allah is the one God.'

'Oh. You mean she died?'

'Yes, Tommy.'

'And yer Uncle Ahmet took care of you.'

'Since I was small.'

'Knee high.'

'Knee high.'

Tommy could not think what to say next, so he looked away towards the Cathedral steps.

'Wanna look inside?' He pointed.

'Yes. It is beautiful?'

'Oh yes.'

Tommy stopped briefly.

'Now who were them blokes?'

'Blokes?'

'The men. Back there.' He jerked his thumb back the way they had come.

'Men from the boat.'

'*Aurora.*'

'*Aurora*, yes.'

'They were very … kind to you. Why was that?'

'I not know. They are not kind, I think. But I not know why.'

'Maybe it's what pa was getting at. Maybe it's somethink to do with yer uncle and the murder. You reckon?'

'I not know.' His open, honest face, scar and all, looked straight at Tommy.

'Can I ask you summink?'

'Ask.'

''Ow did that 'appen?' He pointed at the scar. Every boy has a fascination with scars.

'I not know. When I was …' He hunted for the phrase. 'Knee high. A baby. I not remember.'

Hassan decided that he had told Tommy Jackson enough.

'Leave him be,' said Lucy. 'It's 'is business.'

There were many little groups standing in the Churchyard, passing the time of day. Some were already eating: a pie here and a penny loaf and cheese there. They had probably been working since dawn. Two men in black tail coats and pristine top hats were discussing business. A man pushed a barrel organ across the yard, perhaps heading towards the pleasure gardens to find a good spot for the afternoon. The monkey on his shoulder darted curious looks at people, and a lady in black shrank back as he passed.

As they started to walk, three people watched them. One had followed from Bishopsgate Street, and now sat on a bench some distance away, his chin resting on the top of his cane. With his brisk strides, he had had no trouble keeping up with running children in a crowd. Whenever he caught somebody's eye, he took a sudden interest in the brass eagle's claw on top of the cane, and then rested his chin again and resumed his study of the three youngsters. He could see that the boy and girl were related, probably brother and sister, but what of the boy from the east? He was sure he recognised him.

The other two stood out in the crowd, dressed as they were in their sheepskin coats and *lunghees*, watched as well as watching, and waited as Tommy and Hassan walked towards the Cathedral.

'What shall we do now?' asked Aziz, as unsure as ever.

'We wait,' said Khodar. 'We wait and see what they will do. If they enter the building, they have to come out. We can wait for them here. You think Ahmet Qaderi knows his nephew is entering the infidel church?'

'What does it matter?' asked Aziz. 'He has a good heart, after all.'

'A good heart? What is the point of a good heart if you walk away from Allah?'

'With a good heart you can never walk away from Allah,' said Aziz. 'My father told me.' He was pleased to put it so clearly.

'Look. They are going in.'

Groups of people stood and talked, so that Hassan and Tommy were soon hidden.

The inside of the Cathedral was unlike anything Hassan had ever seen, and he walked under the dome and looked up, his eye tracing the edges of the Whispering Gallery. The space, he thought, could contain three of the biggest buildings he had ever seen.

Lucy sat in a pew quietly. She looked at Hassan to make sure he was watching her. One day, she hoped, he would need to know how to sit in a pew. Tommy watched him too, and saw that now there was a reason for his silence. In fact, he realised that there had always been a reason for it. Tommy had known families who had arrived from the countryside with their sun-tanned skin and their cracked hands and their amazed silence. It had taken them weeks to get used to the city. On top of that, Hassan hardly knew English and was being dragged around a busy city by himself. 'I'd 've bin quiet an' all,' he thought.

Still Hassan looked around him, and wandered over to a gigantic statue in the south transept. A man stood on a giant pedestal, leaning on an anchor, the other hand under his jacket. Hassan wondered what colour the jacket might have been. A woman dressed rather oddly, Hassan thought, in a military helmet with feathers, stood beneath him, holding a man who seemed to be wounded. On the other side of the pedestal was a rather timid-looking lion.

'Nelson,' said Tommy. 'Lion. He pointed at the helmeted woman. 'Britannia. The lion showed 'e died in a battle.'

'Battle?'

'War.'

Hassan was surprised. Was this a celebration of some sort? Did everybody who died in a war have a statue like this in a church? Was there a statue of his father somewhere?

Outside, the man who had followed them from Bishopsgate Street watched from the main entrance behind them, his gold-topped cane still placed thoughtfully under his chin. But then, when he looked again for Khodar and Aziz, they had vanished. He darted back down the steps, turned left and strode back into the yard beside the Cathedral.

He was surprised to see Aziz and Khodar ahead of him at the side door. He slowed his pace and watched carefully. Perhaps this could still be avoided.

From a distance, he saw Hassan, Lucy and Tommy come out into the chill breeze which blew from Ludgate Hill and under the railway bridge. A few dead leaves skittered across the pathway. Khodar stood directly in their way.

'So, my young friend. How are you enjoying your visit?' asked Khodar, in Pashtu. Again, the mouth was smiling but the eyes were not. Tommy understood nothing the man had said, but he wasn't born yesterday, and he understood the eyes and the mouth. He also understood the hand clutching Hassan's shoulder.

'And where are you going today, with your new friend?' He took a long look at Tommy, who glared back at him.

'I do not know, Khodar.' The grip tightened just a little, so that Tommy did not notice. 'Truly, I do not know!'

'I think you know exactly where you are going. You are going to meet the keeper.'

'Keeper?'

'We found your uncle's letter, Hassan. In Kabul. We know all about your … what is the word? … Your search. We have known about it since the month the *feringhees* left Kabul to be slaughtered at Khoord Kabul and Tezeen and Jugdulluk and Gandamuk.'

Hassan was blank with astonishment and confusion. What was this man talking about? He looked at the other man. Aziz looked anxious, his eyes now darting between Tommy and Hassan and his cousin, and now looking along the path. Lucy he ignored. He seemed to think that she was either unimportant or unthreatening.

'Khodar. Please stop this,' said Aziz. The boy knows nothing. I have said it to you before, but you will not listen. It is not ours. We do not know where it is. Nobody knows where it is. Who says it is anywhere? It is impossible. The boy is just a wayfarer, and an orphan. Let us leave him be.'

'Weak as ever! You know how long we have dreamed of this! It is a tale worthy of the *Thousand and One Nights*! A great treasure! We have crossed the seas for it, ninety-four days working like slaves to get here. And you will give up now?' He released Hassan and pushed him gently against a wall so that he could not escape. Somehow Tommy stuck by him as this happened, so that they were trapped together. Lucy stayed outside the circle, and looked around her. She caught the eye of a tall, bearded man in a top hat and a yellow waistcoat.

Then Khodar spoke again to Aziz, an edge in his voice. He spoke loudly enough, perhaps deliberately, for Hassan to hear him.

'I will have this treasure! The treasure is ours: brought to our country, and our country destroyed: the fortress of Ghazni, the walls of Jalalabad, the streets of Kabul! It is an Afghan treasure. The *feringhee* owes it to us! And it will be paid!'His voice lowered again. You know what it is like to kill?'

Aziz was unable to breathe for a moment.

'No.' It was a crisis of belief as much as an answer.

Khodar lowered his voice to a bare whisper, not because his Pashtu could be understood by anybody other than Aziz and Hassan, but in order to chill his cousin's marrow. 'I know,' he hissed. 'It is easier than you think if you want to.' He turned to Hassan. 'You see, I have already killed once. I killed a man who could not mind his own business. I can take my knife to your throat if you wish it. Just say the word.'

Aziz's eyes widened and he could barely whisper.

'My cousin! What are you telling me? What have you done?'

Before he could say more, Aziz had a knife under his chin. For the second time in London, Hassan felt the world contract into a pinpoint of fear. Neither Khodar nor Aziz could speak any more: Khodar out of rage and Aziz out of terror. Aziz felt like a man on a cliff top, feeling the plunge before it had started.

At first, neither of them noticed that Tommy had gradually shuffled around them. As they did so, a gap opened between Aziz and Khodar, and suddenly all three of them bolted for the nearest adult they could find, and almost ran straight into that same, black-coated, top-hatted stranger who had followed them from Bishopsgate Street and who, of course, had watched *Aurora* arrive in the East India Docks the evening before.

'Now then, my ...'

'Quick, mister! A man with a knife!'

Hassan searched desperately for the words.

'He kill a man! Yesterday! I see him dead!' Tommy gaped palely at Hassan, eyes like saucers. 'I tell truth, Tommy. Khodar tell Aziz. Right now. We tell your father.'

Mr Dickens looked from Hassan to Tommy.

'And how would you know that, pray?'

'Murder in the docks last night, sir. I seen him. So did 'Assan an' his Uncle. An' 'e just said it, in 'is own language.'

'Yes, in Pashtu,' said Hassan. 'My language also'.

The man raised both eyebrows, lowered one, and then frowned.

'Very well, let's make enquiries, shall we?'

Dickens had no fear of getting involved with the law. He had once been a witness in court, against a man accused of ill-treating a horse.

'It was 'im: 'im there.' Tommy pointed at Khodar, who had been watching intently. Dickens and the two boys stood still as Khodar approached them. He spoke calmly.

'My name is Khodar. A fine morning, sir.'

'Indeed,' said Mr Dickens. 'Are these young gentleman causing you trouble, sir?' He looked from Khodar to Aziz, and noted Aziz's nervousness. 'It may interest you to know that I have been in the courts myself once or twice. Should I take these two ruffians away from you?'

Mr Dickens looked hard at Khodar. He was a quick judge of character. A fine actor can always understand the tiniest details in others: a twitch in the jaw line, a pursing of the lips, a spark in the eye. Already he saw something in Khodar that he loathed. Already he suspected there was poison in the man's heart. Was it just the colour of his skin? He hoped not. Indeed not: for when he looked at Aziz he saw a very different man. And the boy's open face, beyond the scar, and his honest eyes were different too.

'The boys are no trouble, sir, thank you. Aziz, my cousin, and I are quite well. I thank you for your kindness.'

Mr Dickens looked again at the quiet man. Again he brought his dramatic interpretation into the game. Aziz could not look at him for some time. Dickens persisted, and eventually Aziz looked up. His eyes were just a little wider than they might have been, and there was just a little sweat on his brow. Then, just perceptibly, a quarter of an inch or so, he shook his head.

'Well, my dear sir, I shall remove them in any case. 'I have in mind a dear friend of mine: one Inspector Bucket of the Metropolitan Police. Perhaps you have heard the name?'

'No sir, I have not.' Again, Khodar smiled.

And then, suddenly, there was a flash, and Mr Dickens found a small knife blade in front of his face.

'Yet perhaps one day you will hear again from me. Now leave us!' He pressed his hand firmly on Mr Dickens' chest, making him take a step back.

Having brought the stranger to this case, Tommy decided that it was time to leave. Quickly he grabbed Hassan and thrust him away, and they took to their legs as though running from a volcano. All Lucy could do was watch.

Hassan and Tommy ran straight into a wall of dark serge trousers. It was a constable, who looked straight over their heads to see which of the innocent gentlefolk in the crowd had been robbed or murdered. He thought he saw a knife being lowered and pocketed, but before he could be sure, Khodar and Aziz had melted away. Dickens wandered across, looking a little pale.

'Why, Mr Dickens, sir.' He looked at the great man as though entranced, and then noticed his complexion. 'Are you quite all right, sir? I get you anything? 'ere, take a seat. Take the weight off your legs for a hinstant.'

'I am perfectly well, thank you, Mr Dixon. I must thank the Fates, however, that you arrived when you did. I have just had a knife placed at my throat and a threat has been made upon my life.'

'It's true, Constable,' said Lucy. 'e did. Didn'e, Tommy?'

'Good Lord, sir!' He looked at Hassan, and grabbed him by the jacket. 'I am arresting you on a charge of robbery and battery against this genelman. You will come with me straightways. Thank you and congratulations, Mr Dickens!'

'Not him!' shouted Lucy. 'It was the men by the church. Two on 'em. Just now.'

'And who might you be?'

'Lucy Jackson.' There was a lengthy pause whilst the Constable looked at her. She was learning nothing from her father. 'Constable.'

'The young lady is quite correct, Dixon. They were two grown men. From the east, I should say.'

'Shadwell, sir? Rotherhithe? You know their addresses?'

'A little further east, Dixon. I should say Afghanistan or India or somewhere. I regret that I cannot be more precise than that. I do know, however, that both I and these boys may be in continued danger. There is more to this than a simple case of robbery in the street. The men have followed this boy half way across the globe and have followed him since he arrived in London. There is a great game afoot, I fear.'

'Well, thank you sir. What do you suggest now, sir?'

Mr Dickens thought for a while.

'I shall take care of them, Constable. I shall find them a place of safety, and listen to the tale they have to tell me. Who knows? The tale may come in useful one day!'

'Very well, sir. If you're sure, sir. I shall make my reports in any case, sir'.

Mr Charles Dickens, Lucy and Tommy and Hassan turned from the policeman and walked away. Tommy had suddenly recovered his voice, and after a few steps, he turned back and spoke in a loud stage whisper to Hassan and Lucy.

'I wonder what my father, SERGEANT JACKSON will make of this when I tell 'im. Constable DIXON, 'is name was.'

They walked for some time, through Fleet Street, up Chancery Lane with its lawyers' wigs and papers tied up with red ribbon, onto High Holborn and then northwards. As they got further from the river, the cheap terraces of Holborn gave way to the fine houses of Russell Square, with their private railings to keep out the ophicleides and the marrow-bones players and the Punch and Judy man and the barrel organ and the hawkers, and then a little further into Tavistock Square, where the houses were the finest Hassan had seen since he had left Malabar Hill. Here indeed were homes fit for the heroes of *A Thousand Nights and One Night*!

Mr Dickens took out a key and opened a gate, and they entered a garden with a great carriage drive, shaped hedges, shrubs and masonry.

''Ere!' said Tommy, rather too loudly. I know you! You're that Mr Dickens, the writer genelman! Mr Picklewick an' Oliver Twist an … an …'

'Mr Pecksniff? Uriah Heep? Smike? Wackford Sqeers?'

Tommy could only nod at the names, not having read any of the books himself.

'Me pa – that's the Sergeant Jackson I was talking of earlier – 'e loves your Picklewick.'

I am quite delighted to hear of him,' said Mr Dickens, smiling, 'and I hope that he is well.'

'Very well, sir, I thank ye. Cor! Just wait 'til I tell 'im I've bin in Mr Dickens's 'ouse!'

'You shall, and very soon. But first, you have a wonderful tale to tell me.'

Chapter Thirteen

November 1855

They stepped the short distance across the garden and up to the front door, which nestled behind great pillars supporting a heavy stone porch. Then, in an instant, they were inside Tavistock House. Behind the door there was a large hallway, lit even this early in the day by gas lamps. Hassan followed Mr Dickens warily, looking at the walls as he passed. There were pictures of the oddest people: pen and ink drawings in dark wooden frames, hanging by sturdy chains from a rail. Hassan glanced at them in turn, torn between keeping up with Mr Dickens and taking in the pictures. Tommy pushed gently from behind, and Lucy held his hand.

'Come on, 'assan. Git moving.'

The first picture was of a pretty young woman in a wood. She was crossing a rickety little bridge over a stream, looking vaguely around her. In the background was a large house. Hassan thought she seemed lost; he could not tell whether she was happy or not. Then an innocent girl, quite young and wearing a long dress and a bonnet, sat in a graveyard. Thinking about death, Hassan thought.

Then a vicious looking woman, much older than the others, spooned something into the mouths of a queue of boys – orphans, perhaps? – and one turned away clutching his mouth, and others were fighting in the background. But it was the last picture that stunned Hassan, because he had seen it before. It was of a fat man in a barrow, in a pen surrounded by pigs, just waking up with his hat cock-eyed, a huge dog barking in his ear and a huge crowd of people laughing at him. Hassan stared. It was surely one of the drawings that he had in his book?

He could not help himself. He reached inside his *poshteen* and pulled the book out for the first time that day. He looked for the picture, found it and compared them. Just the same. The picture on the wall was well copied! Lucy looked over his shoulder.

'Why, they're ezackly the same,' she said.

He glanced at Mr Dickens, who had stopped to wait for them and was now combing his hair in a large mirror.

'Put the book back, young man! I cannot bear to have books lying around. Put it back tidily if you please!'

Seeing Hassan's confusion, he strode back up the passageway and took the book. He tried to replace it on a shelf in a little alcove behind Hassan, but saw that it was full. He looked puzzled, and then saw Hassan holding his hand out. He turned the book over in his hand, opened the cover and stared in astonishment.

'Your book? Surely not? I haven't seen one of these for some time. A first complete edition! Well done, my young friend! Always delightful to meet a customer! ... Ah, a gift I see. Yes. Yes. So you are ... Hassan?'

'Yes sir. I Hassan.'

Dickens held out a hand.

'Charles Dickens. Delighted, I am sure. And a gift from your loving father...' He looked completely lost for a moment, as though remembering something from long ago.

'Come along now. There is a lady I wish you both to meet. Tommy looked at Hassan and shrugged slightly.

'And you, sir. Your name, if you please?'

'Tommy Jackson, sir. Son of Sergeant Jackson of 28 Evans Street. And this is my sister, Lucy.'

'A soldier?'

'No sir, my sister.'

Dickens laughed loudly. 'No, the sergeant, I mean.'

'Policeman, sir. As I told the constable earlier.'

'Yes, of course. Splendid! That may be useful. Now: my drawing room. I have a visitor. A most important visitor whom I would not wish to keep waiting for the world!'

And he sprinted up the stairs two at a time, the boys running after him. The room upstairs was huge. It ran nearly the whole width of the house, except for a little room at the far end revealed by sliding doors. The furniture was sumptuous: chairs dressed in silk, rich woods and fine side-tables, a high-backed leather chair with its back to the door. A fire blazed in a marble surround, and the room was lit by lamps and gaslight. A young lady sat at a writing desk adding up numbers. Lucy stood admiring the prospect, looking up at curtains and pictures, her hands clamped together in case she thought of touching something. Tommy looked out of the window, and Hassan picked out the pattern in the carpet before looking up again.

'Like it? Been here since the summer of '51. All finished now.' He took off his coat and handed it to a maid who had appeared as if by magic. 'The fashion now seems to be for gloom: dark furniture, dark walls, dark wainscot. But as you will see, I like my colour! He swept his arm theatrically at the mint green walls and the salmon pink curtains. Then his voice changed into that of a comic turn. 'Many a man would 'ate it, guv'nor, but I never could stand the gloom, oooh, no, sir! Jus' look at me weskit!' The waistcoat was an even more stunning canary yellow. Mr Dickens put his hands on his hips and twirled.

'Mamie, my dear! We have three extra visitors. We must get a message to the Jacksons' parents. Jackson, 28 Evans Street. Get one of the servants over there, would you?'

'Yes, father. Miss Burdett Coutts is here, father.' And she nodded at the leather chair.'

He strode into the centre of the room and the boys followed.

'Ah! My dear Miss Burdett Coutts!'

In the leather-backed chair was a tall, well-dressed but very plain lady. She wore a royal blue dress, well-laced ankle boots and blue beads.

'I am so sorry we are late. I am late, I should say. We have had, if I may say so, something of an adventure involving a dangerous man

139

from the east, a sharp knife, treasure and an innocent and most delightful young man in a sheepskin jacket. And carrying with him a most remarkable novel by a most gifted young writer called Dickens. I wonder what happened to him?'

Mrs Burdett-Coutts smiled, as she always did when Dickens was in this mood. Dickens looked back, and Hassan saw his expression changed.

'But Mr Dickens, I wonder if you are perhaps serious? Who are these young people?'

'We shall soon know. They are here to tell us their story. However, it is quite true, I assure you, madam, that there has been something of an adventure, and I must sound the depths of it.'

'Very well. Field Lane can wait a little. I too shall be delighted to listen.'

Dickens sat on a sofa opposite, bolt upright, and combed his hair again.

'Now then! The court calls one Thomas Jackson of Evans Street. Tell us your story, Mr Jackson.'

'Yes sir.' He took a deep and rather nervous breath. 'This boy 'assan and 'is Uncle Ahmet comes from Bombay on the *Aurora* yesterday jest as it was getting dark an' they gets off the boat and they says goodbye to a Hindian man, sir, and then they sees him dead and my Pa he's a sergeant in the police like I told you earlier sir and he takes 'im home to our 'ouse or to be ezact, sir, he tells me Ma to take 'em 'ome and I goes to git the Hundertaker. An 'e comes quite quickly and the man's already dead stabbed in the chest with a long knife I should say and blood all over the floor sir and when we gets 'ome we 'as stew and Pa talks to Uncle Ahmet and 'Assan, like, an' they tell 'im they don't know what's 'appened but I saw 'Assan's Uncle Ahmet looking out the window last night like 'e was scared of somefink and then this morning we was walking towards Blackfriars Bridge 'cos I wanted to show 'Assan the pleasure gardens and the cathedral and these two men stopped us at a breakfast stall and I didn't like the look of 'em one little bit, well not the big one called Khodar, so we run for it and then we ran down 'oundsditch and up

140

Ludgate 'ill and into the Churchyard and then we saw 'em again and this time one on 'em 'ad a knife and he said he's killed a man, well that's what 'Assan says anyway, I don't know which man maybe it was the Hindian off the boat, and I ran off and bumped into a constable and he thought 'Assan 'ad the knife and then Mr Dickens 'ere come up and rescued us. Thank you, sir.'

There was a lengthy pause. Even Miss Burdett Coutts seemed slightly breathless, just from listening. Finally she spoke.

'Thank you Tommy. A most exciting story, I am sure. Mr Dickens, do you believe all the details? And do you consider the boys to be in danger?'

'I believe the details entirely, madam. No one of this boy's education would be able to dash it off the top of his head.' He looked at Tommy. 'Beggin' pardon sir, I'm sure. No, I am quite sure of it. It is simply all too consistent and too credible. And there is one thing that Tommy has not told you. I arrived before the constable. Lucy gave me one of those strange looks, you know the sort: a wictim seeking rescue. And then, I was the one with the knife at his throat. Far from rescuing the boys, it was I who was rescued: by Tommy and the constable he summoned.'

'My goodness! Are you recovered now?'

'I am quite well, I thank you. Now, what to do?'

'It seems to me that the these young folk need a place of safety. But where?'

Dickens had come to this conclusion himself, but went through his thoughts again.

'Evans Street is surely too dangerous. It seems likely that the villains know where it is, for we may assume that they have been in the street and watching the house. They could strike at any time.'

'Or here?'

'Quite out of the question, I fear, at least for any length of time. The men may know who I am, and might find my address from any passing child. Whilst they may not break in, we would be unable to move. No – they cannot stay here after tomorrow.'

'At my house, then?'

You are a lady with female servants, an elderly butler and a footman who is always on the back step smoking his pipe.' He smiled at her. 'An exaggeration, I know. But you must take my point.'

'Yes, Mr Dickens, you are quite right. I agree.'

'We need a place of safety in which there are people more than capable of defending these two young men...' Lucy gave a theatrical cough, and looked up at the ceiling. '... and this young lady even more so. Defenders who would strike out without hesitation. In a place which is at once out of the way and yet nearby. But of course, they can stay here just for tonight, if we keep a careful watch. Then we shall have the evening to think the matter over.'

Mr Dickens took a step back as the maid brought in tea and a sliced cake. He held up his hand as the maid started to pour, and managed that himself.

'In the meantime, we have to consider Field Lane...'

He stopped abruptly and they looked at each other, both recognising the stroke of luck at the same time. Miss Burdett Coutts arched her eyebrows and smiled. Dickens laughed so hard that his hair shook, and he had to walk back to the mirror with his comb.

'Children, would you leave us for a moment?' Lucy looked a little put out. A young lady one moment, and the child the next, indeed! 'Miss Burdett Coutts and I have to speak in confidence. He pointed to the small room at the end, and followed them into his study.

'Kindly touch *nothing*.' He looked at them with raised eyebrows to make his point. Then he turned, went back into the drawing room and shut the sliding door behind him.

Lucy grabbed her seat first, and sat in the winged chair at Mr Dickens' desk. She held her hands, palms down, a few inches above the desk, again fearing to touch. Hassan and Tommy sat in two rocking chairs and looked around. The whole room was fantastically tidy. Everything seemed placed precisely to the inch. There was not a speck of dust.

'Me Ma would love it in 'ere,' said Tommy. 'She could jest sit and do nuffink. It's a real wonder, innit?'

Hassan was most struck by the writing desk. He stood and walked over to it. In the very centre, perfectly square on a sloping ink blotter, was a pile of thick paper. Placed at the far edge of the desk was a series of items: a quill pen with a steel nib standing in an ink pot; a paper knife for opening letters and slitting open the folded pages of new books; a pair of fat bronze toads who seemed to be squatting on guard over the paper; a bronze cast of a man and a pointing gun dog. Like Lucy, Hassan did not dare to touch anything.

The door remained closed for more than an hour. Several times they heard clocks chiming through the house in perfect synchrony. For the first time in London, Hassan had time just to sit and wonder. He had now been in England only for a day – it seemed impossible that so much had happened in only twenty-four hours. He had a host of questions, which nobody around him could answer, and which he knew would reduce his uncle to silence.

Why would Uncle Ahmet not tell him the whole story? Was it fear? Was he ashamed of something? Was he in trouble? Ever since they had been in London ... Now Hassan had no idea where he would spend the night, or how he was going to be safe from whatever was going on. He did not like this place, with its wheels and its soot and its crowds. He yearned for Bombay.

Bombay, where Hassan had always felt himself in his father's footsteps. Sometimes, he longed for Kabul too, even though he had never been there, at least not so that he could remember. But London? Even if his father were here, he did not like the place.

Was his father still alive? If so, where? Why had he never tried to find his son? Why had Uncle Ahmet waited all these years? And he still did not know the whole story of what had happened to his mother.

He looked at Tommy and envied him. He was not a great rich man. He had no chance of being a hero of *A Thousand and One Nights*. He would never be powerful. But then he wasn't poor either. And he laughed, and talked to policemen, and tried to nip their toes off with string. Not the world's greatest achievements, perhaps, but they were happy ones. And he had a father, and a mother, and two sisters who were full of joy and certainty. And a peaceful house in a peaceful street. What did Hassan have, apart from missing parents and a strange country that he could not love?

He soon regretted thinking like this. He had Uncle Ahmet. He loved his uncle as he would a father. He was a good and kind man. He had given Hassan everything: his meals, security, his books, his learning, his wisdom and his heart and soul. And he knew that Ahmet would find his father if he could. Or find out about him.

Eventually the door opened, and Mr Dickens beamed at them. Then he looked concerned, and even though nothing had been touched, he strode to the desk and tapped the toads and the dog handler on their heads, picked up the paper and tapped it straight again.

'Now, my dears, we have plans. Tommy Jackson, you will kindly explain to Hassan that your father and his uncle are being informed of this morning's events. Tonight you will stay here. As you can see, there is plenty of space. I shall find you a room on the top floor, furthest from the front door. Tomorrow, I have a place in school for you, and you will be taken care of by Mr Woodhouse and his ...' For the first time, he struggled for a word. '... his assistants. It may not be entirely agreeable to you, but it will be safe. Fairly safe, at any rate.'

Lucy looked worried.

'Tommy, I've a confession to make.'

'Crikes,' said Tommy, grinning, 'you've never done that before, Luce. Must be somefink terrible.'

'Not so terrible,' said Lucy. 'It's jest that pa never told me I could come. That were a lie, Tommy. An' I shall be in such trouble when I get home. Even more if it's tomorrow. Mr Dickens sir, I need to get back there now. Why don't I show your servant the way?'

'Well, I suppose that you won't stand out in London quite as Hassan would, and nor will you be remembered by those villains quite as Tommy would. I'll tell you what, we'll find you one of Mamie's dresses and a coat and a spare bonnet just in case. Will that suit?'

Oh yes, thank you sir.' She gave a little curtsy. 'You've been most kind to us, sir. I thank you ... we all thank you from the bottom of our 'earts.'

'Yes, 'Assan and me thank you an' all,' said Tommy.

'There is really no need, said Mr Dickens,' beaming at them all. Mamie! Would you kindly go to your wardrobe...'

'Yes, father, I heard you,' said Mamie, with ever so slight an edge in her voice, and she smiled at Lucy and took her hand.

*

Later, when Lucy had gone and Hassan and Tommy were tucked away upstairs, Mr Dickens and Miss Burdett Coutts talked in the drawing room. Mamie was again working on the household accounts. Miss Burdett Coutts had stayed rather longer than usual, but they had only just finished the business of the day.

'I fear for them,' said Miss Burdett-Coutts.

'For whom? The Field Lane mob, or just these two?'

'All of them, of course, but these two in particular. What do you think will happen to them?'

'They will be quite all right, my dear Angela. You will see. And if they are not, why, we have assuredly done the right thing'.

He walked to the window and looked down across the garden.

'I know their fear as well as I know my own. There is something I have never told you: indeed, only one man knows of it.' His voice thickened. 'Did you know that I once worked in a bottle-blacking factory for six shillings a week, and that the rest of my little family lived in the Marshalsea? Yes, my father was in the debtors' prison. You have picked up my *David Copperfield*, I am sure. *David Copperfield* by Charles Dickens. DC by CD. Does that not strike you?'

'It is you. I had wondered. I have looked into your eyes sometimes, when we have been at Field Lane or Urania Cottage. There is something in those people you recognise, I suspect. Something you are running from. Perhaps you are running from your own reflection. Do you think so?'

'Perhaps you are right. Yes, certainly you are right. Now let us say no more about it, and I beg of you not to repeat this, not to write it down, not even in your private journals.'

He looked back into the fire.

'My point is that each of us must do what we can. And only what we can. We can do no more than is possible. You see, in this room, this colour and warmth and – dare I say it – friendship, there is comfort and security from the worst the world can throw at us. But we know also what is out there in the darkness. There are people in rooms with the dead, people waiting for cholera, people choking on the smell from the river. The river itself is full of filth from our sewers and our factories and our shipping. There are dens of crime and opium and prostitution. Only a few will ever be saved by Urania Cottage. There are children throughout this wonderful city of ours going to dank rooms with strangers for the price of the family's weekly needs. Yes, even sitting here I fear it. I fear that one day I may return to it.

'Sometimes, you know, I feel quite exhausted by it, by my own running and the hopelessness of it all.'

'But Charles, as you said yourself, you do what you can.'

'Too little! There is no hell, you know. I sometimes wonder whether there is a heaven, but there is certainly no hell. Except for the hell we have made for ourselves. How can we save ourselves from it?'

'You need saving?'

'You know I do. As much as anybody! So do we all.'

'Very well, Charles. Let us have this one small victory. As you said yourself, we can only do so much. But do it we must.' There was a noise of carriage wheels outside. 'Now I must leave you. Shall we meet tomorrow?'

'Yes. Until tomorrow, then. Friday. Things will be well enough, I am sure. Friday is my lucky day, you know.'

'Yes, my dear Charles, I do know.'

And she was gone. Dickens stood at the window and looked out at the gas-lit square and watched until the carriage was hidden from view. He saw that another fog was descending, drew the silk curtains and sat in his velvet chair. He moved the nearest oil lamp a quarter of an inch so that its base was just precisely central on its table, and combed his hair once more.

Chapter Fourteen

November 1855

Early the following morning, Hassan looked out across the garden three storeys below. Or rather, he tried to, for the day was thick with fog. Nearby the shrubs glistened with its moisture, and a little further away the railings were barely visible, like thin lines drawn with the hardest of pencils. Beyond that the world was a blank sheet, devoid of any detail other than a faint aura from a lamp.

Tommy was still sound asleep, and Hassan decided to explore. There was something he had to look at again. He headed down three flights of stairs, treading softly, and into the passageway. Again he looked at the pictures, and again he wondered at the coincidence. There was the fat man again, and Hassan smiled at the way this man had followed him all the way from Bombay. Mr Pickwick was like a thread that had followed him through his life: apart from Uncle Ahmet and Akbar Khan's knife, and the letters, the only constant thing he had known.

He stepped further down the passageway, and looked at a bust he instantly recognised: Mr Dickens, staring sightlessly out of a corner. And then, above the dining room door, a large round stone carving of a woman. But not just any woman: she was surely some sort of *jiniri*, for she carried a flaming torch, and was fluttering over the ground as though weightless, strewing flowers around her. Yet

147

she was human too – she had a child on her back. There was a matching carving over another door: a different woman – or *jiniri* – with flowers in her hair, this time carrying two children, both asleep. An owl looked down on them.

Hassan was lost in the engravings for a moment, but was then jolted back to his senses as the door opened and a lady came out. She shrieked as she saw Hassan, and immediately a door opened down the passageway. Mr Dickens stepped out, dressed in blinding white trousers and a purple waistcoat.

'Now, my dear, nothing to concern yourself with, really. This young gentleman is Hassan. He and his friend Tommy found themselves in a little difficulty yesterday, and I have made it my task of the day to offer a little assistance. I trust that you do not mind.'

'But Charles, why ever did you not tell me?'

'Simply because I did not wish to trouble you, knowing that you were unwell. And, of course, Miss Burdett Coutts was here.'

Hassan had taken a step away and was admiring the engravings again. Mr Dickens was soon beside him.

'Night!' he announced. He pointed at the woman, then at the children. 'She is Night. The children are sleep and...' His voice lowered a little after a pause. '...and death. My poor, dear Dora! You know what this is?' He pointed at the owl.

'Bird.'

'Yes. To be precise, an owl. You have owls in Bombay?'

'Yes. Perhaps. I never see.'

'Now. Look at the other. Night and ...? What?'

'Day.'

'Yes. And here is Aurora, casting flowers about. And the little boy is the morning star.'

'No, sir. *Aurora* a ship.'

'A ship?'

'My ship. From Bombay. *Aurora*.'

'Why of course! I saw it come in. To the East India Dock! Day before yesterday. Fate! And Friday is my lucky day!'

Hassan said nothing.

'And you know who Aurora is?'

'I not know.'

'Aurora is the goddess of the dawn. You know dawn? When the sun comes up!' He cupped his hands and moved them slowly upwards, as though over a horizon. Perhaps today will be a dawn – a new beginning!' He took out his pocket watch, lifted the cover, checked the time and snapped it shut.

At that moment, Tommy appeared at the bottom of the stairs, wiping the sleep from his eyes.

'Good morning, Master Thomas,' said Mr Dickens. 'Have you had a good night's rest?'

Tommy looked at him blankly.

'Evidently not. I'm sorry to see it. Now, let us see about some breakfast.'

In the dining room, there was warm toast and butter, smoked herring and a little coffee. Mr Dickens started to explain his plan to Tommy and Hassan.

'Before nine we shall ...'

He suddenly stopped as Mrs Dickens let a jam spoon clatter onto her plate. She looked at him nervously and he looked back. She scraped marmalade from the cloth.

'Before nine, we shall take a walk towards the Farringdon Road. And what sights we shall see! The Foundling Hospital for those who have been abandoned by their mothers, and the Middlesex House of Corrections for those who have been abandoned by the rest of us!'

'Oh!'

Now Mrs Dickens had spilled tea on the table cloth. This time Dickens glared at her.

'Your stay with my friend Mr Woodhouse need be only for a short period,' he promised. 'I understand that a ragged school may be disagreeable to you: you are certain to meet with some rough characters, be quite sure of that. Nevertheless, the kindness of Miss Burdett Coutts has seen the building greatly improved, and at least it will be safe from your persecutors. Who would ever imagine that you were there? Your father, Tommy, has been apprised of your whereabouts and the reasons for your retirement. Am I to understand that he was already familiar with the circumstances of Hassan and his Uncle Ahmet?'

'Yes sir. They was talking about it only yesterday morning, and I'm sure they spoke of it last night too. But 'e'll want to know ezackly where we are, sir.'

'Oh, he will know, you may be assured of it. Now it is time for us to leave. Goodbye, my dear. I shall return shortly.' He hardly looked at his wife as he led Tommy and Hassan to the front door. Mrs Dickens looked a little sadly after them. Hassan noticed this, and wondered what was wrong. Mr Dickens was full of life, full of enthusiasm and energy, but none of it was directed at his wife. She seemed weak and defeated. What had happened between them?

Outside the fog had thickened. Mr Dickens wrapped a scarf around his throat and looked upwards. A gas lamp flared weakly.

'Little chance of seeing the sky today, I fear. Not with a thick fog in November. The poor old sun simply cannot manage it!'

They went into Tavistock Square and then into Woburn Place, along the edge of Russell Square and left into Guilford Street, Tommy and Hassan having to run for two steps in every five to keep up. Mr Dickens came to a merciful halt and pointed at a building almost dissolved in the fog.

'The Foundling Hospital,' he announced, half way between pride and grief. 'For children who have lost their parents or, more often, have been lost *by* their parents. Given up. Left on the street. Too many mouths to feed. The trustees do a fine job of work, of course, but their task is considerable. The burial ground is at the rear.' As they passed, a small group of the most miserable children Hassan had ever seen gathered at the gate and looked yearningly at the building. Were they looking for a brother or sister? Or dreaming of living there?

Then Dickens and the boys were off again, and soon reached the Grays Inn Road, where the traffic was heavier. Dickens stopped for a few minutes to speak to a smiling man carrying bundles of paper tied with red tape, and then they crossed the road. Dickens gave the sweeper a penny for his trouble, and they walked straight ahead into Calthorpe Street. An ominous building reared up on their right.

'Coldbath Fields,' Dickens announced. 'Close your eyes and imagine what is within. Perhaps you already know, Tommy, since your father is a police sergeant. Within those walls are hundreds of men with numbers on their backs. Men on a treadmill and men moving pyramids of cannonballs back and forth, back and forth, all for no purpose. The treadmill powers no mill and no machinery, and the cannonballs just pass back and forth, back and forth. Perhaps one day your friend with the knife will join them.'

They were now heading towards Blackfriars Bridge, and the fog was noticeably thicker as they got closer to the river. Hassan started to wonder where he was being taken. Why had they not tried to explain it properly to him? Mr Dickens was hard to understand, and Hassan could only ever pick up the odd word. But Tommy knew, and Hassan was sure that he would explain it later.

Again, the buildings quickly became grimier and tattier, and there were soon greater numbers of dusty and aimless people, sitting on steps and looking hopefully but fruitlessly at passers-by. A man in trousers with shiny knees smiled and held out his hat. Dickens marched straight past without a glance, and then darted into an alley on the right. Again, as in Houndsditch, they stepped out of one world and into another, but this time they had fallen into a far deeper abyss than before. Closely-packed three- and four-storey buildings blocked out the light, so that it was almost dark apart from the occasional handfuls of light scattered from a candle or an oil-lamp in a window. The first people Hassan saw, a small group of children, aged from two or three to eight or nine, scavenged among the rubbish. They were utterly filthy.

'This,' said Dickens, 'is Field Lane, Saffron Hill. This is where, young Tommy, I came across Fagin and the Artful. You may have heard of them. Perhaps ...' He smiled at Hassan. '...perhaps you know Fagin?'

Hassan's face lit up. At last he could say something.

'Yes, sir. My Uncle Ahmet says Mr Fagin a very bad man. I must not speak to him or go to his house. My father told him so.'

For some reason, Tommy and Mr Dickens both laughed, attracting the attention of a clothes dealer in a squashed hat.

'Please excuse me, Hassan. You are quite right to avoid him.'

'I should say,' said Tommy with a smirk.

At the other end of the alley was Field Lane proper, and they headed towards it, and towards the light. The ground had sucked the moisture out of the air, and was coated in a layer of damp and slippery mud. It was the filthiest place Hassan had ever been in. The floor was covered in all the domestic debris imaginable: vegetable peelings, broken china, broken toys, newspaper, a rotting chair leg. Hassan jumped as a rat darted across his path, and then another. Against the wall was a dead cat.

Fortunately, Hassan could see nothing beyond the houses, for this would have explained the foul stench that had already prompted Mr Dickens to put a handkerchief to his face. Nor could he see inside the high, narrow rooms, each containing thirty people or more. He could not see the dead child in the room above him, or the dark chambers with their floors missing because they had been taken up for firewood. He could see the wretched looks in people's faces down here in the street, but he had no idea of the defeated blankness on the faces which were hidden from view.

Out in Field Lane a few were trying to make a living: a barber waited, cut-throat razor in hand, at his door; they passed a beer shop, almost empty apart from a few drunks. The salt-smell of a fish warehouse wafted down the Lane, mingling with the other smells. Dust and soot clung to the boarded fronts of buildings, and from a high gable, a tattered flag of indeterminate colour flapped in the wind.

Soon they came across a crowd of people of all ages, gathered around a doorway. A long row of windows looked out from a large hall, and the words *FIELD LANE RAGGED SCHOOL* were inscribed above them.

Dickens put his hands on the boys' shoulders, slid through the crowd and went through a doorway and up two wide flights of stairs. They came out into a room of unexpected and gigantic contrast. Almost everything was wooden: the roof, the great arched beams, the floor. The walls were covered with a rough plaster on which at regular intervals were hand-written instructions in foot-high letters: *WELCOME;* and *HE IS ABLE ALSO TO SAVE THEM TO THE UTTERMOST THAT COME UNTO GOD BY HIM; and HUMBLE YOURSELVES UNDER THE MIGHTY HAND OF GOD;* and *CASTING ALL YOUR CARE UPON HIM;* and *FOR HE CARETH FOR YOU.*

But what surprised Hassan most of all was the extraordinary tidiness and cleanliness of the place. All that soot and litter and human filth, the rats, all that stink of humanity... and then this. The walls were clean and well painted, the windows gleamed, and the floor looked as though it had been scrubbed overnight. The dirtiest things in the hall by far were the people, especially the children. And even they were cleaner than those they had seen outside.

The hall was long and wide, but had been neatly divided with screens about three feet high, as though into different rooms. As they stood looking out across the space, Hassan saw the heads of hundreds of people. Even Tommy was amazed, for the school was not just for children: there were women with babies, fathers with young sons, and old men with grey beards and worn out hats.

Mr Dickens led them into one of the larger partitioned areas near the windows, and stood quietly.

Fifty or sixty small chairs were arranged in rows, and at each sat a boy with his back to the visitors. Some were seven or eight, most were nine or ten and a very few were perhaps the same age as Tommy. These were hunched over their desks, their backs bent. Some of the older boys were disfigured in some way: one had lost a foot and one a hand. Another had a curved spine and a stunted left arm. A fourth stared into space with a fixed grin, drooling from the side of his mouth. All had pale eyes and grimy faces, and wore tattered, threadbare clothing, and scuffed shoes if they were lucky.

There were five adults in the space. By the window was a small man in a black suit and a white collar, reading intently from a small black book. His cheek was creased from holding in place an eyeglass attached to his jacket with a black cord. Behind him on the wall was a large wooden cross. As he spoke, few seemed to be listening, and no-one noticed the visitors. A second, older man in workman's clothes patrolled between the desks. Every now and then he would tap on the desk with a fingernail and point towards Mr Woodhouse. The boy would look to the front or wake suddenly. The lesson continued without interruption.

'And round about the throne were four and twenty seats and upon the seats I saw four and twenty elders clothed in white, and they had on their heads crowns of gold ...'

There was a loud, hawking, coughing sound from the back of the class. A boy just in front of Mr Dickens spat on the floor. The speaker paused and fixed kindly eyes on the boy before continuing.

'... and out of the throne proceeded lightnings and thunderings and voices: and there were seven lamps of fire burning before the throne, which are the seven spirits of God. And before the throne there was a sea of glass like unto crystal, and in the midst of the throne, or round about the throne, were four beasts full of eyes before and behind.

'And the first beast was like a lion, and the second beast was like a calf, and the third beast had a face as a man, and the fourth beast was like a flying eagle. And the four beasts had each of them six wings about him...'

Mr Dickens had coughed quietly, and now did so again, more loudly. The teacher looked up.

'Why, Mr Dickens! We are most honoured, sir. Boys, please stand and say hallo to Mr Charles Dickens, of whom you may have heard.'

Silence. Then, after a short time, laughter. Two small boys pointed at Mr Dickens's shiny black boots and white linen trousers, and then at his waistcoat. Four boys stood and whistled loudly. The low hum of work from the neighbouring classes suddenly stopped. Mr Woodhouse raised his voice in a way that amazed the three visitors.

Si ...... LENCE!'

He simply did not look big enough to shout like that. *Praps he's 'ad plenny of practice,* Tommy thought.

'You do not know of Mr Dickens? No, well. Be kind enough to welcome him in any case. Mr Dickens has been most kind to us and to many others. Those of you who can read well should look at the piece about Field Lane Ragged School from *The Daily News* which I have pasted on the back screen. It was written by Mr Dickens himself, and helped us considerably. And without the kind assistance of him and Miss Burdett Coutts, we would still be in the small rooms we had some years ago and still have no water or washing facilities.' He scanned the class to ensure that they had heard. 'Mr Gaskell, please be kind enough look after the class for a minute or two. Perhaps you would care to come this way, sir.'

Mr Woodhouse led them across the hall. In the smaller classes they passed, they saw girls quietly practising their darning and their sewing in front of two rather fierce women, and some boys being shown how to mend shoes. 'Well furbished,' said Mr Dickens, winking at a small boy. In the next class, younger boys were being shown how to mend their own clothes. They went through a side door out of the hall and into a narrow passageway which led towards the back of the school.

'I trust you are well, Mr Woodhouse?'

'Tolerably well, I thank you sir. The Lord has been kind to me.'

'A most interesting choice of text for the class, I thought. I am not familiar with it.'

'From the Book of Revelation, sir.'

'And what do you think your young people learned from it?'

'Well, sir, the difference between Heaven and Hell, perhaps. I know of no other text which describes it so clearly. And I was about to remark that God's eyes are everywhere, like the eyes of that creature mentioned in the text. That those eyes will see all, and will send each soul to its rightful place.'

'Have you never suspected that these children know hell already, Mr Woodhouse? I see that we shall never agree on this. But for all that, you do the office of a true Christian, a saint even.'

'No, no, Mr Dickens. We must all do just a little. There is, as I said to you last time, a very great deal to do. Not the least is the necessity to keep these young people away from the prisons, the graveyards, the hospitals and the dens of vice. Never mind the gallows. Indeed, I wish I could do more.' He beamed at Tommy and Hassan. 'Now, we have young visitors.'

'Indeed. Hassan and Tommy, this is Mr Woodhouse. Mr Woodhouse, Hassan and Tommy. Tommy is a Londoner by birth and by upbringing, but Hassan is somewhat more exotic! He is from Bombay. Indeed, originally from Kabul. I must not go into *par-tick-lers* ...' Mr Woodhouse chuckled at the stage constable's voice. '... But they are in a little difficulty, indeed in some danger. Rest assured, my dear sir, that they have done nothing wrong, and I shall endeavour to extract them from the mire into which they been plunged at the earliest opportunity. In the meantime, I should like to lodge them here: as both lodgers and students if I may impose on you for two or three nights.'

'Why, most certainly, Mr Dickens. I shall give them a place on the form – together I suggest. I shall tell cook to provide a little extra, and then they shall both be scrubbed clean and their heads shaved.'

Tommy exploded.

'Ere! Wassat for? I ain't avin' me 'ead shaved!'

'Tommy, old chap, I cannot think that it will be necessary. Mr Woodhouse?'

'It is our usual practice. All of the boys who come here suffer mostly from complete ignorance, but most also suffer from their filthy conditions and from lice, of course.'

'Ere! I ain't hignorant! And I ain't filthy. And I ain't got lice!'

'Tommy,' said Mr Dickens as Tommy edged towards the door, 'it really won't be necessary. We have heard what you said ...' His eyes lit up. 'But wait! What a wonderful form of disguise for you both! A change of clothes from Mr Woodhouse's supply and shaved heads. Bob's your uncle! Nobody – not even a man who had spent three months on a ship with you and was hunting you down, would ever be able to recognise you! Quite brilliant, Mr Woodhouse!'He looked at Tommy again and smiled. 'Your hair will grow back in just a fortnight or so. And you will be so much safer.' He changed his voice again: 'Jus' think of the adwenture! What a lark!'

'No sir. No! I shan't 'ave it done! 'Assan, he wants to chop all yer 'air off. Don't let him!'

'Air off?'

Tommy took the end of his hair in one hand and mimed scissors with the other, then pointed at Hassan's head. He soon understood.

'No! Why?'

'For disguise. To hide you.'

'No. He pointed at his own skin, and then at his scar. 'They see me. No cutting hair.'

'Very well. A change of clothes then. New clothes. A new coat. Then you can go out.'

'No sir. I stay here. I not know London. Tommy go out. Tommy have hair cut!'

Tommy was appalled. 'It would be a good idea, Tommy,' said Mr. Dickens. Then you could get home with messages if you need to. They'd never recognise you.'

'What if they did see me, though, they could follow me back, couldn't they? Then they'd find 'Assan, for sure.'

Mr Woodhouse spoke at last. 'I believe he is right, Mr Dickens. If they are in danger, they should both stay here – or in my own rooms at the end of school. Rest assured, sir, that I shall ask no questions.' He dropped his voice so that Hassan and Tommy could not hear. 'I shall try to persuade them to accept the haircuts later.'

'Very well.' He looked at Hassan and Tommy. 'It only remains for me to bid goodbye to you both. However, I shall see you again soon, and I shall pay a visit to your father to see that all is well. May I stay and watch the lesson for a short while?'

'You would be most welcome, Mr Dickens, I am sure.' And Mr Woodhouse bowed slightly, his hands held neatly behind him. 'Hassan and Tommy, there are two seats at the back.'

Hassan and Tommy went back into the hall, but Mr Woodhouse and Mr Dickens continued to talk for a moment in the passageway. Hassan and Tommy soon noticed that the noise had changed; not louder, nor softer, but different. As they re-entered the class they saw why.

Mr Gaskell had found himself in rather a pickle. A boy was calling out, just loud enough to be heard by his friend, but not by those in the neighbouring classes.

'Baines! The winder! Open the winder!'

There was a hum of excitement. The other large boy expanded.

'Open it, Bainesie! We've got 'is 'at!' He waved a rounded, shiny hat with a tiny brim.

Baines shoved up the sash window, and the other boy strode across to it, holding the hat at arm's length. He held it tauntingly out of the window, and they all heard yells from the street below.

Mr Gaskell made a dash for the window too, and for some reason the boy with his hat did not move. Mr Gaskell bent to retrieve the hat, and was now below the level of the partition, so that he was hidden from the rest of the hall.

Then five of the largest boys made a silent rush towards him, and everybody else in the class seemed to hold their breaths.

A boy whispered to Tommy. 'Gawd! They're gonna dangle 'im! Aven't seen that for a good while. And I never saw it here, neither.'

'Watcher mean, dangle 'im?'

'Out the winder!'

Mr Gaskell leaned out of the window and made a grab for his hat. Like lightning, the boy leaned just a little further out, and then just a little further still. And then, as quick as another flash, one boy put a strong hand on the back of Mr Gaskell's head, and two grabbed each of his legs. They lifted him swiftly, until his stomach rested on the window sill, and his head pointed downwards. There were cheers from people down below. The school was too full for them, but this more than made up for their disappointment.

Mr Gaskell was too terrified to shout loudly.

'No, I beg you! whimpered Mr Gaskell. What've I done to deserve this treatment?'

Two girls who had somehow found themselves in the boys' class screamed. One, a plump girl with red hair and a pock-marked face, decided to take action. She strode furiously across the space.

'Jest you leave 'im, you great pair of lumps,' she shouted. The boys cowered in front of her. 'What's poor Mr Gaskell ever done to you, eh? Jest tryin' to 'elp, innee? Poor man. Leave 'old of him!'

She spoke loudly enough for a few young heads to pop up over the screens on either side. Now that the secret was out, the boys could only give up their prisoner. One at a time, they released their hold, and Mr Gaskell slunk towards Hassan and Tommy.

'Where is Mr Woodhouse? Where?' Then he regained his strength suddenly as the shock subsided. 'Where is Mr Woodhouse?' He shouted. He slunk from the class, and sat in a chair in the hall, staring at the floor.

Mr Woodhouse rushed in and yelled for silence. To Tommy's amazement, he got it, and then surveyed the class critically. Three chairs had been turned over, and the floor was covered in chalk, balled-up paper, most of it ripped from books, and the books themselves, some with their covers torn off. This did not seem to bother Mr Woodhouse, but soon he saw something which made him shake with rage. Yet still he said nothing. Instead he walked back to his box, stood on it and put on a mask of stone. He spoke quietly, but with a menacing edge to his voice.

'Tunks! Kindly remove that Bible from the floor and bring it here.'
The larger of the two rebels obeyed.
'Now stand at the back, facing the screen. And the same for you, Phillips.'
The other boy followed.
'Now, Miss Malone, pray explain what has just happened. ...'
The red-haired Amazon took a deep breath.
'... In short sentences if you please.'
Forty-five or so cropped scalps, and almost the same number of threadbare coats, and nearly twice as many eyes, turned to face the girl Malone. Mr Dickens sat on a chair with his back to the screen and watched carefully. Perhaps this would be useful one day.

"Twere Tunks and Pipsie, sir. Soon as you left, sir, I thought I should come over. They've done it afore, you know, when you're not here, like. I eared the ruckus, like, and Miss Watson said to come

down. She knows I can do business with the boys, more than the grown-ups see, beggin' pardon. An' I saw Tunks 'n Pipsie bundling Mr Gaskell out the winder, sir. And Uriah 'oldin' 'is 'at.' She pointed at a boy with greasy trousers. Mr Woodhouse turned towards a reliable-looking boy of eleven or so.

'Is this true, Zebedee?'

'Yes sir. Zeb, sir. I asked Mr Gaskell, as he was reading about the beasts and the 'arps in 'eaven, if 'e'd 'ave a look at me pictures. Pictures of 'orses and stuff. An' when 'e knelt down, Uriah took 'is 'at. And Tunks and Pipsie and them two grabbed 'im, sir.'

Mr Woodhouse went and looked over the partition.

'Mr Gaskell!' Mr Gaskell came back into the class. 'Mr Gaskell, I understand the concern you have for the younger boys and their endeavours. It is wonderful to show an interest in their creativity. But please remember, sir, that there are fifty others. They need complete attention, and will take advantage of you if only you give them a moment.'

'Yes, Mr Woodhouse. I see that well enough, sir. I shall in future watch like an 'awk sir, each one of them indi-widge-ually, just in case they attempts to dangle me out at winder, sir. That is, if I ever sees 'em again, sir.'

And he attempted to stride, but ended up shambling, across the hall. He removed a coat from a hook and turned to survey the class and the visitors one last time. In a flash he was gone, and the boys heard his feet clattering down the stairs, and other footsteps coming slowly up.

Then another and entirely different man came into the class.

Chapter Fifteen

November 1855

He wore a bell-shaped cloak. Underneath were a plain black jacket and trousers, and a waistcoat with plain black cloth buttons. Only his collar stood out with two little tails at the front, in starched white. The children stood as one, and silence descended upon Mr Woodhouse as well as on his charges. Mr Dickens sat quietly, as yet unnoticed by the visitor, and Tommy and Hassan shuffled onto a hard bench.

'Good afternoon to you, gentlemen.'

'Good afternoon. Mr Rough, sir.'

Mr Rough walked slowly around the class, his heels clicking loudly on the wooden floor. Every now and then he would suddenly but very casually decide to pick something up for inspection: a book, a piece of chalk or a boy's pocket Bible. Once he flicked a boy's earlobe to engage his attention and pointed at the desk, shaking his head.

Finally he reached Hassan and Tommy. He looked at Hassan quizzically, and then at Tommy.

'Two new boys, I see. And where are you from?' He asked.

'Evans Street, sir,' said Tommy.

'Evans Street? And you, young sir?' He looked at Hassan again, and Hassan quailed under his gaze. 'Speak up, boy!'

'B...b...bombay, sir.'

A whisper went around the class. Mr Rough soon put a stop to it.

'And you come from Bombay every morning, do you?'

Laughter.

''e's stayin' with me, sir. Tommy Jackson, sir, son of Sergeant Jackson, sir. 'is name's 'Assan, sir.'

'I am sure that Assan can speak for himself, boy.'

'Yes sir. Hhhhassan, sir.'

'And what are you, boy?'

'Boy, sir.' It was the truest word he ever spoke, but it seemed to confuse Mr Rough.

'I mean to ask, are you Christian or Hindu or Sikh or something else?'

'Else, sir. I am Muslim.'

'Muslim? A Musselman, you mean? Good Lord! Whatever is happening here, Mr Woodhouse? You are admitting heathens to the class, is that it?'

'The two boys are in danger, Mr Rough, he said quietly. 'I cannot go into details just now. However, I can tell you that they were brought here for sanctuary. They will cause no trouble, I assure you. Their goodness has been vouched for by someone who is known to you.'

'Do you not understand that every foreigner is bound to have a knife about him? Can the boy speak English? Will he understand the words of Our Lord? Will the little heathen blaspheme against them if he does? I would remind you, Mr Woodhouse, that this class is established for the purpose of spreading the Word amongst the poor Christians of this parish, not welcoming every little Arab with a dagger.'

Mr Dickens, still unnoticed, was having a strange day today. In the past, he had hardly ever thought of people like Hassan. He rarely saw them, and they were only ever servants in his stories.

Now he realised that even Hassan had been a kind of appendix, for really it was Tommy that Dickens had wanted to look after. What would he have done had both the boys been Afghans? Would he really, as he now suspected, have walked away?

But no. Surely not. And nor would he walk away now. It was a revelation to him. He stood and coughed quietly.

'Good morning, Mr Rough. You may recall that we were introduced at your recent committee meeting?'

'Of course, of course.' He looked embarrassed, perhaps thinking that the Great Writer would use him as some sort of comic character in a story about a churchman. 'Mr Dickens, of course. I hope I find you well. And Mrs Dickens? And the children?'

'Well, indeed, yes. And Mrs Rough, I trust? And the baby?'

'Coming along well, I thank you.'

'I am sure that he will be privileged ... to have a father of such moral stature. Such ... principle. One who can spread the word of God with such wonderful passion.'

Mr Rough blushed. What was Dickens trying to suggest?

'You are too kind sir, really. I am a mere servant of the Lord, of course. There is no greatness in me whatever.'

'Not so, Mr Rough. Why, you visit us here at the school most frequently, I believe. More so than I do myself. Why, there is even roast chicken and stuffed pigs' heart to provide nutrition for the wee waifs. Your conduct is that of a saint, sir. Why, it is wonderful that you have been so kind as to help us to find a place for the poor here. Even for young Hassan here, motherless, fatherless and wandering in a strange land.'

He glanced at Mr Woodhouse, who was suddenly shy and looked down at his shiny shoes. Mr Rough looked more and more troubled.

'And the boy is ... most, ah... welcome, Mr Dickens, sir. Yes, Hassan and Tommy Jackson, you are indeed most welcome.'

''s'only for three nights anyhow,' said Tommy. 'My father's a sergeant, you know.'

Soon, Mr Rough made his goodbyes and left down the back stairs.

Shortly afterwards, just as Mr Woodhouse was getting back to the Book of Revelations, a small, ferrety-looking boy with a shock of dark hair came dashing into the hall, the redness in his face just visible beneath the soot and grime.

'They're 'ere agin!' he shouted.

'Dear Lord, not again,' cried Mr Woodhouse. 'Monitors, tell the other classes! Fox, ask Mr White to bolt the street door! Good lad!'

As one, the children rushed to the windows. Tunks and Pipsie got there first, taking charge. Hassan thought that he heard a chanting

163

from below, rhythmical and menacing. It grew gradually louder, and the words became distinct, even to him. There was a regular banging sound, the sound of wood on steel.

'Pull it down! Pull it down! PULL IT DOWN!'

'Malone, get out of the back door, quickly, and run for a constable. Run for three constables. Tell them that this is worse than before.'

In a swish of cheap cotton, Malone was gone, throwing the bolt and clattering down the stairs just as Mr Gaskell had done. She got out just in time, to judge from the sudden wave of caterwauling and beating drums which reached their ears from the front of the building before Foxy had shut the door behind her.

The door was rattled, but the bolt made little difference.

'Smash it down!'

'Sparky, come 'ere! Put yer shoulder to it!'

They heard the door being buffeted again and again, and then there was a splintering sound, as though the door had been ripped from its hinges, or the bolt and hasp had been sheared. A door banged against a wall, and there was a clattering on the stairs before an ugly crowd surged into the hall. Many were carrying old saucepan lids which they carried as shields and were banging with hammers and scraps of wood.

Hassan had never seen anything like it. Never in Bombay had he seen this sort of spectacle. Never had he seen this sort of filth, this sort of squalor, drunks in the street and a hundred people begging at once. Was this city really the centre of the world?

What surprised him most of all was the placidity of the besieged. Had being in this hall quietened them? Were they frightened? Perhaps: but surely there were enough of them to stop this? Perhaps they were just hungry; Hassan had seen the hungry in Bombay, silent, staring, passive.

He had got separated from Tommy, and could no longer see him. But he could see Mr Dickens, and tried to skirt the class towards him. As he reached the front, he came across Mr Woodhouse, under his desk. Hassan quickly moved on.

The mob wreaked havoc. Desks were broken in two, slates smashed against the wall, and books thrown across the class. One boy looked up at Mr Woodhouse's printed placard: *THE LORD'S EYES ARE EVERYWHERE*. He gazed at it, uncomprehending, and scowled angrily. He could not read, and therefore wished all books (and signs) were burned. He climbed onto a chair and knocked the placard from the wall. Then he pushed up the sash, tore the placard in two and threw it into Field Lane.

Dickens looked on, his anger rising swiftly. He had always pitied the poor, but he had never lived in Field Lane or Seven Dials. He had always had food and clothes. He had been taught to read and write, despite the blacking factory and his family's time in the Marshalsea. But he had escaped all that, and now he feared returning to poverty as other men fear drowning or being burned alive.

In any case, this was worse than human poverty. This was the mob. Blind, hateful and beast-like. How he might have pitied them if they were sitting quietly in a doorway, or dying of cholera! How angry he might have been on their behalf! And how he hated them now!

He stood and delivered his best stage roar.

'MMMMEnough!'

There was just the briefest window in the noise. Dickens was used to commanding attention, and waited a moment too long. All he could do was look.

'Look at 'is trarsers!' yelled a bull-like boy in tattered woollens.

There was a roar of contempt, and the momentary stillness was broken as the destruction continued. A few of the school's bigger boys tried to retaliate, but most ended with bloody faces. One lost a tooth.

Then, as suddenly as it had come in, the filthy tide ebbed away, still jeering and banging. As the last of the mob reached the bottom of the stairs, Mr Woodhouse scraped his way out from under the desk, his hands shaking. There were splinters of wood in his hair and his knees were covered in dust. As he stood, a police constable arrived in the hall. He surveyed the damage, gaping.

'All well, Mr Wood'ouse, sir?'

'I am all well now, thank you. The same can hardly be said for the school, however.'

'Rascals, sir, hain't they? Niver mind, I'm sure you'll manage, jest as you did last time.'

'Do we know who these wretches are, constable? Is there no punishment that can be imposed?' asked Mr Dickens.

'It's the usual gang, sir. But you tell me the purpose in punishing 'em. They can't pay fines, an' they're a bit young for prison, most on 'em. What they need is a bit of 'ope, like. You must have seen their condition, sir. "Ardly my place to say that as a police hofficer, but still...'

'So this conduct continues, with Mr Woodhouse's efforts going to waste?'

'Well, sir, we shall 'ave to think about it. P'raps heventually they'll stop it, sir.'

'Very well, constable, thank your for your assistance. We shall indeed think on it. You might give me some names, however. Perhaps I shall try a little persuasion.'

'Wery vell sir.' He took out a notebook and a small pencil, which he licked and held up to the light. He wrote for a minute or so, tore the page out and gave it to Dickens. And then he left, clomping down the stairs.

'How many more could you get in here, Mr Woodhouse? Into this space, I mean?' He asked.

'Well, ah, perhaps a few more.'

'Twenty?'

'We could try. With ... with another adult. Or two.'

'Excellent!'

Dickens smiled, winked at Tommy and Hassan, shook Mr Woodhouse's hand and left in a very great hurry.

Mr Woodhouse recovered himself, gradually. He was embarrassed at his physical cowardice, at his terror in the face of the mob. But then, he thought, there are times when terror is perfectly sensible. And he would never desert this place, or these children. Not for anything.

'Boys and girls! Gather around me if you please. They shuffled towards him silently, cleared some furniture and sat on the floor around him. As they did so, there were movements of furniture, scrapings of chairs across the partitions throughout the hall. 'I wish to speak to you about the future.' A small girl in front of him sobbed, and Woodhouse put an avuncular hand on her head. 'No, my dear. I wish to tell you what we shall do about this, about how the light of the human spirit will shine in the darkness of this wretched world. Let me tell you about the courage we shall have.' A boy laughed. It was Tommy. 'Oh yes, Tommy Jackson, I know that I hid under the desk. All of you hid behind something – something real or something in your heads. And let me tell you this. Without fear, there can be no courage. We are not courageous when we walk up stairs, or when we eat our dinner.'

'We are at 'ome, Mr Wood'ouse, when me Ma does 'er marry-bones or 'er pigs' 'earts.'

Some of the children laughed.

'Take my point, Sally. We shall overcome this. We shall triumph. Now, do we leave this hall like this, or do we put it all back together again?'

There was a silence. A few children sloped off across the hall towards the door. But Foxy was there, and made his views clear enough.

'You stay in there, and let's get this done. We'll start agin.'

There was a cheer, and a flurry of activity. Broken furniture was piled in a corner, ready for repair. Books were repaired with punched holes and string, and piled neatly. Malone fetched a broom and started to sweep the floor of broken slate. Sally, who was perhaps her younger sister, held a tin dust-pan for her. The placards, those that were left, were put back on the wall.

Now, Malone, you are monitor today. You have done a fine job. Here are three shillings. Go and find plenty of bread, three large chickens and ... and – ah – whatever else you like the look of. Off you go now.'

It was clear that nothing more would be learned from books that day. Small groups formed on the floor, and Hassan found Tommy sitting with Tunks and Pipsie, Baines, Foxy and Sally. Tunks asked all the expected questions about Hassan and Ahmet: why they were here if they could already read and were so clean, why Hassan had come to England, how his parents earned their crust, and so on. Eventually, the questions were exhausted, and they resorted to playing games while they waited for Malone to return.

'Chuck farthen,' announced Tunks.

'Chuck farthen to you also,' said Hassan, thinking that it was some sort of greeting.

Tunks laughed as he took a small coin from his pocket, and the rest of the circle, bar Tommy and Hassan, followed suit.

'Not for money, I don't,' said Tommy. 'Me dad would have me guts for garters.'

'Awright, matchsticks then,' said Tunks, flashing his eyes at the roof and then yawning.

Hassan watched carefully. The others took it in turns to throw the coins at the wall. When everyone had done so, Tunks and Pipsie judged the distance of the coins from the wall beneath the window. Like many simple things, it engrossed the children completely, and ten minutes went by in a flash.

'Pitch and toss,' Tunks announced. 'Matches agin. Anyhow, Mr Wood'ouse won't let us play for money, and he's bin watchin' us carefully. One match each.' He placed two farthings on the back of his hand, flipped them into the air, caught them in his other hand and slapped them on the back of the hand they had started in. 'One heads, one tails. Again. One match each.' The matches were thrown in front of him, and the pitch was repeated. 'Two tails!' He laughed, and took all the matches. 'One match each. Two heads'. He gave a match back to each player. And so it went on until Malone returned.

She emptied a sack onto Mr Woodhouse's desk: several children groaned. Three scrawny chickens, fifteen small loaves, a cake and three bottles of beer, all dumped in a little storm of feathers.

'However did you manage, Malone? Well done!'

''Sall right, sir. Me dad helped. 'e's not working today. Ware 'ouse is quiet.'

When Tunks, Pipsie and Foxy had gutted and plucked a chicken each, Mr Woodhouse took a skewer and a ball of string from his desk drawer, tied the string to the skewer and drilled it through each of the chickens. Then he hung them in the fireplace and posted Baines to keep watch. Baines occasionally poked the chickens to make them turn slowly in the heat.

Chapter Sixteen

November 1855

Much later, after the chicken and the bread had been wolfed down, Mr Wright arrived to take an evening class in woodwork, and the girls went off to practise their darning and embroidery once more. As soon as Mr Wright looked around him, he could see an excellent project for the evening: furniture repair, including perhaps a little upholstery on the master's chair.

'And remember, young men, our Lord ...'

'Was a chippy, Mr Wright.'

'Good lads. Now let's get started.'

Hassan and Tommy left with Mr Woodhouse, who had decided for their sake to have a rare evening away from the school. He lived just the other side of Holborn Hill, in a two-room apartment above a locksmith's shop in Fetter Lane. Now Fetter Lane was not so far from the law courts in The Strand, so by day the whole area from Lincoln's Inn Fields, across Chancery Lane and as far as here, was dotted with lawyers and messengers, white linen paper and red ribbon. Yet now, after dark, pale lights glimmered in the windows as they walked up the street. Already the creatures of the night were appearing to replace the lawyers and the skilled folk – printers and stationers and copy-writers – who served them. Now there were bundles of rags in the doorways, and footpads looking for prey.

'How much, Guv'nor?' It was a grating voice, and even Hassan was sure that the man was up to no good.

Mr Woodhouse swung round, equally unnerved.

'I beg your pardon?'

'Ow much, I said. For the pair on 'em?'

A man with a sweaty face – odd, thought Tommy, since it was so cold tonight – looked the boys up and down. 'Worth a penny, these two.'

Mr Woodhouse, quick as a flash, pulled a cudgel, wooden, curved, five inches long and weighted with lead, and held it above his head. The man soon fled.

Both Hassan and Tommy were glad to be back in a safe place, but it was a ramshackle house. Mr Woodhouse had never married: he wanted to teach the poor, and he had never met a woman who shared both his beliefs and his willingness to give up all thought of comfort. None of the women he had known as a young man would have married into a life like this.

He lit a smoky, grey tallow candle and they mounted the stairs. He brought out another key to get into the apartment, found a taper and lit two oil lamps from the candle, which he then snuffed out. The first room was piled high with books and papers, a collection which he had started as a child and continued through Oxford and since. There were only two pictures: one of a ship at sea and one of a grey-haired sea captain.

'My father,' he said. 'God bless him.'

They sat on chairs covered in velvet – the only items of any sort of luxury in the room. Mr Woodhouse lit the fire, and Hassan and Tommy sat, mesmerised by the flames, whilst their host went off to find coffee. Then the three of them looked at each other briefly, and Mr Woodhouse smiled. He took off his coat as the room warmed up, revealing the dusty black jacket he had worn in the school room. He swept a hand over his greying hair, looking fifteen years older than he really was; Tommy thought he must be forty-five, but Hassan, because he was used to the wind-burned faces he saw in the port in Bombay, was much closer. About thirty, he thought.

Mr Woodhouse nursed his coffee, and looked deeply into the mug, as though delving into some mystery. Then he looked up and broke the silence.

'A most disagreeable day,' he announced.

'Right you are, sir,' said Tommy, with his usual mixture of respect and chumminess. Woodhouse looked a little uncomfortable at first, but then understood him.

'And what is your view of our little predicament?' he asked. 'Why does it happen? What can be done to cure it, do you think? I mean, Tommy, it is easy to see these vagabonds as villainous. Yet we must consider the hell that they have come from. London is a horrid place for people to spend their lives in.'

''S'not, sir. Not all of it. My bit's all right, I 'spose.'

'So what do you like about living there?'

'Well, I likes the cathedral, I likes Vauxhall Pleasure gardens and Ranelagh. I likes looking down on the river at sunset, and watchin' 'em buildin' the railways. An' I likes the street bands and Punch and Judy. An' me Pa takes us to an Oyster bar sometimes, and once we went to Astley's Circus: when it was still called Astley's. Long time ago, it was. You won't find all that in the country.'

'Very true, I suppose. I'm a country man, you know. Or I was, until …' He looked embarrassed for a moment, and watched Tommy warily. He had suffered enough today without risking his beliefs again. Then he saw that all was well. '…until the Lord revealed to me what my life's labour should be. The church. And now this.'

He smiled weakly, as though a part of him was unconvinced. Faith was always like that, he thought. It had to be. There had to be a seed of doubt from which the best things could grow. Of course, he had never said anything like this to Mr Rough.

'Now then. What to do?'

Hassan understood this. He had now started to think in English for the first time, and had been seeking words for that question himself. And there they were, jumping out into the air in front of him.

'Now then. What to do?' he repeated.

Tommy laughed and Mr Woodhouse smiled kindly.

'What are you thinking, Hassan?'

'I think Mr Dickens a good man. He help you. You and Mr Dickens good men, sir. He has much money and is a good man. You no money, and you a good man.'

Mr Woodhouse laughed gently.

'You are most kind, Hassan. But I do not know what a good man is. It is difficult to pick out a good man in a crowd, or even in our committee room'.

He winked at Tommy.

'Assright, sir! Like that Mr...'

'No, Tommy! I should not have said that. Leave it be. *Judge not, lest ye be judged, for as ye measure it shall be measured unto you ...*'

'I tell you what I think is a good man,' declared Hassan. '*Happy are believers, who humble in their prayers, who speak seriously, who pay poor-due, who are modest with their bodies – but not to their wives – who are shepherds of a promise, who listen to prayers. They go to paradise, and live there forever.*'

'Most beautiful words, Hassan. You sound just like a Christian already!'

'Oh no, sir, these are the words from *my* Book. My uncle Ahmet taught me to say them in English.'

'Yet they sound so like the words of mine!' said Mr Woodhouse. '*Come, ye blessed of my father, inherit the kingdom prepared for you from the foundation of the world. I was hungered, and ye gave me meat; I was thirsty, and ye gave me drink, I was a stranger and ye took me in, naked and ye clothed me, I was sick, and ye visited me.*'

'Who say this?' asked Hassan.

'Why Jesus said it.'

'And Jesus in my Book also!' cried Hassan.

Tommy was looking confused, and then rather cross, as this conversation went on.

'But what are we going to do?' he exploded.

'Ah, yes, well. What to do?'

'Mr Dickens find a way,' said Hassan. 'He a good man.'

And there was another lengthy silence.

'Your school wash and teach the poor,' said Hassan. 'You and Mr Dickens pay the poor due.'

'But not for everybody,' said Mr Woodhouse. He was starting to look tired.

Silence descended once more.

'So what we do,' said Tommy at last, 'is this. Fink about it. You bring in me and Hassan 'cos we're in danger. You bring in the dirty and the 'ungry and the hignorant. But those childern today was the dirtiest and the most hignorant in London. Most of 'em seemed strong, but I'll betcher they've got 'ungry people at 'ome. So bring 'em in! P'raps they just need teaching.'

'Yes, Tommy, we've all realised that. We understand the need well. The other children hate the school because they cannot be welcomed into it. And they cannot: we are not keeping them away by choice, dear boy. We simply haven't the space or the teachers. Or the means to control them. To many, the task is not, after all, a very attractive one.' There was a flicker of fear in his eyes.

Shortly afterwards Mr Woodhouse wished the boys goodnight and retired to his room. Tommy was soon asleep, and Hassan stood and looked out of the window. So much time, he thought. *So much time looking out of the window looking for danger.* He rarely felt in danger in Bombay, but in this city it was constant.

He looked over the grubby chimney cowls and rusty weathercocks to the west. Rain fell in drops the size of farthings on the soot–streaked window ledge, and the street below became a shiny, dirty charcoal. Soon, forks of lightning started to appear over the roofs to the west, and the charcoal world outside grew still darker in the contrast.

Hassan had not prayed last night. He felt like the *jezailchee* he had once heard of, who had given up praying because his horse had been stolen as he bowed to the east. That was not a good reason to give up prayer for ever, thought Hassan. But last night was different.

The storm gathered and Hassan shivered. He turned his back on the storm and faced the middle of the room.

'In the name of Allah, the kind, the merciful. Praise be to Allah, Lord of the worlds, the kind, the merciful. Owner of the day of judgement. You alone we worship, you alone we ask for help.

'Show us the straight path, the path of those you have favoured, not the path of those who earn your anger nor of those who go astray.'

He bowed.

'To the unbelievers, Allah is like a rainstorm from the sky, with darkness, thunder, and flash of lightning. They thrust their fingers in their ears because of the thunder claps, for fear of death. Allah includes the disbelievers in his guidance.

'The lightning almost snatches away their sight. As often as it flashes forth for them they walk in the light, and when it darkens again they stand still. If Allah willed, he could destroy their hearing and their sight. Lo! Allah is able to do all things.

'Allah has appointed the earth a resting place for you, and the sky a canopy; and He causes water to pour down from the sky, thereby producing fruits as food for you.

'And give glad tidings, O Mohammad, to those who believe and do good works; that there are gardens underneath which rivers flow; as often as they are refreshed with food of the fruit thereof, they say: this was what was given us aforetime. There for them are pure companions; there for ever they will live.'

He knelt and placed his forehead on the carpet. Tommy stirred, and Hassan returned to his chair and slept.

*

At four in the morning he was woken by the clock chiming: why he wondered, had he not been woken at one or two or three, as he had in Mr Dickens's house? He shivered, perhaps because the fire was almost exhausted: he could now see only the silhouette of the coal bucket and firedogs, and the edge of Tommy's chair. He went to the fire and picked up a poker, and stirred the embers for a little more warmth. By their glow he looked for Tommy.

The chair was empty.

Chapter Seventeen

2nd November 1841

As Smith had recovered those two years ago, there was no need of the surgeon, for Nasrin had dressed Smith's wound every day. The bullet had passed through his shoulder from behind, and had left a neat piercing the size of a sixpence. The exit wound was slightly larger and more ragged, but better than it might have been. Smith's greatest problem was immobility, because for months the simplest of actions, such as dressing, shaving, dining or mounting a horse, caused untold agony, and occasionally distressed him even now.

He had loved Nasrin from the first, of course. Not joyously, not at first, but in a way that disturbed him, left him fearful and restless. It was their betrothal and the first year of their marriage that had lifted him – lifted both of them, he thought – and deepened him at the same time. What struck him now was how well he had come to know her, despite the fractured nature of their words to one another.

Yet it was in her care of him, both before and after they were married, that had mostly revealed her nature to him. Her open face, the lightness of her fingers, the little frown and the pursing of her lips whenever he winced, and her relieved smile when the wound had been re-packed, all spoke volumes to him.

Yet even with Nasrin's tender care, Smith struggled to recover his fitness for soldiering. So he had become a political officer with a shattered shoulder who knew Pashtu. At first, he had been pleased, but soon missed his men and the soldier's life. His time now was spent in meetings and carrying messages about, and persuading people to promise things they had no intention of doing.

*

For weeks now, they had all been hungry, for food in Kabul was becoming scarce; the surrounding land and the grain sellers struggled to support an extra twenty thousand people, even this soon after the harvest. And there were also new problems. Some merchants had refused to provide wheat and flour to the army, and others had increased prices five-fold. The Kabulis responded to this with a bitterness perhaps born of fear. In the last few days, the more rebellious Kabulis were threatening to cut off the water supply into the cantonments.

For more than a year, the mountain passes, the only route to Jalalabad and back to India, had been protected by the Ghilzyee chiefs. But the Company had always been worried about money: that was why there was no room in the cantonments for stores of food and ammunition. Then, just a month ago, Sir William had decided to halve the money paid to the chiefs, and in the blink of an eye the only road to India and safety was blocked.

At the beginning of October, Smith had said goodbye to his men, for Sale's brigade was packed off to Jalalabad, just before the passes were closed. Only Sergeant Pooter remained to assist Smith, and seemed suddenly to be taking his natural place in the world. Lomax was promoted to Sergeant and temporary platoon commander, but Lieutenant Revell would watch over Smith's old platoon as well as his own. Smith would have preferred his old friend James, but poor James had left the service a few weeks after they had arrived here. Smith had arranged, quietly, that James be picked to take a message to Jalalabad with a small escort, and he had never been seen again. For a short time, Smith had received letters from him, the last from Sukkur, but there had been nothing for months.

To a man, Smith's platoon had declared that they would 'see him in Jalalabad if death doesn't overtake us first.' The autumn sun glittered in many a watery eye at their parting.

As soon as the news was out, the atmosphere in Kabul began to change. Many Afghans shared in the sorrow: some from love of the men, some from love of their money. Others, the harder-faced among them, saw their chance. How much easier it would be to rid their land of the *feringhee* when they were halved in number!

Before Sale's departure, Major George Broadfoot had been ordered to go ahead with Colonel Monteith to make sure the passes were clear and to ease the way for Sale. Broadfoot went to the bazaar, to the smoky, rasping hot dens where the blacksmiths worked, and ordered spades and pickaxes. At first they had refused to make anything at all. 'We all too busy making our own weapons,' one had said, with a glint in his eye. Broadfoot had set an armed guard on the workshops to force the men to work.

*

This morning, Smith had found an hour to read, and was sitting in front of a small fire on which Malik had set a kettle for coffee. He looked up from his book. His lovely boy, now aged ten months, awake early as usual, sat on the floor, fat little legs splayed, pointing at the threads on the rug as though trying to untangle its little world: birds and bushes and plants, and an odd little figure – a crown? a precious stone? – in the centre. Every now and then Smith peeped over his book and clucked, and the little boy chuckled and clapped his hands. He had just started to crawl, and often Smith would feel a little hand patting his boot.

That was not the only distraction this morning, for Smith found it harder and harder to think of anything other than the trap they had found themselves in. War, he thought, must have a habit of getting more complicated once you were in it.

One such complication was the Shah. He seemed to hate his people, and wanted only to rule over them, as though it were his

God-given right. English kings had once thought like that, of course. Shah Soojah seemed to have no sense of the good of the people, or of nationhood. Smith felt this inevitable, because this was a country of small cities separated by vast plains and mountains, and with a constant flux of kings and princes and tribes and dynasties. No single centre of power would ever be able, he thought, to assert itself over the region. Typical of the British, he wanted to say, with all their influence across the world, to think that the Afghans would ever understand, let alone give in to, the larger view. Smith, Eyre and Sturt had often wondered how the politicals had ever expected Soojah to run Afghanistan.

There had long been doubt amongst his friends. The first chink in the armour was the shooting of Leary. Then three sentries had been killed one night at the camp at Siah Sung, where the bulk of the army had moved after being thrown out of the Balla Hissar. They knew who had done it: Malik, perhaps in hope of another reward, had given the names to Smith one evening. Smith had gone straight to Sir William, and Sir William had ordered that the men be left alone unless there was firm evidence. 'And if you have sufficient evidence, they should all have been shot already,' he said.

Lady Sale, whom Smith had seen regularly during the year since they had moved into the cantonments, was furious.

'Is it any wonder,' she had said to Captain Sturt, 'that the Afghans are starting to push us? While politicians are in charge of the army, and our officers may not do what is military?' She also complained that often the officers *chose* not to be military. It was said that Brigadier Shelton often fell asleep in meetings with General Elphinstone, and that he had once taken bedding in with him. Captain Bellew argued with everybody, and always found an obstacle in the way of a good idea. The General always agreed with everybody. So no decisions were ever made, and meanwhile the threat grew and grew, both inside the city walls and out across the mountains. Poor Elphinstone, thought Smith - old and sick and dithering, and quite out of his depth.

In the meantime, Smith's heart became boundless. As he loved Nasrin, so he loved his son. And as he loved his son, and saw the many kindnesses showed him by the Kabulis, so he started to feel something like a permanence in his relations with them. He and Nasrin learned one another's languages, sometimes quite formally, with exercises and the rote learning of the names of fruits and birds and plants, and furniture and domestic items, and sometimes impromptu, with much laughter.

Sometimes, these lessons were revealing. Smith would often correct something she had said, half lover and half schoolmaster, and then ask her for other examples. One day she had got stuck on the word *only*, and Smith had explained patiently. Eventually, she picked it up:

'I have no girls – I have only one son. I have no horses – I have only one camel.' Then her eyes shone. 'In Afghanistan we have no cowards – we have only brave warriors.'

She immediately regretted what she had said, and struggled to correct it. But Smith had assured her that this was quite right, and there was no shame in saying so.

*

Now, as Smith peeped at Hassan over his book, and Hassan shrieked again, there were fleeting, light footsteps, and Malik came into the room. He had changed a lot over the last few months. There had been a time when he had said little. Perhaps he was still trying to work out who was going to win this war: or, as Leary might have put it, which side his bread was buttered. He had refused to shout either for Leary or for Ahmet in the wrestling match two years ago, and during the ice-skating excursion, he had said nothing to Smith or to Ahmet or to anybody else. He hedged his bets, with odd jobs for the Kabulis and gradually, over a few weeks, by spending more time at the camp at Siah Sung and working as a *cossid*, a messenger and carrier, for the army. More and more, until this last summer, he had felt sure that the British were his best bet. They ruled the country, they had all the cities, and of course they had all the money. And for him, there was no going back to Ghazni. He knew what he had done there, and what his people must think of him. He would need to get his family out of there, one day, when it was safer. They could all be together again. He still felt hopeful about that. And he had grown to like Smith. Perhaps that was how, over the last few weeks, he had come to understand that Smith was … frightened? Not exactly, but certainly worried. He could see it in the way he looked at his wife and son.

He had also seen the lines in other faces, the frowns and the narrowed eyes, and he had heard the edge in their voices. Yet he did not falter: still he served Smith, and still he brought him news. Usually he brought a little something for Hassan, and often he gazed at Nasrin, perhaps, Smith thought, slightly in love with her.

Now, though, he gabbled excitedly.

'I have news, Misser Smith, sir. I hear many things, all bad things. Sir, a *cossid* return from Gandamuk. He tell me much fighting in the pass of Khoord Kabul. Difficult fighting.'

'Yes, of course. A few *jezailchees* up on the top, firing down into the ravines. Any dead?'

'Many dead, sir. Twenty thirty. Mr Sale gone through to Jalalabad. And the pass …' He motioned downwards with the edge of his hand. 'Still closed. No Jalalabad for you. And at Siah Sung, they try to kill Mr Melville.'

'He has survived?'

'He live, sir.'

'Good. What other news?'

'Much talking, Misser Smith. Much talking indeed. Amenoolah will try to stop water today. Will stop canal. You must gather water now in many barrels.'

Amenoolah Khan was a man Smith had always doubted. He was happy to serve the Shah as it suited him, and he was happy to collect the Shah's taxes on the end of a British bayonet. But at the same time, he saw which way the wind was blowing, and Kabul was a remote place. It would not take much to turn him if Dost Mohammed came from over the hills, or sent instead his son, the apple of his eye, the warrior chief Akbar Khan.

'I thank you, Malik. I shall inform His Excellency at once. He must already know of the fighting at Khoord Kabul.'

'Sir. Much talking in city. They want *feringhee* army to leave.'

'Yes, Malik. They have long wanted that.' He remembered the wrestling, ice-skating, horseracing and cricket, and how the Afghans had seemed to love them. How brittle shiny things were!

'Also they want *feringhee* treasure. Today they want attack Captain Johnson's treasury and also his house. They take everything. People in the town now. Today there will be much trouble, Misser Smith.'

Smith thought for a moment. He looked up at Malik and saw him nervously stroking his beard.

'And also kill his house, sir. Everybody. And sir ...'

'Yes, Malik? What is it?'

'They want kill Sir Sikundur Burnes. Today they go to his house and they kill him. I tell Taj Mohamed. Taj Mohamed a good man, and he go to tell Sir Sikundur. And Sir Sikundur very angry. He shout and beat Taj Mohamed on the head. He shout 'Nonsense! Nonsense!' What we should do, sir?'

'Of course they want to kill Sir Alexander, Malik. That does not surprise me in the least. There are some who want to kill all of us. Is Major Broadfoot with Sir Alexander?'

'Yes, sir. Major William Broadfoot. He there.'

'Good. Then I am quite sure that all will be well. I shall visit Sir Alexander shortly and His Excellency straight afterwards. Now, Malik, are you well? Have you had news from Ghazni?'

'I well sir. My family well. And your family well. Your treasure well.'

And he looked at Hassan and pulled a face at him. Hassan chuckled, his perfect round face filled with delight.

Thank God he knows so little, thought Smith.

He threw on his uniform and a blue greatcoat and boots. Nasrin, an echo of five millennia of soldiers' wives, gave him his sword, kissing its hilt. As he had done every day, he took her face in his hands, kissed her on the forehead and said goodbye. He picked up Hassan, took his little hands and drew them ticklishly across his stubble, so that Hassan shrieked with glee. He kissed him, left the house and walked briskly to the bastion at the south-eastern corner of the cantonments. Six soldiers were keeping watch. It still seemed strange that Pooter was helping with political papers instead of out here.

There were flashes from the Balla Hissar and from the city.

'What firing is that, sergeant?' he asked.

'Afghans have got guns into the city, sir, and they're training 'em on the Balla Hissar. Looks like Captain Nicholl is returning fire from the Shah's battery up in the citadel, sir. Wish we was up there with 'im, sir. Lot safer 'n 'ere, sir.'

'You are not the first man to have said it, Sergeant.'

'Thank you, sir.'

'Have you seen Captain Sturt this morning?'

'Just gone to seek orders from General Elphinstone, sir. He may not be back for hours, sir.'

'Very well. I require an escort – say six men – to accompany me on a visit to Sir Alexander Burnes. It will not be a lengthy visit: in any case, I have to return to Sir William shortly after daybreak. Be ready in half an hour, if you please.'

'Sir.'

Smith walked back along the wall and paid a visit to Lady Sale, who was always awake before dawn and often watched the sun rise from the fire-step. Whenever Sturt was engaged on his engineering work, as he was most of the time, Smith would offer Lady Sale what help he could. His best service, he often thought, was to listen to her complaints about the leadership and never repeat them.

This morning she was, as ever, pursuing her passion – her *shoke*, the Afghans called it – for her garden. The land around about may have been something like a desert: rocky, dry, mountainous and covered in thick snow in the winter, but plenty could be grown on the plains, even sweet peas and geraniums which Lady Sale had brought from India. There were hairy little Afghan lettuces, cabbages and, on a wall, gigantic grapes. Next year, she said, she would plant peach and plum trees, and wrap the fruit in tissue paper for the winter just as the Afghans did. Smith watched her energetic passion for living things as he approached, and wondered what would become of it all.

'Ah, good morning Captain Smith.'

He bowed.

'Lady Sale. Have you heard news of Sir Robert?'

'A wound in the ankle, I believe. The bone was shattered, but the ball passed through and was left under the skin, so that the surgeon was able to remove it with ease.'

'Sir Robert wounded, Lady Sale! I am most surprised!'

She laughed.

'It will take more than a ball from a *jezail* to halt his progress, Mr Smith.'

'Just so, my lady. I wonder, in Captain Sturt's absence, is there any service I can do for you?

'Not at present, I thank you. But let me show you something. It may be of use to you later.'

She took him across to the outer wall of the cantonment. There was a round tower known as Sale's bastion, simply because it was behind the Sales' house. For some time there had been a breach in the wall in a narrow V-shape which reached from the top of the wall to about six feet from the ground, and below it was a large rock which the engineers had never wanted to move. Lady Sale climbed up and peered through the gap. Then she got down and invited Smith to do the same. He did so with a stab of pain in his shoulder and looked out.

The view was a good one, for the sky had lightened. Lady Sale could just see a small fort – Mohamed Sharif's fort, the Afghans called it – and behind it the King's garden with its little slatted gate. This may be useful, thought Smith, as a loop hole if cantonments came under attack.

'I would urge caution, Ma'am,' he said. 'I believe that we are about to enter dangerous times.'

'Nonsense!' exclaimed Lady Sale, and not for the first time Smith could see why even Sturt, her son-in-law, called her the Grenadier in

Petticoats. 'They would never dare to threaten me. They know what would happen.'

Smith smiled.

'Nevertheless, my lady ...'

'Yes, indeed, Captain. There is always some nevertheless or other, is there not?'

And at that moment, a gigantic *nevertheless* interrupted them: gunfire from the Balla Hissar, a single boom, soon followed by a second.

'The Shah's guns, I am told,' said Smith.

'Yes,' she said. 'And yet I cannot understand why they would be firing, or at whom. Surely the Balla Hissar cannot be threatened. That is precisely why our garrison should be up there instead of in this preposterous place. Perhaps you would find out for me.'

'I shall do my best, ma'am.' He felt that he was talking to a commanding officer.

There was a sudden shouting from the direction of the cantonment gates. For the second time in his life, Malik was ushered into Smith's presence on the end of a bayonet. Two privates and a sergeant saluted Smith as best they could.

'This man is a trusted servant, Sarnt Williams. You know that.'

Malik interrupted urgently.

'Sir, it start now! We save Sikundur and the treasure!'

Williams ignored him.

'Yes, sir, but as he was running like a lunatic and screaming, sir, and in the present circumstances, like, I thought I should be sure, sir.'

'Circumstances, Williams?'

'Whole city's up, sir. Rioting and that. Shops turned out, mobs 'eading fer Sir William's 'ouse and the treasury, sir.'

'Have troops been sent in?'

'Nothing 'appening at all, sir. Saw Captain Sturt, sir, just now, goin' to the General. When he saw the fire, he said he was goin' to advise the Shah on defending the Balla Hissar. But you know what it's like, beggin' pardon, sir. He's a good officer, sir, but they won't listen.'

'What's the firing about?'

'Captain Warburton of the Shah's service, sir. Firing into the city to get everybody back inside, sir. Not really working as yet. It's a riot, sir. Or worse.'

'Very well. I have an escort ready. My Lady, I shall visit Sir Alexander and then Captain Johnson at the treasury. I shall return to you with news as soon as I can.'

Smith had rarely ridden since he had been shot, and he now climbed stiffly into the saddle. He led the men through the gates and wheeled right towards the distant city walls. The Siah Sung hills stood out dark against the lightening sky, for the sun would soon peep above the horizon at the start of its low, shortened autumnal sweep across the sky. The city walls were dully visible in the gloom, with the Balla Hissar rising away to their left.

Behind the city wall and straight ahead of them, there was an orange aura, a glow of flame. It peaked and dwindled as the wooden roof of a building fell in, and then another would start nearby. Lights were showing in the Balla Hissar and in the Shah's palace just below it, and there was an occasional flash from the citadel followed after a split second by a dull thud as the sound followed the light.

As they approached the Kohistan Gate, they just caught the sounds of tumult: shouts, the occasional scream and clashing of wood and steel. Then there was flame over to the right, and the frenzied whinnying of horses. Smith wondered at this: were they really firing at the stables, the *yaboo kaneh*, or were the horses just spooked by the surrounding flame and noise?

The guard opened the gate, and they entered the city. Smith was surprised to find the first street peaceful and almost deserted, except for an officer with a few soldiers. It was Captain Sturt.

'Captain Smith. William, I should say! Mighty glad to see you. Where are you heading?'

'I have urgent news for Sir Alexander: there is a plot against his life. I fear that Captain Johnson's treasury will soon be under threat also.'

'Yes, so my Afghan friends keep telling me. You see how it is: Sale gone, and nobody here to make decisions. What we need at present, of course, is three hundred men in the town with muskets.

But who will give the order for it? Brigadier Shelton has ordered me up to find out what is happening. The Shah demands a force be sent in, the Brigadier wanted to come, and everybody else dithers. In the end, Shelton came anyway. Lawrence had the same difficulty. D'you know, he had to run an Afghan down on the way up to the citadel: fellow was trying to kill him. None the wiser when he got there.'

'But I must get to Burnes. He will not listen to the Afghans: he thinks he knows more than they do. He may listen to an officer.'

'Very well, dear chap. But take great care.' He stood with mock self-importance. 'But don't expect me to come with you, for I have an audience with his Majesty the Shah Soojah al-Moulk.' He laughed unconvincingly, and then he became serious again. 'Quite honestly, he has already done more with his troops than the combined might of the British army has managed. You missed a rare sight when his infantry went rampaging into the streets to calm things down.'

'And were they successful?'

Sturt smiled.

'Have you ever led a platoon through those tiny passageways with bayonets fixed? There's no room to turn around, let alone perform any sort of execution. Twenty of them were cut down by *jezails* from the rooftops. They left their guns and ran for it back to the Balla Hissar. The Brigadier had to cover their retreat and collect their weapons for them. Such an indignity!'

'What can we do?'

'Do, my dear friend? Three hundred troops come in, and then we retreat to the Balla Hissar and hold out for Sale's return. Or, if the passes are blocked, appeal to General Nott at Kandahar. Quite obvious. But it won't happen, of course. Between ourselves, I'd say the game's up. Time to negotiate for all we're worth. You know how it is: nobody listens.'

And he walked away, bearing left towards the citadel and the King.

Smith took a road straight ahead, ordering the escort into silence and expecting a shot to ring out at every turn. But the place was, for the time being, surprisingly quiet. Had he entered a lull? Had the rebellion petered out? Had it failed already? The quiet unnerved him after what he had seen from outside the walls, and he felt that he was being watched from the rooftops and the gardens and the passageways hidden away on either side of the streets. As he treaded the dusty, narrow, winding alleys towards the houses of Sir Alexander and Captain Johnson, past the shuttered workshops, the odd wilted tree, he could see the signs of what had happened: a broken blade, a lead ball nestling in a corner, a shattered cannon ball, a tumbled wall, a missing door. Shop after shop had been broken into, its shutters splintered or lying in the streets, and the frustrations of a hundred people revealed in the scattered produce: fruit and half-finished tools and pottery.

After a few hundred yards, he signalled a halt. The men closed behind him and he whispered urgently.

'Listen.'

They heard it too: a murmur, like a distant sea. Nearer and nearer. Voices: shouts and chanting. A faint smell of burning. Nearer still. Then around the street corner from the right they came, a mob of forty or fifty, unarmed, but their faces filled with rage. A man looked straight at Smith, measuring his strength, glancing at his sword and his pistol and at the muskets carried by the men. He carried swiftly on, jostled by his friends.

Friends? Or comrades? Smith wondered, and ordered the men forward slowly.

Soon they reached the street between the two most important British-occupied buildings in the city: Sir Alexander's house on the right, with its thick cedar-wood door, shuttered windows and a painted balcony overlooking the street; and on the left, Johnson's treasury building, with its crude vaults, and his house, nestling alongside.

A crowd was already gathering, looking up at Sir Alexander's house. They shouted and raged and rattled things. Out for blood, Smith thought, and was glad of the muskets.

Soon, three figures in uniform appeared on the balcony: Sir Alexander stood proudly, in dress uniform complete with fluttering feathers and shining epaulettes. Smith pitied him: he was trying desperately to show that he was still in charge, and looked less and less convincing by the minute. Lieutenant Burnes, his younger brother, and Major William Broadfoot stood by him, standing tall but equally uncertain. Sir Alexander shouted loudly down at the crowd, but Smith could hear nothing as the words were drowned out by the rage from below.

Then Smith saw five men with *jezails* arrive at the back of the mob, and raise their rifles. He shouted an incoherent order.

But he was too slow.

A shot rang out, and on the balcony William Broadfoot dropped forward, his arms and chin on the balcony, staring at the crowd with a frown. He was dead before he fell.

The crowd cheered, and was suddenly silent.

A servant – or was it Taj Mohammed? – ran onto the roof and yelled at the *jezailchees*, tears of rage in his voice. He stood in front of Sir Sikundur, and spread his arms wide, protecting him. The *jezails* were lowered, but the crowd roared. Another servant appeared on the balcony and beckoned the Burnes brothers inside.

Still the air was tinged with smoke, and it grew quickly thicker, rasping at Smith's nose and throat. A thick plume arose from behind the house, and the soldiers soon heard a sound dreaded by every countryman: a frantic neighing of horses, and then the desperate clatter of hooves.

'Withdraw!'Smith shouted, and led his men round the building and through the gardens. There was a crazed scene: horses and ponies ran blindly and in circles through the plants, scattering earth and dust behind them, trampling cabbages and the last dying flowers under their hooves. Their flanks and their breaths steamed in the chill air.

'Sir! Sir! Please help me, sir!'The voice was filled with panic. Smith turned, alarmed at the voice, and struggled to make anything out through a think cloud of smoke. Then it cleared to reveal a soldier tugging at a twisted, smouldering stable door as a pony whinnied – screamed almost – from inside. The soldier was enraged at the weight and stiffness of the thing, and as his rage grew his strength faltered. Smith joined him, picking up a musket on his way across the yard, and rammed it up to the stock in a gap in the door. Terrible abuse of a weapon, he thought, but needs must. Somehow he got the fingers of both hands through the gap, and heaved with all his might. The door gave all at once, and a small white pony, with a smouldering scar on its side, ran in terror between them.

And there was Ahmet the wrestler, throwing a pail of water over the horse, and urging others to help him save the *kaneh*. Some helped, forming a chain to the well, passing buckets swiftly from hand to hand. Others were too caught up in the imminent defeat of the *feringhee* to care about the stables, and gathered in the garden to look up at the rear of the house. Soon it was clear that the stables were beyond saving, even by the heroic Ahmet. He was wise enough to see it too, and placed his pail on the floor with a fatal resignation.

Smith looked across the gardens to the house. Three Afghans in *lunghees* and robes emerged through a door, and Smith was sure he recognised them. One was the servant who had appeared on the balcony and taken Sir Alexander and his younger brother away into the house; who were the other two?

Surely not?

Smith soon had his answer as the three moved into the crowd and away towards the street. The Afghan grabbed the *lunghees* of the other two and threw them into the dust.

'See here! See here!' he shouted. 'Here are the great Sir Sikundur and his brother!'

This time, Smith was quicker to react, and raising his sword he took a step towards the Burnes brothers. The crowd, looking inwards towards Sir Alexander, was unaware of Smith as he moved.

Smith felt his shoulder gripped by a vice.

'No, my friend. Three is enough for one day.' He turned to look into the eyes of Ahmet. 'This is not your day to die, Captain Smith. Quickly, come with me.'

Smith stood transfixed, watching the swirling crowd in front of him. Somehow they had not seen him: what with the burning stables, the fleeing horses and the drama unfolding in their midst.

The crowd roared. There was a flash of steel, and another and another. The brothers soon disappeared from view, hidden from Smith by a flurry of arms and whirling blades.

Smith felt himself being moved as if by an unseen hand, unwilling to go and quite unconscious of what he was doing or where he was going. His men followed, muskets pointing outwards.

Behind them, the dust was stained with blood, and the tumult grew. Ahead the Balla Hissar loomed up, and Smith noticed one of the men looking across at its secure walls. He caught the man's eye, and understood the thoughts behind it.

'Safest place sir. They may require our assistance, sir. Or there may be messages to take back, sir.'

'Yes. Just so. On the double, then.'

Smith allowed the men to lead the way, running at a brisk trot. Normally he would have been at the front, but now his mind was a blank, temporarily stunned by what he had just seen. He did not even wonder whether this was the end of things, or whether it was some new challenge, like the charge at Ghazni. He understood only the rage and the noise of the mob, and felt sick of it all.

They soon reached the Balla Hissar, and were allowed quickly through the gate.

'Thank God!'

'Sir?'

He pointed. It was Sturt, staggering along in front of him, his face fixed on the floor as though searching for a lost coin.

'Captain Sturt!'

Sturt seemed deaf to everything outside his own contracted circle. Smith swiftly overtook him.

'Sturt! What is happening? I ...'

Smith stared into Sturt's face. He was drenched in his own blood, which coursed from a long gash in his cheek and an inch-long puncture wound in the side of his neck. There was also a growing crimson circle under his left arm.

'You!' He did not know the soldier's name. If only Leary or Pooter were here! 'Fetch a *palkee* from the citadel! We must get him back to cantonments. To his wife.'

Later, he did not know why he had said that. Was he arranging a death scene or a healing?

Sturt gripped Smith's shoulder and shook his head, unable to speak. He pointed feebly forwards. Smith nodded and put himself under the wounded man's arm. A soldier took the other side and they moved with surprising speed towards the king's audience chamber. The Shah's body guard, the *Hazir Bash*, leapt aside, and in a flash they were in the Shah's presence, in that room with the fine shutters, the throne and the new silk furnishings which had suddenly appeared as the people's rage and hatred had grown.

The Shah tried hard to look composed, but could not quite carry it off. He stood - Smith had hardly ever seen him stand in this room – and he stared. His hand shook visibly before he stilled it by gripping the edge of a table.

They sat Sturt on one of the silk chairs, which was soon covered in specks of blood. He coughed, and the back of his hand was spattered red.

The Shah had been speaking to Captain Lawrence. Lawrence was, of course, much more experienced in political work than Smith, and had the Shah's ear rather more often. But now he too was silent, and Smith noticed that the sleeve of his red tunic had been almost sliced off. How had he escaped wounding?

'There is a *palkee* on its way. We shall need to get him back to cantonments,' said Smith. 'Are you able to assist us?'

'Why, certainly. I have to return in any case.' He lowered his voice. 'I seem at the moment to be going backwards and forwards a great deal. You know how it is: from the Shah to Elphinstone to the Shah to Macnaghten to the Shah...'

'Lawrence, the whole place is up. Burnes ... I fear for Burnes. William Broadfoot is dead. Shot right next to the Burnes brothers at the house. And clearly, the treasury is next. I would not care to be in Captain Johnson's position at present. We must do something, surely. Where is Shelton's force? And ...' It was his turn to lower his voice. '...and the Shah's infantry?'

'They have been out. Rescued by Shelton, actually. He's here. Waiting for orders. Waiting, waiting.'

'What happened to you?'

'It's nothing, really. Fellow leapt out at me. Decent-looking chap, but as you say, the whole place is up. Ran him under my horse. Properly mangled, God willing.'

The *palkee* soon arrived, and Sturt was laid on it. He took a little water, and wheezed noisily. Four soldiers took a corner each, and they left the room. Neither Smith nor Lawrence felt the need to make their usual obeisances to the Shah. He looked at them like a man under sentence of death.

The way back was again surprisingly quiet, other than a distant murmur from the direction of the treasury. Before eleven they were back in the cantonments. The first person they saw as they approached the Sale house was Sir William Macnaghten, standing next to the very same horse he had been riding when the Dost Mohammed had surrendered and asked for mercy. He was deep in thought.

Here he was, out of his splendid house beyond the cantonments, out of his gardens, out of the opulent offices from which the Afghan campaign had been waged for more than a year. Here he was, back on the safe side of the wall.

Chapter Eighteen

S omehow, Sturt fought on. The great, open gash across his neck and throat had surely been mortal, and yet he lived. For days his wife and Lady Sale watched him, waiting for the end. He could not speak, his breath at times came fitfully, and his back arched in agony. The worst was that he could not drink without terrible pain, and his lips became dry and cracked. Yet three days after he was wounded, he woke, turned towards a sunny window and said faintly 'Better... better'. Perhaps he would see India again after all.

For a while, nobody knew what had happened to Sir Alexander Burnes, the British Resident in Kabul. Communication between the cantonments and the city were all but non-existent, senior officers were still unable to make decisions, and every piece of news contradicted what had gone before. But at last, and almost in desperation, the junior officers were starting to make decisions for themselves. Smith had made his report to Sir William, and informed him that he believed Sir Alexander to be dead.

'Enough of your croaking!' Sir William had said with his quiet certainty, and Smith had left. Later that day, the Shah had reported in anxious notes that Sir Sikundur was a prisoner, then that he was wounded.

Finally, Naib Sharif, an old friend of Sir Alexander's, arrived at the cantonments to see Sir William. He had enjoyed many a pleasant dinner in the Residency, telling tales of his family and listening to the Resident's adventures, all told in Sir Alexander's marvellous Pashtu. But now his face was as sombre as could be, and he seemed to feel that a golden age had come to an end. Sharif did not take his eyes off Sir William, who eventually turned and stared out of the window.

Naib told how the Burnes brothers had died, and left no detail out. The address from the balcony, the shout of betrayal in the garden, the men being cut down in a hail of steel and rage.

Afterwards, said Naib Sharif, Sir William had been cut to pieces which were hung upon the trees in his garden. His head could not be found; perhaps it would be sent to the Dost as proof that the *feringhees* had been defeated. Sharif had paid for a private burial before sunset, according to his custom, but still blood dripped slowly from the branches.

True to Malik's prediction, the treasury had been ransacked. Twenty soldiers of the Shah's service and all of the servants had been massacred. Captain Johnson, by one of life's strange flukes, had been spared. He had received no warning, not even from those he had thought to be his friends; he had simply been absent at the time.

Now, food was still in short supply, and the soldiers had been put on half rations of food and water. The animals were no longer being fed. Every day two or three died. Their putrefying bodies were left outside the gate, and the air stank with them. As Smith looked over the wall one morning, looking north along the Kohistan road, half expecting a great line of hostile Ghilzyee and Kuzzilbash to appear at any moment, all the movement he could see in the dead landscape was a fly-bitten collection of horses and ponies, stripping the bark off a few fruit trees and pounding at it with their yellow teeth.

Ahmet Qaderi was filled with pity. He had been treading a careful path. He was neither an Afghan farmer nor an English soldier; but as a grain merchant, he relied on both. His wrestling had made him popular with the *feringhee,* but it had also been vital for him to win in front of his own people. When they had been ice-skating, and many times since, he had spoken to the British as an Afghan through and through. They would surely be defeated in the end, he had always said.

So he had never drifted from his own people. But some had been watching him resentfully. Never mind what he had said and done, he spoke too much to the *feringhee*. Why, his sister had married the officer, and his own nephew had the blood of the *feringhees* in his veins. He would need to be watched carefully.

Ahmet liked Smith openly, for Smith was a good husband. He was also the father of little Hassan with the bright eyes and the pudgy legs, and Ahmet dreaded to think what might happen to the child and Nasrin if Smith were taken from them.

And Smith would be taken from them, one way or another: even now, with the cantonments still intact and the fortifications of the Balla Hissar still available to them, Ahmet Qaderi feared for the British. Like everyone else in the city, he had heard that Akbar Khan, the great warrior son of the Dost, was on his way, with perhaps five or six thousand men. The British would be outnumbered, and they would be facing a choice between starving in the cantonments, holing up in the Balla Hissar (Oh, *why* would they not move there now? asked Eyre) and making a rapid march to Jalalabad as the winter drew on.

It was the last of these that the Afghan chiefs wanted, followed by a withdrawal from Jalalabad itself. But there were conditions, and as so often, the city knew about these before most of the British officers and men. This was why Ahmet and Malik went to see Smith as soon as they heard of them. Malik stood silently, his eyes cast downwards, as Ahmet stated the case. Smith sat in an elbow chair he had bought in a workshop on the Old Kent Road just before he had sailed.

'Your army is in great danger, Mr William. Akbar Kahn arrive in ten days, perhaps nine. Sir William speaks of leaving Kabul?'

'Yes, he is to be Governor of Bombay.'

'But the army will leave also?'

'Perhaps.'

'Perhaps you have no choice. Akbar Khan want to take you to Jalalabad, through Khoord Kabul, Jugdulluk. Very dangerous without him. Without Akbar to protect you, the Ghilzyees kill you.'

Smith thought for a moment. How did Ahmet know all this?

'But there will be fourteen thousand of us! And soon the snow will fall! How long will it take?'

'Sir William thinks nine days. I say longer: perhaps fourteen.'

'And the guns? Can they get through the passes?'

'No.'

There was a long silence, and Malik and Ahmet glanced at one another.

'Guns stay here,' said Malik. 'And also ......'

'And also what?'

Involuntarily, Malik looked through the doorway at Nasrin and Hassan, who were playing together on a divan in the tiny sitting room.

'You leave all your guns. You leave all your wounded. You leave Kandahar, Ghazni, Herat and Kabul, and then you take your wounded home. You leave ...' He struggled with the words.

'I see. We leave our Afghan wives and our children? Here in Kabul? And who will protect them?'

'Akbar Khan protect them. He promises.'

18th November 1841

Nasrin sat at her tiny cherry wood table, writing in a thin slant of sunshine which picked out every shade of the grain. Her husband had brought the little table from his homeland, and it had been one of his first gifts to her.

Now, she was carefully copying a piece of Smith's writing. She had been surprised at her own skill, and as the weeks went by the daily task was becoming much easier. Each day, dear William wrote out a short piece from his book and gave it to her, always touching her cheek.

She knew little about the book. William often laughed when he was reading it, and she was reminded of a story her mother told her, a story from *The Tales of a Thousand Nights and One Night*. Ali the Persian has had his bag stolen in the market in Baghdad. He takes the thief to the Kazi and pleads for justice. 'But the bag is mine,' says the thief. 'It contains eye-powder and two gold cups and two candlesticks and two tents and two plates and spoons and a cushion. And two leather rugs and two jugs and a brass tray and two basins and a cooking pot and two water jars. And a ladle and a needle and cats and two dogs and a wooden plate. Two sacks, two saddles and a gown and two fur coats. And a cow and two calves and a she-goat and two sheep and a lamb. And two green pavilions and a camel and two she-camels and a lioness and two lions and a she-bear and two jackals. And a mattress and two sofas. And two saloons and two sitting rooms and a kitchen and a whole company of Kurds who will tell you that this is my bag.'

The Kazi raised his eyebrows and tried hard not to smile. He looked at Ali.

'But no,' said Ali. 'The bag is mine. It contains one thousand fighting men, a sheep fold, one thousand barking dogs, gardens, beautiful slave girls and singing women, marriage feasts, great tracts of land, prisoners, robbers with swords and spears and bows and arrows, drinking companions, drums, flutes, flags, banners, boys and girls and five Abyssinian women and three Hindi maidens and four damsels and twenty Greek girls and eighty Kurdish women and the Tigris and the Euphrates. And a thousand rogues and stables and a mosque. And the Kingdom of Solomon."

And the Kazi did not believe either of them. He told Ali to open the bag, and Ali took out some bread and a lemon and some cheese and a few olives. He threw the bag on the floor and left in a bad temper.

Now *that* was a funny story! How they had always laughed! Was William's book as funny as that? Sometimes, she had taken the book down and looked at the pictures. They were all pictures of *feringhees* in their own country. How odd they seemed! There was a man on the roof of a wagon, with a crooked hat and a bottle in his right hand. Ragged children were chasing him, and a man waved a club in the air. The fat man with glasses, who was in most of the pictures, was leaning out of the window looking up at the man on the roof.

In another, the same man was playing the game they called cricket: Nasrin had seen this in Kabul. She found neither the game nor the pictures funny. Perhaps one day, when she could read the writing...

She continued to copy.

'Now, attend, Mr Weller,' said Sergeant Buzfuz, dipping a large pen into the inkstand before him, for the purpose of frightening Sam with a show of taking down his answer. 'You were in the passage, and yet saw nothing of what was going forward. Have you a pair of eyes, Mr Weller?'

'Yes, I have a pair of eyes,' replied Sam, 'and that's just it. If they wos a pair o' patented double million magnifyin' gas microscopes of hextra power, p'raps I might be able to see through a flight o' stairs and a deal door; but bein' only eyes, you see, my wision's limited."

Nasrin sighed and put down her pen. Perhaps William would explain when he had time.

23rd November 1841

Captain Johnson had been working hard in the grain stores of Beymaroo. Prices were high, but there was plenty of grain to be had if the merchants and farmers could be persuaded to sell. In part, they saw the desperation of the British and their followers and were sure they would pay. However, they were also wary of what the Dost might say when he arrived. They had heard that he had a forgiving nature, but they needed to be careful. There were also plenty of *jezailchees* near at hand, and the merchants became involved in a careful balancing act between carrying on their trade and collaborating with the enemy.

Johnson did well to maintain the supply. He spent hours in the village, talking and smiling and drinking mint tea with great lumps of sugar.

However, the night watch raised a hue and cry in the early hours of 20th November. Sergeant Pooter roused Smith by banging on the door with his fist, which for him was unusually violent. Up on the fortifications of the cantonments, they looked across at Beymaroo. The sky above the village was glowing orange, and even from that distance they could hear the screaming of horses.

The following morning, Smith looked across at the village through his eyeglass. It looked almost deserted, but as he watched he started to notice a few people ambling through the blackened streets. Here and there a house had been reduced to a few charred beams and lumpen piles of mud bricks. Later, cannon fire from the hills started to land in the cantonments. They called it a dropping fire, but Smith felt that this sounded far too gentle. The Engineers, directed by Captain Sturt from his bed, had worked for the rest of the day to repair breaches in the walls.

Sir William had ordered that something be done. For once, he seemed to understand the threat. Last week, Shelton had taken the hills, declared victory and promptly returned with his men to Kabul. Immediately, the Afghans had returned to the ridges. Yesterday, Major Swayne had tried to shift the Afghans from the hills, and failed completely. Before dawn today, Brigadier Shelton, very much against his will, had taken more than two thousand infantry, more than four hundred cavalry and a hundred engineers into action. Smith, Sergeant Pooter and a few sentries watched from the walls of the cantonments as the force headed out towards Beymaroo village just before dawn.

'Good luck to them,' said Smith very quietly.

'I should say they'll need it, sir,' said Pooter. 'What are numbers, against all those *jezailchees* popping up and down in the rocks, sir?'

'Never mind, Pooter. They have at least taken the guns out with them. And the Brigadier is just the man for this.'

'Just the one gun, sir.' They looked at one another. Smith could hardly believe what he was hearing. He looked through the eyeglass again.

'So I see. Nevertheless, Pooter, we have a strong force.'

'Yes, sir.' But Pooter still looked very doubtful, and watched the hills anxiously.

*

Just a few hours later, they had seen enough. Once more Eyre, who had joined them at the wall, despaired at Shelton. Yes, he was brave, but he needed to be brave after the mistakes he had made. And his bravery cost the lives of other men rather than his own. He had marched into the hills with only one gun. He had formed his foot soldiers into two great squares on a ridge, to defend against a cavalry charge which could never have made it up that slope. Of course, the squares were a wonderful target for the *jezailchees*, which had far greater accuracy and range than the British muskets and rifles. Eventually, the infantry had made a run for it, knowing that if they stayed they would surely be shot down.

In Beymaroo village itself, there was a similar disaster. Sergeant Mulhall had turned his gun on the enemy, showering them with grapeshot so that they had been forced to find shelter in the village, many of them in burnt out houses. Major Swayne was ordered to take the village, but instead of walking in through the main gate as he could have done, found himself at a barricaded side gate instead. There the *jezailchees* found him and his men, and pinned him down for a terrifying half-hour of splintered wood and shattered brick before he was forced to retreat.

So it was white faced and shaking men, covered in dust and sweat, who returned to the cantonments that afternoon.

3rd December 1841

It started to snow, and the bodies of the soldiers left on the Beymaroo heights froze. They included the corpse of poor Colonel Oliver, headless and handless. He was worn out, and too fat to run, and had walked slowly towards the enemy, fully intending to be shot dead. Only a week or so earlier, when Captain Johnson had announced with pleasure that he had found some grain, Oliver had questioned the need for it. 'None of us,' he had said, 'will be alive to eat it.'

Now, the cantonments were hungry again. Nasrin spent much of her time asleep, worn away by giving much of her ration to Hassan and by worrying for her child, her husband and her homeland. Her beauty became blighted; her eyes hollow and her skin dry and pale. When she looked at Smith, her eyes glistened and her breath was short.

However, there was some good news. As before, Captain Johnson had managed to find more grain, this time from a Hindu merchant who had agreed to leave a hundred sacks full at the Mohamed Sharif's Fort during the night. Smith also heard rumours that a friendly Afghan merchant had agreed to join him.

Sure enough, the delivery was made, and Smith's platoon were among those who helped to carry it in. For a few days they ate again, albeit frugally. Nasrin returned to her copying for an hour or so each day, and Hassan was heard to babble and chuckle even more often than usual.

*

It was at about this time that Ahmet and Malik disappeared. They were often together, and of course Malik usually accompanied Ahmet on his visits to Nasrin. Now, suddenly, there was no sign of them.

Nasrin pleaded with Smith to find out what had happened, and Smith did all he could. Ahmet Qaderi was a familiar figure in Kabul, and most of the officers knew him, at least by sight. Smith asked Johnson, Eyre and Sturt. He spoke to Lady Sale, Brigadier Shelton and even General Elphinstone. He asked the men, and the mullahs. Nobody had seen Ahmet Qaderi the wrestler for several days.

Early one morning, Sergeant Pooter visited Smith whilst he was reading reports.

'Awfully sorry to interrupt, sir. We've found a body, sir.'

'Is it Ahmet Qaderi?'

'Hard to say, sir. Rather a mess, sir.'

And so it was. The long clothes were soaked in blood from hem to breast, the hands were missing and there was empty space and blood-red soil between the unravelled lungee and the neckline.

But it was not Ahmet Qaderi, Smith found when he drew up the sleeves and looked at the severed arms. Even with the hunger, Ahmet Qaderi would not have been as reduced as this. He was altogether a bigger man.

No, this was Malik, who had risked his life by throwing in his lot with the British forces at Ghazni. Smith had always expected him to sue for peace with Ghazni, and return home to his family. Now he would be buried here, next to the other hundreds of dead. Smith decided that he would see to it that Malik's family were told, before realising that he knew nothing of them. He did not even have a tribal name for him.

Before the body was taken care of, Smith went through the pockets and folds of cloth looking for clues. All he found were a few rupees and, to his amazement, a letter addressed to Nasrin. He wondered what to do with it. What might it contain? For a moment, he wondered whether it was some distant declaration of love or admiration; perhaps he should burn it. But, he thought, letters should always be delivered. Perhaps it was this that Malik had died for. So as soon as he returned to the cantonments he left it on Nasrin's little rosewood table.

Later, Smith heard her sobbing, and went to comfort her. She had in front of her two letters, both in her native tongue. One, she said, was addressed to her, and one to Hassan. She was translating one of them into English, and had broken down in mid sentence. Smith put his hands on her shoulders and kissed the top of her head. Together, they sat at the little table and completed their translation – Nasrin's translation, mostly – of Ahmet's last letter to Hassan.

It was strange, but well after dark, when Smith came back from another interminable and inconclusive meeting, Nasrin seemed much calmer. She even managed to smile.

'Shall we have one more look at the letter, my darling?'

She looked down.

'There is no need, dear William. It is finished.' She looked into his eyes. 'And now I know that my dear brother is well. I never see him again, perhaps. But ... I know that he is well. He was here. After you went out. Perhaps he waited. He don't like to say goodbye to you. But I am a sister. He must say goodbye to me. And I give him the letter. To remember.'

*

Meanwhile, on the tops of the Beymaroo hills, thousands of Afghans were lined up, looking down on the cantonments and waiting.

Chapter Nineteen

The snow had now fallen heavily, and lay in great drifts against the walls of the cantonments. At times, the wind blew fiercely from the east, whipping up the snow and bringing tears to the eyes of sentries. Food was still more scarce, for the threats of the mullahs had cowed the merchants into submission. Still there were Afghans willing to bring grain into Kabul, but often at a terrible price: now it was the Ghazees who intercepted the army's grain outside the gates. Many of the merchants were killed or left for dead, and the grain, already paid for, was taken away. Again, Smith realised, the army could do nothing to stop the plunder.

Still there was no sign of Ahmet Qaderi, who seemed to have vanished from the face of the frozen earth. Her own letter Nasrin had kept to herself over those days, but Hassan's letter she had copied several times, with Smith's help, into English. Each time she threw her earlier, less perfect efforts into the fire, except for one or two which Smith managed to rescue and hide away. She gave Hassan's Pashtu letter and its English copy to Smith, and he placed them carefully inside the book from which Smith had been giving her lessons.

Copying the letter seemed to satisfy Nasrin, Smith thought, and he noticed that every now and then she smiled a little as she wrote. Sometimes, Hassan would grip of the leg of the small table and stand and watch her, and Smith was touched beyond imagining to see it.

Smith knew that he may soon need to write letters also, as final farewells and keepsakes to those he loved. He had again heard the talk of Afghan wives and children being left behind when the army headed into the mountains. Often now, he looked out at the crystal beauty of the Hindu Kush, and the deep blue sky beyond. For all the beauty, he dreaded his arrival in the first of the mountain passes, but this was nothing compared to his thoughts on his departure from Kabul.

Akbar Khan had seen that the time was right to come down from the hills and to negotiate for the surrender and retreat of the British army. There had been many negotiations, which came to no firm conclusion. Akbar wanted a shameful and abject surrender, but the Envoy was treating for more than just the lives of his men. He also wanted an honourable retreat.

Yesterday, Sir William had gone out on horseback to meet Akbar, his cousin Osman Khan and assorted chiefs by the Kabul River. This evening, Sturt, Eyre and Smith sat in Smith's little sitting-room to tell one another what they knew. This was not much, of course, so the rest of the evening was spent in guesswork.

There would have been some talk, Smith said, of the British army being in Afghanistan only to help the Afghan people. He wondered what the chiefs would have thought of this. Sturt smiled, and winced slightly as he did so.

'We should give the Afghan chiefs their due,' he said, in his new gravelled voice. 'They know our interests as well as we: Russia, Persia, India, the great game and so on. And their people will know of this also.'

Eyre and Smith nodded their agreement.

'We have always underestimated the Afghans,' Sturt continued. We think them brutal and gluttonous and chaotic, and sometimes cowardly. True, they sometimes kill a sentry or a camel and run away. You saw for yourself, Smith, how they killed Burnes and the Broadfoots. What they did to me was a long way short of even-handed. And yet that is not the whole truth. We saw them fighting on Beymaroo heights, and in the village. We saw them charging our lines at Ghazni. So we know that they are a most courageous force, and that they know what is what. They do not have an Envoy who keeps things to himself. It seems to me that they share their intelligence... Well, let us say that the Afghan knows more about events across the region than the men in your platoon, Smith.' Smith looked him in the eye. 'Do not mistake me, William. Your men knew more than most.'

'Quite so,' said Eyre. 'But where does all this leave us? As a military force, we are finished, and the Afghans must know it. Why, we are even unable to secure our provisions against attacks by a few ungoverned Ghazee rebels. What chance do we have of fighting our way to Jalalabad? Or Peshawar, or wherever the Envoy chooses to send us?'

'Surely Sir William has no choice,' said Sturt. 'All he can do is promise to withdraw from the whole country – Ghazni, Jalalabad, Kandahar. And then plead for food and safety and pray that Akbar keeps his word. And, of course, that Akbar has the power to control the passes for us.'

Just then, Nasrin came into the room. It was most unusual for her; normally she would leave Smith in privacy when he had Army visitors. Sturt and Eyre stood quietly as they always did when a woman entered the room, then bowed very slightly and smiled woodenly. Nasrin had nothing to say, but just looked at the officers with a little frown, as though seeking something from them.

'Good evening ma'am,' said Sturt.

'I trust you are well?' said Eyre.

'I find myself very well,' said Nasrin. 'We all a little hungry, perhaps.' This at least was convincing.

'And your son?' Sturt enquired.

'Sleeping, *inshallah*.'

Sturt smiled. 'And when he is awake? Something of a soldier, I should say? Why, soon he will be out exploring.'

'Perhaps, sir. But there is little here to explore. The world is too dangerous. Never he leaves my sight outside. And a soldier? Certainly I hope not! Soldiers leave their mothers. And their wives...'

She could not go on, and raised their hands to her face and slid from the room.

'So sorry, William,' said Sturt.

'Not at all,' said Smith. 'You were merely being courteous. However, perhaps we should all question the value of English courtesy in this place.'

They sat down again, and Smith lit a pipe with a taper from the fire.

'So what next?' asked Eyre. 'What do you think our glorious Envoy has offered to the chiefs? The Koh-i-Noor diamond? India? Wagon loads of rupees?'

They all smiled wryly, knowing the seriousness which often couched itself in Eyre's humour.

'Well, Sir William will have offered to withdraw from Afghanistan: from Kabul, from Ghazni, from Kandahar. It is possible...' He looked at Smith. 'It is possible that he will offer hostages: some wounded, or the sick, or Afghan families. I'm sorry, William. It has to be faced, you know. What will you do? About Nasrin and your little boy, I mean?'

'One thing I cannot do,' said Smith, is to take them into battle.' He took his pipe out and looked at them earnestly. 'To tell the truth, I have considered this at length. Indeed, I have thought of little else. The Afghan chiefs may be brave, and they may be knowing, but that does not mean that we should have blind trust in them. We cannot rule out an attack by Akbar Khan as we make our retreat. So Nasrin and Hassan must stay here.' He became distracted for a moment, and took a long draw on his pipe. Sturt and Eyre could barely see him through the smoke, but his voice was cracked. 'Nor can I forget that Nasrin and Hassan have nobody here to protect them.' He felt a lump in his throat, his voice all but cracked. 'God help them, I don't know what to do.'

There was a long silence as Sturt and Eyre considered the situation.

'Perhaps,' said Sturt, 'it is a blessing that you have little choice but to trust in the Afghan chiefs and to come back for Nasrin and Hassan when Kabul is properly under Afghan control. It seems that

I shall do the same for my wife and her mother. Even General Sale can do nothing to help, since we can no longer communicate with Jalalabad.'

'Yes, I'm sure you are right,' said Smith. 'We can only hope.'

23rd December 1841

So the negotiations had continued, on and off, for the next ten days or so. Smith and his friends heard that Sir William Macnaghten had succeeded in persuading the chiefs to guarantee food supplies and safe passage out of Afghanistan. At one point, it was even reported that the garrison would leave within three days. However, just as those in the cantonments started to hope for food, the Ghazees again attacked the merchants without any response from the British or the Native regiments or the Afghan chiefs.So the chiefs could not be trusted.

It was about this time that Pooter fell sick. It started with a trivial incident: a boy had thrown a small stone over the wall and hit Pooter on the back of the hand. It seemed to be nothing, and Pooter had not bothered with a bandage. But two days later it was a weeping sore, and Pooter took a fever. The cold and the lack of food had weakened all of them, and now there were a number of sick in the sanatorium. Smith feared that he might lose a second sergeant. He could only hope.

In other ways, the situation looked more promising. Sir William Macnaghten felt, despite warnings from his Afghan friends, that he should turn to Akbar Khan. More rumours were spread, usually by Afghans who had been present at the meetings. When the British left, they said, Shah Soojah al-Moulk would be allowed to stay on the throne after all, and Akbar Khan would be his Vizier. The British would stay for a few months, and be properly looked after. Akbar, of course, would be given large sums of money with which to rule; and for a little extra, the head of Amenoolah Khan, the ringleader in the killing of Sir

Alexander Burnes, would be placed in a bag and given to Sir William. Needless to say, Sir William had rejected this offer with disgust.

Eyre and Sturt were worried that if the chiefs or Akbar Khan knew that Sir William was trying to make agreements with both at the same time, the army would never be safe. And if Akbar could persuade Sir William to betray the chiefs, he would know that one day the British might betray him.

So the British army had no way of knowing who their protectors or their enemies might turn out to be. None of them would guarantee the supply of food. If the chiefs got wind of an agreement to make Akbar Khan Wazir and to keep Shah Soojah on the throne, there would be complete revolt. Captain Mackenzie and Captain Lawrence, as well as loyal Afghans, tried to warn Sir William about the dangerous game he was playing. And so it went on, until this snowy morning two days before Christmas.

*

Smith and some other officers and a few sentries were watching nervously from the wall, showing their usual interest in what was happening beyond. It was another clear day, and away to their right the Balla Hissar glowed in the sunlight. A short time ago, a fine cavalcade of Afghans, a dozen chiefs and their followers, had come up a gentle slope to a stretch where the snow lay thin and powdery. In places, the wind had blasted the snow to reveal patches of bare earth and tufts of grass. Through his eyeglass Smith spotted the man who must be Akbar Khan, the wind ruffling his beard and making his lungee dance about his head. He was wearing Captain Lawrence's pair of fine double-barrelled pistols, which Macnaghten had generously bought and given to him the day before. A few men dismounted, and spread a large carpet on the ground. They all seemed to be talking, but occasionally laughter broke through the crisp air and reached the ears of the observers.

Shortly afterwards, a small party of British left the Western gate and headed along the frozen road, and over the canal to where the Afghans were waiting. Why so little protection? wondered Smith. The party included Sir William, Captain Mackenzie, Captain Lawrence, and Captain Trevor, and a few *chuprassis*, armed soldiers who acted mostly as messengers and assistants. There was also a fine unmounted horse, trotting nobly, its head held high, alongside Captain Mackenzie. This, Smith realised, was Captain Grant's pride and joy. Not another gift to Akbar Kahn, surely?

As the British party reached Akbar Khan and the chiefs, Akbar raised a hand in salute. Through his telescope, Smith could see him smile. Macnaghten and Akbar spoke briefly, and Akbar patted the pistols he wore at his side. Captain Grant took the bridle of the riderless horse, and drew her towards Akbar, who threw his head back and laughed. He held his right hand out, palm upwards, to invite the British to dismount and sit down. A man stood at the reins of each horse.

For some time, Smith had been watching two hundred or so armed Ghazees gradually approaching and encircling the group.

'My God,' said Smith. 'Why is Akbar letting them get so close?'

Even from this distance, he could just hear Lawrence shout and point outwards at them. Again, he saw Akbar Khan laugh, and held out his hand to guide Lawrence to his place on the carpet. Instead, Lawrence stood behind Sir William, and then went down on one knee with his hand on the hilt of his sword.

Smith could not work this out. Had the Ghazees been brought along by Akbar, or under their own steam? Were they supporting Akbar, or in opposition to him?

What happened next was a blur. A sentry was the first to notice.

'Sir! The Ghazees is getting closer, sir! And the grooms is moving away with the 'orses, sir!'

There was a shout from down on the slope. Smith could see Akbar pointing furiously at Macnaghten and his officers. Lawrence was grabbed by the arms and his sword and gun were taken from him, and Mackenzie had a pistol pointed at his head. Trevor was taken captive at the end of a dagger. Akbar and another man had grabbed Sir William by the arms. In a picture which Smith would never forget, Sir William stayed on his knees for as long as he could and looked pleadingly at his captors. The men on the ramparts could just hear his cries, but could not make out the words.

Lawrence, Mackenzie and Trevor were forced up on to horses behind their riders and ridden furiously away to the right along the banks of the Kabul River, kicking up powdery snow and earth. Soon they were being chased furiously by a dozen or more men from the crowd of Ghazees, who were shouting wildly and waving swords. Smith could see that the Ghazees wanted to kill the three captains, and the chiefs to use them as hostages. Captain Trevor, unable to hang on in the rush, soon fell and was pounced upon and cut to pieces, but Lawrence and Mackenzie arrived at Mahmoud Kahn's Fort well ahead. They turned to face their pursuers, and in all likelihood their deaths, but before the first blow was struck Akbar Khan swept into their midst, sword raised, and beat down the Ghazees' weapons. The Afghan captors and the two British officers got into the Fort and managed to bar the door. A Ghazee pointed his musket in at a window, but fell as the weapon was twisted from inside.

Smith turned his small brass telescope back towards Sir William. He lay in the snow, partly concealed by Akbar's men.

*

Inside the fort, Mackenzie and Lawrence sat exhausted on a bench, and stared ahead of them. They shivered, partly with cold, as the sweat from their panicked ride cooled them. In his imagination, McKenzie could still feel the barrel of the pistol against his forehead, and Lawrence could think only of Trevor falling from his horse and being sliced to ribbons by the Ghazees. McKenzie spoke first.

'I shall never understand this country,' he said. 'At one moment, I was sure that Akbar and his men would kill us. The next, they were desperately trying to save us from the Ghazees.'

'Of course,' said Lawrence. 'We are not much use to Akbar as corpses. We may only be Captains, yet there is a ransom in us for all that. Who knows what Akbar may gain from keeping us prisoner? Especially in the midst of negotiations?'

'And will he keep Sir William? As a hostage? He must surely have more value than us.'

'Perhaps, but remember that we are without fault in his eyes; whilst Sir William has been trying to trick him this last month.'

'So they will kill him?'

'We cannot say, Mackenzie. But I fear his life is more in the balance than ours.'

The noise from outside, which had ebbed and flowed for the last hour, rose again. McKenzie, who understood Pashtu better than Lawrence, translated for him.

'They are shouting for our blood, dear chap. "Why protect the accursed? Kill the infidels! Shed the *feringhee* blood! Kill them!" '

'Merry Christmas!' said Lawrence, and forced a strangled laugh. He looked at Mackenzie, and they shook hands.

The noise outside rose again, and there was a hammering on the thick door. A lone voice screamed with rage, and the two captains remembered their own different scenes from the sacking of Ghazni.

'Look at the window! Look at the window! In this you see your own future. The *feringhees* will surely die!'

They looked, and framed by the window, with the mountains and the blue sky as background, was a bloody hand with the ring finger missing. The hand was pale and bloodless, and gore ran down the sharpened stick on which it was fixed.

25ᵗʰ December 1841

It was an unusual and memorable Christmas dinner. Smith, Nasrin and a few others had been invited to spend it with Lady Sale. Despite everything, the Grenadier in Petticoats was in good form. They sat on cushions on the floor, for the gigantic mahogany table which fighting Bob had brought from Bombay had by now been broken up and burned. They drank from solitary wooden beakers, for the goblets and glasses had been sold for what little food remained. Lady Sale had dug up the remainder of her vegetable garden before it was razed by others. She had used the last of her dried fruit, wrapped in tissue paper in the dark of a small outhouse. And she had ordered the slaughter of a camel, on its last legs in any case, and shared it between carefully selected friends. There were no plates, and they ate from makeshift wooden trenchers saved from the remnants of the table.

Smith looked across at Nasrin, who leaned listlessly back against a wall. Hassan was sitting between her feet. Smith winked, and Hassan chuckled, innocent of the outside world and of what used to be in this very same room.

All they could do now was to wait. Of course, they did not know what they were waiting for. Perhaps for the arrival of General Sale from Jalalabad or General Nott from Kandahar. Perhaps for safe passage through the mountains. Or perhaps for death, and an eternity in beautiful gardens under which rivers flow.

6ᵗʰ January 1842

Smith had been awake all night. He had visited Pooter late the previous evening, and had afterwards been in an agony of indecision. Pooter was out of danger, but eventually Smith realised that he could not risk taking an invalid into the passes. The sergeant would have to take his chances as a prisoner.

Smith had finally got up and dressed long before dawn. He kissed Nasrin gently on the forehead so as not to wake her, and then did the same to Hassan. He lifted a little hand and put his copy of *The Pickwick Papers*, with uncle Ahmet's letter and his mother's translation tucked inside, beneath it. He had struggled to think of the best words to write in front of the book, imagining a dozen circumstances in which it might be read. In the end, he ran out of time and wrote one simple sentence. Hassan stirred a little and murmured, but slept on.

Smith opened the door and stepped into a foot of snow. 'Just the thing,' he said quietly.

Already, soldiers and wagons, a great train of camp followers and their children, a few sorry-looking camels and a braying troop of mules, were milling around. The camels were laden with *kajavas*, the great panniers slung over their backs and bulging with the soldiers' pitiable last few possessions. Smith remembered twenty times as many camels in the Bolan pass just two years before, burdened with cigars and pewter cups and dress uniforms and armchairs and mahogany dining tables. He smiled as he remembered Nasrin's story about the thief and the bag. *And an army of occupation and fifty-two artillery pieces and four thousand camp followers and their children......*

Without thinking what he was doing, Smith lifted the flap on a *kajava*. Perhaps he wanted to see what his army had been reduced to; perhaps he would see the mahogany table reduced to a single candle stick or a silver goblet. Instead, he was shocked to see a small pair of dark eyes looking up at him in terror. The child must have been three or four years old. For all the bitterness of the moment, Smith smiled; and the child, now pacified, smiled unwillingly back. Smith walked away, remembering his first meeting with Nasrin and the hopes that had carried him to a frozen lake such a long time ago.

*

More than an hour after sunrise, the great train of the army of the Indus was finally ready to leave Kabul. Smith could delay no longer. He had to say goodbye to his wife and son. So he went back to his house for the last time, remembering vaguely the plans that he and Nasrin had made for their future. Not that they were plans, of course: they were just a list of possibilities. Perhaps he would spend the rest of his life in India. Perhaps one day he would be a colonel. Or perhaps they would take a chance and return to Surrey, he and his Afghan wife. Who could say?

He went first to Hassan's cot. It was empty. Nasrin must have taken him to her bed, ready for the last goodbye. He moved across the room, dreading the next moments. He reached for her hand and called her name.

The bed was empty.

He searched the house: the pantry, the parlour, the vestibule, even the closets. He grew increasingly desperate, dashing from room to room over and over again. There was a shout from outside, the sound of a whip and a braying of a donkey. He called her name, and he called his son's name, over and over. Nothing.

Then he realised. He remembered how she had been over the last few days: indeed, over the last few weeks. Withdrawn, sometimes tearful, and more wrapped up in Hassan than ever. She had been avoiding him, and he had hardly noticed. They had stopped talking about the future. And now, because she could not bear to see him go, she had taken Hassan away to avoid the leave-taking.

There was shouting again, and braying. He heard a soldier's curse. Now he had no choice but to go into the cold, mount his horse and leave Kabul. His fate now was largely out of his hands. Whether he lived or died, whether or not he saw Nasrin and Hassan again, was in the hands of Akbar Khan, the Ghilzyee chiefs and the snow and ice. God seemed to be nowhere.

Captain Sturt was directing operations.

'Captain Smith! Best of luck to you, sir!' His voice was still a little croaky, and Smith wondered whether his wounds would give him trouble in the cold.

'Thank you, Sturt. Why the delay?'

'I am quite sure that you would be able to hazard a guess, Smith. Nevertheless, I should explain it to you. You see the breach in the wall?'

There was a great gap, perhaps twenty feet across, in the wall of the cantonments, and some of the rubble had been gathered into neat piles on either side. The remainder had been used to fill up the canal to provide a road across it.

'Such is the reward of all your effort,' said Smith.

'I do not mind that so much. It was the delay that concerned me. We have little time as it is to find a safe encampment in the pass before nightfall. This has delayed us for hours. We should have left at dawn, or even before, and it is now ten o'clock. All that work and delay just to stop people from getting their feet wet! Why, they know they have to walk through the snow for ninety miles in any case!'

'I trust that you made your usual representations to the General?' Smith smiled grimly.

'As always,' said Sturt, and he laughed with a hollowness that Smith had not heard from him before.

'And our chances?'

'That is just what they are. Chances. Do you remember a time, Smith, when chance had nothing to do with the matter? When our fate was in our own hands, not in the hands of God, or the weather, or the enemy?'

*

The departure from Kabul was chaotic. It seemed to take hours to get across the canal, and then to ford the river. Again and again, they stopped and waited. In panic, realising that their chances of a safe overnight encampment were slipping away, crowds of people fought their way across, slowing down the escape even more.

Occasionally, there was the noise of gunfire from behind. Smith's stiff shoulder prevented him from turning around with ease, but eventually, in a bend of the road, he twisted in his saddle to see the cantonments ablaze, and the occasional flash of a *jezail*. He looked forward again, and tried to empty his mind of everything except his wife and child.

Behind them, but not so far as Smith had thought, a young and beautiful Afghan woman held a small boy, who clung to a book and a letter with a red seal. They bumped slowly along, with the flap of their *kajava* pulled low over their heads.

Chapter Twenty

6ᵗʰ January 1842

T hey stopped, yet again, at four in the afternoon, in the murk of dusk. As they had left Kabul, in the fearsome jostling and struggle to cross the canal and the river, all the planning, poor as it was, had fallen to pieces. There was an advance guard led by Brigadier Anquetil; Brigadier Shelton commanded the main body and Colonel Chambers' rearguard followed. But mixed in with the army were twelve thousand camp followers, wives and children and two thousand camels over-laden with baggage.

As they left, Zemaun Shah, who seemed to regard himself as King once Shah Soojah's protective army had joined the retreat, warned that food and firewood had not yet been gathered, and that the start should be delayed again. The rearguard waited while the thousands in front carried on, and when they finally left they were slaughtered in their hundreds, the snow stained with blood and pocked with the bodies of children. Clothes were stolen even from the living, and Captain Mackenzie would remember for the rest of his life the sight of a naked two-year-old Indian girl looking up at him with wide and darkened eyes as he passed. He rode on, knowing that there was nothing he could do. Why should this child be different from so many others? Perhaps, he thought later, because she was beautiful, and because she had looked straight into his eyes.

Now, at Begramee, they were to pass the night in the snow with no food, no firewood and no tents. No candlesticks, no pewter tankards and no cigars. Just six miles into the march, most of their possessions had been pillaged. The one remaining luxury was a supply of sherry which many used to keep themselves warm. If only they had known that in the long run sherry would make them colder, not warmer.

A few small fires were started; later, a returning traveller would find the leather cover of a Bible surrounded by a sprinkling of grey ash. Some were shown by friendly Afghans how to keep warm in the snow by lying in a circle, their feet towards the centre and *poshteens* on top of them.

In the morning, Captain Lawrence found old Conductor McGregor lying peacefully in the snow, uncovered and ice cold. It was no wonder, thought Lawrence, that the man who had spent so much time gathering stores and providing for others should now decide to lay down and die. Perhaps he no longer had a purpose in life. There were others too, and they could neither be buried in the hard ground nor taken to Jalalabad.

7th January 1842

The following day, the force covered only 4 miles, as far as the village of Boothak, so that they had still not even entered the Khoord Kabul pass, which they should have cleared on the first day.

Early on, Smith became aware of troops of Afghan horsemen appearing on the sides of the column. He asked Sturt what it might mean. Was this the guard promised by Akbar Khan, or was this yet another danger to them? Smith looked carefully at the Afghans, and they looked carefully back. Unusually, Sturt was silent, and his wounded face tightened in the icy cold.

8th *January 1842*

Finally, they entered the Khoord Kabul pass. At daybreak two hundred Afghans blocked the entrance, until the 44th charged at them with fixed bayonets to force them out of the way.

Otherwise, discipline and order had flown, along with their hopes. At seven in the morning, without orders, the advance guard, the main corps and followers decamped together, mingled chaotically in an urge to make progress towards the safety of Jalalabad.

There were now only three tents between the ten thousand of them, and no food or water at all. Smith had seen Indian Sipahees with swollen, purple tongues and sunken eyes; in their raging thirst they had been eating snow.

Before the army moved on, he had taken a hammer and helped to knock ice from the hooves of horses. As they took their first steps on the new day's march, he saw more frozen corpses: a mother and child, two children clutching one another, and a naked Indian messenger with the ashes of his clothes next to him. He must have decided to be warm one last time before he died.

The sheer, cliff-like sides of the pass grew higher and steeper, until the sun was entirely shut out beyond the sliver of sky. The pass seemed like the gateway to hell. There was no sound from the heart, no laughter, no conversation, not even any order. For hours, all Smith could hear was the muffled clop of hooves, and the ringing and gushing torrent of the narrow river which had gouged this path between the mountains.

As the day wore on, the cold was numbing his senses. He could hardly have held a sword, let alone thrust it at an enemy. When others spoke to him they seemed very far away, and he could barely feel his feet. He started to count the steps of his horse, looking downwards all the while except to glance up every time he reached one hundred. His shoulder, for the first time in months, was stiff and sore.

The half-conscious lover in him feared for his wife and child. He expected that by now Shah Soojah would be dead, and he could only hope that Zemaun Shah would protect them. If not, how many might seek vengeance on the wife of the infidel?

For all that, the soldier in him was glad that Nasrin and Hassan were not with him in this waste. Wherever they were, it must surely be a better place than here.

By midday, he was sensing movement on the high ridges above, and at first wondered whether he was losing his mind. Surely nothing could live up there? But shortly afterwards, his mind was forced to focus by the glint of a *jezail* behind a few rocks hastily built as a firing point. It would only be so long now.

*

The firing started shortly afterwards, as the first soldiers crossed the icy river for the umpteenth time. As through a haze, Smith saw an officer in front of him - he did not know who it was - shot in the throat. He sat still in his saddle for a moment, and his right hand made a vague, questioning movement towards his face. Then his hand fell and lay still, and he slid from his horse. For a moment, his boot caught in a stirrup and he was dragged through the snow, leaving a great streak of blood.

Further ahead a camel, one of the few remaining, was hit. It fell to its knees, its head dropped into the snow and it died where it knelt, leaning on a grey rock. The flap of the *kajava* was pushed open by a small hand, two small eyes looked out, did not like what they saw and disappeared again. There was a wailing from inside.

Smith did not stop, for there was no point. The only point now was to continue.

All around, men and women were falling. Smith looked up again, and counted - for he could still count - more than twenty *jezailchees*: each, it seemed, with more than one weapon, and a boy to load for him. The rate of fire was extraordinary given the nature of the weapons. For almost an hour, perhaps until they ran out of ammunition, the weapons flashed and smoked, until finally all was silent. Those who followed would have to pick their way carefully across mounds of bodies and through the sweet smell of blood and the freshness of snow and ice.

Thank God they are not here, thought Smith.

An hour or so later, Smith heard a familiar voice; perhaps any voice would have sounded familiar in that silence, but this was Captain Sturt.

'My dear Smith!' He sounded exhausted, and his throat rasped a little. 'It is good to see a face I know. What do you make of things now? Do we have a chance?'

Smith stared at him blankly. He felt like a drunk. It was strange, because drunks normally had so much to say, but he could think of nothing. There was a long silence as the two horses plodded side by side. Then Sturt spoke again, and his words were like lightning.

'I am surprised that you decided to bring your wife and child on this outing. You seem to enjoy these social excursions into the snow, dear fellow. However, I must reserve judgement on the wisdom of the expedition. You might have delayed until the weather was kinder.' He tried to laugh.

Smith felt that he must have misunderstood.

'It is not so, John - may I call you John? - after all, we are two old friends in the last days of our lives. No, it is not so.' He paused to recover himself. For they are safe in Kabul.'

'I am so sorry, William. I felt sure that you must have changed your mind on the matter. I have seen them, in a *kajava*. Halfway down the column. I saw Hassan peeping out. I am quite sure of it. I passed them shortly after we crossed the river the last time.'

Sturt turned and looked behind him.

Smith needed no further direction. He shook Sturt's hand and wished him well, turned his horse and trotted him back through the pass, dodging past horses and their lolling, vacant riders, past trudging Sipahees and even a British woman carrying a baby. Most looked at him as though he were mad to be heading back towards the blood.

The trotting of the horse and his working in the stirrups gradually warmed him a little, and his perceptions started to recover. He remembered the fallen camel, and realised with a painful convulsion that he had failed to recognise his own child.

Soon, he found the camel's carcass. He dismounted painfully and staggered almost unwillingly from his untethered horse. He stepped through the camel's blood and reached the *kajava*. He hardly dared to lift the flap but grasped it in his hand. It was rough and icy on the outside, but warm within. He looked inside, and two terrified pairs of eyes with large black pupils looked up at him.

Nasrin gasped with astonishment, and laughed. Hassan beamed and clapped his mittened hands. Smith put his face in his hands, in a strange paroxysm of joy and rage. He felt something surge in his heart. Then he heard himself speak.

'Why are you here? What in the name of God made you do this? Why have you brought Hassan into this murderous place? You promised me that you would stay where it was safe!'

She looked at him tearfully. Or was it just the cold? Her eyes darted nervously about his face.

'But dear William, I could not stay in that place. You saw what was happened. I heard what they want to do with me.' She looked down at the mop of tangled black hair. What they would do with Hassan?'

'Why? What did you hear?'

'Some want to kill us. A few, but enough. Even the new Shah, people say he want to put us in prison. Maybe …' Her voice cracked and she gave a trembling sigh. 'Maybe I never see you again! Better here with you dear William.' She drew a hand out of the *kajava* and touched his frozen glove.

He thought hard, his mind scanning the darkness in search of a small light. They could not stay with him, for to be near him would be much more dangerous than fending for themselves. Smith knew that he was more than likely to die, and he could not bear the thought of Nasrin or Hassan taking his lead ball for him. Even if he survived, what kind of life could he live after that?

He looked behind him. Still there were people trudging past. Few were able to lift their heads to look at him, until a small group of Afghan camp followers walked steadily towards him. There were many Afghans on the march: hundreds of them had helped Sturt to build the cantonments; others had worked as servants to British officers; others were half friend, half spy, keeping their ears to the ground, advising and warning, and eating and drinking with those who paid them for their help. Smith thought he recognised one of these men: was he one of Sturt's labourers? A carpenter? But he could no longer think.

The man came over to him.

'Terrible days, sir. You know this woman and child?'

'My wife and son, sir.'

The man looked surprised. So you are Mr Warburton, with the Afghan wife? And there was another man, I think. Smith?'

'I am Smith. My wife is the sister of Ahmet Qaderi. He has gone, and I do not know where. I have asked and asked, but nobody knows.'

'Ah, yes. I remember him. The poor grain merchant. A good man.' He put out his hand, and Smith shook it. 'You are worried, sir. I see it in your face. You are afraid for your wife and child. You think that they cannot travel with you, for you are a soldier. You have your duty, and to be with you is a danger. What can we do?'

Smith was silent.

'Sir, allow me to help you. To help your family.' He held out a hand, palm upwards, to encompass his companions, hardy-looking men in *lunghees*, thick *poshteens* and cloth footwear instead of leather boots or shoes. If only the British had thought of that!

'Sir, we know the passes well. We hope to live. Let your wife and child come with us.'

Smith did not have long to think. The cold was biting into him again, and numbing his brain. He thought he could trust these men, at least more than the *jezailchees* if Nasrin and Hassan were near him. So he let them take the *kajava* from the back of the dead camel; four of them carried it between them with Nasrin and Hassan still inside.

Smith kissed his son and then his wife.

'Goodbye, my darlings. We shall meet in Jalalabad, *inshallah*.'

223

He could say no more, and Nasrin's eyes darted across his face again. He shook the hand of his new friend, and watched as the *kajava* continued on its way. He mounted his horse and overtook them without a downward glance.

*

'Smith! Where the devil have you been? Thought you were dead. Whatever has happened to you?'

Smith stared at him. Who was he? Brigadier Sale? No, he must be in Jalalabad by now. Or was it Bombay? No, that was a long time ago.

'Stop gawping, man. Smith! Come to!' He felt himself being shaken by the shoulders.

Shelton? No. A memory came to him: Brigadier Shelton was at the front of the column. Sturt? No: neck wound. He remembered that.

Perhaps it was Mackenzie or Eyre.

'Sturt was telling me before he died... you know he's dead? He was telling me about your wife and child. Did you find them?'

That made Smith look at him properly for the first time. He was a little older than Smith, perhaps in his late twenties. Of course: it was Captain Lawrence.

'Smith!' He was shaken again. 'Did you find them? No? I am sorry, dear fellow. But there is always hope, even here. And listen, old fellow, Akbar Khan has been to see us. His miserable failure to protect us through the passes – or his deliberate treachery, who knows? – does not stop him from paying calls. We could hardly say that we were not at home. He wants hostages. As if the wounded left in Kabul are not enough. He wants hostages to make sure that we leave Kandahar and Herat and Jalalabad. He wants some officers, and he wants the women and children. You must go along with your wife and son.'

'No.' Still, Smith could not think.

'But don't you see? This is your chance. The three of you can survive. Come with us. If it helps us... some of us... to reach Jalalabad then why, it is your duty. Perhaps it will help to remove the *jezailchees*

224

from up there. Perhaps there will be food and water for the rest. Can you not see? If you do not do this, you will surely die, and so will your wife and son. You have a duty to them also. The army is doomed. We must save what we can. Here – take some brandy.'

Smith took two large gulps, turned his horse and headed back once more into the pass. He had never realised that they had come through it. He never drank brandy, but it left him completely untouched, except for a brief little warmth. And he was able, for a while, to think again.

The streams of people coming the other way became thinner and slower. There were wounded people, people with cut heads and crippled arms, people limping, and one with a missing hand. Still there was the occasional fire from the cliff tops, and Smith was hit below the eye by a fragment of rock. He hardly noticed.

And then he saw what he was looking for, and also what he dreaded. There was a small group of wiry Afghans, one with bloodied feet. He soon realised that they were the friends he had met earlier, but there were fewer of them now. How many, and how many fewer, he could not tell, for he was unable to count.

They recognised him immediately.

'Captain Smith.' The voice was dry. 'We so sorry, my friend. We can do nothing. The *jezailchees*. They shouted we are traitors and start to shoot. My two brothers, they are dead. We sorry. We cannot save your wife or child, and we cannot bury them in the snow and ice.' He turned to indicate the abysmal pass behind him. 'We leave them. One hour.'

Involuntarily, Smith carried on. He had to find them. Whatever had happened, he had to be certain before he left this place. And perhaps his friends were wrong. Perhaps... but he could not think of it.

Progress was very slow. His horse had to pick his way through the pass, unwilling to step on the corpses. Never had Smith seen so many bodies in the same place. He had been appalled by Shah Soojah's butchery at Ghazni, but that was nothing to this. Few seemed to have died of the cold; for no one would have stopped here by choice, and the snow was again stained with crimson.

Here and there, a body lay untouched and peaceful, but without clothes. Smith wondered at this: he had seen people burning their clothes for warmth, but here there were no ashes; it seemed that their clothes had been taken, either for warmth or for money.

*

He found her body half a mile back into the pass, in a place of the completest gloom, untouched by sun for most of the year. Already, before two o'clock, it was almost dark. The cliffs rose sheer to either side, and seemed to gather towards each other near the top.

He closed her pellucid eyelids, lifted her out of her blood and laid her in fresh snow. He brushed the snow from her clothes, and held her icy face in his hands. He kissed her forehead, as he had always done when he left the house, and remembered her kissing the hilt of his sword. Her warmth, her words, her smile, her touch... None of these entered his mind. Simply, she was not there. Braced against the cold, his mind all but empty, he staggered to his feet and looked around.

What of Hassan? He walked and stumbled and searched, scanning the bodies near and far. Of his son there was no sign.

The hard cliff faces echoed with his desperate yells. He could see nothing bar delirious visions of Hassan in the little house in Kabul, alternately snuggled into the red tunic and covered in his mother's blood.

Chapter Twenty-One

9th January 1842

S mith could remember nothing. The torture of the day before and the numbing cold had rendered him semi-conscious. His only thoughts were made of disconnected pictures from a life he had lost. He had no perceptions of the present and no understanding of his next steps. He had slept in the snow and somehow woken again, and now he wandered mute and aimless.

10th January 1842

He awoke to a jumble of voices. There were an English lady, chattering children and a crying baby. Two women chatted noisily; they sounded like soldiers' wives. There was a quiet, murmured Pashtu and the crackle of a fire. He smelt earth and straw and smoke, and was gradually brought to his senses completely by the smell of rice and ghee and meat. Was it lamb? He remembered eating lamb with the men before they had left.

There was a sudden silence and a wisp of chilled air. A powerful voice spoke. Smith opened his eyes at last.

'Welcome to you, my friends. Allah will be pleased that you live. Now it is I who can *pay the poor due, and care for the traveller and the widow and the orphan.*'

'Are we to understand that you are Akbar Khan?' asked the English lady.

'I am'.

'I trust, sir, that your care of us here will be better than your care of us on the march. You gave us your word...' she spat the words out, '... you gave us your word that you would protect us from the Ghilzyee chiefs. And you have led us to slaughter and starvation. For you, sir, I have seen children freeze to death.'

Smith looked up at Akbar Khan. Close-to, he was poised and intelligent-looking as much as fearsome. He had black, arched eyebrows, a fine, well-trimmed beard and a thin and lengthy moustache. He was dressed for the weather, in a *lunghee* with a bright red border, a thick scarf, a heavy *poshteen* and crude boots.

Yet it was the eyes that transfixed Smith, for they never wavered. Smith could imagine him both in battle and holding court.

'I did all that a man can,' he said solemnly. 'I do not want your destruction, because you are good people, and I also know that to destroy you would bring fire upon us. No people is beyond the desire for vengeance. What purpose would it serve to kill you all?'

'And yet you have done so! Twelve thousand people! British and Indian and Afghan! And you think none of us knows Pashtu? You think we know only Persian? You really think none of us knows that you ordered your men to stop firing in Persian, and to slaughter us in Pashtu? Yes, I know this. I know it from one I can trust. You will most surely be damned for it.' One of the soldiers' wives gave a little gasp of astonishment at the lady's use of such shocking language.

Akbar Kahn was silent for a moment. Smith noticed two children, a boy and girl, gazing at the great warrior in awe. Akbar Kahn looked back at them and Smith thought that in the flickering firelight he saw a glistening in those dark eyes.

'I say again, Lady Sale.' He paused. 'It was not what I wanted. Now what I must do is ensure that you are safe and warm and fed. You understand that this is necessary? You will not be safe if you try to go to Jalalabad now. And I need you here to be sure that your husband and his forces return to India. When they are gone, you will be released.'

And he bowed at Lady Sale and turned on his heel, leaving another icy blast.

'Wretched man!' hissed Lady Sale. She looked across at Smith, who was trying hard to raise himself on an elbow. 'It is easy for him to blame everything on the Ghilzyees. We know them of old, of course. We remember paying the money to keep the passes open, and we know how soon the passes were closed as soon as that poor fool Macnaghten ceased paying the levy. Yet I cannot credit Akbar Khan's claim that he bears no responsibility. Unless, of course, he is less competent than he seems.'

Smith could only stare back. He noticed that her sleeve was soaked in blood.

'I trust you have heard about poor Sturt?'

Smith nodded.

'My daughter and I...' she looked across at Emily, whom Smith had not noticed before. 'We thought that he might just survive. He had recovered so well. And then he came across Major Thain's horse and had to go back to seek his friend. He took a ball in the stomach. Lieutenant Mein here brought him back down, despite his own wound. Dr Bryce could see it was hopeless, although he did not tell us so. And dear John died some hours later.' She took her daughter's hand. 'We buried him. He was the only man I saw given Christian burial.'

Still Smith did not speak. He urged his mind to piece things together again, but he could still see only disconnected images: a body, a special body, one among thousands. A small child clapping his hands; and an empty snowbound space, empty at least except for the blood and the lifeless humanity and the boulders beneath the sheer cliff walls.

As his mind struggled, he stared about him. His eyes were taken by the flames, and then by the faces around him. He searched the faces of the children, and they shrank away from him.

*

Just a little more than six miles east of the end of the Khoord Kabul pass, near the village of Kalata, a shepherd zigzagged down the hillside towards his home. That morning, after checking on a sheep, he had headed towards the tops which looked down on the pass. It was curiosity which had brought him there; he had heard much of the *feringhees*, but had hardly seen them. He wanted to see their splendour for himself, for he was sure that it would be a splendid procession back to their homelands, wherever they were.

He had heard much hatred for the *feringhees*, and of course hatred was right. They should not be in his country, collecting taxes to keep their own king on the throne. They should not have killed so many at Ghazni. Yet he had also heard that they rarely executed people. But still they were wrong, since they were invaders.

Whatever his thoughts of right and wrong, he had been shocked by what he had seen below him in the pass. Of course the whole region was covered in snow, and a man would have to be mad to go out into that weather without a good lungee and a *poshteen* and properly clad feet. And plenty of nourishment of course, and the means to light a fire. Yes, these people must have been mad. He looked down at the corpses in their pools of brown blood, and saw that some of them had shed no blood at all, but seemed simply to have laid down and died. These were the bodies wearing no clothes, and the shepherd was surprised at the colour of their skin. For they were not all white as he had heard; many were brown, perhaps from just beyond the Hindu Kush. How strange!

There were a few *jezailchees*, Ghilzyees he supposed, picking from the bodies. There were right to do so, of course, for there was no point in allowing the dead to wear good clothes when the living could make use of them. And there would be money of course, and things that could be sold. Perhaps the better men would use the money to add to the poor due, and the less good would pay extra for what they bought.

Horrified, and perhaps also a little disappointed, he decided to head back towards Kalata. For it was cold, and his wife would be worried.

Just then, he heard a cry echo up the cliffs. It was a strong cry, a little cry of rage and terror. What was it? A woman? No: more like a child. His brow furrowed and his eyes wrinkled up as he peered downwards. The pass was still and apparently lifeless, but there was still that cry. Had he imagined it? He could not be sure, but just as he could not have left a bleating lamb, he could not turn his back now. He had to be sure.

He was a small man, but immensely strong. Just as he always did, he picked his way downwards, checking each placement of his nimble feet and steadying himself with his mighty grip. At last, he was at the bottom and stepping into a foot of snow.

Again he heard the cry. It was to his left, and surprisingly nearby. That was why he had heard it the first time: the sound had bounced straight up the hard rock face. He turned and saw a neatly folded *poshteen* wedged between a rock and the cliff face. It was well hidden from the path, but from his position next to the cliff a shepherd could see it clearly. Who would have hidden it there? And why hide it at all with a child inside it? It was surely madness. Yet there was much madness in this place.

Again there was a cry. The shepherd did not hesitate, but ran quickly to the parcel. He gently loosened the folds, and his hand came away sticky with blood. He found, wrapped up in the *poshteen*, a book and some papers and two strangely fashioned pieces of metal. He put them aside carefully. Another cry. More folds, and more blood. Surely the child could not survive this.

But it had, and it must be hours since it had been left here. Finally, the shepherd reached the warm bundle inside the *poshteen*. The face made him blanch, for it was covered in blood from a wound descending from the cheek. But the blood in the *poshteen* could not be the child's, for the wound was too small. He - for the shepherd soon realised that this was a little boy - really seemed quite well. Perhaps the cold had numbed his wounded face, for he reached up with his little hand and grabbed the shepherd's beard. In the midst of all that blood and death, the icy cliffs rang with the shepherd's laughter.

*

He took the child and tied him safely in his *poshteen* with the book, so that he could climb back up the cliff using both hands. He left the worthless steel in the snow.

The shepherd wondered what his wife would make of this gift. They had been married ten years, and still there was no child. His neighbours said all sorts of things, he was sure. And he himself had asked why Allah had not granted him this one gift, this life in a drop of blood.

Yet as he had become older, he had learned not to question his God, for he now knew that *Allah is the light of the heavens and the earth. His light is as a niche wherein there is a lamp. The lamp is in a glass. The glass is as it were a shining star. The lamp is kindled from a blessed tree, an olive neither of the east nor of the west, whose oil would have almost glowed forth of itself although no fire touched it. Light upon light. Allah guideth unto his light whom he will. And Allah speaketh to mankind in allegories, for Allah is knower of all things.*

And he was just a shepherd in the gloom, and he knew very little.

There were lamps in one or two of the houses as he entered the village. Perhaps they too were kindled from a blessed tree. He saw his wife outside the door, looking out for him. He called to her, and she ran to him. He saw at once that she was angry.

'Where have you been? It is almost dark, you stupid man!'

'I am sorry, my love, but I have something special. Let us go into the light, so that I can show you properly.'

Inside the house, he gave her the *feringhee* book and the *feringhee* letters.

'And what do you have in that *poshteen*,' she asked, for the *poshteen* had fallen still and silent as he had come down the hillside.'

'That is the best of all,' he said, and she shrieked as the little face was revealed to her.

'But who is it? Where did you find it? It cannot be ours, you wonderful, silly man!'

'Oh yes, he can. I have saved him, and what I have saved I can love and tend. This boy is surely an orphan, and you know what the Prophet tells us. *Righteous is he who giveth his wealth, for love of him, to kinsfolk and to orphans and the needy and the wayfarer and to those who ask, and to set slaves free.* We have no wealth, we have few kinsfolk. In this place there are few wayfarers. But what we have, we shall give to this child, Allah be praised.'

For the first time in months, she laughed. And for the first time in longer still, she took his face in her hands and kissed him.

'You are right,' she said. *'And verily thy lord will give unto thee so that thou will be content.'*

Chapter Twenty-Two

November 1855

In a small set of rooms on the top floor of a two-pair-of-stairs building in Montagu Street, Whitechapel, above a small baker's shop, a man sat looking into a dying fire. It needed more coal, or at least a good stirring with the poker, but the man looked puzzled, as though adding more coal was too much of a challenge. Once or twice he seemed about to stand, and then changed his mind, quite bewildered.

The room grew chill, for it was a wet and windy morning, and cold air was finding its way through the window frames and under the doors. Still the man sat, staring into the fire. It was only a little after eight, but he had been sitting here for at least two hours. Sometimes he smiled a little, and then caught himself and frowned again. He had in his hand a long clay pipe, which he sometimes raised to the mantelpiece as though making a toast.

The room was small, but the man had not managed to fill it. Most rooms like this were cluttered with ornaments, or pieces of small furniture, pictures and fire screens and vases, pokers and pots and pipe racks, a book or two, and the dozen other small things that told the story of a life.

Here there was very little, and looking into the man's eyes, a visitor might easily imagine that he must carelessly have left his life somewhere else. For there were no books to advertise his interests, no pictures of horses or cottages or lake-land scenes; nothing related to a profession or whatever else had been his life's work; no pictures of a wife or family; only two armchairs, one pipe, a small table with a decanter of sherry and a half-full glass. On the floor in front of the fire was a book, turned to page 18. There were a few oddments in the hearth: firedogs, a coal bucket and a toasting fork.

There was nothing on the walls, not even very much paint or paper, and here and there a few red bricks showed through. The door frames and wainscot had been varnished, but their sheen had dimmed with time. The paint on the window frames had dulled and peeled also, but the paint clumsily smeared on the edges of the glass still looked like new.

There was no rug, and the warmth of the bakery below rose up between the floorboards. Hanging on the back of the door was a large, thick, rough piece of cloth, somewhere between a shawl and a blanket. Sometimes on a cold evening the man put it over his knees. Even though he was not yet forty, he seemed old.

People rarely came to see him; those he had known best were spread far and wide, and even those who had come back to England came only occasionally. But perhaps, he thought, this would be a lucky day.

*

Later, there was a sharp rap at the door. The man jolted awake, and saw that the fire was out completely. He rose, a little shakily, took a long sip from the sherry, straightened himself as best he could, and called out.

'Yes. What is it?'

He knew what it was already, for the rap had been unmistakable. It was Mrs McCready, probably asking for her rent. He always paid his rent on time from his army pension, and she knew he had been an officer, but that did not change her suspicious nature.

'Visitors, Mr James. And don't forget...'

He opened the door, and was met by three faces he had never seen before. A police sergeant, a girl of 12 or 13, and a man who looked as though he might be from India, perhaps even from those wastes beyond the Khyber pass. James wondered whether he did not look slightly familiar, but how could that be?

He looked straight at Mrs McCready, and drew himself up still straighter.

'No madam. I shall not forget, no more than I ever have.'

'Thank you, sir, I'm sure. These are Sergeant Jackson and his daughter, Lucy. You did say Lucy, sergeant?'

'I did indeed, Mrs McCready. And this, Mr James, is Mr Qaderi'. James and Ahmet nodded at one another. 'Now, I should like to speak with Mr James, if you don't mind.'

Mrs McCready said nothing of Ahmet Qaderi, but it was clearly he who drew her interest.

'Most certainly, sergeant.' She fussed a little, as though wanting to be asked a favour, but under Jackson's stare, she eventually withdrew and clumped down the bare wooden staircase.

At last, they entered the room.

'I am very sorry that you have caught me so unprepared,' said Lieutenant James. 'I do not generally receive visitors, as I am sure you can see.'

'Please do not worry, sir.' Jackson sounded as he was: a sergeant addressing a lieutenant. 'I thank you for agreeing to speak with us.'

'I only hope that I can be of assistance,' said James. He quickly snatched up the sherry glass and placed it behind his chair, and then dragged a small wooden settle in front of the fire and invited Lucy and Ahmet to sit on it. Sergeant Jackson sat himself in the other armchair, and placed his palms, rather officially, on the arms.

James looked earnestly into Ahmet's face.

'Forgive me, sir. We were not properly introduced. I am George James, once of the 13th Light Infantry, and now... well, now I am as you see me.' He did not wait for a response from Ahmet, but went on, caught up in what he had to say. 'My current situation, I am pleased to say, is only temporary. I am now deciding upon my future arrangements. I have a number of opportunities, and I must choose between them.'

'Just so, I'm sure,' said Sergeant Jackson.

'Now then, will you take something to keep the cold out?' He realised that the fire had died entirely, and spent some time with the coal bucket, a wheezing pair of bellows and the poker. He looked at his visitors in turn.

'Hmmm? Perhaps a little toast? Tea? Rum and water? A little pineapple? I have nothing else at present, I am sorry to say. I have not yet got anything in.'

'Tea would be most kind, I am sure.'

'And for me also,' said Ahmet with a little bow of the head.

As he made the tea, James continued to talk, although to little purpose. Finally, he poured from the pot and beamed.

'This rather reminds me of the Afghan campaign,' he said. Four people in a tent, pouring tea. He looked out of the window. 'The weather was rather different, mind.'

There was a silence, finally broken by Ahmet.

'We came to speak of Afghanistan,' he said. 'We are looking for a man. A dear friend. We believe you may know of him.'

'Why, I knew many men in Afghanistan. I believe that most of them are dead. I trust you have been to Astley's circus, sergeant?'

'Of course, sir.'

'The tale of the wondrous Lady Sale shooting the natives?'

'Yes, indeed, sir! Mr Qaderi and I spoke of it just this morning.'

'There were many who did not find it such an adventure,' said James. 'History may perhaps tell the story of the 12,000 men, women and children who were slaughtered on that retreat, but it will not tell it often, at least not in England. We do not like to hear of defeat and death.'

'And you were there?' asked Ahmet. 'It is strange; I do not remember you. And I remember most of the officers in Kabul. Why, the man we seek was an officer in your regiment.'

James looked long and hard at Ahmet, whose face grew more familiar. He tilted his head a little, and frowned, but still the recognition would not bloom. He dropped a spoon on the floor and bent to pick it up again. He looked around at his visitors, who were clearly waiting for something.

'Ah … yes. It is a difficult story for me to tell,' said James. 'To cut it short, I was in Kabul only for a few weeks.'

'You were wounded?'

'In a manner of speaking, yes.' He put his hand on his heart. 'Although I did not shed any blood. Yet I saw blood, and plenty of it. What I saw at Ghazni would make a man's hair stand up on end. I would not speak of it in front of the young lady. In short, a dear friend of mine requested that I be sent to Jalalabad on leave, with a message of some sort to give my passage the semblance of honour, and this was granted. To my shame, I did not return, but was appointed to different duties in India. I was told that I lacked steel, or a backbone or some such.'

The tone of his voice had changed completely, and he could no longer look Ahmet or Sergeant Jackson in the eye. Instead, he smiled at Lucy and darted the toasting fork into the fire.

'A little cheese, perhaps?' Lucy shook her head. 'I soon tired of the army, and resigned my commission and returned to England. I had not seen London in nearly ten years. Such changes! Railways, Battersea, Bermondsey, all those places!'

'As I say,' said Sergeant Jackson patiently, 'we are in search of a man you may have known. There has been a murder, you see. And it is just possible…' Lieutenant James was staring into the fire again. The silence caught his attention, and he looked up. 'It is just possible, sir, that he … that is, Captain Smith, can help us to find an explanation.'

'Smith, did you say? Well, I'm blessed! Smith! Yes, I knew Smith. I spoke to him often, especially after duty. A good man. A good friend. Indeed, Smith it was who spoke to the Brigadier about me. We might say that he saved my life, if not my honour.'

'And when did you last communicate with him? Did you ever see him after you left Afghanistan? In Sikkur, for example?'

'Not in Sikkur, no. I left there before the hostages were freed.'

'Do you know where we might find him, sir? It is most important.'

'Why, I would think on his estate. He lives at Southlands, near Newdigate, not far from Redhill. You know where that is? Smith returned from Kabul in the winter of 1842, I believe. Terrible time he had of it. Perhaps my commanding officer was quite correct when he said that I lacked backbone. A few deaths, a few cold nights, a little blood, I was fit for nothing more. But Smith ... he lost his sergeant, you know. He lost his wife. And he believes that he lost his son, although that is unclear. I wrote to him you know, a dozen or more years ago.

'As I have said, even in the heat of the campaign, and even though he was very young, he was once able to care for me. I wanted to... hah...' His voice broke a moment, but he soon recovered himself. 'I wanted to recompense him somehow. At least, to give the thanks I owed him. I made my enquiries of the army in London, and received no immediate response. Still they had not forgiven me, I suppose. But then I received a letter from the elder Mr Smith, to whom my letter to Horse Guards had, I suppose, been forwarded. I was most surprised by it.'

'And why was that, sir?' Sergeant Jackson had often wavered between police officer and friend; now he was most definitely police officer again.

There was a long silence. Lieutenant James stood and walked slowly to his bookcase. Beneath the shelves there was a small chest of drawers and a little folding desk; he opened the desk and drew out a letter. At last, thought Ahmet, a sign of the man's past. James stood for a moment with his back to them, and when he turned again, his face was full of anguish.

'Please... take the letter and read it. And then you will understand.

Sergeant Jackson unfolded the letter and started to read it to himself. Molly reached across and tugged at his sleeve. 'Pa!' He looked down at her with a look that was supposed to be withering, but failed completely. She smiled and started properly.

'Sergeant Jackson, sir. Please may we hear the letter?'

The sergeant looked around him. Ahmet did not seem to mind, and James nodded quietly before looking down at the floor.

'Very well.'

*

Southlands,
Nr. Newdigate,
Surrey,
13th March 1844

Dear Lieutenant James,

Thank you for yours of 5th inst., in which you kindly enquired as to the health of my son, Capt William Smith, late of the 13th Light Infantry.

I regret to inform you that Capt Smith is at present in very poor health. When he returned from overseas duty, he was, as you may imagine, in very low spirits. Indeed, it took me some time to encourage him to speak to me at all, let alone of what was most concerning him. Eventually, some weeks later, he told me what I most feared; that his wife and child had been lost on the retreat from Kabul. There had been some news printed of the conditions on the retreat, and the horrors there can hardly be imagined. Even as I try to imagine my son in blinding snow and frozen waste looking for his loved ones, my own being is as though frozen to the core.

It now seems that there is little that can be done for him; he exists from day-to-day, sometimes helps his brother a little on the estate, although in silence, and just occasionally going further afield, but rarely where he will find his fellow men. Perhaps time will heal him, but I have always doubted whether time of itself is the healer that men claim it to be. William will need more than just that.

It may interest you to know that I have received a letter forwarded to me from India. It was written by a man claiming to be my grandson's Afghan uncle, who tells me that the boy is still alive. If that is the case, the English seems to be uncommonly good. Perhaps it was translated by some English clerk, or perhaps it is in some way fraudulent. I have no evidence either way.

In any case, I consider it to be quite impossible that the boy would have lived; those who have spoken to me since, and the reports I have read in newspapers, not to mention the memoirs of officers who survived, make it clear to me that no survival would have been possible in those passes for one so young.

Moreover, it is very much against my wishes that my son should be concerned in this matter, even if the boy is his own, which in any case seems impossible. As I have intimated, his well-being at present is at a low ebb, and his medical men have questioned whether any great degree of recovery is possible for him. To raise his hopes falsely would be cruel in the best of circumstances, but in the situation in which he currently finds himself it would be extremely dangerous to his chances of recovery.

I have instructed the War Office and the Regiment in Bombay that I wish my son to be left in peace; and whilst I am sure that your intentions are honourable and kind, I should be grateful if you would do the same.

Yours,
Charles Smith.

*

James looked up from the floor. He was now the centre of attention, and the room was silent again until he spoke.

'Then he lost his father, although at an advanced age, in 1845. His elder brother inherited the estate in Surrey. It carried an income, I believe, of some £2000 per annum. William helped to administer it, for the brother was not always the most... how shall I say?... the fittest of men, for all his brains. And then, just four or five years ago the brother died also, aged only in the early forties. Of course, the captain had no choice but to persevere. Yet he was a much reduced man. He lives there now; I saw him shortly after the death of his brother, for I thought that I could lend assistance and at the same time find a better situation for myself.

'But Smith seemed to feel the association between myself and his past. He would not meet me, and communicated with me only through his steward, one of his men from the old days. The steward was most civil, of course, but nevertheless directed me on my way. Perhaps it was loyalty and tender care on his part. Perhaps he never even told Smith that I had visited. That would certainly accord with the wishes in his father's letter. Or perhaps, having helped me once, dear Smith was unwilling, or unable, to help me again. I would not blame him for it.'

Ahmet Qaderi was now keen to enter the conversation. He had not felt warmly welcomed by James, who had made no enquiries about him. Surely James knew that he was an Afghan. Perhaps, like Smith, he wanted the old days buried.

'What did you know of the wife and son?'

'Smith married in Kabul, you know. I was never acquainted with his wife, of course. However, I was informed by others that she was most beautiful. She died on the retreat, and I have heard that Smith found her. Their son must surely have died also, but his body was never found. That is no surprise, in the circumstances.'

'It would not be strange,' said Ahmet. I have spoken to many who saw the passes soon after. Even when I came through more than two years later, I saw terrible things. What caused the most pain was the children. There were very many. So who would recognise Hassan?'

'My dear sir! You know his name! You knew Smith? And his wife and son?'

'Why yes. You have not asked me, sir, why I have come all the way from Bombay to see you. My name, sir, is Ahmet Qaderi. Captain Smith was married to my sister Nasrin. As you say, she was a most beautiful woman, and also a good one.'

'Gracious me! You are Ahmet Qaderi! Ahmet Qaderi the wrestler! Smith's man told me about you. You would be the boy's...'

'Uncle.'

'Uncle, why yes. But I still do not quite understand you, sir. What is the purpose of your coming to England?'

'Sir, the boy did not die. He lived, and is alive still. He is here in London, and the sergeant here knows where. It is my hope that Captain Smith and his son can be ...'

'Brought together? Reconciled?'

Sergeant Jackson drew himself up proudly. 'Just so, sir. But we also seek a murderer. A crewman on *Aurora* – the ship that the two genelmen from Bombay arrived on – was knifed in the docks. We believe there is some connection with Kabul.'

Lieutenant James looked from Ahmet to the sergeant and back again. Lucy smiled at his amazement.

'But why have you waited all this time? It must be, what? thirteen years?'

'There were two reasons, sir. First, I did not have the means to come to England until now. Now I am making good livings, and I must come to England for business. Second, I have written to ask of Captain Smith many times to the Regiment in India, and also to the War Office at Horse Guards in London. I had one short reply, from Sikkur, saying Captain William left the army. Nothing else. I do not know why. Perhaps writing to an Afghan merchant in Bombay was not ... usual. Often, I have thought of a grand man opening up my letter, and thought of the look on his face. But now I am here, I wanted to find what happen to him. For him and for his son there is a great treasure awaiting.'

'Indeed? A treasure? Smith never struck me as very keen on treasure. What do you propose to do?'

'It seems that we have little choice,' said Sergeant Jackson. 'This is too big an opportunity to let it pass by, begging pardon. We must take our chance, and hope that all will be well.'

It was getting dark, and James had moved to the window. He stood there with his back to them, looking out into the street.

'I quite agree,' he said. 'I wish you well, and pray that you are more successful than I was. How I wish I had known of this before.'

'That is hardly your fault,' said Sergeant Jackson. 'You did what you could. Now we must make fresh endeavours. Would you care to join us, sir?'

'Why, most certainly, Sergeant Jackson. I had so hoped that you would ask me. It will be most pleasant to be of service.' He looked at Ahmet. 'Will your friends be accompanying us also, Mr Qaderi?'

'My friends, sir?'

'Why yes, the two fellows in the street outside. Are they not your friends?'

Sergeant Jackson flew through the door, quickly putting his whistle to his lips, and they heard him rattling down the stairs and removing the door chain and bolts. Then they heard his whistle and the patter of feet on the pavement.

Soon, he returned, red and breathless.

'The sooner we get to Surrey, the better, he said. We shall meet you at Victoria station at nine o'clock sharp tomorrow. They all stood, shook hands (except for Lucy, who bobbed politely) and went down the stairs.

As they did so, Mrs McCready appeared.

'Is everything well, sergeant?'

'Yes, madam, I thank you. Mr James seems a fine man. I only hope that his new arrangements come to fruition shortly.'

'New arrangements, sir? Mr James has never told me of no arrangements. Mr James never has arrangements, of any kind. At least, not in the twelve years he's been with me. A good man, as you say sir, but not adventurous, like.'

*

In the street, Jackson wondered about the next day. He was surprised by his sense of loyalty to these people whom he did not know, and whose customs and habits were so very different from his own, but whose hearts seemed so very similar.

As they walked, Ahmet Qaderi seemed to be thinking deeply, and indeed he was. He was thinking of a way to express his admiration for the sergeant. Eventually, he found it.

'You do not know the Qur'an, Sergeant Jackson?'

'Er, not well, I must confess.'

'There are some beautiful verses in our Holy Qur'an, sergeant. And there is one which tells of the generosity of good men such as you and the mercy of Allah. *For lo, Allah wrongeth not even of the weight of an ant, and if there is a good deed, he will double it and will give the doer from his presence an immense reward.* One day, *inshallah*, you will find the reward for the good that you have done.

'Well yes, perhaps, sir. I am not sure that we shall ever know.' He seemed a little embarrassed, and quickly changed the subject. 'Now then, perhaps we should think of tomorrow. Not least, we must inform the young man in question of what we have found out, and of our plans. I shall head straight to Field Lane; perhaps you would be so kind sir, as to escort young Lucy home for me. It is not so very far, and Lucy knows the way.'

And Lucy took Ahmet's hand and started back towards the Whitechapel Road.

'One moment, sir. What shall I say to the boy? I don't wish to raise his hopes, like.'

'Why, sergeant, well... Just tell him treasure is safe. He know what that means.'

'Very well, sir.'

*

As the three figures receded, two more figures, one large and one smaller, watched them from their hiding place in the alley.

Chapter Twenty-Three

November 1855

That same Sunday morning, Mr Woodhouse had knocked on his parlour door, and Hassan had awoken immediately. Mr Woodhouse soon noticed that Tommy was missing.

'Now where is your young friend?' he asked.

'I not know, sir,' said Hassan. 'He not here when it dark early. I sorry sir for sleeping.'

'You have done nothing wrong, Hassan. And I am sure that young Tommy Jackson knows how to take care of himself, even in this part of the city.' For all that, Hassan thought that he looked worried.

They walked to Field Lane. It was a grim morning, with a white-grey sky and a drizzling mist. Muffled people stood in doorways, staring silently as Mr Woodhouse and Hassan walked quickly through the filthy streets. Here and there a child cried, or a stray cur barked.

There was no laughter and no speech, and there were only a few dull birds. When he thought of Bombay, Hassan often remembered his uncle's garden. It was a golden place, filled with frangipani and betel nut and a host of smells; and with birdsong. It was in that garden that he had learned the beauty of the Qur'an: *and Allah brought you forth from the wombs of your mothers knowing nothing, and gave you hearing and sight and hearts that haply ye might give thanks. Have they not seen the birds obedient in mid-air? None holdeth them save Allah. Lo! Herein, verily, are portents for a people who believe.*

Could Allah be in this place? Why did he not command the birds here also? Were there birds outside the Jacksons' house? Could his uncle see and hear them? He could not remember seeing a bird since he was on *Aurora,* except in cages on those dismal streets.

The drizzle turned to rain, light at first. As the sun rose, a little unwilling life sounded. A cough from an upstairs window; the soft lowing of cattle from Smithfield market; the crash of a door. Then, as they turned into Field Lane, Hassan flinched as a church bell tolled out. As the chime died, others rang in the distance at odd intervals. He had heard bells before, of course, in the distance at quarter hour intervals. But never so nearby, and never for so long.

Mr Woodhouse noticed Hassan's unease. 'I see you are disconcerted, Hassan,' he said. He saw Hassan's puzzlement. 'Forgive me. I mean that the bells are very loud to a newcomer.' He pointed into his ears, and Hassan nodded and smiled. 'You are more used to the *muezzin.* A more human sound, perhaps.'

Hassan held his fists to his mouth, trumpet-like, and nodded again. 'They all go to mosque? ' he asked.

'To the church, yes. At least, many do. Not as many as twenty years ago. Now there are not so many churches, and it is difficult to believe in God's mercy when your children die around you and you can hardly see the sun.' He saw that he had lost Hassan completely, and was glad of it. He took a large key from his pocket. Whatever Hassan had seen of the Field Lane Ragged School on the previous afternoon, and however dangerous things seemed, he was glad to arrive.

The school was quiet. Normally, even on a Sunday, Mr Gaskell would have opened up, but Mr Woodhouse was not sure whether this time he would return. He had resigned many times before, but had always come back for his pittance. However, Mr Woodhouse thought that this time may be different, for the children had never before gone so far as to hang him out of the window.

No sooner were they inside the building than there was a knock at the door. Mr Woodhouse clattered upstairs - he very rarely clattered anywhere - and looked down out of the window. He never just opened the door nowadays. Strange: it was a police sergeant. And yet it was too early for any further assaults on the building to have taken place! And it was a Sunday! Mr Woodhouse returned downstairs, finding Hassan at the end of the passage, as far from the door as he could get.

'It is nothing to worry about, Hassan. Just a visit from a friend, I am sure.'

He opened the door, and Sergeant Jackson stepped in, touched the rim of his helmet and asked to speak to a Mr Woodhouse, please sir. Hassan stood silently.

'Why, I am Woodhouse. How may I help?'

Sergeant Jackson looked over Woodhouse's shoulder at Hassan.

'I have news about the young gentleman, sir. Young Hassan Qaderi here.' He pointed.

'Why, Hassan. Do you know the sergeant?'

Hassan beamed. 'I know him, sir, yes. He Tommy father.'

'Of course,' said Woodhouse. 'For some reason, I was thinking of a soldier.'

The sergeant drew himself up and looked official. 'May we speak in private, sir? It concerns the boy, sir. And at present, sir, the less he knows the better.'

'Why certainly, Sergeant. Let us go to my study. But surely Hassan can be with us. After all, he is unlikely to understand a great deal of what we say. Let me take your cape.'

'Thank you, sir.' He shook the drizzle out at the doorway, and handed the cape over.

Hassan stood silently in the corner of Mr Woodhouse's study, but could understand little of the conversation. He understood most of the words, but not what they meant. It seemed like the riddle of a jinn. The treasure was safe, the sergeant had said, and the story would be finished tomorrow. There was no rush; indeed, it may be better to keep Hassan hidden for another day. And Tommy would cop it later, he said. Then he had put his cape back on, touched the edge of his helmet with a slight nod and bade Mr Woodhouse good day.

Whatever could it mean? It was strange that the idea of treasure kept coming up. His uncle had mentioned it in his letter, and occasionally since. But surely it was just a story? Or was it? Khodar had talked of it, and now the sergeant had spoken of it most mysteriously. Was that why uncle Ahmet had brought him to London, to find some treasure? Why would he not tell him so?

Mr Woodhouse busied himself in the pantry, and brought back a mug of hot cocoa and a slice of toast with butter and cheese.

'You must be hungry,' he said, and patted his stomach.

Hassan smiled to himself. Why did everybody think that he understood no English at all?

'I understood nothing of what the sergeant said, although he seems a good man.' Woodhouse busied himself with odd items on his desk, and spoke constantly to himself, then to Hassan, then to some absent person. 'After all,' he continued, 'not everybody in London would have walked so far for a stranger. Not even a police sergeant. You saw the mud on his boots, and the rain had got into his hair.' He made a raining motion by wiggling his fingers above his head. Hassan nodded enthusiastically to show that he had understood.

'For it is as the book of Matthew says: *Then shall the King say unto them on his right hand, Come, ye blessed of my Father, inherit the kingdom prepared for you from the foundation of the world: For I was hungry and ye gave me meat: I was thirsty, and ye gave me drink: I was a stranger, and ye took me in: Naked, and ye clothed me: I was sick, and ye visited me: I was in prison, and ye came unto me.*

'*Then shall the righteous answer him, saying, Lord, when saw we thee hungry, and fed thee? or thirsty, and gave thee drink? When saw we thee a stranger, and took thee in? or naked, and clothed thee? Or when saw we thee sick, or in prison, and came unto thee?*

'*And the King shall answer and say unto them, Verily I say to you, inasmuch as ye have done it to one of the least of these my brethren, ye have done it to me.*

'In his way, the sergeant has done the work of God.'

Hassan looked at him blankly, and Mr Woodhouse smiled back.

There was another knock at the door, this time rather urgent, perhaps because the rain was now falling heavily.

Mr Woodhouse put on a strange voice, rather as Mr Dickens had. 'Why, bless my soul, another wisitor.'

Again Mr Woodhouse clattered upstairs to look out of the window, and then came back down again to open the door.

It was Tommy Jackson. 'Lor, what a day! Beg your pardon, Mr Woodhouse.'

Mr Woodhouse was suddenly stern 'Now where did you go to last night? I have had people out looking for you this morning. Your father is most displeased.'

'Sorry, Mr Woodhouse, sir. But I had an idea, and I had to do it straight away, like. And I've got news, sir. '

'An idea, Tommy? Pray tell me. I shall be most interested to hear it.' He looked doubtful.

'Well, sir. It's them two gentlemen, sir. I couldn't help but think, sir, that maybe they'd be hangin' around outside your 'ouse. So I went out, and sure enough, there they both was. 'Ow they found us, I shouldn't like to guess. But they was there, I saw 'em clear as day. Soon as they saw me, they made 'emselfs scarce, like.'

'I am most concerned to hear it,' said Mr Woodhouse. 'We must hope that we can avoid trouble. I wonder whether they know of Sergeant Jackson's interest? More to the point, do they know you are here?'

'Dunno, sir.'

'I shall send somebody straight away to tell the sergeant what has happened.'

'Please, sir, lemme go, sir!'

'No, Tommy, I need you here. But you may fetch Malone. Run quickly.'

'Where to, sir?'

'Why, Hosier Lane, of course. Know where that is?'

'Think so, sir.'

'There must be no *think so* about it, Tommy. Down Victoria Street, as though you are heading for Blackfriars Bridge. When you get to Holborn Hill, left into Snow Hill. Keep your wits about you there, Tommy. Halfway up Snow Hill, Hosier Lane is to the right, by the hospital. The Malones live at number 22, upstairs room. Now, quickly - off you go!'

And Tommy was gone in a flash.

'Hassan, let me give you a book for a moment. You may find it difficult, but it will keep you from worrying.'

'Thank you sir, I try.'

Mr Woodhouse left Hassan alone. The study was cold, and whilst it was clean and tidy, Hassan could hear noises from beneath the floorboards. He looked around him, and saw odd ornaments: an ornate inkwell, a glass paperweight and a cheap vase. There were two pictures: one of a splendid man with grey hair, a silver beard and a strange white collar, and the other of a young woman, perhaps very beautiful but painted very simply. The rest of the room was filled with books. Every wall was covered with shelves, even below the one window, leaving just enough space for the door they had come in by and another, lower door on the other side of the room by the window. The ceilings were quite high, but there was a small ladder so that Mr Woodhouse could retrieve books from the top. Hassan did not touch the books, remembering how Mr Dickens had spoken to him in Tavistock Square. He just gazed, and tried to read the golden letters on the spines.

Still Mr Woodhouse did not return. Perhaps he was looking for just the right book. Soon Hassan grew bored. He looked out of the window and rattled the handle on the second door. It was open, and he peered out. The building opened into a tiny cobbled yard, with high brick walls on the other three sides and another door with a large key in it which seemed to lead into a narrow street. The rain had stopped, and Hassan took a step onto the cobbles.

He leapt in fright.

For there, his head just looking over the wall, was Khodar. Hassan could just make out the top of another turbaned head next to him. Aziz seemed to have his back to the wall, as though keeping watch. As always, Khodar's attempts at friendliness made him all the more sinister. He showed his few teeth in a forced grin and spoke to Hassan in Pashtu.

'So there you are, my friend!'

There was a scratching on the outside of the wall. Soon Aziz's face appeared. He looked straight at Hassan and gave him a frightened smile. His feet scraped on the wall again, and he was gone.

Hassan's nerves made him speak a little too loudly.

'Why have you come to see me again? Why do you keep following me wherever I go? What do you want with me? Are you going to kill me?'

'My dear friend! Why would I want to kill such a dear friend as you, and such a young gentleman? Did you not know that you are a gentleman? With a fortune? Indeed, you are a very wealthy young man. Or you soon will be if the treasure that was taken from Kabul comes into your hands. What is it, this treasure?'

'I know nothing about treasure,' said Hassan. 'Perhaps you should ask my uncle, Ahmet the wrestler. Or perhaps you should ask Sergeant Jackson. I am sure that he would be interested to meet you. He wants to ask you about the murder in the docks. Certainly, you were very nearby, and you knew the man.'

Aziz's tousled head moved as he took a step away from the wall and turned. He seemed to have forgotten again that he was on lookout duty. He looked silently at Hassan, and seemed to cower away from his cousin.

The door behind them clicked open. Hassan stepped away from the wall and turned to see Mr Woodhouse with a book in his hand.

'Hassan! Why are you out here? I have a responsibility for your safety, which I cannot meet if you must be out of doors on a whim. Now, go back inside straight away.'

Hassan pointed behind himself at the wall, and turned to look at Khodar and Aziz. But again, they had flitted from view.

*

Back inside the school, Hassan read his book. Or rather, he looked at it. He might have understood had the language been spoken to him, but today he struggled to make out the letters. It was hard to tell what it was about; for there were no pictures, and the cover was plain, and the print was tiny.

Mr Woodhouse sat at his desk, polishing the lessons for his Sunday school which would start in half an hour. Still Malone and Tommy Jackson had not returned; Tommy should have been back by now, and yet again Mr Woodhouse was a little worried. Perhaps there had been some delay at Malone's rooms, or perhaps Tommy had been distracted by something. After all, he did seem to be frequently distracted.

Mr Woodhouse lit a pipe. Hassan coughed, and Mr Woodhouse opened a small casement window. As soon as he did so, a murmur came into the room. It grew gradually louder, until Hassan realised what it was. Shouting. A crowd shouting! Soon Mr Woodhouse noticed it too, and put his pen back in the inkwell and his face into his hands. In no time, they could both hear the clash of metal on metal, and the shouting grew to a rhythmical chant. They could not make out the words, but Mr Woodhouse felt sure that it was coming this way.

'Hassan, stay here, I beg you. It is not safe outside, do you hear?'

'Yes, sir. Stay here.' And he pointed at the floor.

Mr Woodhouse went out of the back door, and Hassan heard him opening the door into the alley. The noise was now bouncing off the walls and roofs. Soon, Mr Woodhouse came back.

'Quickly, Hassan, come and see.'

Outside, at the end of the alley on Cowcross Street, a crowd had gathered, made up entirely of children. Hassan recognised Malone, Pips and Tunks, and many of the others from the school, but most were strangers. In the middle, however, was Tommy Jackson, and Hassan was hardly surprised. Tommy started shouting, and the noise was quelled.

Mr Woodhouse walked slowly towards the crowd, and then turned back. He would rather have Hassan with him than leave him alone in the house.

Hassan wondered why the banging and shouting had suddenly ceased, and felt half prepared to run.

''Assan! Look who I found.' He beckoned Hassan towards him.

It was Aziz, who lay on the ground and looked up in terror at the faces around him. He looked pleadingly at Mr Woodhouse, who with a sudden determination pushed into the centre of the crowd, put out his hand and helped Aziz to his feet. He looked furiously at Tommy Jackson.

'What in the Lord's name has happened here?' he snapped.

Many of the children spoke at once.

'Si-LENCE!' He waited for a moment, looking into the eyes of each of the thirty children in turn. He had often said that the eyes were as windows to the soul, and he wondered, not for the first time, about the souls he had in front of him.

'Malone. Kindly tell me what has happened.'

'Well, sir, Tommy Jackson bangs on our street door, and then he comes up the stairs and bangs on the door to our rooms...'

Mr Woodhouse grew impatient.

'Yes, Malone, I'm sure he did. What happened in the street?'

'Yessir, it did.'

'What did, Malone?'

'Well, we come back up 'Osier Lane, like. And jest as we gets back to the main road, Tommy grabs 'old of me 'n pushes me in a doorway. I wasn't 'aving that, was I? I 'ardly knows him. What would me father say?'

'But sir, it weren't like that. I didn't want them to see us,' protested Tommy.

'I'm quite sure you didn't!' said Malone, with narrowed eyes.

'I didn't want 'em to see us 'cos they're dangerous, ain't they? One of 'em's got a big knife.'

'Tommy!' Now Mr Woodhouse was getting really impatient. He spoke very slowly. 'Please tell me ... how it came to be... that this gentleman found himself ... on the floor ... surrounded by twenty noisy people looking as though he has had the life almost frightened out of him. Who is he, and what ... has ... happened?'

'We saw 'em, like I said, like, on the corner of 'Osier Lane.'

'But who are they?' Woodhouse shouted.

At last, Hassan found his voice. He pointed.

'He Aziz, sir. We came together from Bombay. On *Aurora*. He here, this morning.'

'Aha! So here is one of the gentlemen behind the wall?'

'What, they was 'ere this morning? Well, I'm damned!'

'Kindly do not use that foul and blasphemous language here,' snapped Mr Woodhouse.

'Sorry, sir,' muttered Tommy.

'Now, we shall remove this gentleman into the school where he will be safe. Where is his friend?'

'Run-off,' said Malone. 'Funny thing is, we weren't even trying to nab 'em. This lot...' (she pointed at the unfamiliar half of the crowd) 'was coming along, makin' a racket. I was finkin' they was on their way to the school again, to smash it up, like. And then from where we was hiding,...'

'It were my idea, sir,' said Tommy. I just kind of shouted, like. *THIEVES*, I shouted, and this crowd, and the school crowd, just kind of chased the pair on 'em together. One of 'em, the biggun, the clever one I reckon, saw us first and made a beeline. This one just kind of stood there, gawping, not knowing what to do. By the time he started running, 'e was too late, and we caught 'im easy.'

'Very well,' said Mr Woodhouse. 'Malone, did Tommy Jackson tell you about your errand?'

'No, sir. 'e were just about to, when he decided to grab me and pull me in the doorway.' She looked at him, still resentful.

'I would like you, Malone, and you must tell your father first, to go to Evans Street, just off Commercial Road, and visit Sergeant Jackson. People will know where he lives. You must tell Sergeant Jackson that we have his suspect - or at least, one of his suspects. It is best he comes here to speak to him.'

'Yes sir!'

And she was gone, looking back twice at Tommy.

'Why can't I go with her, sir?' asked Tommy.

'Because at present it is better for you, and quite possibly for Miss Malone, that you stay here,' said Mr Woodhouse with a very slight smile.

*

Mr Woodhouse, Hassan, Sergeant Jackson, Tommy and Aziz were crammed into the study in Field Lane. Mr Woodhouse had made tea, and had even given them a few small cakes which had been baked by the girls on Friday. Even after two days, they were just edible.

Aziz had at first been terrified, and this had not changed much during Sergeant Jackson's first few questions, which were translated by Hassan.

'You are in great danger, sir. Your life hangs by a thread, as your body may soon do.' He put his hands to his own throat to make the point. 'Does he know hanging?' he asked.

'Oh, yes, sir. He know it well.'

As though to prove the point, Aziz opened his eyes wide and shook his head gently.

'Now, then. Tell me where you are from.'

'He say Kabul and Bombay on *Aurora*.'

Why are you here?'

He thinks for trade, with his cousin. They have goods.'

'Thinks? Does he not know?'

'He says yes, for trade.'

'What did you do when you got off the boat?'

Now there was a hesitation.

'They say goodbye to their friends, they pray, and then they look after their goods.'

'And where did they sleep?'

'He not remember, sir.'

'Ask him to tell me about his lodgings. The room he slept in.'

'He not remember, sir.'

Sergeant Jackson raised his eyebrows and levelled his gaze at Aziz. Aziz soon faltered, and started to talk again.

'Aziz and Khodar not sleep, sir. They stand in the street.'

'And where was this?'

'He not remember.'

'Very well. Ask him to describe the street. And no more delays!'

Aziz answered hesitatingly, pointing at Sergeant Jackson as he did so. As he spoke, Hassan looked across at Sergeant Jackson, his mouth slightly open.

'He say they watch your house.'

'My house? Why so?'

'He don't know, Mr Jackson. He says it his cousin's idea. His cousin is seeking treasure.'

Sergeant Jackson smiled knowingly, and Aziz smiled too. And then the smile was withdrawn abruptly, and Sergeant Jackson levelled his gaze again.

'So,' he said slowly. 'You have followed Hassan Qaderi and his uncle Ahmet from the dock to Evans Street. You have followed Hassan Qaderi and Tommy Jackson around London. Indeed, it seems that you have followed him all the way from Bombay. You have threatened Mr Dickens, one of our finest citizens, with a great big knife. Most of this I already know.' Hassan translated, but Sergeant Jackson left a long silent gap to give his next words the greater impact, all the while looking fixedly at Aziz. 'I said that you may hang.' As Hassan translated, Sergeant Jackson fixed his eyes on the bridge of Aziz's nose, and then he hesitated again. Aziz, like a fish played on a line, had had the freedom of a few smiles and even a laugh, but now he was being reeled in again, and the colour drained from his face.

'I am sure you know that a man died on the dockside the night you arrived. From *Aurora*, he was. A member of the crew, I am led to believe. Killed with a knife, quite a large knife, I'm told. Tell me what you know about this. And tell me about your cousin.'

Aziz started to panic, looking from face to face, and between the faces at the wall behind. He had trouble finding his words, but once he found them they came spilling forth in a torrent. And he told the whole story of the letters in Kabul, the search for Hassan, the story of the treasure and finally the killing of the little Indian.

'He not see the Indian die,' said Hassan. 'His cousin tell him later. I hear him, by the mighty mosque. Aziz not want the treasure, but his cousin frighten him. Khodar... Aziz thinks Khodar kill the Indian. Indian know about the treasure.'

'Tell him if they were both looking for the treasure, they are both to blame. And like as not, they will both hang. They will go before a judge, there will be a short trial, the judge will put on his black cap, they will go to prison, and then they will be taken from that place and hanged by their necks until they are dead.'

Hassan translated as best he could, and Aziz went to his knees, put his face in his hands and wept. Sergeant Jackson sat back in his chair and watched for as long as he could bear it.

'But...' said Sergeant Jackson, and to Hassan's surprise, laid his hand on Aziz's quaking shoulder. 'But there is another way. A better way, I should hope. Khodar must be brought to justice, and Hassan and young Tommy must be made safe. If Aziz can assist us in the matter, perhaps it will be the better for him.'

Sergeant Jackson reached into a pocket and took out two pieces of paper. He unfolded them and shook them to attract Aziz's attention. Aziz looked up with a pale, tear-stained face and red eyes. Jackson pointed at the writing on the paper.

'Treasure,' he said simply. 'Give Khodar this. It shows where the treasure can be found. There is even a railway timetable to help him. And tell him nothing else. For if the two of you try to escape, you will be run to ground, and both of you will surely hang.' Hassan translated, and as he did so Sergeant Jackson reached out a hand and pulled Aziz to his feet. 'Now go to your cousin.' And he pointed at the door to the yard. They heard the gate shut with a click.

Sergeant Jackson sat forward again, looked at Hassan and then at Mr Woodward, and raised his eyebrows. 'Well, then. What a to-do. I never heard of such a thing. Perhaps I should speak to the inspector. What do you say, Mr Woodhouse?'

'I am sure, Sergeant Jackson, that you are handling matters most admirably. I trust that you will be heading into Surrey tomorrow? For you know Hassan, and I judge that you are trusted by his uncle. Surely, it is your business.'

'Yes, I believe you are right, sir.' He thought for a moment. 'What I find difficult to fathom, however, is why Mr Aziz, in a strange land, should suddenly get so honest.'

They sat in silence for a moment.

'What do you think, Hassan? Why did Aziz tell the truth so easy?'

'He frightened, sir.'

'Perhaps,' said the Sergeant. 'Of being captured, of prison and hanging, of course, in a strange land'.

'And being alone, taken from his cousin', said Hassan. 'And also of Allah. *Allah knows everything in the heavens and on earth. When three meet, he is the fourth and when five meet, he is the sixth. He is always with them, and at the resurrection, he tell them what they did.* So Aziz fear Allah. When he dead, he want to be in the garden. So in our holy book, we learn not to hide the truth.'

'I am a little concerned about his prospects, Sergeant,' said Mr Woodhouse. 'Will he really escape the gallows? And if he does, surely he will spend many years in some godforsaken gaol?'

'That's as maybe. We shall need to know how closely he followed his cousin, and how far he supported his dreadful actions. Indeed, whether he took part in them. I think it unlikely, for he does not seem to me to be either a great thinker or a man of action.'

Hassan, of course, had always rather liked Aziz; it was Khodar with his familiarity and closeness who repulsed him. He remembered what he had learned from his uncle Ahmet: *those who do real deeds and afterward repent and believe - lo! For them, afterward, Allah is forgiving and merciful.* Hassan could only hope that for Aziz the garden, despite all its wonders, was some way off.

Chapter Twenty-Four

March 1844

I t was springtime in Kabul. Fruit trees were coming into bloom, and the shepherds tended their teeming flocks of goats in lighter clothing.

Once again, the city had settled. In April 1842, three months after the slaughter in the frozen passes, Akbar Khan and his army had been heavily defeated. The hostages he had taken had been rescued by General Sale and returned to India. In September, General Nott had swept down from Kandahar with his Army of Retribution to wreak a bloody vengeance on the Afghan chiefs, and reduced large parts of the city to ruins.

Now, even the few sick and wounded British had left Kabul, and much of the city had been roughly repaired with the dun-coloured mud bricks. They had had a better harvest, and fewer mouths to feed, so now there seemed to be plenty. The orchards had been largely untouched, and piles of peaches and plums were wrapped in the stores. The markets, now vibrant again, were splashed with colour and the smells of bread and meat and spices hung lightly in the air. Today, the sun had warmed Kabulis' backs, and their senses had been awakened as if by hope. All in all, they were glad to be free again.

Early in the afternoon, a man walked steadily along the Jalalabad Road, and wondered what he might find ahead of him.

He had not been here for more than two years; he had no idea whether he would be welcomed as a traveller, or flayed alive as a traitor. He was reminded of a verse from the Holy Qur'an, and spoke it aloud.

'Unto Allah belongeth whatsoever is in the heavens and whatsoever is in the earth. He knoweth that which is in front of us and that which is behind us, while men encompass nothing of his knowledge save what he will allow. His throne includes the heavens and the earth, and he is never weary of preserving them. He is the sublime, the tremendous.'

So a small part of the man's imagination was ready to accept his fate. Yet at the same time, he lived in hope.

*

Soon the man had reached the Jalalabad Gate. He walked through the narrow streets, unchallenged. A woman at a stall nodded to him, and a man gazed perplexedly after him. Had they recognised him? Surely somebody would know him. What would happen when they did?

He walked on, looking straight ahead and often into the eyes of strangers. He walked up the steep slope to the Balla Hissar, and rested for a moment in the shadow under the walls. An Afghan guard watched him, but again there was no challenge. He had planned what he would say to gain admission; and for the thousandth time he rehearsed the words that he would use in front of the Dost Mohammed and Akbar Khan.

He walked through the portico, and at last he was spoken to by a man with a diagonal scar on his chin which was partly covered by a full red beard. He had deep brown, honest eyes.

'Where are you going, my friend? This is not a place for you.'

'I wish to see the Dost, and Akbar Khan if they are here. I believe that they are here, for I have been told so by many on my journey.'

The guard roared with laughter, but his humour soon faltered. The other man did not divert his gaze. He was evidently serious.

261

'And who are you, who wishes to see our King? I can see that you have travelled far.'

The man hesitated, and this gave his words an extra weight.

'I am Ahmet Qaderi. I have important business with the Dost.'

The guard showed a flicker of recognition and called to a boy who soon ran from within.

'Tell the vizier's man that the Dost has a visitor. Perhaps an important visitor.'

*

An hour later, having been kept waiting for a suitably dignified length of time, Ahmet Qaderi entered the audience room of the Dost through a high archway framed with bright red cloth. Around the room were guards, most armed with a variety of swords and daggers, and a few with *jezails*. Here and there were serious-looking but unarmed men, all standing as still as stone. The Dost sat on cushions on the floor, one hand on his thick grey beard. He was dressed finely, but without extravagance, in an immaculate light blue turban and gently brocaded coat. A younger man stood above him dressed in blue, and immediately Ahmet knew that this was Akbar Khan. Akbar seemed to suspect a threat, for he stiffened as Ahmet approached.

Ahmet Qaderi bowed low and silently, then straightened and looked the Dost in the eye. This was a dangerous tactic, but after much thought Ahmet had decided it would be necessary. He wanted to be both respectful and strong. He waited with an absolute stillness as the King surveyed him. Some of his attendants looked a little nervous. Finally, the king spoke.

'So you are a wayfarer from Jalalabad,' he said. 'Why did you not come to see me in Jalalabad, since I have been there for so long?'

'Because, Highness, my business concerns Kabul. What I seek is nearby, I hope. I beg in the sight of Allah that you will help me to find it.'

There was another silence. The Dost gently lifted a hand and nodded, and Ahmet continued.

'Sir, I seek my nephew, my sister's son. I pray that he is still alive after the slaughter in the passes two years ago. I have not seen him since, and I wish to find him, or to speak to one who saw him die so that I know he is in the Garden.'

He stopped as though waiting for a further question, but there was none.

'My nephew is Hassan Qaderi. Perhaps some would call him Hassan Smith. He is the son of Nasrin Qaderi, my sister, who married an Englishman in the eyes of Allah. Hassan's father was Lieutenant William Smith of the *feringhee* army. The three of them left here three winters ago. Before the slaughter in the Khoord Kabul, Jugdulluk and Tezeen.' He paused, and his eyes passed over his attentive audience. 'Hassan was then two years of age, or thereabouts. So now he will be four years of age. He has dark hair, like his mother's. I can tell you nothing more, for I have not seen him since I left Kabul before him.'

'To go to Jalalabad. As you have said. Why?'

'I had enemies here, sir. Enemies who wanted me dead. Perhaps they still want their vengeance. My life is in their hands, or in yours.'

He paused again, and this time he was determined to wait for the Dost to speak.

'And the boy's mother? Where is she?'

'She is dead.'

The Dost softened, almost imperceptibly. His eyelids dropped just a little, and the corners of his mouth relaxed. He looked up at Akbar Khan and spoke crisply but quietly. Ahmet noticed the similarity between the two men, and felt a close bond between them. The younger man bowed to the older as Ahmet had done, and remained silent.

'I shall entrust this to you, my dear son, for *Allah will care for those who believe and do good works: such are rightful owners of the Garden under which rivers flow. They will live there for ever. And remember, Allah chooseth for his bounty whom he will, and Allah is of infinite bounty.*'

'Thank you, my father and king. May Allah bless you also, for you have cared for the orphan and poor, and you have given your bounty. I shall do my duty to you, as you shall command me.'

263

It was now that Ahmet needed his greatest strength. The moment had come sooner than he expected, for he had not expected Akbar to be with his father.

'Highnesses, I came through those same passes to reach here,' he said. 'Even now, what I saw can barely be described. I am sure that you have seen it too. Perhaps, unlike me, you saw the blood in the snow shortly after it happened. Perhaps you saw the dead women and children being eaten by birds. I did not see these things, and that is why I did not know what happened to my nephew Hassan. I pray that you will tell me, sir, if indeed you know.'

A shadow passed across Akbar's face, and his eyes glistened a little. When he spoke, his voice sounded tight and dry.

'Indeed, Allah commands that we give unto orphans their wealth, and exchange not the good for the bad in our management of it, nor absorb their wealth into our own wealth. Lo! That would be a great sin.' There was no pride in the words; no righteousness. Rather, a sadness which was something like a quiet grief. 'I shall ask my chiefs to pass the words to their peoples, and I trust that we shall find out about the boy, for good or bad.'

'I thank you sir.

In the name of Allah, the beneficent, the merciful.
Praise be to Allah, Lord of the worlds,
The beneficent, the merciful.
Owner of the day of judgement.
Thee alone we worship, thee alone we ask for help.
Show us the straight path,
The path of those whom thou hast favoured;
Not the path of those who earn thy anger nor of those
who go astray.

When shall I return to you?'

'There is no need to return, Ahmet Qaderi, for there is no need to leave. The wayfarer will be tended to, and whilst you rest enquiries will be made.'

It had been easier than Ahmet had dared to imagine. As he laid his head down that night in his comfortable room, after a meal of lamb and peaches and cool water, he slept the sleep of the just.

*

Late the following afternoon, Ahmet sat in a small courtyard. He smelled hibiscus and distant cooking, and felt the sun on his face.

He remembered the letter he had sent, translated for him by a friendly clerk, from Jalalabad to Captain William Smith, c/o the 13th Light Infantry at Sikkur. He asked only for news of his sister, his friend and his nephew, and sent polite best wishes to those he had known.

In reply, a letter had arrived some weeks later over the signature of a Major Collins. The letter started with the usual formalities, but the next words were shattering.

> *Captain Smith identified the body of his wife shortly before being taken hostage by Akbar Khan in January 1842. There is reason to believe that Hassan Smith, even in the absence of his body, is also deceased.*
>
> *Most regrettably, Captain Smith, who has not been in the best of health, has resigned his commission and returned to England.*
>
> *It is most unlikely in the circumstances that Captain Smith will have any future connexion with Afghanistan, or that he will wish to be reminded of his experiences there.*

*

At dusk a week or so later, Ahmet Qaderi heard the door open behind him. He turned to see Akbar Khan, dressed this time in plain grey and shiny English boots. Ahmet stood immediately and bowed.

'You seek a young boy, four years of age.'

'Yes, Highness. My nephew.'

'There are many boys of that age in this country. And also there were many who died'.

Akbar Khan waved at Ahmet's chair, and they sat down opposite one another. There was a long silence, as though Akbar was searching for words. Ahmet looked at him carefully, daring for this moment to see him as an equal. Akbar looked aimlessly up at a wall, perhaps tracing the fine cracks that were growing on it. His throat was exposed, and Ahmet saw him swallow.

'You know that I never wanted that. No man would want to kill children. Not even the children of his enemy, for such a man would soon find his own people against him. And what of my enemy? You think that I wanted them to be killed also? I wanted them to be gone, that was all. You did not see how I bargained and argued with the chiefs. I wanted their safety. But you saw what happened in the passes. You saw it as you came back here from Jalalabad. I saw it myself as it happened. I swear to Allah, there was nothing I could do. I had no power over the Ghilzyee chiefs, and they were full of rage.

'And you must understand that rage. The passes are in their territory, and also their livelihood. They felt they had the right to have their share of the *feringhees'* wealth. You had the profit from the grain, I believe, and they had the profit from their protection. And then Sir William, most unwisely, insulted them by withdrawing the money. Even the *feringhee* officers advised him not to do this. Then the army demand safe passage through the passes. I thought that I could save them by bargaining. But, may Allah forgive me, I was wrong. Perhaps money might have saved them.'

Ahmet Qaderi was dumbstruck at this openness. It was more like a confession than he had ever imagined. He looked up at Akbar and saw that his eyes were full of tears. He wiped them harshly away with his thumbs.

'I am sorry, my friend. And this is not the first time that I have shed tears for those people. I hope that you do not feel me weak.'

Again, Ahmet was silent and waited for Akbar to continue.

'It is right that you should care less for my feelings than for your own, and your sister and nephew. I sent out a dozen messengers into the passes and villages around, asking for news. One returned this afternoon. He has heard of a boy, living in a small village in the hills. The village of Kalata. The parents have the most unusual possessions, and have made no secret of them. It is most odd, I think, that a shepherd and his wife who can neither read nor write even in their own language, should own letters and a book written in a *feringhee* tongue. Here is what I suggest.'

At this point Akbar reached into his robe and took out a long dagger from beneath his arm. It was a thing of deadly beauty. It was sleek rather than ornate, with the handle of burnished steel inlaid with brass, or even gold perhaps. Something green sparkled in the light.

'Take this knife as a gift from Akbar Khan. They will understand my wishes, I am sure. I shall send an escort with you.'

He stood, and so did Ahmet. As Ahmet started to bow, Akbar took him by the shoulder.

'No, my friend. Now it is I who must serve.'

And he turned briskly on his heel and went back into the citadel.

*

Late in the afternoon, three days later, three men, one of them Ahmet Qaderi, rode through the hills above Kalata. As they descended into the village, Ahmet suggested that they dismount as a sign of respect, and they led their horses by their bridles into the midst of a dozen or so tiny houses with thick walls and flat roofs.

The shadows rose up the mountain to the east as the sun set, and at this altitude, and this early in the year, the air was chill and damp. A weather-beaten woman looked up from her door as they passed, and there was the bleat of a goat.

In moments they had found the house they were looking for. Inside, a man sat alone, eating rough bread and fried goat. He looked up as they came in, and froze with a piece of fatty meat in his fingers. Only for a moment: he was hungry, and the meat was soon in his mouth.

However, he soon guessed at the importance of his visitors, stood quickly and bowed, wiping his hands furtively on a cloth. The escort spoke first.

'Good evening, friend. We are seeking the shepherd, Tariq and his wife.'

The shepherd looked worried, as though caught in a dreadful deed.

'I am Tariq,' he said. 'But sadly, as you see, I am alone, for my wife is now with Allah.'

The escort smiled gently.

'The Angel of Death, who hath charge concerning us, will gather us, and afterward unto our lord we will be returned.'

Ahmet looked at the shepherd. As when he was before the Dost in Kabul, he had rehearsed his words carefully.

'We are searching for one who is very dear to me. I too have suffered loss, for my sister is in the Garden under which rivers flow. I am seeking her son, my nephew, and I believe that you can help me to find him.'

'What would I know of your nephew, sir?'

'You have a son?'

'I have. A boy of 4 years old, I believe.'

'And is he truly your son? Did Allah make him from a drop of your blood? Or have you taken him in and given him the love that is due to an orphan?'

The shepherd took his face in his hands, and took a few deep breaths. As he looked up at Ahmet, a tear fell into his beard. He spoke in a gravelly voice.

'It is true. I heard him crying in the pass below. It was a terrible place, like the road into Hell. I saw a thousand dead, many women and children. Never have I seen so much blood in one place. So much blood. I went to see, not to steal, no, not to steal, but to see. Only to see. I soon wished that I had not, that I had stayed above the pass with my goats. But then, as I stood in all that waste, I heard a noise. A cry. I had no choice but to go to it. I did not steal the child, for it was alone and I......'

'Be easy, my friend. *For you believe and have done good works: such are the rightful owners of the Garden. They will abide therein.'*

'And I brought the child here to my wife, and we cared for him. He had a terrible wound on his face. Who could have done such a thing? To a child? *There are fires, and he will abide therein.*'

'And this was two years ago?'

'Two years, yes. In the depths of winter. The snow was deep, I remember. It took me two hours to walk here with the child, and I thought he must surely die. But when I came here, he was living, and still he lives.'

At last, trying hard to contain himself, Ahmet was able to ask the vital question. He forced himself to speak slowly.

'The boy is well now? And where is he?'

'I can no longer care for him. He is too young to be on the hills with the goats. My sister cares for him while I care for the flock.'

As the shepherd said this, a woman shouted outside.

'Not so fast! Stupid child!' And then she laughed, and there was a high-pitched squeal, and the clatter of the door, and a breathless young woman entered the room carrying a wriggling child. She stopped, and was silenced. She pulled her scarf down a little over her forehead, and nodded jerkily to the three newcomers.

The boy, not used to strangers, hid in her skirts, and then behind her. After a few moments, he peeked around and looked up into Ahmet's face. Ahmet breathed in sharply as he saw a bright, gently curving scar running from the corner of his eye to the corner of his mouth.

The next thing to catch Ahmet's attention was the look in the boy's eyes, half shy, half recognising. The child frowned slightly. Two years is a long time in a small boy's life, yet not long enough to forget Ahmet's face.

Ahmet knelt, and gestured to the boy, who soon came to him. Ahmet touched his hair, and then took his little face in his hands, so that he looked straight into the boy's eyes.

'Do you remember me, Hassan? Do you remember your uncle?' The boy was silent, and frowned a little. 'Perhaps not.'

'I remember your face, sir. But I am not Hassan. I am Tariq, like my father. Why do you call me Hassan?'

269

Ahmet thought for a moment. What should he say, and how much should he say?

'Your name was Hassan a long time ago, before you came here. You had an adventure, and you were in great danger. If this good man ......' – he pointed at the shepherd – had not found you in the ice and the snow, you would not have lived.'

'My father has told me the story of the ice and snow many times. He is not my real father, you know. And my mother was not my real mother. This aunt is not really my aunt. My real father and my real mother are lost, and I know I will never see them again.'

'And do you remember them?'

'Not very much, no. But sometimes I dream of a man who is very tall, much taller than my father. He has a book, and he smiles at me. And he speaks words that I do not know. Sometimes I have some very strange dreams. I dream of a man smiling at me and making strange noises. Like a bird.'

'Do you remember anything else of your father?'

'Oh yes. In all my dreams, he wears a red jacket, the colour of a lovely flower. I never see clothes of such colours when I am awake.'

*

Now, with Hassan sitting in front of him on the horse, his head nodding as they plodded back through a cliff-sided pass from which the spring sunshine was shut out entirely, Ahmet looked back over the negotiations of the last few days.

Discussions had not been easy, for the Shepherd had a strong bond with his little son, and because the boy was a link, the only living link, with his dead wife. On the other hand, Ahmet was determined to reclaim his nephew, because the boy was his only reminder of Nasrin, his dead sister. And he had powerful arguments: the boy should be with his family, and the escort had made it clear that Akbar Khan wished to see the boy returned to his uncle. There was powerful proof in what the boy had said about his dreams, but the final tipping points were the dagger, which promised a bond with the great Akbar Khan, and the dire poverty of the shepherd. Certainly, he shed tears at the boy's leaving, but knew it was for the best.

Within two days, Ahmet could see the walls of Kabul in the distance. As always at this time of year, the city seemed to hang in the light, as Ghazni had before Sergeant O'Leary and Hassan's father those six years before. Ahmet wondered how much of Kabul Hassan would remember when they reached it.

Chapter Twenty-Five

November 1855.

S ergeant Jackson collected Hassan from the school just before
dawn. They made their icy way to Victoria, their breaths like
spirits upon the air, where they found Ahmet and Mr. James
waiting for them. Mr James carried a mysterious-looking wicker
basket. Straight away, Ahmet gave Hassan back his book, with the
letters tucked in the back, and then the dagger given to him by
Akbar Khan.

'Today of all days, you may need these,' he said.

'Why today, uncle? Are we in danger? Or we are returning to
India?'

Uncle Ahmet smiled a little, and looked evasively at a passing
omnibus, pretending to take an interest in it. He said nothing to
Hassan about the purpose of the journey. He simply said that it was
'business'. Hassan wondered at this, and also wondered what his
uncle had been doing over the last few days. Certainly, he had been
speaking to the sergeant, probably about the terrible thing they
had seen in the docks. And perhaps he had met some buyers at the
warehouse. Yet once again, Hassan felt that he was being held at a
distance from his uncle, and wondered why. He would have to watch
and listen carefully.

The sergeant had already bought tickets for the London, Brighton
and South Coast Railway. There was a train due to leave at 9.40,

and they found it standing under the canopy, gleaming brass and green paint with a line of mahogany coaches behind. Already, it was swathed in steam and smoke.

They arrived at Redhill in less than an hour. How very different were the experiences of Hassan and his uncle! For Hassan, this was the greatest of adventures, still more exciting than departing from Bombay on *Aurora*. For the entire journey, he looked out at the rapidly changing landscape. He saw the splendour of the Thames, dotted with barges and small boats, and downriver The Vauxhall Pleasure Gardens. Soon they passed through Battersea, its tiny houses clustered along the banks like an infestation. Then across green fields and farms to Clapham, and then across more green fields, before they stopped briefly at Purley. Another ten minutes took them through Ahmet's most terrifying moments as they entered the tunnel at Merstham, in a blast of wind and smoke as though they were entering some nether world. To Ahmet a minute or two of darkness seemed like twenty, and even the man who had walked the Jugdulluk Pass in winter was ashen as they reached Redhill. It had not been so long since experts had predicted the inevitable death by suffocation of every passenger who dared to enter a tunnel on board a fast moving train; and even as they came into Redhill station, Ahmet would have believed them.

In the station yard, Mr James managed to hire a cart to take the four of them to Southlands, which was apparently ten miles away and would take more than an hour to reach. 'All the more time for thought,' he said.

They sat sideways in the cart, with their backs to the view, Ahmet and Sergeant Jackson on one side and Lieutenant James and Hassan facing them on the other. Hassan did his best to peer at the scenery between the men opposite, and over the head of the driver, but eventually settled for a combination of looking to the rear, through the clouds of dust kicked up in their wake, and twisting round to look behind him.

There was the crack of a whip, the squeaking of wheels and the jangling of harness. Occasionally the driver would call to the horses through his muffler, and often swapped his whip from hand to hand to try to keep both warm. The cart creaked slowly on.

Ahmet did not understand Hassan's fidgeting: he took his excitement for impatience.

'Hassan, do not worry. *Man is made of haste. Allah will show you many portents, but ask him not to hasten.* All in good time, my nephew.'

He had forgotten, in his own anxiety, that Hassan had nothing to be impatient about. Soon he realised that he was projecting his own nervous expectation onto the boy.

The countryside looked barren. Beyond the hedgerows, Hassan made out the burned stubble of harvested crops, and on the horizon great clamours of rooks and crows, their gigantic nests exposed against the sky by the fall of leaves. Here and there he saw a ditch filled with ice, and in one low spot the whole road was covered in a crazed and speckled icy mirror. Hassan remembered the plenty and warmth of Bombay, whilst Ahmet's thoughts were further back, packing fruit in Kabul. He looked across at the cold, hard ground, and as often, he sought the comfort of his faith. *Lo! In the creation of the heavens and the earth, and the difference of night and day, and the ships which run upon the sea with that which is of use to men, and the water which Allah sendeth down from the sky, thereby reviving the earth after its death, and dispersing all kinds of beasts therein, and in the ordinance of the winds, and the clouds obedient between heaven and earth, are signs of Allah's sovereignty.*

'I am looking forward to the spring already,' said Mr James.

At a turnpike, the driver had to knock at the lodge, where the sleepy pike man took his sixpence and gave grudging directions to Southlands, which he described as being 't'other soide o' Russton', before turning on his heel and slamming the door behind him. Seeing his face at the window, the driver raised his whip, perhaps in thanks, and they carried on their way.

Now they entered a woodland in which there were trees that Hassan and even Ahmet had never seen in such number before: oak and chestnut, and silver birch pointing upwards like cadaverous limbs. Hassan took a sudden interest in the ground as they sped over it, captivated by the prickly shells of conkers and the varied colours of oak leaves. At Russton, a man with bandaged feet, scraggly hair and a dirty face lifted his dead pipe to them as they passed.

There were signs of industry, but not of work. There were poor, deserted houses around a small brick field, each surrounded by broken fences and nettles. The fields too were deserted, and even in the gloom of a dull autumn day the houses were unlit.

Soon afterwards, they arrived at Southlands, and the three men looked anxiously across at the manor house, which lay a quarter of a mile away on the side of a gentle valley. They came off the road, and followed an avenue of elm trees until the house reappeared in front of them. It was a fine structure, of red brick and sash windows, with a roof of uniform and straight slate tiles, but a combination of sun and rain and frost had yellowed and peeled the paintwork and varnish.

'Two years since I was here,' said Mr James, 'and it needed some work even then. The place has gone down a long way since. Poor Smith.'

Ahmet laid a hand on Mr James's wrist.

Hassan wondered at this. Poor Smith? Surely...?

'Let me go first,' said Mr James. 'After all, I am known here, and I stand a greater chance than you.'

They watched him walk up the short path to the door, across a carpet of moss and weeds and gravel. Either side of the door was a plant which had once been fragrant, but was now straggled and dead looking. Mr James reached for the door knocker, and Hassan's heart missed a beat as he saw that it was a T-shaped length of steel, quite sharp on one edge. Somewhere, he had seen something like this before.

The door was soon opened by a man a little older than Mr James, wearing a long tailed black coat and no shoes. It was clear to Hassan that he and Mr James knew one another, for they both smiled. Hassan heard the words 'sir' and 'not at present'. Then Mr James turned and pointed at the cart, and Hassan heard the word 'Jackson'.

Mr James beckoned, and the sergeant got down from the cart and went to join them.

Shortly afterwards, Hassan and Ahmet were invited over. They got down from the cart and it rattled away. Mr James made introductions.

'I present Mr Ahmet Qaderi and Young Master Hassan Qaderi, Mr Pooter. It is on Hassan's behalf that we are here.'

Mr Pooter looked at Hassan calmly, but his calmness masked huge surprise. 'Ah, Master Hassan,' he said, with a gentle smile. 'And you would be ...? Tell me, how old are you?'

'I fourteen years, sir.'

'Yes, of course. Fourteen. Well.' He looked up inquisitively at Ahmet, and there was a brief flash of recognition, followed by a warm but silent handshake.

'Mr Smith is presently indisposed,' said Mr Pooter. Or, I should say, he is presently consulting his doctor. One of his doctors. When he is free, I shall of course ask him if he is willing to receive you. I suspect that in the circumstances...'

'Thank you, sir,' said Ahmet.

'There is really no need to call me sir, Mr Ahmet. After all, I am the servant here.'

*

They sat in a room lined with books. There was a fine view of the gently sloping valley side, crisscrossed with neat hedges and here and there a line of trees or a small copse. James stood at a window with his back to the others, as he had done in Montagu Street. Hassan surveyed the books but did not touch, remembering again what had happened at Mr Dickens's house. He looked along the spines, and soon came across a set of volumes in the same colour, and of the same size and style, as his own. At the left-hand end of the set, there was a book sized space, covered with the same dust as the tops of the books. How strange!

Half an hour later, Mr Pooter returned.

'Dr Morris has now left,' he said. 'He has detected some signs of improvement. Perhaps in another year or so... Please come through to Mr Smith's study. I would urge you all to absolute silence, for it takes very little to upset Mr Smith. Please.' And he extended an arm to indicate the way.

They walked along a windowless, wainscoted passageway lit only by a few dim candles mounted on the wall. They soon reached the door, and Mr Pooter put his forefinger to his lips and pointed at the sergeant's shoes, and then at everybody else's. Hassan understood first, and reached down to pull his boots off. The others followed suit.

Mr Pooter put the finger to his lips again, and gently, ever so gently, knocked on the door and pushed it open.

It was dark inside, but it seemed very tidy, indeed almost bare. The glass of picture frames glittered slightly, reflecting very little light coming between the curtains. A lamp burned on a small table in the corner, and the aroma of oil and tobacco filled the room. At a desk, facing the window, and with his back to the room, was a man. He sat very upright and very still, his left hand on an open book which surely he could not read in this light. Occasionally he tilted his head to look through the space in the curtains.

Mr Pooter coughed slightly, and said 'Mr Smith, sir. Your visitors. Do you still wish to see them?'

There was stillness, and absolute silence. Nobody moved, or seemed to draw breath.

Hassan felt lost, as though in some storm that was whipping desert sand into his eyes. And yes, his eyes pricked a little, and not because of any sand.

Still they stood there and waited.

It was Hassan who realised, somehow, what had to be done. He looked at the man, and the book, and remembered the space on the shelf. Ever so gradually, so as not to make a sound, he opened his own book to a page on which the corner had been turned over many, many years ago. He crept forward in the gloom and put his slight hand on the wrist of the man at the desk. The man looked at the hand, as though studying it, before slowly turning to Hassan. As he did so Hassan distracted his attention by presenting him with the book, open at a picture of the fat little bald man being hit over the head with a leg of beef.

The man chuckled a little, then caught himself and frowned. He took the book and gripped his chin as though in pain. He leafed through the pages for several minutes, reading the odd paragraph and smiling, while the four men and Hassan watched in stillness and silence. Soon he felt something at the back of the book with the fingertips of his right hand, and pulled out a few folded sheets. He opened them, and touched the words gently with his finger in the light from the window. Hassan heard him swallow.

They heard him gasp for breath, and saw him clutch the arms of his chair, and Mr Pooter strode forward to support him.

For the first time, the man spoke.

'What is this?' He turned to face the others. 'Who are you? Why are you in my private quarters?'

'These are the gentlemen I told you of,' said Mr Pooter gently. 'Do you remember? You agreed to see them.'

The man frowned again, and then suddenly looked straight into Hassan's face. His head shook slightly, and his mouth made the word "no" soundlessly.

'Pooter! For God's sake, let me see him! Let me see him!'

'He is still here, sir.'

'But let me see him! Open the curtains! Let some light into this dreadful room!'

'If you are quite sure, sir.' And soon a chill winter sunlight flew into the room, catching specks of dust in its shafts.

The man was revealed, and Hassan's senses were numbed by what he had not seen before: cropped grey hair, buckles on shiny boots, and a scarlet tunic with gold braid and epaulettes.

Captain Smith, late of the 13th Light Infantry, took his son in his arms and wept.

'My boy. My dear, dear boy.'

And at last, Hassan wept also.

When Hassan was eventually released from his father's grasp, he looked up to see that the others had left. For the first time in twelve years, father and son looked into each other's faces. The father seemed not to notice the son's scar.

*

Later, Smith took his son - already he was calling him Hassan Smith - outside. As they crossed a lawn, Pooter (ex-Sergeant Pooter) kept a watchful eye from a short distance, having been advised by Sergeant Jackson, his brother in rank, of the need for care. 'I am fully aware of the need for caution,' Pooter had said with a smile, 'for I have taken it these last twelve years, day in and day out. I have known the slightest circumstance to have the most terrible effect on the Captain. Yet what amazes me at this time is the ease with which he has accepted the greatest shock one can imagine.'

'No. That is hardly surprising, Mr Pooter. I cannot see it as a shock: more of a wonderful surprise. This has been a most strange tale, sir, and one that will be worthy of much retelling, not least in a court of law.'

'Oh yes. But that is not all, Mr Jackson. Earlier, in Captain Smith's study, you saw me open the curtains. And you saw the light come into the room. I have wondered whether the curtain might fall in tatters, for that is the first time that proper daylight has been admitted to that room for seven years, and that last time only briefly. It may surprise you to know that the Captain has only infrequently set foot outside this house over the last ten years or more. But now, I wonder. Perhaps this is a new dawn for him. A new light, if you will.'

'There will be difficulties, of course.'

They watched as Smith and Hassan walked along a gravel path; the father pointed at a withered stem and cupped his hands, as though describing the new growth of the following spring.

'Of course,' said Pooter. We must ask the young man about those. And his uncle. Do they, do either of them, wish to live in England? If so, what will become of the old man? Where will he live?

And how? And then there are all sorts of questions about education. Captain Smith has faith, of a sort, but what of Hassan's? And what of his uncle's, if he stays? I have been in Afghanistan, Mr Jackson, and whatever we make of the people in our theatres and our books and our newspapers, I have seen them to be a social people, a people for whom friends and family are of vital importance. In short, how will they manage? At the very least, there will be much to learn.'

'I am quite sure of it, Mr Pooter. But meantime...' He looked urgently into Pooter's face. '... there is another matter which I must acquaint you with. It is most urgent.'

'Surely not so urgent in these circumstances,' said Pooter, smiling.

'Indeed, Mr Pooter. It is most specially urgent: now that ...'

'Now that Mr Smith and the boy are together? Now that Hassan is here?'

Smith was showing Hassan the view, pointing across the valley at a cluster of cottages.

'Just so, Mr Pooter.' Having played the part of earnest friend for a good few minutes, Mr Jackson became Sergeant Jackson again, and stood a little taller. 'Indeed, we have reason to believe they are both in mortal danger, something to do with treasure, I believe. One man is dead already. Couldn't make head nor tail of it myself, like. It's to do with their country, where they come from, where you and Mr Smith were all those years ago. I've seen the letter Hassan handed to Mr Smith, but I can't see why they're in danger, it all seems so... hedged about, like. As clear as turnips, Mr Pooter, begging your pardon. I...'

They were interrupted by shouting. It sounded like Mr James, whom they had left speaking to Ahmet in the library. And indeed it was: for soon two strangers appeared on the lawn with their hands in the air and their heads bowed, and Mr James followed with a pistol. The larger of the men, who had barely any teeth, tried to make himself look smaller; the smaller man kept very close by his side, as though for protection.

Hassan and his father turned and looked at the men. Soon Ahmet arrived, rubbing his eyes.

'Whatever is this?' said Smith, as Sergeant Jackson moved swiftly across the lawn.

Hassan immediately recognised Khodar and Aziz. On any farm, and in any lane, each of them would have stood out, as Mr Dickens would have put it, *like a dolphin in a sentry box*.

Aziz saw that he had no choice but to obey Mr James's instructions, and his movements were fearfully placid. But Khodar was still enraged, and when he saw Captain Smith, his red tunic unbuttoned, he stood transfixed at the sight. For a moment he seemed about to lunge at him. Jackson strode between them and silently held up a hand. He handcuffed Khodar, and looked a little confused as he surveyed Aziz. Eventually, he decided that Aziz posed little threat, and left him alone. Then he stood tall, perhaps the tallest he had ever been.

'I am taking you both on suspicion of a murder. You will be taken to Lunnon as soon as a conweyance and a spare hofficer is found. Unnerstand? Your search for your great treasure is over, d'you see?'

Ahmet translated for them. Khodar's eyes widened, and Aziz swallowed hard and looked appealingly at Sergeant Jackson. Surely he would let him go soon?

There was a silence, broken by Captain Smith. He smiled benignly. He nodded slowly and narrowed his eyes, a man brought to a sudden new understanding after years in the darkness. A short while ago, he hardly knew who he was himself, let alone the great truths about his visitors. Now, suddenly, he was the only man in the garden who understood everything. He turned to Khodar and spoke slowly in Pashtu.

'Ah, yes. I understand. For I have read the story every day; after all, it is my story. You have my Pashtu letter. Yes, my letter! Tell me, where did you find it? Did you find the body of my dear, dear wife? Did you find it in a *kajava* on the back of a dead camel? Or did you just buy it? However it was, you have been seeking a great treasure. A treasure that was sent across the seas. A treasure that would make a man rich *beyond the wealth of Kings*, as Wordsworth puts it.'

Khodar did not know of Wordsworth, but he clearly got the gist.

'May I see the letter? It is mine, after all.'

Khodar jerked his head to his *poshteen*. Sergeant Jackson lifted the fabric and withdrew a few folded sheets, just like the sheets in the back of Hassan's book, and the ones owned by Ahmet.

'Shall I read it to you? It is a poor translation, I am afraid, and rather sketchy. I believe that I was somewhat distracted when I wrote it, and there was no time for my dear Nasrin and me to work on it properly.' He swallowed hard.

*

Long ago, there was a boy who was so rich that men dreamed of being his equal. His father was good, and his mother was beautiful. He was born one winter, when it was very cold. His treasure came from blood, and was given to him by God.

Some of the treasure came across the sea with his father, but most of it came from his own country. Only he and his mother and father, and one uncle knew of his riches. Nobody else, not even the Shah, knew about his treasure.

The uncle was a poor merchant whose people loved him, for he lived by Allah's commands. His people might see him wrestle, and they loved his joy.

But then the people hated Ahmet Qaderi. He did a good thing, in the hope of winning a great prize himself. But his people were unjust to him, and he fled for his life across the deserts and mountains.

We must pray that he is safe today, still hoping for his prize. We hope that he is working hard in his new country, and that he has found a loving wife and children. Yet we may also be sure that he is sad to have left behind the boy and his riches, and he fears the traveller who may one day come to him bearing bad news.

The uncle knew that the boy was living in a time of bloodshed, and that the people would learn to hate him too. They wanted the treasure, all of the treasure, to be taken across the sea, and some wanted it to be destroyed, for they said it would cause much sorrow.

The riches disappeared, and were never seen or heard of again. Some men said that it was worthless, but that is not true. Still, it is beyond the wealth of Kings, and any man who has it under his hand would be the happiest man alive. Some say that it went over the sea again, and is now far away, being watched over by loyal guards. Some think that it is nearby, looked over by a trustworthy shepherd. The boy himself is lost, and has no idea of his riches.

However, uncle Ahmet knows where to find the treasure, and he knows that one day he and the boy, Hassan, will travel together to meet it again.

*

'This letter...' he waved it in front of Khodar and Aziz. '... this letter is, unfortunately for you, a poor Pashtu translation, written by an Englishman of little ability, of an English translation by an Afghan woman who, for all her beauty, was as yet no scholar in the English language, of a Pashtu letter written by a man in a very great hurry. God knows, we all needed the practice in letter writing, and had so little time for it. It is no surprise that the letter you found, or bought, has led you, dare I say it, away from the straight path.

'I suppose you will have looked in Kabul for this treasure. Perhaps you went out into the wilderness in search of it. Perhaps you followed the army through the passes. Perhaps you searched in Jalalabad and in Bombay. Perhaps then you realised that the treasure had been stolen away overseas. Perhaps you thought that the poor young man was dead, or did not know that the treasure was his, and therefore would not miss it.'

Khodar's rage had quickly become entrancement. Perhaps still, this could turn out well for him. Aziz became more and more puzzled.

'This young man, my son, is the rightful owner of the treasure. It is a treasure that belongs here, in England, and should never have left. Only ...' For a moment, he could not continue, his voice constricted and his eyes fixed on a small patch of turf in front of him. Then he gathered himself again. 'Only, had the treasure not left England, there would now be no young man to seek it.' He put a hand gently on Hassan's head. 'The world would be short of a fine young man.'

Hassan looked up at him. Like Khodar, he got the gist. Unlike Khodar, he felt it too.

'So where is this treasure, do you think?' He moved his hand expansively around the garden, towards the house, over the valley. Then he looked straight at Khodar. 'You want to see the treasure?'

Khodar nodded.

'You can see it now. You are looking at it. I am the treasure that Hassan has thought of all his life. The treasure came to India, then to Afghanistan, through the passes and back to India, and then to England. I hope that I am a great treasure, the half of it that Hassan has not lost. It is the treasure of a father's love for his son.'

For the second time in twelve years, and the second in a few minutes, Captain William Smith wept. Hassan stood close to him. Ahmet took great interest in his own tired eyes; Pooter turned his back and looked up at the roof, as though checking for loose tiles, and Sergeant Jackson took a sudden interest in lawn weeds, and stroked his moustache.

*

A little less than two hours later, Khodar and Aziz had left for London under the escort of Sergeant Jackson and the local constable. In the dining room, hastily (and not entirely) swept of dust by Sergeant Pooter, a transformation had taken place. Smith had disappeared for half an hour and returned a changed man, in a suit of his father's. He had ordered tea: a crisp white tablecloth, jam and silver spoons in glass bowls, cakes and pastry, honey from his own hives. With hands that rattled the cups and saucers, and wide eyes and hair standing up a little, Smith poured the tea.

Ahmet and Hassan were amazed that such a man could provide all this, and smiled openly and thanked him.

'Do not thank me,' said Smith. This is all, all of it, the work of Pooter. The man who has saved me, who somehow kept me living for this day. Don't stand there like a butler, Pooter. Come and sit down, dear friend. How he did it all alone I've no idea.'

'I had more help than you realise, sir,' said Pooter. 'People have really been very good.'

'And all friends shall taste the cup of their deservings! Shakespeare, almost. To start with, you must all stay here for as long as you wish. I have been out of circulation for long enough, and besides, we have a great deal to tell each other. Only, you must forgive me on the occasions when I fail you. As I say, it has been a long time since I undertook business or engaged in a lengthy conversation. The only words I have spoken have been – well, to myself, I should say. Yet tomorrow, I shall introduce you to the country round. For one day, my son - how I have longed to say this - you shall be lord of all you survey!'

Perhaps Hassan did not understand this, or perhaps he was just put off by the taste of honey, the finest thing he had ever eaten.

He looked up, his finger in his mouth, to see the other five observing him smilingly over their teacups.

Chapter Twenty-Six

December 1855

Aziz was remembering a time, perhaps twenty years ago, when he and Khodar had been looking after their families' goats in the foothills near their village. The cousins had looked at the peaks of the Hindu Kush, their fifteen miles of distance foreshortened by the crystal air to an arm's length. On one side of their valley the mountain lay in its own perpetual shadows, but on the other, jagged triangular summits reached up from behind a ridge, and long, dappled fingers of snow seemed to grab them as if to tear them from the earth.

It was spring, and as in previous years, Aziz felt the beauty of it all flow through him, and his heart was caught in a surge which resounded in the crash and rattle of the stream which bore the melted snows through the valley. He looked at what was close by: the parti-coloured goats, the flattened space of closely cropped, luminescent grass, the rocks worn smooth by the stream, and the sunlight on everything.

He could not remember what he and Khodar had talked about, but a picture of him had fixed itself in his mind. Khodar had been standing on a rock, but not to keep an eye on the goats, for with his hand shielding his eyes from the sun, he was looking far along the stream, out to the end of the valley. Aziz knew that as always, Khodar was dreaming of the world beyond.

Why, of all the things he had seen, was this the one that filled his waking hours? Why that view of Khodar? Why that view of the home valley? And why, for pity's sake, had he been made to leave it?

*

The trial had been brief, on one of those late autumn mornings where shafts of sunlight come in through the windows and make us narrow our eyes. The Crown had put its case with due solemnity, and had called the witnesses: Mr Dickens and Sergeant Jackson and then, briefly, Ahmet Qaderi and Hassan, before calling Khodar and Aziz to tell their own version of events. A small elderly man, seemingly from their own country but settled in London, acted as interpreter.

Strangely, at least to Aziz, whose mind had struggled to keep up with events, and whose English consisted of only a few nouns, the Counsel for the Prosecution seemed much kinder to him than to Khodar. When Khodar was examined, he was addressed with a raised voice; there was much wagging of the finger and turning to the jury. The judge, seated high above, listened intently, occasionally smiling slightly with his finger on his lips. Somehow, Khodar remained calm, and gave quiet, lengthy answers to the interpreter, who passed them on to the court. He often gestured at Aziz, his palm upward. Just occasionally, there was a catch in his voice. If only Aziz had been able to hear him from the other side of the court! He wanted to help Khodar, in his simple way, to try to mitigate his guilt with the love and understanding of a cousin. Yet how could he, in this alien place with its unknown tongue, and its dark oak and musty ceilings and fearsome quiet? And how could he, knowing Khodar's guilt?

And then he heard his name called, and a gentleman in black beckoned him to the witness box. As they passed, Khodar put a hand on his cousin's shoulder, a tear in his eye. Counsel asked Aziz about his cousin, about how they had got to London, about the little Indian on the boat, about Ahmet Qaderi and his nephew Hassan. About their meeting with Mr Dickens outside St Pauls, and about the treasure that they were seeking. Of course, Aziz had never spoken to the little Indian, except to talk about the weather, and sometimes about the food on the *Aurora*. He knew nothing of Ahmet Qaderi, although his cousin seemed to like Mr Qaderi and Hassan. He knew nothing of any treasure; he had not understood what the treasure was, or where it might be found.

And it was now that the man in a white wig started to raise his voice, and his eyes flashed, almost like those of an angry man. Aziz could not understand the questions, because they weren't really questions. Even through the medium of the interpreter, the questions sounded like accusations. The man in the wig sometimes indicated Khodar, but in translation the interpreter stood very still and placidly, his arms by his side, and spoke quietly and matter-of-factly.

And soon, it was over, and they all stood as the judge and the twelve men of the jury left the courtroom. They were not gone for more than half an hour, whilst Khodar and Aziz sat silently in the dock, waiting. Khodar seemed unable to speak or even to look at his cousin. Often, he might have taken Aziz's hand, or put his arm across his shoulders, but not now.

Then the jury and the elderly, distinguished, ermine-trimmed judge returned. The entire court, the defendants, the witnesses, the lawyers, reporters who had been scratching away with their pens, and the entranced general public, stood as one. When the judge was seated, they all sat down again. A man in the jury stood up and said a few words in response to a few questions from that same gentleman in black, and then sat down again. The judge looked at Khodar, and the gentleman in black indicated that Khodar was to stand. The judge spoke softly, and carried the greater authority for it. Soon, Khodar covered his face and wept, and was led from the court. Then Aziz was made to stand. The judge looked at him sternly for some seconds before speaking, and then spoke severely. Then there was a pause, and the whole court held its breath. The judge reached down and picked up a black cloth, or so it seemed. He looked at it abstractedly, turned it around, and placed it on his head. Still the court held its breath, and then the judge spoke for one last time, in a way that reminded Aziz of poetry. The court exhaled softly. Aziz was gripped firmly by the arms and led through a door and down some steps into the dark.

*

Now, as he sat in that cell in the chill dawn, waiting for the terrible thing that would soon be done to him, Aziz wondered where Khodar was now. For he had not been to see him, had written him no letter and sent him no gift. And all Aziz could remember of him was that young man standing on the rock looking out to the valley's end, dreaming of escape to the world beyond. Perhaps even then he had been thinking of treasure.

A key rattled in the door, and there were voices outside. Three men in black, one with a white collar, came into the cell.

'Begging your pardon, sir. It's time to go.'

For the last time in his short life, Aziz saw the goats in the pasture, and felt the Hindu Kush and his cousin in his heart.

Chapter Twenty-Seven

April 1856

Hassan had been excited by the snow, for it was the first thing he had seen in England which had reminded him of the mountains. True, the snow was not as harsh or as deep, but its crispness smelt the same, and even in these lowlands, the clear light sent him a little echo of the Hindu Kush.

One day, his father had gone out in boots and a thick coat and returned with a snow-speckled fir tree which he had put up near the fire, and then decorated with little candles and a star.

They did not go to church at Christmas, of course, and Smith and Pooter had understood that. In Afghanistan, the separation of faiths had been almost complete, even when their ideas came so close to touching. Rarely would an English soldier or a sepoy have gone to the mosque, even to admire it, and the Afghans were never seen at communion or evensong.

Always, after a church service, there would be a small and distant cluster of Afghans who had listened to the alien melodies, and then watched as the Christians went their separate ways. And the soldiers of Army of the Indus, when they heard the Muezzin's call to prayer, paused only for a moment as the Kabulis made their way to the mosque.

The real sharing of faith was more intimate. There were the Afghans' conversational references to the Holy Qur'an, to its birds held in the sky and its love for the traveller and the orphan, the *inshallah* after every casual wish. And every so often, an Afghan might, in the middle of some revelation about a soldier's brother or a parent or soldier friend, hear a Christian *thank the Lord* or *God willing*.

*

And here they were, back in the East India dock. It was shortly after dawn, for the clipper *Erytheia* would be leaving on the early tide. She rose above them, her black hull shining in the dawn, and her decks and rigging swarming with men and boys. The very tops of her masts dulled into a light mist. For April, the air was bitterly chill.

Beneath *Erytheia's* prow stood a small group of people, mostly silent apart from the odd, tense word here and there.

Mrs Jackson stood silently with Lucy, Tommy and Lizabet, her matronly hands on the girls' shoulders. She had given Hassan a terrifying hug, held his head in her hands, looked him in the eyes and wished him well, and Lizabet had given another of her well-practised curtseys. Lucy had made a strange bow, fixed him in the eye, given him a meaty handshake and then swallowed hard. Now she stared downriver with a pained, and yet slightly stubborn, look on her face.

Hassan, Smith and Pooter stood a little apart, watching those around them as though aware of some imminent danger. For the first time in more than fifteen years, an observer might imagine that Smith had once been a soldier.

Mr Woodhouse spoke quietly to Sergeant Jackson, perhaps – who would ever know? – of the poor, or learning, or Christ, or of Aziz, whom Woodhouse had seen in all his agonised separation the night before he died. Whatever it was they talked about, neither man smiled.

Ahmet arrived at the dockside, looked down for a moment at the shiny reflections in the damp cobbles, and then over at the row of moored vessels, and walked softly towards his nephew. Hassan walked towards him, and they met halfway. Ahmet did not explain where he had been; maybe in a warehouse checking over the goods he had bought to take back to India: luxuries for the British, perhaps, wine and cigars and silverware. Or even some essential or other for the new mills.

Before he reached Hassan, Ahmet looked up at the prow of *Erytheia* and stopped. Suddenly his face was full of quiet fury. Only Smith noticed, and followed his gaze to the ship's rail. There stood Khodar, framed against a dull sky. He held Ahmet's stare for a short while, then turned and shuffled away across the deck. Smith looked again at Ahmet, and saw that he had murder in his eyes.

Hassan looked towards the River Thames. As before, on the evening back in December when he and Ahmet, and Aziz and Khodar, had first arrived in London, the water was laid out like silk. Hassan imagined setting out on it, and then the nightmares of the Bay of Biscay and Cape Horn and the monsoon, if it came early. And Bombay, which he would be seeing again in a slow ninety-odd days.

*

Hassan had spent happy weeks with his father, mostly. They had talked and talked; Smith had recovered some of his rusty Pashtu, and Hassan had started to polish his newly found English. He was not yet ready for Mr Pickwick, but he could soon hold his own with his father at mealtimes, for his young mind learned quickly.

His father had shown him everything: the rich grassy land, covered in snow and then frost, land being ploughed in the spring; grown lambs on the slopes; the dairy cattle in their byres, and later in the fields, the horses in their stalls. Over the weeks he had explained everything, too: what would be planted this year, and how he would rotate the crops; where the lambs would go to market, and the price they might fetch; how the cattle were milked. He talked of hunting, and Hassan learned to say and to define the strangest of words, such as covert and den and beaters. His father took him into the copse, and pointed out scurrying pheasant, and then returned to the house and showed him the shotgun that had belonged to his own father and grandfather. He taught him the meanings of stock, trigger and trigger guard, muzzle and barrel and cartridge.

Hassan always felt Smith's intense yearning, his burning eyes. Sometimes the intensity was too great for him to bear, too demanding. It seemed as though his father wanted to possess him completely, never to let him out of his sight, to determine the rest of his life. Sometimes, his father would be placid and calm. Perhaps he would look distantly into the fire, or stop his horse fifty yards from Hassan's and look out over the landscape, as though once more separate and alone. Yet even then, Hassan feared - just a little - his father's new strength. For at times Smith seemed driven by something; by some daemon or mania. Where might it end?

What Hassan would never know was the fevered way in which Smith had met his tenants and asked them question after question, how he had gathered his books and his father's journals, and how he had wracked his brains well into the night to relearn the life he had forgotten. How many hours he had spent talking to Pooter, going over the smallest details of his work over so many years. And all of this, the sudden recovery after years of darkness and incapacity, was for Hassan. And it was *because* of him, too. Smith had a son now; a reason to work, a purpose for a new engagement in the life of his land.

But despite Smith's best efforts, Hassan's connection with this place ebbed and flowed like a tide. At first, of course, he had been thrilled to have found his own father. It was perfectly plain that he was his father, for Hassan had openly sought out (and found) his own features in his father's face; and Smith had stroked Hassan's scar with tenderness and pity. Their hands too were alike, in shape if not in shade, the ends of their little fingers curved gently and familiarly inwards. And they shared earlobes, eyebrows, nostrils, foreheads.

One evening, Hassan had wanted to show his father his dearest treasures: and they sat for three hours in front of the fire, Smith interrupting only to fetch another log or to coax the fire into life with the poker. First, the dagger.

'What a beauty!' Smith had exclaimed. He held the edge to the light. It tapered to nothingness, just as it should. 'Never been used to cut anything, I'll wager.' He held the weapon gently by the blade, and looked admiringly at the handle, at the workings of steel and brass, and two small emeralds winking in the firelight. 'Beautiful work. Wherever did you find it?'

'It was given to me, sir ...'

Smith raised a forefinger. 'There are no sirs here, remember. Many English boys call their fathers sir, but not here!' He smiled kindly.

'It was given me by Akbar Khan, my father. A gift. Akbar cried tears when he gave it me. "I am most sorry for you, and for your mother and father," he said. "Take this to remember my sorrow". I was only four years of age, but I remember the day well. I remember Akbar shaking my uncle's hand, and touching his shoulder.'

They had looked too at Hassan's *Pickwick Papers*. As before, Smith took the book like a lover's hand, and then held the spine's gold lettering up to the light, and looked along it as he had looked along the blade of the knife. He opened the yellow-edged pages, and flecks of dust fell from them. He turned the pages over until he found uncut leaves, and took a silver paper knife and sliced gently through the folds. He looked intently at the first page of a new chapter.

'I almost finished this. Goodness me, I remember reading it at Ghazni. That evening before the attack ... the last evening before James ...' He looked into the fire for a moment, and then back into his son's eyes. 'I shall read the rest to you, Hassan. It will be a labour of love. And perhaps one day you will read it yourself from the beginning. It will be hard work for you, but there will be a mighty reward. Perhaps together, we can read the rest.' He squeezed his son's shoulder gently, and returned to the story.

'Mr Tom Roker, the gentleman who had accompanied Mr Pickwick into the prison, turned sharp round to the right when he got to the bottom of the little flight of steps, and led the way, through an iron gate which stood open, and another short flight of steps, into a long narrow gallery, dirty and low, paved with stone, and very dimly lighted by a window at each remote end.

'"This," said the gentleman, thrusting his hands into his pockets, and looking carelessly over his shoulder to Mr Pickwick, "This here is the hall flight".

'"Oh" replied Mr Pickwick, looking down a dark and filthy staircase, which appeared to lead to a range of damp and gloomy stone vaults, beneath the ground, "and those, I suppose, are the little cellars where the prisoners keep their small quantities of coals. Unpleasant places to have to go down to; but very convenient, I daresay."

'"Yes, I shouldn't wonder if they was convenient," replied the gentleman, "seeing that a few people live there, pretty snug. That's the Fair, that is."

'"My friend," said Mr Pickwick, "you don't really mean to say that human beings live down in those wretched dungeons?"

'"Don't I?" replied Mr Roker, with indignant astonishment; "why shouldn't I?"

'"Live! Live down there!" exclaimed Mr Pickwick.

'"Live down there! Yes, and die down there, too, wery often!" replied Mr Roker;" and what of that? Who's got to say anything agin it? Live down there! Yes, and wery good place it is to live in, ain't it?"'

Perhaps Smith found this less funny than he would once have done, remembering the fate of Aziz. He closed the book.

'Perhaps another time, Hassan. Let us read something else.'

And then they read Ahmet's letter together. Three copies of the letter were now together: Ahmet's first Pashtu copy and the English version which Nasrin had lovingly and beautifully translated into English, both folded into the back of Hassan's book; and Smith's Pashtu letter, which seemed to have caused all the trouble. They followed one from the other like Chinese whispers.

As often, Smith and Hassan spoke in a casual mixture of Pashtu and English. Smith understood that this allowed them to speak as equals.

The English letter especially Smith held lovingly, smelling it and once or twice touching it to his lips. He ran his finger gently over the name of his wife Nasrin, which appeared in small fine print at the bottom of the last page. He folded the letter gently and put it safely to one side, and they looked again at the first Pashtu version.

'Tell me, Hassan, did you ever understand this letter?'

'A little. I thought it just a story. But I also thought there was something more in it. A meaning. Something about me. Now I understand it a little more, but not all of it.'

So slowly, over the next hour or so, they reconstructed the story. Smith taught it as a lesson, interrogating the words, asking Hassan for his ideas and checking and re-checking his understanding. And of course, like the best of teachers, Smith was a learner too. After all, Hassan knew his uncle better than Smith did.

They talked for a long while, and all through the conversation Hassan sensed his father's mind drifting back and forth, through the happy days that he had lived, and perhaps also through the days of blood. They talked a little of the wildest dreams of men, of what it meant to be rich, of all the things that men may treasure, of the fortune that other men may not envy, but which are the greatest fortune of all. They talked of the poor trader, who had lost the love of his people, of what it meant to pay the poor due, and to care for the widow and the orphan. They talked of what these things meant for Hassan and for Smith and Nasir and Ahmet Qaderi. Somehow, the letter eased Smith in the midst of all his pain and his sudden awakening; more and more, he remembered the living Nasrin, and saw her face in his son's.

Smith asked Hassan why it was that Ahmet Qaderi had never married or had children of his own, and Hassan said that they had never talked of it. Smith smiled, because this was something he had already guessed.

The hardest thing for Smith was the business of the treasure being sent back across the seas, for he was the treasure himself, and the treasure too had suffered. It was the one flaw in Ahmet's tale. Towards the end of the story, they had smiled at the idea of Khodar wanting to go off into the desert and dig for treasure; Smith wondered at the idea of digging up a red tunic full of sand, and Hassan chuckled, almost as he had as a small boy in Kabul. Lastly, they wept for the loyalty of Ahmet Qaderi.

*

A month passed, the snow melted and then even the frost cleared for a few days, and Smith started to teach Hassan to ride. Hassan remembered trotting on a horse in Afghanistan, but that was long ago, before he was five years old. He had never handled a horse himself. At first, Smith put him on a small pony which he held by the bridle. Then the horse trotted gently in the meadow, in a large circle at the end of a rope. And after a few days, they took gentle rides through the woodlands and across the fallow fields. Hassan imagined one day riding up Malabar Hill, his uncle following and the taste of betel on his tongue, and the scent of frangipani in his nostrils. They had not discussed the future, not properly, and Hassan felt unsure of it.

Once or twice during these times, he had felt his uncle's presence fading a little, moving away into the distance. Most obviously, he saw less of him as he travelled the district, but even when they were together there was a space between them. He supposed that it was right for Ahmet to do this whilst he was with his father, because they had so little time, but still it hurt. After all, Uncle had been father for so many years. Hassan remembered no other. Sometimes, Ahmet obviously expected Hassan to stay, but had not quite said so.

Many of his sentences now began with the words 'When you become a man...' or 'When I return to Bombay...' or 'One day, when I visit you...' There was always a subtext: 'We shall separate... You will become an English landowner... You will be Smith, not Qaderi...You may never see me or Bombay again...' Gradually, he felt himself torn. The unspoken words became: 'You will spend your life in this land of ice and snow... You will never see a mosque or hear the muezzin again ... This life is not your life...'

And then there were the great unspoken questions, unspoken by anybody: 'How can you change yourself? How will you ever come to love this country, with its rattling coaches, its smoking chimneys, its scarecrows and its soft green hills? How will you avoid standing out like a red tunic against a desert sky? Will there be hatred alongside your father's love?'

So ... whilst Hassan sometimes imagined staying here, he knew that it could never happen. How could his uncle have imagined such a thing? How could he, Hassan Qaderi, ever stay in this country, with its white faces and its green fields and its great populations of workers and machines and temples which hid their gods inside themselves? How could he possibly? This thought stayed with him always, even in his joy at what he had found, and in the love that grew within him.

*

One day, Smith took Hassan to the windmill. They were met by the miller and his wife, and a son about Hassan's age, standing expectantly together as their visitors dismounted; perhaps the boy had been looking out from the top of the mill and had seen them coming.

The mill was not working, for the miller had obviously been up a ladder mending the sails. He approached them wearing a cream coloured apron covered in smears of paint and dust. He wore thick boots, for the thaw had started and the ground was muddy. A tidy grey beard met a grey Derby hat with a ribbon around it. His jaws clenched, perhaps from the little clay pipe which he now held in his right hand. His head bobbed a little, and he touched the brim of his hat.

'Welcome, sir, I'm sure,' he said to Smith, but looking at Hassan. 'We are most honoured, sir. That you should come such a long way just to see us, like. Such a long way!'

'Not so far, sir,' said Hassan. 'My father's house is near here, you know.'

For some reason, the miller and his son laughed loudly.

'A lovely wit he has, sir' said the miller, this time looking at Smith. 'A fine young feller, I'm sure! Some tea, Izzy, and a crumpet or two, if you please.' And Izzy, her long dress flying, scuttled off towards a tiny thatched cottage next to the mill. They all turned and followed her.

Once inside, they hung their coats in the chimney as the boy put a log and some kindling into the fireplace, lit a lucifer and coaxed the fire into life. As he did so, Hassan looked more carefully at his hosts. The miller was a short, stoutish man, perhaps in his forties, although it was hard to tell. Now that he had removed his hat, his hair seemed clamped to his head, and he ran his hand through it to let the air to his scalp.

'I beg your pardon, Mr Fuller. I haven't introduced you,' said Smith. 'This is my son, Hassan, as you will have heard. I was married, you know, when I served in Afghanistan. Few people here know of it. Hassan, this is Mr Fuller, Mr George Fuller, and his son John. John is - how old, Mr Fuller?'

'Fourteen come April 4th,' said Mr Fuller proudly.

John came forward and offered his hand, but with a suspicious glance, as though doing what he was expected to do, rather than as he wished.

'Pleased to meet you, Hassan, I'm sure,' he said.

'And I am pleased to know you also,' said Hassan awkwardly. Then he turned to George Fuller. 'What is your work, please, sir?' he asked.

'Mr Fuller is a miller,' said Smith. He takes the wheat or the corn and he turns it into flour. And with the flour we make bread and biscuits and cake.'

'With flowers? And how you make bread with flowers?' asked Hassan, astonished.

Again, George and John roared with laughter, and this time Smith looked at them just a little disapprovingly. George soon put things right.

'I'll tell you what,' he said. 'John, you take young Master Hassan and show him the mill. Show him the flour, and the stones and the hopper and such. And meantime, Mr Smith and I shall talk business, for there is a little business I believe, Mr Smith?'

'I am quite sure we shall think of something,' said Smith with a smile.

John held out his hand to Hassan and pulled him from the little stool he had been sitting on. They took their coats down from inside the ingle and were soon outside. The wind had whipped up from the east, and the sky was darkening with threatening grey clouds. Hassan shivered.

'Let's run,' shouted John. And he tore off across the fifty yards to the windmill's door. By the time Hassan caught him up, he had lifted the latch and the door had creaked open on its hinges.

Inside, all was silent. Tiny and unconvincing shafts of light fell through small and grubby window panes. Hassan could see next to nothing, and his eyes seemed to be stubbornly resisting adjustment to the dark. But soon, he could make out tools hanging on whitewashed walls: long, two-man saws, a couple of rusty scythes, forks and spades and a pitchfork. John Fuller was nowhere to be seen. Hassan called out.

'Mr John! Where you are gone?'

There was silence; neither reply nor the sound of movement.

There were steps ahead of him, and a wooden handrail curved its way around and upwards. Hassan found himself on the bottom step, and kept calling John's name as he ascended the staircase.

Then there was a yell, more a sort of cackle, and the air was full of dust. Hassan coughed as he breathed it in, and felt it settling in his hair and on his face. He coughed and coughed, fighting for breath, and as he regained control he heard the cackling again from above. It was the sound of a jinn; an English boy might have thought of something halfway between a witch and an ogre.

'Gotchoo! ' shouted John from above, thrilled with his easy victory.

Hassan moved up the stairs until he stood in front of a small window, and saw that he was covered in white flour. John stood in front of him roaring with laughter: for the third time, Hassan thought. For the first time in many years, a thin sliver of bitterness entered his heart. Why come here, to this dark and windy place, to be laughed at three times?

John, no longer laughing, looked straight at him and narrowed his eyes a little. Hassan glared at him, and then patted down his clothes and his hair to remove as much of the flour as he could.

Still they stared at each other, both wondering when the other would strike the first blow. Then John Fuller turned and continued up to the first floor.

'Come on up,' he called. 'Let me show you the workings.'

They continued up for more flights of open stairs, their steps resounding against the brick walls and wooden beams. At last, they could go no further. John used a lot of words that Hassan had never heard before, and Hassan relied on his pointing instead. A great shaft came in through the wall, and two large wooden cogs intersected at right angles, and a further shaft went down to the floor. John pointed out of the window at one of the sails, and then at the cogs and then at the floor. He led the way back down two flights, until they came to two gigantic circular stones laid one on top of the other. The top one had a hole through it, with a large funnel resting in it. Again John pointed at the sails, and made a large expressive circular motion with his arm, then pointed at the shaft going from mill stone to ceiling, and made a smaller circular motion with his finger. Then he pointed at the mill stones, and made another circular motion before bounding down the stairs. At the bottom, a tube came through the ceiling, and below it there was a pile of sacks. One of the sacks was half full of flour. This time, John put his hand gently into the sack and held it out to Hassan. Hassan held out his hand to receive a little powder.

'Flour!' proclaimed John.

Hassan smiled. 'Flour! Not flower!' He held an imaginary flower to his nose and sniffed. John laughed, probably pleased that his accidental cruelty was now in the past and had been forgotten. But still they had to go back and face their fathers.

They stepped back out into the biting wind, and this time the race to the miller's cottage was closer. Hassan got there just ahead of John. They laughed together, and John lifted the latch and led the way in.

'Good Lord!' exclaimed Smith. 'Hassan! Whatever has happened to you? You look like a ghost!'

'A ghost? I don't know ghost.'

'Of course you don't. There are no ghosts in Afghanistan. Just the jinn, and they are so much more fun!'

Mr Fuller took things more seriously.

'John, explain yourself!' he barked.

''Twere an accident, father. There were a weedy sack on a shelf, and it fell.'

'Jest on Master Hassan, and not on you? How so?'

John was silent again.

'We'll speak on it later, then.' He looked back at Hassan and then at Smith. For some reason, Hassan would always remember his next words. 'At least it makes you look a little more like the rest of us, I 'spose.' He smiled at Smith, but the smile was met with a blankness. Smith turned, pretending to have heard something outside, and spent some time bent over and peering out of the window at some imaginary event.

'Now, let's get you cleaned up a bit. Let me tell you, flour is the very last thing you want on you when it's threatening rain. Izzy!' And soon Izzy Fuller was there, leading Hassan out of the room. George and Smith sat in wing chairs, and John stood silently.

Smith struggled with something to say, caught as he was between the anger of the protective father and the embarrassment of the teatime guest. So he said nothing. What he would have said in those moments would soon have been interrupted anyway, by a loud shriek from the pantry.

'God bless us! Please! I've done you no harm!'

George Fuller leapt to his feet and rushed to the door. Smith followed a second behind.

As they did so, something crashed to the floor in the pantry.

They soon found Izzy Fuller pressing her back to a wall, holding Hassan's dusty shirt in a panicky ball. Hassan was standing feet away, stripped to the waist. In his hand was Akbar Khan's bejewelled dagger. Smith strode towards him, grabbed the dagger, held him by the wrist and dragged him back into the parlour.

'Good God, Hassan! Whatever are you doing?'

Hassan looked up at him, wide-eyed. The corner of his mouth twitched, and his scar moved a little. He could not speak, but gazed vacantly over his father's shoulder, his eyes flitting from a candle stick to a small clock, and then to a vase. He picked out patterns in the cracks on the chimney breast, and the first time in years he saw the little yard outside his father's office in Kabul.

'Hassan! Look at me!' He took his son's chin in his hand and turned his unwilling head. 'What is it?'

Finally Hassan spoke. 'I show her. Like this.' He held his arm out straight, the tip of the blade towards Smith. As he did so, George and Izzy Fuller stood in the doorway.

'So, Mr Smith, sir...'

'Mr Fuller, please accept my apologies. Hassan meant nothing by it. You see, this is his proudest possession. He has owned it since he was a small boy. It was the gift of a Prince, you might say. Akbar Kahn. In Kabul. Hassan says he was merely showing the knife to Mrs Fuller. Honestly, he meant no harm. Please believe me.'

Smith turned the knife around, held gently by the blade and posted handle first to Izzy Fuller. She took it, trembling a little.

'Yes sir, a beauty I'm sure. But to carry such a thing. It did frighten me rather.'

'Not for carrying around, I'd say,' said George Fuller. 'Could cause trouble, that.' He took the knife from his wife and passed it back to Smith. 'I daresay it's the done thing in his country. But not in ours. He has a lot of learning to do about us before he goes back, I'd say. With due respect, sir.' And he gave a last, severe look at Hassan. Izzy looked from behind him, and even John kept a careful distance.

Soon, Smith said their farewells and they left.

It was dusk already, but there was a strong moon. Somewhere a dog barked, and a few birds sang. Smith put his hand on Hassan's shoulder. He wondered at the world he lived in, and its lack of understanding. There was nothing so mysterious about Hassan really. In these parts, his hair and his eyes and his skin, and the scar on his face, were unusual certainly, but not so unusual that Surrey could not get used to it.

On the other hand, would John Fuller have thrown the flour, had Hassan been a local shepherd boy or farrier's son? He doubted it. And did Izzy really need to be so terrified of a jewelled dagger, held by such a boy as Hassan? He doubted this too, and then thought again of the future. He must speak to Ahmet.

*

One evening, after Hassan had gone to bed, Ahmet and Smith sat into the small hours by the fire; Pooter joined them after a while, at first with a pretence of mint tea, then staying to stoke the fire, and finally being invited by Smith to draw up a chair.

They sat silently for a while, Pooter sucking on a clay pipe, and Smith and Ahmet looking once more into the flames. It was Pooter who revived the conversation.

'Young Hassan seems to be adapting well to England,' he said. He had already understood that this was the main thing on their minds, but was confused by their response. Smith frowned, and Ahmet stroked his beard. Neither spoke, but Pooter persisted.

'I suppose, sir, he must find England as strange as we once found Afghanistan.' Still silence. 'Only more peaceful, of course. Mostly, at any rate.'

Some minutes later, Pooter tried a new strategy. 'I should be interested, sir, to see how his education proceeds. Will you send him away to school, or employ a tutor?'

At last, there was a response.

'I am indeed most troubled by all of this,' said Smith.

'Troubled? Why so, sir?'

'Do you not see, Pooter?' His voice cracked a little. 'You know the work I have done. You know how hard I have tried. With your considerable help, of course. But I see now – I have long known – that to keep Hassan in England is a foolish idea. I told you what happened at the mill. Can you not imagine something like that happening to Hassan almost every day? Wherever he goes, whatever he does?'

Ahmet Qaderi stared into the fire. His face gave nothing away. So again, Pooter spoke instead.

'But he will learn, surely? And *nation shall speak peace unto nation*, as they say. And people here will learn, too. In just a few

304

years, it will be as though Hassan has always lived here, as though he were born here, as though you had met Nasrin...'

There was a silence for a while.

'It is not merely a question of nations. Or a question of the boy's mother, if you will,' said Smith. 'I am also extremely anxious about the life here. The life of an estate owner, a farmer, a landlord. Hassan was not born into it like I was. You know, Pooter, how much I owe you...'

Pooter held a hand up.

'No, really. I do, I really do. I know you have been my manager, I know this has been a good living for you. But that does not mean that you have not saved me, saved this estate. Kept it moving on whilst I was able to do nothing. Ten years it was, more than ten years. But at least I was born into it. I know the language and the customs and the work. I know the markets. I know the region. At least, I know enough to learn them afresh. Indeed, over the last few months I have started to learn again and – as I hope you have seen – I have learned quickly. But Hassan does not have my advantages. He knows nothing of this life, and I fear he will really struggle to learn it. Put simply, he will never fit. It will be hard on him, too hard. And what do you think, Mr Qaderi?'

Ahmet lifted his greying face into the light and looked straight at Smith.

'I think, Mr Smith? What I think... He is your son. It is not my right to say.'

'But you know him. You know him better than I. You have been...'

'Yes. And I love him like a son. But he is only *like* a son to me. That is why I have no right to say. I never have a son, you know.' He looked back into the fire for a moment. 'Once, perhaps I may have done. But you know what happened in Kabul. And then... to Bombay and work and business. And people who were not my own.'

'Just so,' said Pooter, moving into Smith's line of vision. 'The people were not his own, sir. But Mr Qaderi has survived, has he not? And not just survived, but survived with great success. And surely Hassan can learn what you and your brother learned, given time. Can he not? With your care and guidance?'

'But still I cannot believe it possible,' said Smith. 'and even if it were possible now, when he is younger and under my protection, you know that none of us live forever. I am more than forty years of age. And my health ... What would Hassan do if I were not here to protect him?' Pooter tried to interject. 'Yes, yes I know. But you are older than I, Pooter. In better condition, perhaps, but still older. What would happen to him? If he were 20 or 25, and nobody to protect him? And what of marriage, children? In such a small society as this? Would settling him here, educating him, teaching him everything I knew, loving him... Would it condemn him to a life alone? A life half lived?' He paused. 'It is so hard. So, so hard.'

They settled back in their chairs, with nothing more to say.

*

Hassan did not see his father the next day, nor the day after. He heard him sometimes, shuffling in this study, and sometimes he heard him talking with Pooter. Once, uncle Ahmet was with him, and their voices were low.

When Pooter took Hassan out with him to arrange repairs to a tenant's cottage roof, they looked across the lawn at his father's study window. The curtains were drawn, just as they had been when Hassan and Ahmet had first arrived all those weeks ago.

Chapter Twenty-Eight

April 1856

By now the mist had cleared, and Hassan could make out the very tops of the masts against a brightening white sky. He looked around him at those who had come to see him off, and remembered, in a seemingly random order, some of the events he had shared with them.

Mr Woodhouse was still talking to Sergeant Jackson. Both their heads were bowed, as though in mutual reverence: Jackson for the man of God, and Mr Woodhouse for the constable. Hassan remembered that cold night in November when he and Tommy had been taken away from the terrible danger of Field Lane, only to find themselves in a gloomy street, with that ordinary but terrifying man offering to buy them from Mr Woodhouse. As he remembered it, Hassan could almost smell the dark night air, and feel it against his skin. He especially remembered the dim gas lamp trying pathetically to light the scene for him.

From there, his mind scampered on to that same night, when he had woken to find that Tommy had disappeared, and he was alone – or very nearly alone – in a city he knew nothing of. He remembered looking out of the window the following morning, across the shiny black slates to the drizzling sky. From the dead sun just above the horizon, he had known that he was facing east, but how far away that east had seemed!

Mr Woodhouse and Sergeant Jackson were talking about him, obviously: for every now and then they glanced in his direction.

Hassan looked across at Molly Jackson and her daughters. Lucy smiled at him unconvincingly. Lizabet looked up at her sister, and then at Hassan, and soon she hid her face in her mother's coat. Mrs Jackson gave a little wave. Hassan remembered the very first evening in London, when he had arrived on *Aurora*, when the little Indian had lain by the dockside surrounded by a crowd of strangers, breathing his last in a foreign land.

Hassan would miss the Jacksons, for they had shown they cared for the traveller and for the orphan that Hassan then was. It would have been easy for Molly to walk away that first night, and how different things would then have been!

For the millionth time, Hassan felt his uncle's hand on his shoulder. Ahmet guided him gently forwards, towards Pooter and his father. Later, Hassan would wonder if Aziz had felt something like this as he walked to the gallows. He wanted this moment to be over, but he also wanted it to last forever. Uncle Ahmet put the question beyond doubt.

'It is time, my Hassan,' he said, with a gentle involuntary squeeze. And for the last time, Hassan walked towards his father.

Smith watched as he approached. He too saw this as an ending. Pooter took two steps away from him, and discreetly turned away, looking abstractedly downriver.

Smith held a hand out to Hassan, and Hassan shook it limply. They looked directly into one another's eyes. Smith spoke firmly, but Hassan could see that he had to work hard to achieve this.

'Not like that, my boy. The handshake must not be like a vice, but nor must it be like a wet fish. If you remember nothing else of England, remember that.' He smiled, as limply as Hassan had shaken his hand. Hassan tried again, more firmly. 'Better. Now, goodbye my dear son. You have made me very proud. And remember: you can always come back to England, when you are a great merchant in Bombay, or the Dost's great adviser in Kabul. Perhaps one day...' It seemed that he could speak no more. He took Hassan in his arms, remembering a thousand joys and two great sorrows. Then he held him at arm's length, and looked into his face.

'Promise me two things, Hassan.'

'Yes, father. I shall.'

'One day, go back to the Jugdulluk Pass, where your mother died. Take my love with you, and lay some flowers, for that is what we do in England. All those years ago, I never had the chance. And write to me every week, or as often as you can. And I shall write to you also. Let us remember each other always.'

'Always, father. I thank you. Always I will thank you.'

Again, the hand on the shoulder.

'Now. Your uncle is ready to go. Go, my boy. Go into the world and be a good man.' Hassan saw his father swallow hard.

Other, lesser, farewells then followed. A proper firm handshake for Pooter, who had shown him so much, and who probably, so Hassan thought, had wanted him to stay in England.

Ahmet had a few words for Mr Woodhouse. They had met for the first time just that morning, but Ahmet knew what he owed him. He held on to Woodhouse's hand.

'*I worship not that which ye worship; Nor worship ye that which I worship. And I shall not worship that which ye worship. Nor will you worship that which I worship. Unto you your religion, and unto me my religion*. Yet we are both believers in the one true book.'

'Indeed, sir, and I wish you well. We both believe that there is one God, and we only worship Him in different ways. The most important thing is that we live good lives. As you have said, we must pay the poor due and care for the traveller and the orphan. As you have always done. I see it in Hassan's eyes.'

'And so do you too, Mr Woodhouse. I thank you with all my heart'.

Smith overheard this and took a few steps towards them so that he could speak quietly. It seemed to those who watched him that this was a distraction from his pain.

'Paying the poor due. I remember the expression from the east. Tell me, Mr Woodhouse, are you so determined to stay in this part of the world, ministering to the young folk of Field Lane? Can I not tempt you to take a living in Surrey? There is a living vacant, you know. A good living. Better than you have been used to, I'll warrant. Forgive me: I do not know you well, but I have heard much that is good of you. There are needy people in Surrey also, you know!'

'Thank you, Mr Smith, but my work is far from finished here. It may be hard at times, but I am blessed in my love of it. Most of the time, at any rate. Here I shall stay.' He broke off, caught by something he had seen coming from the dock gate.

'Goodness me! Look! Look who is coming!'

A man in a long grey coat and a silk top hat was approaching them. Only one man any of them knew would have walked so quickly. As he reached the separated group, Hassan made out his glittering eyes and alert manner. Involuntarily, Hassan and Tommy Jackson ran to him. He welcomed them with outstretched arms, and his laughter boomed across the space.

'Well, well! And you are leaving us, Hassan?'

'Yes, sir, Mr. Dickens,' said Tommy Jackson. 'E's off back to Bombay, 'e is. Don't think e's liked it too much in Lunnon, sir. What wiv the cold and the murderin' and such'. Going back wiv 'is Uncle Ahmet. Back to make 'is fortune in the east.'

'And quite right too, I should say. I rather doubt that London is the place for you. A wretched place for the young, too often. And for the grown ups too, of course. Your poor friend Aziz, for one. Poor man. I have always wondered what a man must face in his last hours in such a place. Perhaps you have read about my Fagin, Tommy?'

'No sir.'

'No?'

'Well, not yet anyways. My father, Sergeant Jackson, I should say, 'e will of done, I'm sure.'

'Well, anyway, as you may read one day, if you do not already know it...' He looked over their heads towards the eastern horizon, out beyond the bank of the river, down the river to the sea and further still. *'The most wretched sort of affair this world is. Somebody's always dying, or going and doing something uncomfortable in it. Do you see? But I am become morbid. Let me lift my heart a little.*

Where shall I look? Yes, of course. Here we are.' Mr Dickens lifted his chin and frowned, summoning up his memory. *'There are dark shadows on the earth, but its lights are stronger in the contrast...* and you, young Hassan and Tommy, you are two of the brightest of lights. And remember, Hassan, as you go your ways, that there are...' And he called up the memory again. *'There are voices in the waves, always whispering. Of love, eternal and illimitable, not bounded by the confines of this world, or by the end of time, but ranging still, beyond the sea, beyond the sky, to the invisible country far away!'*

Hassan understood none of this, and Tommy Jackson little more. Even the adults who had gradually gathered around looked a little exercised by it.

Now Uncle Ahmet seemed to be growing impatient, or perhaps it was awkwardness at the thought of what he had to do, to remove Hassan from his father, to recommence that permanent – probably permanent – separation. Once again his hand descended on Hassan's shoulder. He spoke in Pashtu.

'Now, my nephew, it is time to leave. Say your goodbyes, especially to your father.'

And Hassan shook his father's hand once more. Why was he taking so long to break this fragile bond? *Erytheia* seemed distant, and his world was focused here. How could he go? Ahmet and Smith faced each other, slowly opened their arms, and embraced, steeling themselves for the separation.

Eventually they parted, and Ahmet took Hassan's elbow and led him away. After the first step, the traverse to the gangplank got easier. Soon, they were there.

Hassan and his uncle Ahmet, his loved uncle, the brother of his mother, the man who would surely care for him for years ahead, walked slowly over the black water with the occasional backwards glance at their new and now deserted friends. They all stood still, gazing, as though they were counting the steps. Hassan took a final look and raised a hand to them, and then could see them no more.

*

Hassan and his uncle stepped down onto the deck, and Ahmet gave their names to a short man with a list and a thick pencil.

'Come, Hassan, it is time to pray as we start on our new voyage across the seas, for there will be many dangers ahead of us.' They went to the *Erytheia's* stern, and faced the east as best they could.

Both raised their hands, their palms facing the east. A stiff easterly blew into their faces; perhaps it was that that brought tears to their eyes. They then held their hands together on their stomachs, and as usual Uncle Ahmet spoke.

'In the name of Allah, the kind, the merciful. Praise be to Allah, Lord of the worlds, the kind, the merciful. Owner of the day of judgement. You alone we worship, you alone we ask for help.

'Show us the straight path, the path of those you have favoured, not the path of those who earn your anger nor of those who go astray.'

Hassan had already prepared a Sura of his own.

> *'The beneficent hath made known the Qur'an.*
> *He hath created man, and He hath taught him speech.*
> *The sun and moon are made punctual, and the stars and*
> *   the trees adore Him, and the sky He has uplifted;*
> *And he has said the measure, that ye exceed not the measure,*
> *   but observe the measures strictly, nor fall short thereof.*
> *And the earth he hath appointed for his creatures,*
> *Wherein are fruit and sheathed palm-trees,*
> *Husked grain and scented herb.*
> *Which is it, of the favour of your lord, that ye deny?*
> *He created man of clay like the potters,*
> *And the genie did he create of smokeless fire.*
> *Which is it, of the favour of your lord, that ye deny?*
> *Lord of the two easts, and lord of the two wests!*
> *Which is it, of the favour of your lord, that ye deny?*
> *He hath loosed the two seas. They meet. There is a barrier*
> *   between them, and they encroach not one upon the other.*
> *   There cometh forth from both the pearl and coral stone.*
> *Which is it, of the favour of your lord, that ye deny?*

His are the ships, displayed upon the sea, like banners.
Which is it, of the favour of your lord, that ye deny?
Everyone that is thereon will pass away;
There remaineth but the face of the lord of might and glory.
Which is it, of the favour of your lord, that ye deny?'

They bowed as usual, and then stood. Uncle Ahmet took Hassan into his arms a moment, and nodded slowly. As he spoke again to a ship's officer, Hassan walked slowly to the bow of *Erytheia*, dodging past a sailor, skirting round a man with two small boys, and almost pitching into a young priest clutching a prayer book. And then, just as he reached the prow, and just as he took hold of the rail and started to scan the dockside below for his father and friends, there was a voice behind him, gratingly familiar, but at the same time hard to believe. A voice which jarred him through and through.

'So, my young friend. Here we are again. All of us together!'

The words alone might have sounded welcoming; they may perhaps have been spoken by a long-lost friend. But the tone in which they were uttered was fearsome.

Hassan turned and there was Khodar, standing gigantically above him. Khodar smiled grimly.

'You know, I have been seeking you ever since my cousin Aziz was taken from me. You should have been easy to find, of course. After all, I have been before to your father's house. But it is harder to find without a map and when there is no one to follow, even when you are charged with a vengeance as I have been. Oh, how I have waited for this meeting! And how fortunate that we should meet now. For soon we shall sail, and we shall be away from the *feringhees'* laws, and they will no longer protect you!'

Khodar now put his face so close to Hassan's that the boy's focus narrowed to the lonely teeth, and his nostrils were filled with the smell of betel. He stepped swiftly aside, so that he was now on the side of the open deck. And then he found his voice.

'Vengeance, Khodar? Why would you seek vengeance against me? What have I done to you?'

'You know what you have done. If it were not for you, and your *feringhee* father and your treacherous mother, Aziz would never have come across the sea to this infidel country, this pit of evil. And if it were not for your love of the *feringhee* and his laws, Aziz would still be living.' He stepped swiftly across the space between them, and tried to clutch at Hassan's clothing. He caught the fabric between his thumb and two fingers, but Hassan managed to pull himself free again. The priest looked fearfully at them, before deciding that what another man did to his son was none of his business. He scuttled away without a backward glance.

'One day, quite soon, you and your uncle will die for this, for what you have done. One day, I swear, before we reach Bombay. You will be shared between my knife and the fishes in the deep sea. And so will your uncle Ahmet.'

Hassan found himself with his back to the rail. His terror had so focused his awareness that he had stopped thinking of rescue. He could hear shouts from the dockside, so he could probably have made himself heard, but his throat was dry and taut, and in any case there would be nothing that his friends below could do to help.

Khodar's bulk blocked his view entirely, and all he could feel in the air was rage, so he did not notice Ahmet's quiet approach. The first he knew of it was Ahmet's voice.

Ahmet spoke in a way that Hassan had never heard from him before. It was quiet, steely, barely audible.

'Leave the boy, Khodar. It is not the boy's fault that he was born of his parents. Rather, blame me. It is more my fault that Aziz is dead than it is Hassan's. I have often remembered, in joy and in sorrow, the day his parents met. Smith and his sergeant – Leary, I think his name was – asked me to find a party of Kabulis to join him on an expedition to a lake outside the city. Perhaps you have heard the story. The smiths of Kabul had made blades for the feet, so that men and women could skate together across the ice.' He paused. Khodar seemed to relax a little. 'One of the people I gathered together was my young sister, the baby of our family. She was very beautiful, and perhaps I already knew what would happen. Later, when I saw them skating, I understood it for the first time. So I was responsible for their meeting, for their marriage, and I became responsible for Hassan.

'I was responsible too for the treasure you had imagined: for it was I, Khodar, who wrote the story. Perhaps you did not know that. And after seeking the treasure for year after year, you finally understood that it was not the kind of treasure you thought it was. That was my fault also. Later, kill me if you must, but in the name of Allah, leave the boy alone, and let him live.'

For all the beauty of Ahmet's simple story, Khodar's rage returned. Perhaps now, in the face of the simple, loving story, he at last saw his own wrongness. Far from softening the rage, the story made it still worse.

'If I kill you first, Ahmet Qaderi, you will die not knowing whether the boy will live or not. That will be the price you pay.'

Khodar took a step towards Ahmet, and Ahmet took a step backwards. A step, and another step, and another. Somehow, this part of the deck was now deserted bar the three of them. Hassan had not noticed the gradual sidling away of the priest and a few sailors, until they were now left alone.

Soon, Ahmet had his back to the rail. Why did he not take a hold of Khodar, as Hassan knew he could, and bring him to the floor? Perhaps it was his age, or perhaps the presence of Hassan. Or perhaps it was because this was no mere sporting challenge, but a challenge instead that could end only in one kind of defeat, perhaps even death. Perhaps it was that, the seriousness of the challenge, that uncle Ahmet was trying hard to avoid.

Still Khodar drew closer. Now Ahmet had to arch his back, his spine pressed against the rail, and looked into Khodar's dark eyes. He felt that he would surely fall into the icy water below, or onto the hard cobbles. The rail creaked a little. Still he stared into Khodar's eyes.

Then Khodar frowned and hissed a little. He bit his lip with one tooth. His eyes widened; his pupils widened to little discs. His hands reached forward. One rested on the side of Ahmet's neck, the other gripped his shoulder.

And then he fell to the deck, yelling in pain. Blood ran from a wound in his side.

Ahmet looked for Hassan. He stood a few paces away, across no more than two yards of deck. In his hand was the dagger, long and bloodied. Ahmet skipped across the space to him, and took the dagger from him.

'I am sorry, my nephew.'

He dropped the dagger into the water below. Then he raised his hand, and struck Hassan hard across the cheek. Hassan felt the blood rushing to his stinging face. He would feel the shock of this for the rest of his days.

'I do this in love.' He took Hassan in his arms, and spoke urgently in his ear.

'Now you must run, back across that gangway. Back to your father. You must stay in this country, where you are safe.'

'But uncle, what will become of you? They will take you and …'

Hassan heard the cry of a crewman, and an answer from the quayside.

'No. No, I shall explain if I am asked. And you must say the same if you are asked. He attacked you, did he not? That is why your face is red. He was trying to kill you. I had to use the knife to free you. And then you ran to your father, to safety. I am sorry about the knife. But I fear for you, with a knife in your hand.' He smiled softly. 'One day, it would have been trouble for you. Now, go. Quickly!'

He pushed Hassan from him, and Hassan found himself stumbling, stumbling, pushing past people, the wrong way across the gangway. He looked back to see his uncle binding Khodar's wound.

'Quick, m'boy!' Called a sailor. 'An if yer leave now, there's no coming back. We're casting off. Quick, now!'

Hassan pushed past him and jumped back onto the cobbles. He ran across the dock, to his father, who stood desperately scanning the rail of *Erytheia*, looking for his son, wanting to wave to him as the cutter slid away.

'Sir! Look!' Pooter pointed at him, and Smith looked at Hassan and then at the prow of *Erytheia* as it moved away from the dockside.

Ahmet did not seem to see them, crouched as he was over the deck. He did not even seem to realise that the vessel was moving until it was some distance away, and he finally looked up and sought out his nephew and raised a tentative hand to shoulder height and waved to them.

'Hassan, whatever has happened?' Smith moved towards his son, and touched his reddening face.

'It would seem,' said Mr Dickens, 'that the boy has decided to stay after all. A curious choice, I would say.' He raised an eyebrow. 'But his choice, for all that. Will he make a farmer, Mr Smith? What do you think?'

Smith could not speak. He and Hassan faced one another, still a small space between them.

'Yes, he'll make a farmer, with some help.' It was Pooter again. 'I shall leave you to it, sir.' And he walked slowly away.

*

After that, there were other walkings-away. Sergeant Jackson strode purposefully across the dock like a police sergeant on duty, which of course he was. Soon he saw some bother at one of the chestnut stalls, blew his whistle and ran from the docks after some scallywag. Mrs Jackson, Tommy, and Lizabet gazed after him, and then turned to Hassan. Tommy shook his hand.

'Welcome to Lunnon, 'Assan,' he said. 'I know you're goin' all that way to Surrey, but I 'ope we can stay friends. An' I'm sure Lucy and Lizabet thinks likewise.' Lucy blushed, but managed to fix her eyes on Hassan's. Lizabet wailed. And the family walked slowly back to business, turning and waving once or twice, or perhaps three times, as they left.

'We shall meet again, I am quite sure,' said Mr Dickens, with a handshake, a little bow and a touch of the rim of his hat. 'For it is rarely that I meet a person of such interest, never mind one so young. I could almost imagine...and yet perhaps not. It would be too different...My readers would perhaps...' And most unusually for Mr Dickens, he trailed off, perplexed.

317

He strode off as purposefully as Sergeant Jackson had, only with even more energy, and Mr Woodhouse strode purposefully after him, struggling to keep up.

Hassan faced his father again. Pooter took his usual few paces away and looked out after *Erytheia*, which now cut the silk of the water just as *Aurora* had done five months before, only in the other direction, now almost on the reaches of the Thames proper. Uncle Ahmet had been shrunk by distance, but still his hand was up, gently waving. Hassan realised with a pang that he had not been watching the space between them, and now both he and Smith turned and waved in big gestures to make up for lost time. They watched until their view of the clipper and of the man who had cared like a father for Hassan for ten years or more was cut off by the rigging and sails and hulls of other vessels.

Again, the hand on the shoulder, but this time it was his father's hand.

'So, are you sure about this, my son?' His voice cracked a little.

'Most surely, my father,' said Hassan. 'but I ask one thing. Please to be called Hassan Qaderi, not Smith? To remember my uncle Ahmet and my mother? Father, I have made my choice.' He looked out across the water again. 'And now, is too late in any case!'

Smith's laughter was tinged a little with sadness. He thought of the man Ahmet, now travelling alone. They walked slowly towards the red brick archway of the dock gate, both wondering in their separate ways about the difficult future that lay on the other side. They had their different hopes and fears, of course, even now untold. Yet still, Smith's hand was on his son's shoulder, and that counted for everything.

Epilogue

October 2009

Captain Qaderi stared for a moment at the spot where the peach stone had landed. How might that garden look in a hundred and seventy years' time? What had it looked like all that time ago? How many times had he asked that question?

He had ancestors who had lived in Kabul. He had never known their names; perhaps here he would be able to find out. What would they have been, great great grandparents and uncles and aunts? No, more than that. Four greats, probably. His grandfather had told him there were some papers at home and some bits and pieces from this place. Letters and books and ice skates, of all things. He couldn't imagine using ice skates in a place like this, although he knew it would get cold in the winter. He must look them out some time.

Strange how history came full circle. The British had been here before, of course. They had started off in the Balla Hissar, now a ruined stretch of mud brick across the edge of a hill. Apparently they had later built a whole little town (cantonments they called it). It was somewhere just next to the road from Bagram airbase to the city. Somewhere on the left, although you couldn't see it now. The funny thing was, Qaderi had seen Russian blockhouses just on the edge of where the cantonments would have been. Nobody seemed to learn anything from history.

Not that he could talk. Somewhere, there was a wonderful history in his own family, but he would probably never bother to find it, and certainly not while he was here. Anyway, he thought, at the moment he had more important things to think of.

'Smith!'

'Yes, sir?'

'Finished with those, Sergeant?'

'Yes, sir.' He passed back the Otterburns.

'As there's nothing happening, tell the men to stand down for a bit. Take some tea if they want it.'

'Sir.'

Sergeant Smith turned and headed back down the concrete steps. Captain Qaderi smiled, readjusted the binoculars and continued to scan the city of Kabul.

Acknowledgements

This story is based on events during the First Afghan War. There really was a 13th Light Infantry, and its route through India and Afghanistan was as I have described. I am indebted to Patrick Macrory's excellent *Kabul Catastrophe: the invasion and retreat 1839 – 1842* (London, 1966) for the essential historical details of the campaign. Any inaccuracies are mine alone.

General Keane, General Elphinstone, Sir William Hay Macnaghten and Sir Alexander Burnes were, in their different ways, really in charge. Colonel Sale really did invite his men to shoot him, and later led his men to Jalalabad. He really did bring back his wife and the other hostages from the hands of Akbar Khan, and there really was a play at Astley's Circus in 1844 called *The Prisoners at Cabool*, which might have been seen by a three-year-old Tommy Jackson. Akbar really claimed to have shed tears over his part in the retreat, although these may or may not have been real. I realise that some historians will think I have treated him overly sympathetically.

There may well have been a Lieutenant Smith in the 13th Light Infantry, but my Smith is fictitious. Captain Warburton really did marry a niece of the Dost Mohammed; their son became Colonel Sir Robert Warburton, who commanded the Khyber Pass until 1898. Lieutenant Eyre, also a talented artist, became General Sir Vincent Eyre. Captain Sturt was really married to the Sales' daughter, Emily. Lieutenant Holdsworth really did take a spear from the tent of a chief, as described in a letter to his father in 1839.

The other officers mentioned really existed, except for Lieutenant Revell and Lieutenant James, who are my own inventions. I am indebted to Lady Florentia Sale's *A Journal of the First Afghan War* (ed. Macrory, 1969) for details of some of the relationships between these men and the problems they faced.

In London, the only real characters are Charles Dickens and Miss Burdett Coutts, a member of the Coutts banking family, who funded both Urania Cottage, a home for destitute women, and the Field Lane Ragged School. If you have never read Dickens, I suggest that like Hassan Qaderi, you start with *The Pickwick Papers.* All italicised quotations, from this and other works by Charles Dickens, are taken from the original texts.

I have taken quotations from Muhammed Marmaduke Pickthall's beautiful translation of the *Holy Qur'an,* first published in 1930. I hope that my motives in using these quotations will be understood and welcomed.

Finally, the Tale of Ali the Persian has been borrowed from Sir Richard F. Burton's 19th century translation of *The Arabian Nights* (2001 edition).